The Tudor

Joanna spent twenty-five years at the BBC writing and presenting for radio and television. Her first book, *Rebellion at Orford Castle*, was a children's novel set in East Anglia. This was then followed by *Island Games* and *Dubious Assets*, set in her adopted homeland of Scotland and published under the name of Joanna McDonald.

Gripped by Shakespeare's history plays, Joanna originally began researching King Henry V's 'fair Kate' as a schoolgirl and the story of Catherine de Valois and the Tudor genesis has remained with her throughout life. Inspired by a chronicle description of Catherine's 'damsels of the bedchamber', the schemes and treacheries of medieval royal courts are brought to life through the eyes of 'Guillaumette', her servant and companion.

Joanna Hickson lives in Wiltshire and is married with an extended family and a wayward Irish terrier.

Follow Joanna on Facebook or Twitter @joannahickson.

By the same author

The Agincourt Bride

JOANNA HICKSON

The Tudor Bride

HARPER

This novel is entirely a work of fiction.
The names, characters and incidents portrayed in it are
the work of the author's imagination. Any resemblance to
actual persons, living or dead, events or localities is
entirely coincidental.

Harper
An imprint of HarperCollins*Publishers*
77–85 Fulham Palace Road,
Hammersmith, London W6 8JB

www.harpercollins.co.uk

A Paperback Original 2014
1

A catalogue record for this book
is available from the British Library

ISBN: 978-0-00-744699-5

Typeset in Birka by Palimpsest Book Production Limited,
Falkirk, Stirlingshire

Printed and bound in U.S.A.

MIX
Paper from
responsible sources
FSC **FSC® C007454**

For Katie and young Hugo
who are my Catherine and young King Henry.

EDWARD III _m._ PHILIPPA
of England   of Hainault

(3rd son)
BLANCHE   _m.1_   JOHN   _m.3_   KATHERINE
of Lancaster   D. of LANCASTER   Swynford
                                            BEAUFORT line
                                            (legitimised)

HENRY IV   MARGARET   _m.1_   JOHN
of England   Holland   E. of Somerset

                              JOHN   2 more sons
                              E. of Somerset

                                           (no issue)

HENRY V   _m.1_   CATHERINE   _m.2_   OWEN TUDOR
of England   of France

                     HENRY VI   EDMUND
                     of England and
                     France

THOMAS   JOHN
D. of Clarence   D. of Bedford
_m._   _m.1_
MARGARET   ANNE of Burgundy
D. of Clarence   _m.2_
                     JACQUETTA of Luxembourg

The ENGLISH ROYAL FAMILY

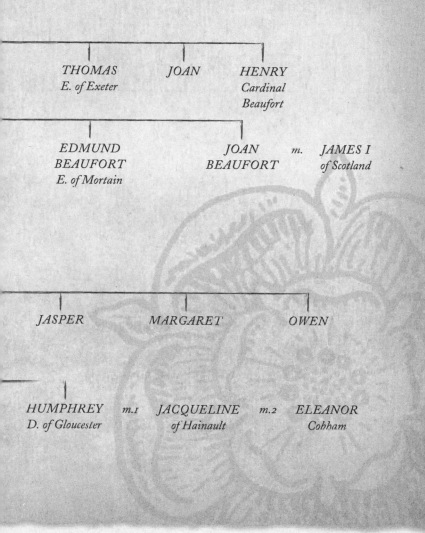

THOMAS	JOAN	HENRY
E. of Exeter		Cardinal Beaufort

EDMUND BEAUFORT	JOAN BEAUFORT	m.	JAMES I
E. of Mortain			of Scotland

JASPER	MARGARET	OWEN

HUMPHREY	m.1	JACQUELINE	m.2	ELEANOR
D. of Gloucester		of Hainault		Cobham

CHARLES VI   m.   ISABEAU
"The Mad"   of Bavaria

| 2 boys, 1 girl died young and 3 other girls | LOUIS Dauphin (d. 1415) | JEAN Dauphin (d. 1417) | m.1 | JAQUELINE of Hainault |

m.2
JOHN
D. of Brabant
(annulled)

m.3
HUMPHREY
D. of Gloucester

The FRENCH ROYAL FAMILY

MICHELE   m.   PHILIPPE   CHARLES (VII)
(d. 1421)   D. of Burgandy   Dauphin
                                             "Pretender"

HENRY V   m.1   CATHERINE
King of England
Heir of France

HENRY VI
of England
&
HENRY II
of France

Southern England, English occupied France & the Burgundian Low Countries 1420-1450

York
Beverley

ENGLAND

North Sea

HOLLAND

Leicester
Coventry
Kenilworth
Warwick
Bury St Edmunds
Hatfield
Oxford
Hadam
Hertford
London
Windsor
Eltham
Canterbury
Dover
Winchester
Southampton

Bruges
Antwerp
FLANDERS
Calais
Lille
Mons
PICARDY
HAINAUT
Agincourt

English Channel (The Sleeve)

Harfleur
Rouen
Beauvais
Compiegne
Reims
Bayeux
NORMANDY
Senlis
St. Denis
ISLE de FRANCE
Caen
Poissy
Paris
Vincennes
Troyes
Melun
FRANCE
Corbeil
Montereau
Chartres
Orleans

N
NW
NE
W
E
SW
SE
S

NARRATOR'S NOTE

The House of the Vine, London, Summer 1440

Respected Reader,

My name is Guillaumette, known to my friends as Mette. Some of you may already know that and yes, I am French but I write this at my house in London, where I live very quietly now. You will understand that the French are not much liked in England today, so I think it best to speak and write in English.

It is not my own story I write; this is the story of my mistress, Catherine de Valois, youngest daughter of the French king Charles the Sixth, whom I suckled as a baby, nursed as a child and tried to console through the troubled years of her girlhood, during which she was offered by various of her male relatives to the invading enemy, King Henry the Fifth of England, as his bride. This she eventually became, not entirely without her consent, in June 1420. By the end of that year, as a result of his extraordinary military success, an alliance with the Duke of Burgundy and a very favourable (to him) peace treaty, King Henry and his new bride were able to enter Paris in triumph, he as the new Regent and Heir of France and she as his queen. Afterwards they sailed for England as a golden royal couple, ready to be féted and celebrated, not least at Catherine's coronation in London. And I sailed with them.

Since France lay devastated by years of constant warfare, you may think it was a relief for me to follow in the new queen's train, but I left France with a heavy heart. I had always been close to my daughter Alys, who with her husband and baby girl lived in Paris, which was now under English rule. My son Luc, meanwhile, had sworn his allegiance to Catherine's seventeen-year-old brother Charles, the former Dauphin, who had been disinherited and declared illegitimate by his sister's marriage treaty and forced to retreat to his loyal territories south of the Loire. Charles would have to fight the combined armies of England and Burgundy if he was to win back his name and his claim to the French throne. Catherine and the Dauphin's father, King Charles, was subject to devilish fits and often confined to a padded room, believing he was made of glass and terrified of being shattered; a living metaphor for the shattered state of his kingdom and, I fear, the splintered state of my family. Regrettably we were typical of French people at the time, the divided victims of violence and political upheaval. I did not depart with a light heart.

Nevertheless, when we embarked at Calais, part of me was glad to be leaving the chaos behind but, I realise now, twenty years later, how little notion I had of what we were sailing into. Catherine had no choice, she was by law the Queen of England, whether the English liked her or not; but for me it was different. I followed her out of loyalty and love, but there were times later, I assure you, when I wondered whether I had done the right thing in boarding that ship . . .

PART ONE

Queen of England
(1421–1422)

1

The grey-green sea looked hungry as it lapped and chewed on the English shore, voracious, like the monsters mapmakers paint at the edge of the world. With her sails flapping, the *Trinity Royal* idled nose to the wind under the walls of Dover Castle, a vast stronghold sprawled atop high chalk cliffs which gleamed in the flat winter sunlight. Visible against this great white wall were the flags and banners of an official welcoming party and a large crowd of onlookers gathered along the beach. Unfamiliar music from an unseen band drifted past us on a dying breeze.

Having almost completed my first sea voyage, I could not say that I was an enthusiastic sailor. I felt salt-stained and wind-blown, my only consolation being that the sea-swell which had plagued my stomach all the way from France had now eased and the ship's movement had dwindled to a gentle rocking motion. Queen Catherine, by contrast, looked radiant and unruffled after the crossing, even when faced with the prospect of being carried ashore in a chair by a bunch of braggart barons, bizarrely known as the Wardens of the Cinq Ports; bizarrely because there were seven towns involved, not five as the title suggested, and some of them were not even ports. Apparently this chair-lift was an English tradition, but personally I considered it barbaric that a king and queen should be expected to risk their lives being carried shoulder high over treacherous waters to a stony beach when they could have made a dignified arrival walking down a gangway onto the Dover dockside. Besides, as Keeper of the Queen's Robes, I, Guillaumette Lanière, was the one who would have to restore the costly fur and fabric of the queen's garments from the ravages of sand and salt-water.

King Henry discussed this singular English honour with his brother, Humphrey, Duke of Gloucester, when the duke boarded the Trinity Royal from his galley, half a league off the white cliffs. That his grace of Gloucester thought himself a fine fellow was amply evident in the swashbuckling way he climbed the rope-ladder, vaulted the ship's rail one-handed and sprang up the stair to the aftcastle deck, where the king and Queen Catherine stood waiting. Gloucester sported thigh-high polished leather boots and his short green doublet clung tightly to his muscular physique, admirably displaying the heavy gold collar and trencher-sized medallion of office which hung around his broad shoulders. His bend of the knee was practised and perfect, accompanied by a flourish of his right hand as he grasped his brother's with the left.

'A hearty welcome to both your graces!' He pressed his lips to the king's ring, but raised his eyes not to his brother's face but to Catherine's. 'England waits with bated breath to greet its beautiful French queen.'

A faint flush stained Catherine's cheeks, but she remained straight-faced under the impact of Gloucester's dazzling smile. If the duke's youth had been in any way misspent, it did not show. I believe few men of thirty could boast such a fine, full set of white teeth as that smile revealed. His face was clean-shaven, smooth and unblemished, in striking contrast

6

with the scarred and care-lined visage of the king, only five years his senior.

'We hear you have a ceremonial welcome planned for us, brother.' King Henry raised a quizzical eyebrow. 'We are to be carried shoulder high through the surf.'

Gloucester appeared reluctant to drag his gaze from Catherine's face. 'Indeed, sire, as is customary for people of great rank and honour. You will be pleased to hear that the surf has dwindled to friendly ripples now though. You may remember that we welcomed Emperor Sigismund to these shores with the Wardens' lift. We can do no less to honour the return of the glorious and victorious King of England and France – and the advent of his beauteous queen – than was appropriate for a visiting Holy Roman Emperor.'

King Henry frowned. 'It is ill-judged, Humphrey, to place the crown of France on my head while the father of my queen still lives.' He made an irritable upward movement with his hand. 'But rise, brother, if only to explain how we are to enter these chairs of yours without getting wet. As you know, I have always avoided such mummery in the past.'

When he rose, Gloucester stood almost as tall as the king and a head taller than Catherine. 'A simple matter, sire!' he declared, gesturing over the side of the ship. 'The litters are fastened ready, there on my galley. The captain will bring the ship as near to the shore as he may, the gangway will be lowered onto the galley and you and Madame, the queen, will walk regally down it. Once safely seated, you will be rowed towards the shore until the water is shallow enough for your Wardens to wade in, take the litters on their shoulders and bear them ceremoniously up the beach. The trumpets will sound, the musicians will play and the crowds will cheer. When he can make himself heard, the Lord Warden

– my humble self – will make a speech of welcome, then your litters will be lifted shoulder high once more for the short journey to the castle.'

'And do I have your solemn word that there is no question of either of us receiving a ducking?' The king favoured his brother with a fiercely narrowed gaze.

Gloucester made an appreciative gesture in Catherine's direction. 'Her grace appears to be made of fairy dust, my lord. I would wager we could carry her from Dover to London without effort. As for your grace's royal person, it can surely rely on divine protection to remain dry.'

'Hmm.' King Henry grunted non-committally.

Catherine suddenly favoured Gloucester with one of her most regal smiles and surprised him by speaking in charming broken English, her voice light but firm. 'My lord of Gloucester is gracious to honour us with this ceremony, but should I not also descend from the chair and set my foot on English soil?' She turned to the king. 'Perhaps we could walk to the castle, my lord? It does not look far. The people will the better have a sight of us.'

King Henry shot a sharp glance at his brother, who shook his head almost imperceptibly and said hastily, 'That might be unwise, Madame. It is a steep climb. But Madame will have the opportunity to set foot on English soil when she reaches the town gate. There, the mayor of Dover waits to present you with the freedom of the town. I can assure you that the populace is out to greet you. Walking anywhere would render your graces susceptible to the attentions of over-eager citizens in the narrow streets, and besides we go in procession to the castle. Teams of hand-picked burghers are waiting to shoulder your chairs, and I think when you witness the exuberance of our English crowds you will understand the need for being raised above the common herd. Also, I trust you will forgive the coarseness of the people's greetings. They will doubtless shout "Fair Kate!" as you pass. It is not meant to offend, but to please. Fair is in praise of your beauty and Kate is a shortening of your name.'

'The king has told me this. If they think me fair before they have properly seen me, such blind devotion cannot be deemed . . . how do you say? . . . an insult,' responded Catherine with a smile. 'And if they call me fair, how can I then not like the name they give me?'

I watched Gloucester bow deeply to Catherine and thought I saw a spark of recognition in his eyes, as if he realised that, like him, she possessed a keen appreciation of the importance of public acclaim. 'You are a lady of great wisdom, Madame. And you are to be congratulated on your grasp of English. Is she not, brother?'

King Henry directed one of his rare smiles at Catherine. 'You will find that my queen grasps many things quickly, Humphrey, including the strategic value of flattery. Now, let us get this adventurous journey started. I think you will need help in mounting the chair-litter, Catherine, however much my brother makes light of the matter! You should summon your attendants.'

There were only three of us to summon because all but one of Catherine's French ladies-in-waiting had been left with their families in France. The exception was the devout and practical Agnes de Blagny, a knight's daughter who had been orphaned and impoverished by her father's death at the Battle of Agincourt. She had come to the French court with Catherine from their convent school, where they had been close friends. The other attendant was a young English beauty, Joan Beaufort, daughter of the Duchess of Clarence and step-daughter of King Henry's brother Thomas, Duke of Clarence. The duchess was also accompanying Catherine to England to instruct her in the protocol of the English court. At nineteen and fourteen years old respectively, my two colleagues in attendance on the new queen were better suited, I willingly admitted, to help Catherine down the gangway and onto the gilded chair-litter that was roped tightly to the bobbing galley. Being the same age as the English king, I am not suggesting I was over the hill in any way, but I confess that my thirty-four years had broadened my beam and made me less agile than my younger companions. However, I think I can safely say that my relationship with Queen Catherine ran closer and deeper than that of any teenage court damsel, for I had suckled her as a babe, nursed her as an infant and steered her through a profoundly troubled girlhood. She had left her mother, Queen Isabeau, in Paris without a second thought, but in order to bring me with her to England she had raised me from the rank of menial servant and given me a courtier's post as one of her closest confidantes. I had journeyed a long way from my father's bakery on the banks of the Seine.

I bustled behind Agnes and Joan, directing proceedings as they did all the bending and tugging, easing the queen's voluminous skirts down the narrow gangway. The king and the duke handed her into the galley and the girls helped her into the litter, tucking the folds of her costly gown around her feet to keep it clear of the water.

As the galley drew nearer to the beach, seven men wearing short doublets and thigh-high bottins started to wade out towards us, the wavelets lapping first at their leather-clad ankles and then rising up their shins. The shingle shelved very gradually and they were a good thirty yards offshore before we came alongside them, at which point the Duke of Gloucester stood up and leaped casually over the side, landing up to his thighs and causing a mighty splash. Muttering under my breath, I hastily brushed the water drops from Catherine's fine worsted skirts as the rowers shipped their oars and those nearest to the chair-litters began to untie the ropes attaching them to the galley.

'Have no fear, my beautiful queen,' Gloucester said as the galley rocked turbulently, unbalanced by the rowers' efforts to heave Catherine's litter over the side and onto the shoulders of the bearers. 'Archbishop Chichele was our last carry and he is twice your weight.' He glanced over his shoulder at the other three men in his team and signalled with his free arm. 'Forward, fellow wardens!'

As they began moving, I saw Catherine raise her chin, summon a fixed smile and lift one hand to wave to the crowd. On the other side of the galley, King Henry was already shore-bound.

The rowers returned to their oars and the galley began to swing away towards the jetty, giving me a clear view as the Duke of Gloucester suddenly sank up to his chest and the queen's chair tilted violently.

I cried out in alarm and the cheers from the onlookers instantly turned to a collective gasp of horror as Catherine lurched forward in her seat, clinging desperately with the one hand that was still clutching the arm of the chair. The duke appeared to struggle to regain his balance, but just as it seemed Catherine must topple forward into the water, he thrust his arm upwards to return the litter to the horizontal and throw her back into the chair. There was no particular reason to think that his stumble had been deliberate, but I could not help wondering. Although he was soaked to the armpits, he did not look greatly troubled when he turned to speak to her and I had the chance to see his face.

'A thousand pardons, my queen. A loose stone attempted to trip me, but as you see it failed. All is well and your adoring public awaits.'

The galley moved out of earshot before I could catch Catherine's reply, but I recognised her expression. It was one of anger and suspicion, as if she too doubted Gloucester's integrity, but it lasted only moments, then her smile returned, growing ever more confident as the cheers of the crowd redoubled. I cast a glance at King Henry to gauge his reaction to the incident, but he was looking the other way and had not seen it.

Marshalled behind stave-wielding sergeants, the people surged forward on the shingle waving evergreen branches and coloured banners and hailing their hero king and his trophy French queen.

'God bless Queen Kate!' Fair Kate! 'Bonny queen!' 'Hail to the conquering king!' 'God bless good King Hal!'

From this moment of her arrival on the Kent coast, there was the same noisy tumult wherever she went. Gloucester had been right in every particular about the people being rowdy, but I was unprepared, even so, for the triumphant mood of the crowd as we passed through the steep streets of Dover in procession to the castle.

This scene was repeated on following days, time and time again, as the royal train made its slow progress towards London. At every village the populace turned out in their best clothes, precious relics and religious banners were paraded out of the churches and petitioners scrambled to catch the king's attention or beg the queen's blessing for their children. Even the weather showed favour, bestowing on the royal procession unseasonal warmth, bright sunshine and blue skies. Despite winter-bare trees and sparse vegetation, the countryside looked fertile and well-farmed, in sharp contrast to the abandoned and unkempt fields of Normandy, from where we had recently come.

It was during our three-week stay in Rouen, before we took ship for England, that Catherine had insisted I take riding lessons. As a baker's daughter from the back streets of Paris, I had never learned to ride and, until I began to travel around France with the court, I had never seen the need. Even though I had been married at fifteen to a groom in the royal stables, apart from our frequent and lusty use of the hayloft above their stalls, I had never had much truck with horses until Catherine decided it was time I did. I had rapidly discovered that now she was a queen, when she made a decision something was done about it.

'You cannot accompany me on a royal progress if you have to ride on one of the baggage carts, Mette,' she had complained. 'I may need you en route and will not want to wait while someone goes to search for you at the back of the procession. Besides, I assure you that it is much more comfortable to ride a horse than to be bounced around on a cart.'

One of King Henry's grooms had been instructed to find a docile cob and teach me the rudiments of horsemanship. It did not take long, for all I needed to do was walk and trot and keep my mount safely reined in behind the horse in front. I was not intending to chase after the hunt or indulge in adventurous gallops across moor and heath. What I had not anticipated, however, were the aches and pains that resulted from sitting on a horse for long periods of time.

However, my legs and rump grew accustomed to it and by

the time we reached Canterbury, I had become quite comfortable in my sideways saddle, and grown fond of the sturdy brown mare which had been procured for me at Dover, reared and broken I was told, on the wild moors of England's south-west. She had been named Jennet, but I decided to re-christen her Genevieve after the patron saint of Paris and hoped she would look after me just as that virgin saint protected my home city.

But my poor mare had begun to limp by the time we arrived at the abbey of St Augustine in Canterbury, where the royal household was to lodge while visiting the city and the tomb of St Thomas à Becket. That evening the king and queen were dining privately with the abbot and I took the opportunity to slip away and check whether any of the grooms had tended my horse's front foot. But when I led her from her stall, I found that she was still lame. Dusk was falling and I had no idea what to do, so I began searching about for some assistance. To my surprise, the only person I encountered was little Joan Beaufort, looking flustered and nervous and very out of place in her elaborate court dress and furred mantle.

'Sweet Marie, Lady Joan, a young girl like you should not be wandering about the stables alone at this time. What are you doing here?' Apart from being the epitome of English beauty – strawberry-blonde, blue-eyed and apple-blossom-cheeked – as the king's cousin and step-niece, Joan was one of the most eligible damsels of the court.

'Searching for you,' she replied, obviously very relieved to have found me. 'I have been looking everywhere.'

'My horse is lame,' I said. 'I want someone to tend her foot.'

An eager look animated the court beauty's face. 'I know about horses. I always preferred the stables over needlework. Has the mare got a stone in her hoof?'

I shook my head. 'I have no idea. How do you tell?'

'Let me take a look. Is that her over there?' She trudged off to where I had tied Genevieve back in her stall a few yards away, ignoring the horse dung and wet straw which mired her slippers and sullied the hem of her priceless brocade gown. Giving the mare a gentle pat, she bent down and expertly lifted her front hoof, peering at its underside. 'Yes, there is a stone in this one.' She placed the foot carefully down and turned to me. 'I need something to prise it out with. A strong stick would do.'

I was about to go off in search of an implement when I suddenly realised that she must have been seeking me for a reason. 'Incidentally, Lady Joan, why were you looking for me?' I asked.

She frowned. 'Oh, I almost forgot. The queen wants you. She is in a frenzy.'

2

If Catherine had ever been in a frenzy it had abated by the time I got to her, but she was certainly angry, pacing around the grand bedchamber in the abbot's house, which he had vacated in favour of his royal guests.

'Where on earth have you been, Mette? I wanted you and you were not here.' There was a strident, peevish note in her voice that was new to me. She could be cross and critical at times, but was not usually given to petulance.

'I am sorry, Mademoiselle. I went to the stables to check on Genevieve.' It was hardly a grovelling apology, but I soon realised that perhaps it should have been.

'Do you mean to say that you abandoned your queen in favour of a horse?' she almost snorted. 'Is there something wrong with your horse?' The sharp tone of this enquiry did not imply any sudden burst of equine benevolence on her part.

'She had a stone in her hoof,' I replied. 'Lady Joan removed it for me.'

This revelation brought her anger fizzing to the surface again. 'This is unbelievable! I have three ladies to serve me and yet when I need their assistance I find that two of them are dancing attendance on a horse!'

Wondering what it was that could have brought on this uncharacteristic fit of pique, I decided that there was nothing

16

for it but to act the truly humble servant. 'Forgive me, your grace,' I said, abandoning my usual, more familiar, form of address. 'I had no idea you were in such urgent need of me. How may I serve you?'

She turned her back and paced away across the room. 'Oh it does not matter now. Clearly my problems are of no consequence compared to a stone in your horse's hoof!'

Agnes de Blagny, who had borne the brunt of the queen's initial outburst, was making faces at me behind Catherine's back. I found her facial gymnastics hard to interpret, but gathered it had involved King Henry in some way.

'Please, Madame – your grace – tell me what it is that has upset you. Does it concern the king? Was it something he said?'

She swung round at that, her eyes suddenly brimming with tears. 'All day people have been calling out my name, begging for my glance, holding out their children for my touch. I am their beautiful queen, their Fair Kate, their Agincourt Bride. But my husband, the one who should have my glances and my touch and whose child I should be bearing, prefers to squander his attention on debating Christian doctrine with the abbot and inspecting the abbey's library of dusty old books. And tomorrow, after he has prayed for an heir at the tomb of St Thomas à Becket, he says he must leave me here and hasten to Westminster to meet with his counsellors. I ask you – where in all the two thousand books the abbot is so proud to display to the king does it say that there has ever been more than one Immaculate Conception? What is the use of praying for an heir if Henry does nothing about actually getting one?'

There was the crux of the matter. She might be the darling of the crowds but, deep down, she would be an inadequate failure as a queen if she did not produce the heir that was so essential to securing the future of the crowns of England and France. Her marriage to King Henry was the very embodiment of the unification of the two kingdoms. She was the living proof of his remarkable conquest of more than half of France, but the joining of the two crowns, set in law by the Treaty of Troyes at their wedding eight months before, would be useless unless there was a male child born of the marriage; an heir to inherit the empire King Henry was creating and to carry it through to succeeding generations. On the surface Catherine was the ultra-beautiful, super-confident Queen of England and presumptive Queen of France, but inside she was a quivering mass of insecurities, all centred on the imperative conception of that child.

I hurried across the room to the abbot's carved armchair into which she had sunk with a heavy sigh. 'His grace will be here soon, Mademoiselle, I am sure,' I said, lapsing back into the intimate form of address I had used ever since we had been reunited when she came to the French court at thirteen, fresh from her convent school. To me she would always be 'Mademoiselle', however many grand titles she acquired. 'He rarely fails to wish you goodnight, even if he works into the small hours.'

Catherine gave me a withering look, far from mollified by my attempt at consolation. 'A goodnight kiss is hardly going to sire the next king of England, Mette,' she complained, fretfully tugging at the pins that secured her veil to her headdress. 'Henry could learn something from his subjects when it comes to enthusiastic outpourings of love!'

I gazed at her ruefully. What she was trying to tell me was that King Henry had not performed his duty in the marital bed for some time and I was guiltily aware that I might be partly responsible for this lack. A month ago, just after Epiphany, Catherine had miscarried. It had not been a well-developed pregnancy, but for a few joyous weeks she and Henry had believed the essential heir had been growing in her womb. Fortunately they had not made any announcement to this effect, having followed my suggestion that it might be best to wait until a few more weeks had passed; so Catherine had not had to suffer court murmurings of dissatisfaction and doubt about her ability to bear a child. But of course it had been a bitter disappointment for the king and queen. To my surprise, the king had not been critical of Catherine or blamed any lack of care on the part of her attendants, including myself, which had emboldened me to advise him that it would be wise to allow her a few weeks to recover before making any further attempt to get her with child. The fact that I had not told her of this conversation was now coming home to haunt me. The king might be scrupulously following my advice, but the queen was misinterpreting his restraint, construing it as lack of interest.

I decided to try a fresh approach. 'I recall the king saying he was eager that you should be crowned his true consort before any heir was born, Mademoiselle. Perhaps he has decided that it would be best even to delay conception until after your coronation, believing that God will bless your union once you are both consecrated.'

The feverish removal of hair-pins ceased suddenly. Catherine now turned to meet my gaze, which she had so far avoided, a flicker of hope dawning. 'Do you think that could be so, Mette? Really?'

I nodded vigorously, glad to have provided at least some crumb of comfort. 'Yes, Mademoiselle. As you know, the king lays great stress on divine approval of his actions. Truly I believe you should not doubt his regard for you or his trust in God's holy will.'

She frowned. 'But if he is convinced that it is God's will anyway, why has he sworn to pray for a son at the shrine of every English saint we pass in our progress through the kingdom?'

I gave her a mischievous smile. 'Why do you attend Mass every day, Mademoiselle, when God must know that you worship Him unreservedly anyway? Is it not to demonstrate your faith to the world?'

Catherine's brow wrinkled as she considered this. 'Actually, I think it is to reinforce my faith, Mette,' she said after a moment.

'Well then, perhaps the king is reinforcing his faith in God's will by giving Him a little reminder now and then,' I responded.

She gave me a reproachful look. 'I have said it before, Mette, you are too flippant in your attitude to God and the Church.' However she spoke more calmly having revealed what was the immediate cause of her outburst. 'Tomorrow the king will be leaving us and going on ahead to London to supervise arrangements for my coronation,' she informed us. 'The date has been set for February the twenty-third. That is just over a fortnight away.'

'And what will you do in the meanwhile, Mademoiselle?' I asked, seeking to glean some idea of when and where we were to make our own arrangements for this momentous event.

'We are to travel to Eltham Palace, which is apparently a royal palace close to London, where we can rest and organise ourselves for the big day.' Catherine turned to young Joan, who had been hovering quietly nearby waiting to assist her to undress. 'You may help me to choose my maids of honour for the ceremony,

Joan. I am told that a number of young ladies are to present themselves at Eltham Palace for my consideration and I believe three of them share your name, or a version of it. It seems that in future I may call "Joan!" and four of you will answer.'

Young Joan Beaufort lifted her chin proudly. 'But I was here first, Madame. The others will have to take different names.'

I was delighted to hear Catherine's laugh ring out and see a twinkle return to her eye. 'You are right, little one! You shall be the one and only Joan and we will call the others something else. Meanwhile, please come now and help me take off this headdress.'

Joan advanced to pick up the discarded veil and remove the jewelled net and fillet which had restrained Catherine's pale gold hair for her dinner with the abbot. Agnes and I exchanged relieved glances; a crisis had erupted and now seemed to have subsided, but I did not doubt there would be many more over the next weeks and months. This had been a warning that for the foreseeable future we would have to deal with a vulnerable young queen whose growing popularity would doubtless continue to wreak its share of havoc with her mood, causing her to veer alarmingly between intense self-belief and a desperate sense of inadequacy, unless and until her confidence was bolstered by the arrival of a viable male child. King Henry would not be the only one praying for an heir at the shrines of the English saints. Very likely I would be creeping in behind him with my own fervent prayers of intercession.

3

Our first sight of Eltham Palace was a disappointment to those of us who measured English palaces against the sprawling, marbled splendour of the French king's Hôtel de St Pol in Paris. Eltham had once been a royal hunting lodge and the densely wooded park around it was certainly extensive, but the demesne itself had been developed in a higgledy-piggledy fashion with a variety of accommodation towers and half-timbered guest houses strung out around the walled bailey, cheek-by-jowl with the kitchens, dairies and breweries, not to mention rows of lean-to wooden stables, kennels and mews, with all their attendant muck and stink. Situated above all this, on a raised mound, were the royal apartments, great hall and chapel which, although built of beautiful mellow stone and modernised with elegant oriel windows, looked surprisingly inadequate for a palace where King Henry's father was reported to have lavishly entertained the Byzantine Emperor twenty years before. However, as we rode up to the gatehouse, I noticed a vast tourney ground laid out beyond the curtain wall and concluded that the entertainment on that grand occasion must have been chiefly al fresco.

My information about Eltham had been provided by a pleasant and unassuming young man called Walter Vintner who joined us during the later stages of our journey. To my surprise he did not seem averse to riding alongside an older, wimpled member of the queen's entourage. As we rode out of Rochester that morning, I had smiled at him, thinking what a personable youth he was, polite, fresh-faced and soberly attired in riding hose and boots, a short dark-brown doublet and cloak and a cheerful green hat with a feather in it. A clue to his employment was an ink-horn which he wore slung from his belt alongside a leather scrip, which I quickly learned contained the quills and paper he needed as one of the clerks of the king's household.

After we had discovered each other's positions within the royal retinue, I took the bold step of pursuing him with flattery. 'You are so kind to speak French with me, Master Vintner, and with such clarity that I am prompted to pick your brains rather than those of your fellow countrymen who speak with accents I am afraid I find difficult to understand.'

'Ah, you have my father to thank for that,' he confided. 'He is so often in France on the king's business that he speaks the language like a Parisian and has teased me into doing the same.'

'Royal service is a family tradition, then,' I remarked. 'Is your father also in the king's employ?'

'Indirectly,' he replied. 'He is a lawyer at the Court of Common Pleas in London, but the royal council has need of his advice on diplomatic missions to Rouen and Paris. I do not ask what these missions are, nor do I think he would tell me if I did.'

My eyebrows probably disappeared under the band of my coif. 'Is your father a spy then, Master Vintner?'

He laughed. 'No, Madame! He deals with confidential legal negotiations between the English and French administrations. In truth I know no more than that. And please, why do you not call me Walter? I am not yet used to being addressed as "Master".'

'Why, how old are you . . . W-walter?' I stumbled over the very English way he said his name, pronouncing the W as I remembered Catherine's younger brother Charles had mispronounced his Rs when he was an infant in the nursery, and Catherine was his adored playmate; the same brother who now called her traitor for marrying his country's conqueror.

'I am nineteen. Although my father thinks I behave more like a twelve year old.'

I was struck by the sudden thought that he was the same age as my firstborn son would have been, had he lived. But he had not lived; instead I had suckled Princess Catherine and come to love her and, for that reason, now found myself here in her train on foreign soil with a lump in my throat.

I coughed, forcing out my next words. 'Fathers can be hard to please. What does your mother think?'

His face grew solemn and he made the sign of the cross. 'Sadly for us all, my mother died last year.'

My heart gave a little lurch to think of his grief for the mother so recently deceased. 'God give her rest,' I murmured. 'But who is "us all"? Do you have brothers and sisters?'

'Two sisters,' he nodded, 'younger than me. They try to run the house, but fifteen and thirteen is too young really.'

'And who guards them while you and your father are away?' I asked with concern. 'They will need protection surely?' Then I heard my own words and felt ashamed of their intrusive nature. 'I am sorry. It is none of my business.'

He regarded me thoughtfully. 'No, do not apologise. It is kind of you to take an interest. In truth it is an awkward situation because our aunt – my father's sister – has recently come to live in the house. She is a widow but my sisters do not like her. Meanwhile, my father buries his grief in his work and does not notice.' He gathered up his reins and clicked at his horse impatiently. 'Hey, Dobbin, shall we get there today?'

I took his impatience with the horse to be an indication that he wanted an end to the subject so, after a pause while I urged my Genevieve to close the gap between us, I reverted to my original topic. 'Have you been to Eltham before . . . er, Walter?' I asked.

'Once,' he admitted, 'on the way to Dover. I was only recruited into the royal household last month to serve the king on his return.'

'It is a royal palace though, is it not? Is it much used?'

'I believe the king has hunted there a number of times and the court came for Christmas a few years ago. I am told that his grace's father liked it particularly, but of course the present king has been out of England a good deal.'

'Yes indeed. He has seen more of Normandy than England lately,' I observed. 'What do your fellow countrymen think of that?'

Walter shot me an appraising glance. 'Well the battle of Agincourt was a great victory, of course, so he is very popular.'

'For us French it was a catastrophe,' I remarked dryly.

I saw his cheeks colour. 'Yes,' he muttered awkwardly, 'I suppose it was.'

'What do the English think about having a French queen?'

His colour deepened further. 'She is beautiful, Queen Kate!' he exclaimed. 'The people love her as soon as they see her, as you have witnessed.'

'Yes, they do,' I agreed, 'and long may it last.'

'Why should it not?' Walter cried. 'A glorious king and a beautiful queen – that is what the people want in their monarchs.'

Catherine may have thought she would miss King Henry's company at Eltham but, in truth, there was little time for moping. Couriers brought letters daily, outlining the developing plans for her coronation and the surrounding celebrations; there were gowns to be tried and adjusted, headdresses to fit, veils and jewels selected to match each set of robes, visiting courtiers to entertain and for exercise, some hawking in the surrounding forest.

In the midst of all this, a group of court damsels rode in for her appraisal as maids of honour and over the following days I was happy to hear Catherine's laugh ring out amidst a chime of girlish giggles as half a dozen young daughters of the nobility did their best to teach her some of the English court dances, while she attempted to teach them the French way to play bowls and they all swapped tips on the art of harmless flirtation. Catherine did not confide her thoughts to me but, as a close observer, I soon assessed which girls I hoped she would choose. Then, just before she was due to appoint them, the Duke of Gloucester threw a stone into still waters when he arrived at Eltham unannounced, bringing with him among his large retinue, a young lady. Within minutes of their arrival, a page came to Catherine's solar to request audience with the queen for his grace of Gloucester and the Damoiselle Eleanor Cobham.

'What does it mean this word "Damoiselle", is it an English version of our "Mademoiselle?"' Catherine asked her sister-in-law, the Duchess of Clarence.

We were all in the great solar, a royal presence chamber large enough to hold upwards of twenty people comfortably and had been listening to a new poem celebrating the royal marriage, penned by a poet called John Lydgate whom King Henry apparently much admired and patronised. It was written in English and, even though it was declaimed with great clarity by a professional player, Catherine had been frowning over the strange language and meter of the verse, so she looked quite grateful for the interruption.

'Yes, more or less,' allowed the duchess. The two royal ladies sat in canopied armchairs, while the young would-be maids of honour had grouped themselves around them on low cushioned stools and benches. 'The title is used at court now to indicate a maiden of birth but not of noble blood. Her father is probably a knight ordinary, a lord of a manor but not a baron. She therefore does not merit the title "Lady".'

'I see.' Catherine turned to Agnes with a smile, addressing her in French. 'There you are then, Mademoiselle de Blagny. It seems that here in England you are a Damoiselle.'

Agnes and I were occupying a sill-seat in one of the solar's long oriel windows, which protruded over the main courtyard of the palace and gave a clear view of the entrance to the royal apartments. We had witnessed the arrival of Gloucester's entourage and exchanged intrigued glances as we watched the duke elbowing a squire away to personally help a young woman down from her horse in a way which had led me to assume she was at least a countess. Not so, it would seem. This must be the Damoiselle Cobham, although with the hood of her cloak pulled over her head against the chill weather, it had been impossible to see her face.

When she walked into the room, it was instantly obvious that Eleanor Cobham was a beauty; small in stature with glossy dark auburn hair smoothed under a little green veiled cap, a pale, unblemished complexion and huge black-lashed eyes the colour of violets. She was also very young, with all the grace of a yearling hind as she knelt before Catherine's chair with her head bowed and her eyes modestly downcast, her robe a simple surcôte of pale-green wool, untrimmed and oddly old-fashioned, over a kirtle of cream linen with trumpet-shaped braid-edged sleeves. Compared to the bevy of stylish, blue-eyed blondes around her, with their bright-coloured houppelande gowns, rich fur trimmings and jewelled headdresses, she looked like a dainty wren among goldfinches.

The Duke of Gloucester bent his knee deferentially to Catherine. 'God's greetings to your grace,' he said with one of his dentally perfect smiles and precise flourishes. 'I beg to present Damoiselle Eleanor Cobham, the daughter of one of my ablest troop captains, Reginald Cobham, the lord of Sterborough. In return for valiant service under my banner at the siege of Cherbourg, I undertook to introduce his eldest unmarried daughter at court. Sadly her mother is too unwell to act in this capacity, but it came to my notice that you were appointing young ladies to your service as handmaids and attendants at your coronation, so I took the liberty of bringing the damoiselle here to Eltham, confident that you will find her entirely suitable for such a role in your train.'

Gloucester did not remain on one knee for long, moving to greet the Duchess of Clarence before stepping back to allow them both to inspect his protégée.

Catherine studied the crown of the little green cap with its pristine shoulder-length drop of white veiling. 'Pray rise and lift your head, damoiselle, so that we may see your face, for I think it is a very pretty face,' she said kindly, watching Eleanor's graceful return to standing and the proud lift of her chiselled chin above the smooth, pale column of her throat. 'But then all these young ladies display English beauty at its best, do they not, my lady of Clarence? Your daughter, Joan, not least among them.'

'Indeed they do, your grace,' agreed the duchess. 'And you have wisely decided to choose your companions according to their sweetness of character and temperament, rather than their looks.'

'Exactly,' nodded Catherine. 'So you see, my lord duke I cannot instantly grant any request to include the Damoiselle Cobham among them until I have enjoyed more of her company.' Ignoring the duke's frown of displeasure, she smiled at the newcomer. 'Meanwhile, we are happy to welcome you, Eleanor, and I will ask Mademoiselle de Blagny to introduce you to the other young ladies and make sure you are comfortable, whilst I retire to learn more of the arrangements for my coronation from his grace of Gloucester.'

She rose from her chair and there was a rustle of skirts as we all rose with her but, before she departed, she cast a second glance at the damoiselle, who now appeared even smaller, measured against the others. 'How old are you, Eleanor?' she asked.

'Fourteen, your grace.' There was a slight hesitation and the girl blushed before adding, 'That is to say, soon I shall be fourteen.'

'Yes, I thought you were very young. Not yet fully grown, I think. Well, time will remedy that.' Catherine addressed the duke directly. 'Let us take refreshment in my privy chamber, my lord. I gather that as Great Chamberlain you have been making all the arrangements for the feast. Will you join us, Madame?'

This last was to the Duchess of Clarence, who expertly swept back her trailing skirt and followed the queen and the duke from the solar. As soon as the door was closed, a burst of chatter broke out among the assembled girls, several of whom clustered around the newcomer asking where she was from and whether they knew any of her family. Eleanor looked slightly startled, but obligingly answered their questions, although it soon became clear that her connections were not recognised.

Listening to this exchange, the French word *parvenu* sprang to my mind, and I noticed that while Eleanor's eyes might be the colour of violets, there was nothing of the shy wildflower about her. In truth, this was a shameful thought on my part because if anyone was *parvenu* in the assembled company, it was me. However, Eleanor's manner and dress were such as to make it obvious that here was a girl who was not from a vastly privileged background and who lacked the sophistication gifted by wealth and social position. I wondered if the Duke of Gloucester had done her any favours by dropping her in amongst these judgemental daughters of the English nobility and was minded to feel sorry for her. But at thirteen she already showed the composure of some young ladies of twenty and the cool self-containment of a high-bred cat; I decided that I could probably save my pity for those who needed it. If and when the Damoiselle Cobham entered the queen's service, I suspected it would be only a matter of days before she displayed all the traits and skills of a seasoned courtier.

I had begun to wonder whether Catherine would ever seek my opinion of the candidates for her maids of honour and had more or less resigned myself to accepting whoever was foisted upon me, since it would inevitably fall to me to break them in, if that was the right term for showing these proud fillies how and in what ways they were expected to serve their queen with grace and humility. There were several among them who I thought might find the humility part of it hard to stomach.

More encouragingly, there were some for whom it would be a natural extension of a careful upbringing. These latter were the girls I hoped would make the grade and I was gratified to have my opinion sought later that night when Catherine retired to bed.

'Which of the young ladies shall I call to serve you tonight, Mademoiselle?' I asked, pushing a poker into the embers of the fire ready to heat her bedtime posset.

She made a face. 'None of them, Mette. They all look at me with such questing eyes, as if willing me to tell them they are chosen. I know their families are waiting and hoping they will be given a position. It is so important to them and I cannot bear to disappoint.' She crossed to the prie-dieu and I thought she was about to kneel and pray, but instead she suddenly turned and wailed at me. 'Help me, Mette! I do not know what to do.'

'About the appointments?' I spread my hands to indicate my hesitation. 'What does the duchess say?'

'She says I should take the ones I like best, but I believe the king would not think that the right thing to do. Some of them are of higher rank than others, some of their families deserve royal patronage more than others, and some would just make better attendants.'

'Then I think you should take those,' I said at once. 'At least they should be at the top of the list. After all, there is no point in having people around you who are lazy or who resent the tasks they are required to do.'

'Are there any who do that?' She seemed surprised at the suggestion.

'I have noticed one or two, Mademoiselle. Of course you would not see the faces they pull behind your back.'

'No, of course not. You must tell me their names, Mette. And what about the Cobham girl – Eleanor? I think she is too young yet to be let loose about the court, but I am reluctant to offend the Duke of Gloucester. After all, he is the king's brother.' By now Catherine had sat down on a stool beside the hearth and was staring into the fire.

'Why do you think the duke has singled her out?'

I tried not to inject my question with hidden meaning, but I must have failed because she glanced up at me, frowning. 'He said it was as a favour to her father.'

'Yes, but when does a royal duke ever owe a favour to a mere troop-captain?' I pointed out. 'It seems to me there is something not quite right about it.'

'What are you trying to tell me, Mette? That the duke has lecherous intentions?'

'I have no cause to think his grace of Gloucester unscrupulous,' I said hurriedly. 'The girl is very young, a beautiful child.'

She held up her hand sharply, cutting me off. 'Yes, yes, I know. You need not say it. A young girl with her looks is always vulnerable, especially if she does not have powerful relatives to protect her. So you think I should send her back to her mother? And you are right. I will tell the duke that I will reconsider her in a year's time. Let him be satisfied with that.'

I pulled the hot iron out of the fire and knocked the ashes off it before plunging it into a jug of spiced wine. A tantalizing aroma of fermented fruit rose in the sizzling steam.

'And the other young ladies, Mademoiselle? Which of them will you have?' I asked, reaching for a silver hanap from the nearby buffet.

She gave me a mischievous smile. 'Unless you tell me they have been pulling faces behind my back, I think I will appoint the three Joans or Joannas or whatever they call themselves – they are all Jeanne to me. I know it will make for confusion, but we can use their surnames and they all seem pleasant and uncomplicated. Also Belknap and Troutbeck are from the north . . .' Her brow furrowed in concentration as she struggled to pronounce the next words. '. . . Lanca-shire and York-shire I believe – and will be helpful keeping me abreast of matters in those far outposts of the kingdom. With Lady Joan and Agnes that will make five. What do you think?'

I answered her question with one of my own. 'Do you not need six maids of honour to carry your train at the coronation, Mademoiselle? I hope you are not expecting me to line up with the young damsels.'

Catherine giggled. 'And have the mother ewe plodding along beside the skipping lambs? No, no, Mette – that would never do. I will ask the beautiful Damoiselle Cobham to be the sixth train-bearer before she returns home to Sterborough – wherever that is. I hope that will appease the Duke of Gloucester as well as compensating the child a little. Now, Mette, tell me I am the queen of diplomacy.'

I made her a low curtsy. 'You are the queen of queens, Mademoiselle,' I assured her, offering the warmed wine. 'I hope this is not so hot it scalds your grace's sharp wits.'

4

'What can I hear, Mette?' asked Catherine when I drew back the bed-curtains at dawn. 'It started a few minutes ago and I have been lying here listening, thinking it might be angels.'

'It is a choir, Mademoiselle,' I told her. 'There are boys dressed all in white on the green below your window and they actually look rather like angels, only lacking wings. They are here to herald your coronation day.'

'That is very special. They sound wonderful.' Catherine made to sit up but hastily snuggled down again. 'Blessed Marie it is cold! Those poor boys, how can they sing in this frost? They need something to warm them. Will you make sure they get hot drinks, Mette?'

'I will send a page with your orders at once, Mademoiselle,' I assured her. 'But do not let your own drink get cold.' I had placed a cup of warm buttermilk and honey at her bedside. I held out her chamber robe and with reluctance she shed the covers, quickly stepping down from the bed to don the fur-lined robe. 'The fire has been burning all night so you can warm yourself at the hearth.'

At last the day of her coronation had arrived and, following a tradition begun by England's first King Henry, Catherine had spent the night in the Tower of London.

The previous morning she and the king had left Eltham at dawn, mounted on white horses, bells jingling on their harness and tasselled trappings of scarlet and blue boldly displaying the lions of England and the fleurs-de-lys of France. They were met on Blackheath Common by the city's mayor and aldermen who had ceremonially escorted them through the narrow shop-lined thoroughfare that crossed London Bridge and into the crowded and festooned streets of the city. I had not taken part in the parade that followed, but Catherine had excitedly described it when she returned at dusk.

'London is magnificent, Mette. Hundreds of bolts of cloth of gold had been distributed by the Guild of London Mercers and hung from the windows of the houses where they billowed in the breeze, turning the streets into a golden pathway. It was truly magical. A holiday had been declared and the roads were free of foul-smelling rubbish and lined with young girls in white kirtles with baskets full of dried herbs and rose-petals to throw under our horse's hooves so that we smelled only fragrant perfumes as we rode. For the duration of the parade the fountains ran with wine, although as you know King Henry has an abhorrence of drunkenness and had ordered it diluted with spring water. Even so, there were plenty of people in very high spirits. Spectators crammed every vantage point, blowing trumpets and horns, and some of the more agile citizens leaned from attic casements or perched on rooftops and even clung to church steeples to get a clear view. I was fearful that someone might fall, but no one did, as far as I know.

'There was plenty for them to see. On raised platforms at each crossroads mummers staged biblical tableaux celebrating marriage and monarchy and outside every church on the route choirs sang psalms and anthems. Fifty knights of the king's retinue rode before and behind us flying their brightly coloured standards and wearing full suits of armour, which glinted in the sunshine. Then, mounted on bright chestnut palfreys behind them were my six maids of honour attracting deafening cheers and whistles – and so they should have, in their blue fur-trimmed mantles and sparkling jewelled headdresses. We made a circular route through the centre of the city, stopping at St Paul's church to hear a celebration mass, and then to a feast in the Guildhall before returning along the river, past moored barges, docks and warehouses all decked with flags and crammed with more cheering crowds of people. I have to admit that today we were more enthusiastically greeted than when we rode into Paris last Christmas.'

I had left the royal cavalcade after crossing London Bridge and ridden with the household servants and baggage straight to the royal apartments in the Tower of London, on the city's eastern flank. The quiet of the inner ward, where I had spent the day supervising the queen's unpacking, was suddenly broken by the fanfare of trumpets. I found a window from which to watch the returning procession as it clattered over the draw-bridge that spanned the moat, past the Lion Tower where the king's animals were housed, through the massive gatehouse, under another gatehouse and into the inner ward. Steam rose from the horses' flanks and the riders' cheeks were flushed bright red, their breath condensing in the icy air as daylight faded. A hot tub awaited the queen before a blazing fire, not only to warm a body stiff and chilled by the February wind, but even more importantly to begin the purification process essential before the divine rite of coronation.

The queen would make a lone vigil ahead of the solemnity of coronation. Having escorted his queen formally to her lodgings, the king immediately rode away again to Westminster, leaving the Archbishop of Canterbury with Catherine in the royal chapel of St John. The archbishop spent an hour explaining the vows she would be taking and the indelible nature of the sanctity which anointment with the holy chrism would bestow. When she emerged, she looked pale and slightly dazed and went immediately to the small oratory beside her chamber, where she dropped to her knees before the portable altar that always travelled with her with its precious triptych of the Virgin.

Each of the maids of honour had been given particular duties regarding the queen's personal grooming – meticulous washing, trimming and brushing and the application of fragrant unguents – but I knew that if Catherine wished to pray, these treatments would have to wait. The wooden tub, draped in fresh white linen and set before the fire in the royal solar, had to be refreshed with hot water and re-draped three times before the queen felt that the preparation of her mind and soul for coronation could give way to the smoothing and soothing of her body and its ritual cleansing.

I waited with her in the little oratory, standing quietly in the deep shadows cast by the flickering wax pillar candles. When she rose from the prie-dieu and turned to leave, she noticed me there, smiled at me wistfully and moved close to whisper, 'I do not feel worthy, Mette. I fear the filth of Burgundy will never be prayed away.'

There was no one else to hear us but, nevertheless, I replied in the same hushed whisper, 'You have said yourself that the crown is your destiny, Mademoiselle. You did not allow that devil duke to snatch this marriage from you and now your coronation will demonstrate forever your high worth in the eyes of God.'

Although nothing had been said, I was intuitively aware of Catherine's fervent hope that the crowning ritual would bring a spiritual rebirth that might banish once and for all the dark memories of the torrid abuse inflicted on her by Jean, Duke of Burgundy; appalling ill-treatment which had ended only with the violent death of the duke, murdered in the presence of, if not by the hand of, her brother Charles. I had prayed that her marriage to King Henry would allow her to set the past aside, but it seemed it might take more than that.

'Perhaps the weight of the crown will finally instil a sense of right,' I added gently; 'that and the birth of an heir.'

She closed her eyes and crossed herself. 'I have been begging Our Lady for both, Mette. I earnestly pray that she will intercede for me and that I will emerge from the abbey tomorrow fortified with God's divine strength and ready to carry the heir that our countries demand.'

When her eyes opened, the expression of determination in their deep-blue depths startled me. Looking back, I had not anticipated how fundamentally the catharsis of coronation might affect her.

Over recent days two of the three Joannas (they all shared the extra syllable to their name) had formed a tight friendship, always keeping together and helping each other in the performance of their tasks. Joanna Belknap and Joanna Troutbeck were both from the north of England and seemed to possess a certain down-to-earth practicality. In order to differentiate between them, Catherine had decided to call them by their family names, a habit which made life easier for the rest of us but which did not please the third Joanna whose name was Coucy, a solitary girl not given to smiling readily or volunteering for anything. She complained out of Catherine's hearing that she considered being addressed only by her surname to be disrespectful. When I suggested that being in the service of the queen and addressed by name at all could only be deemed an honour, she gave one of her habitual, dismissive sniffs. Through careful enquiry I discovered that the Coucy family held, among others, the estate and barony of Dudley, which included possession of a substantial castle, and that her father had served King Henry in France and was recently appointed a court official. The Coucys were what might be described as 'top-rank' and very conscious of the fact.

When all six young ladies came to dress Catherine on the morning of her coronation Coucy, sniffed and sneezed and complained about the penetrating chill of their allotted rooms at the top of the White Tower, but Eleanor Cobham remarked on the glorious view to be had from its windows.

'They are calling it "coronation weather", your grace,' she told Catherine, kneeling to present the first of the queen's fine white hose, embroidered with fleurs-de-lys to signify her French royal lineage. 'From our chamber you can see across the River Thames and miles out over the countryside. I think today you might even be able to see as far as my father's manor of Hever!'

Catherine merely smiled and raised her eyebrows, being distracted by Agnes who was polishing her long pale-blonde hair with a silken cloth to make it glossy, but Coucy gave another of her chronic sniffs and commented tartly, 'Hever? I thought you came from some place with a borough in it, Cobham.'

'Yes, my home is at Sterborough,' Eleanor agreed equably, affecting not to notice the other girl's scornful tone, or her use of the surname. Joanna Coucy had decided that, since she was to be addressed by her family name, she would call all her fellow maids of honour by theirs. 'But my family has rents from more than one manor, as I am sure does yours. Hever is one of them.'

'Not manors,' responded Coucy scathingly. 'My family has estates – and more than one of those.'

Catherine eased her foot gently into the toe of the pale hose and stretched out her leg for it to be rolled up. Without turning she said, 'Is it not your task to raise my skirts, Coucy, to allow Eleanor to pull up the hose? And you might remember, while you boast of your estates, that they are granted to your father by the king and what is granted may also be withdrawn.'

Joanna Coucy flushed bright red, muttered an apology and carefully lifted the skirts of the queen's chemise and chamber robe. I watched Eleanor duck her head to hide a smirk as she tied one cream satin garter and wondered how long Coucy would keep her place at the queen's side.

Catherine wore two kirtles for her coronation – one of fine ivory Champagne linen directly over her chemise and the other of more substantial weight, for warmth when she was ceremonially stripped of her grand outer robes before her anointing. This second garment was a tunic of heavy white silk, lined with a layer of soft shaved lamb's wool and sewn with tiny seed-pearls. It had tight sleeves with long trailing tippets of ermine. Around her neck was draped a white stole of the type worn by bishops and senior clergy, lavishly embroidered in shimmering gold thread. At the anointing, and before the crown was set on Catherine's head, this stole would be removed to allow the sumptuous ivory velvet houppelande gown made for her in Paris to be drawn on and fastened with four fabulous diamond-studded clasps which were part of her French dower, followed by the crested, crimson, ermine-trimmed mantle of state, the train of which was twenty-feet long. Abbot Haweden of Westminster was due to officiate at the anointing, and he would keep the stole as a reward and a memento of his pivotal role in Catherine's transformation from ordinary mortal to one of God's divine representatives on earth.

In the Abbey Church of St Peter, I squeezed into the north transept among the officials of the royal household, where we had a clear view of the raised chancel and the high altar. There the carved and gilded throne stood on a stepped dais in the centre of a beautiful mosaic pavement, laid in squares and circles of brightly coloured stone and glass. Above it heraldic banners hung from the ceiling vault, showing the honours and devices of all the English Kings since William of Normandy. And so, as the ceremony began, I was able to raise my voice in loud approbation along with the great congregation of barons and ladies, when we were asked if we would have Catherine as our rightful queen. She looked modest and graceful in her embroidered white kirtle with her hair tumbling loose from a simple circlet of gold as she was escorted to each corner of the chancel by King Henry and the abbot and their demands for approval were swamped by loud shouts of 'Aye, we will!'

Then she was led to the altar by the Archbishop of Canterbury, where she made her solemn vows, speaking the Latin words fluently and without mistake. A lump came to my throat as I watched her prostrate herself before the great gold crucifix while the choir sang an anthem of dedication. She lay on cushions with arms outstretched in total supplication and inside my own head I could almost hear her fervent prayers that a great and compassionate God would demonstrate her worthiness to be queen by removing her burden of guilt and granting her an heir for England's crown.

Her maids of honour came forward to raise her up and remove

the stole and circlet. While the choristers sang a plangent benediction, she stood waiting, head bowed, under a cloth of gold canopy held by the four highest-ranking noblewomen of the court. Then the archbishop advanced to anoint her with the holy chrism on her forehead, intoning solemn prayers of dedication and intercession. Another anthem was sung while the holy oil was carefully wiped from her skin with a soft cloth, which was carried to the altar and placed reverently in a jewelled pyx. Then she was robed in her coronation garb and taken in procession to be enthroned.

During this procession the train of Catherine's heavy ceremonial mantle was carried three to each side by the maids of honour. Halfway across the chancel, without warning or apparent cause, Joanna Coucy suddenly tripped. By a supreme effort she managed to save herself from tumbling to the floor but not without jerking the mantle and pulling Catherine to a halt.

The procession resumed directly, but the gasp of dismay I had heard reminded me of when the Duke of Gloucester had tripped on the Dover shore. While all attention was on the king, who stepped forward to formally place Catherine in the throne, I kept my gaze fixed on the maid who walked last in the line of train-bearers, a pace behind Joanna Coucy. It was Eleanor Cobham and on her lips there played an enigmatic, smug little smile. I could not help suspecting that Eleanor had deliberately trodden on Joanna Coucy's skirt and made her trip in order to pay her back for slighting her family earlier in the day. Eleanor Cobham may have been the youngest of the maids of honour but she was far from being the meekest.

A glorious fanfare of trumpets and the sound of soaring soprano voices raised in a triumphant 'Vivat Regina!' and 'Long Live the Queen!' announced the moment the crown was placed reverently on Catherine's head by the archbishop. The crown was a precious and ancient relic of English history first used by Queen Edith, consort of the saint-king Edward the Confessor, who was buried behind the altar only yards from the coronation throne and whose shrine and sanctuary was a much-visited place of pilgrimage. We French often expressed scorn for the Saxon people who had been conquered by the armies of Normandy nearly four hundred years before, calling them uncouth and uncivilised, but if the workmanship of that crown was anything to go by such disparagement was sadly misplaced. Dozens of highly polished gems of every size and hue were set in a coronet of gold surmounted by pearl-studded cross-bars centred on a finial carrying a diamond the size of a goose's egg. It was a crown just light enough for a lady's head, but grand enough for an empress's regalia and wearing it, with two gold sceptres placed in her hands, Catherine was transformed from a beautiful young girl into a regal figure of power and patronage, an icon of sovereignty. I could not tell what was going on in her head, but in mine a subtle alteration was taking place. I felt my eyes fill with unbidden tears. The image of the infant Catherine tiny and helpless at my breast seemed to be slipping from my mental grasp, to be supplanted by this awesome figure of authority, crowned with gold and precious stones and invested with the symbols of earthly and divine power.

King Henry did not attend Catherine's coronation feast. He explained that it was because the rules of precedence dictated that if he were there she would not be the centre of attention, would not be served first and her new subjects would not do her full honour, being obliged to bow the knee to him first. Disappointed though she may have been, in his absence she was unquestionably Queen of the Feast. The highest nobles in the land acted as her carver, server, butler and cupbearer, while two earls knelt at her feet throughout the meal, holding her sceptres. The Earl of Worcester made an impressive spectacle riding up and down the centre of Westminster Hall on his richly caparisoned horse, ostensibly to keep order, and the Duke of Gloucester, in his role as Great Chamberlain of England, strode grandly about displaying his physique in a short sable-trimmed doublet of gold-embroidered red satin, brandishing his staff of office and directing the seemingly endless parade of dishes and subtleties.

In truth it was more of a pageant than a meal, a feast for the eyes rather than the stomach, as course after course was presented, each one more magnificent than the last and, because Lent had begun the previous week, all consisting of fish in one form or another. I had never seen so many different sea foods presented in so many guises. Anything that swam or crawled under water and could be hooked, trapped or netted had been turned into a culinary masterpiece; sturgeon, lamprey, crayfish, crab, eel, carp, pike, turbot, sole, prawns, roach, perch, chub – roasted, stewed, jellied, baked or fried, embellished with sauces or topped with pastry confections – culminating in a spectacular roasted porpoise riding on a sea of gilded pastry and crowned in real gold. It was all too much for me, but the great and good of the kingdom seated around me on the lower floor of the hall clearly relished it. From her royal dais, the new queen consort smiled and nodded at her subjects, admired the extraordinary skill of the cooks and, I noticed, consumed scarcely a morsel.

In the absence of her husband, seated beside the newly crowned queen was a pleasant-faced young man who also wore a crown; King James of Scotland who, although a monarch in his own right, did not outrank Catherine because he was a king without a kingdom. It was the first time they had met and his story was one which kept Catherine spellbound for much of the feast and earned her heartfelt sympathy. So much so that she regaled us with it at length the following day.

'King James told me that there are warring factions in Scotland, just as there are in France and that his older brother, David, the heir to the throne, was starved to death in a castle dungeon by his uncle, the Duke of Albany. Fearing that James might also fall into Albany's clutches, his father, King Robert, put him on a ship to France for safety. He was only twelve. Just think how frightened and lonely he must have been. And before he got near France, his ship was boarded by pirates off England. When they discovered his identity, they sold him to the English king, my own lord's father, who then demanded that the Scots pay a vast ransom for him. When word of this was brought to King Robert, he fell into a seizure and died; so Albany achieved his evil ambition, took power in Scotland and the ransom has never been paid.'

At this point she gave me a meaningful look. She was thinking, as I was, of the parallels between this story and the civil wars between Burgundy and Orleans which had shaken the throne of France and led to her own marriage treaty, in which King Henry had supplanted her brother Charles as the Heir of France. However, she made no reference to it and continued her tale of the hostage king.

'King James says the English have always been kind to him, particularly my own lord, the king's grace, and the recent death of Albany has set the stage for the ransom to be paid. So, since under the rules of chivalry it is a queen's prerogative to plead just causes, I mean to ask the King of England to instigate the

King of Scots' return to his kingdom.' She clapped her hands with delight at the prospect of exerting her new powers.

'Incidentally, little Joan,' she turned to address Lady Joan Beaufort, who was gazing absent-mindedly out of the solar window, no doubt wishing she was galloping over wide-open spaces to the cry of the hunting horn, 'King James made particular mention of you during the feast. He pointed you out to me, asked your name and who your parents were. I think you might have made a conquest there.'

Surprised at being addressed directly, Lady Joan went pink, but I think it was more from confusion at being caught day-dreaming than embarrassment at being singled out by the Scottish monarch. 'Oh,' was all she said, casting her eyes down as though she had no idea what the queen was talking about.

Catherine laughed. 'I think most girls would be more excited by the attentions of a young, unmarried king than you appear to be! Perhaps if I told you he has recently purchased a new jet-black destrier from the Earl Marshal's stud you might be a little more impressed?'

Joan's eyes did light up at this. 'Has he, your grace? How much did he pay for it?'

The queen spluttered with mingled mirth and exasperation. 'I have no idea. You will have to ask him yourself, but you may have to wait a while because he departs tomorrow in the king's train. King Henry fears that the Welsh border is too dangerous for ladies to visit at present, so he intends to go there first while we stay here at Westminster and make preparations to meet him further north. Belknap and Troutbeck, I want you to tell me all about the northern shires. Who are their leaders? What are their grievances and concerns? I am to join the king at a place called Kenil-wort.' She stumbled slightly on the pronunciation of the

English name and gazed enquiringly about the room. 'Is that how you say it? Which of you can tell me about this place?'

Joanna Coucy was ready, as always, to air her knowledge. 'It is the grandest of the Lancastrian palaces, your grace, situated right in the heart of England. I went there once with my father who had business at the duchy court. I believe the king spent his early childhood there. It was his mother's favourite castle.'

'Is that so, Coucy?' Catherine beckoned to the girl. 'Bring your stool nearer and reveal to me all you know about Kenil-wort and the king's mother.'

'Forgive me, your grace, but I believe it is pronounced Kenilworth,' remarked Coucy, smirking as she picked up her stool to carry it across the room, deftly dodging Eleanor Cobham's suddenly outstretched foot. Observing this, her second attempt to capsize the big-headed Joanna, I decided it was probably fortunate that, with her coronation duties over, the tricky Damoiselle Cobham would be returning home to Sterborough the following day.

5

The queen's procession arrived at Kenilworth at sunset. Seen through the mist rising off the surrounding lake, the castle seemed to float weightless before us, its tall red sandstone towers glowing in the sun's dying rays like pillars of fire. We were cold and tired after a long day in the saddle, but the magnificent spectacle imbued us with a new energy and the whole column of riders broke simultaneously into a brisk canter which even I, novice horsewoman that I was, found unexpectedly invigorating, especially as the chill March breeze had stiffened my limbs and, despite my riding gloves, almost frozen my fingers to the reins.

I had been to a few castles in my time, but I had never seen one quite like Kenilworth. Even at a distance it gave the impression of a palace rather than a fortress, for its towers were not crenellated, its curtain wall was barely eight-foot high and you could see the sun glinting off scores of delicate glass panes in huge mullioned windows. As we trotted through the first gatehouse to enter the long causeway across the lake, I realised the reason for the lack of apparent defences. Those fine windows were never going to be shattered by a bombardment, for not even King Henry's vast new German cannons were capable of hurling a missile that far and getting scaling ladders and men across the lake would take a flotilla of boats which would simply not be available at this inland location. The causeway was the only dry access to the castle and it was fiercely fortified with stout stone barbicans and gatehouses at both ends, which fortunately stood open to our cavalcade. I learned later that the causeway was in fact a dam, built in order to flood the land around Kenilworth and create a huge lake. In that misty pink sunset, with a group of swans trailing wedge-shaped ripples over the glassy water, it looked to me like the legendary lake of Avalon and when a solitary boat with a crimson sail emerged through the mist, moving slowly towards the apparently floating castle, it might have been carrying King Arthur to his final resting place.

Our accommodation at Kenilworth was the best we had experienced since leaving the Hôtel de St Pol in Paris over two years before. The principal living chambers were on the first floor of a tower set behind the spectacular great hall, where the master-mason had deployed a unique system of heavy oak rafters, permitting a wide, cathedral-like space without any of the usual pillars needed to support the roof above. It reminded me of Westminster Hall, where Catherine's coronation feast had been held, but Walter Vintner, my fount of English history, told me that the Westminster roof was actually a copy of the Kenilworth design. It was this fact that really brought home to me how rich and powerful King Henry's grandfather, John of Gaunt, had been as Duke of Lancaster, for it was he who had initiated the renovation and embellishment of Kenilworth with its soaring towers and gracious presence chambers.

When I started to relay this information to Catherine on the morning after our arrival, she stopped me in mid-sentence, holding up her hand imperiously. 'Do not tell me, Mette!' she exclaimed. 'I do not want to hear anything about the glories of

Kenilworth unless it is from the king's own mouth. Nor do I want to be given a guided tour of its policies by the steward as he offered last night. I am sure the place is heaven on earth but I will only think so if King Henry shows it to me himself. Where is he, Mette? He wrote to say he would meet me here in mid March. Today is the fourteenth. Why is he not here?'

Her fretful query was typical of the mood she had been in ever since King Henry had left for Wales on the day after her coronation. Although her father and mother, the French king and queen, had lived in separate houses within the royal palace and held their own separate courts, for some reason Catherine seemed to expect that she and Henry would be together all the time, making no allowance for the fact that he had not one but two kingdoms to run and a new campaign army to recruit and finance before he returned to his preferred occupation, which was storming more castles and conquering more territory. I do not know where she had got the impression that a marriage between royals meant living a cosy domestic life. Certainly not from her mother, Queen Isabeau. Too late I realised that, unlikely as it seemed, she had a commoner's attitude towards marriage and sought love and a working companionship with her husband, and I fear I was probably responsible for this desire, which was rarely fulfilled at any level of society.

I could not even persuade Catherine to break her fast in the great hall or attend mass in the ducal chapel, which only required a short walk across the inner court. She declared that she would emerge only when the king put in an appearance. Fortunately, later that morning, a courier arrived on a lathered horse with news that King Henry would be at Kenilworth before sundown. There was also a letter for the queen, written under the royal seal and in the king's own hand which, when she had read it, she showed me with undisguised glee, as if to say: 'See? I was right to wait!'

—§§—

To Catherine, my dear and well-beloved queen, greetings,

I trust this finds you already at Kenilworth where, God willing, I expect to be myself within the day. We have hardly seen the hills of Wales, for it has rained consistently but our marcher barons are successfully keeping the peace and we have encountered little unrest.

At Kenilworth I have a surprise for you and ask you not to be too curious about your surroundings until I come to show them to you personally. We have talked of my love for the place and I long to share it with the Queen of my Heart.

I will set out at sunrise and must stop briefly at Warwick, but before sunset I will have you in my arms. God be with you and keep you safe until then,

I kiss your mouth,
Henry

Written at night in Dudley this 13th day of March 1421.

—§§—

Noting the address from which this letter was written, I was thankful that Catherine had not shown it to Joanna Coucy, for we would never have heard the end of it if she had known that the king was staying at her father's castle. I handed it back, a little surprised that she had shown it to me at all, because of its personal nature. I took it as another example of her fluctuating self-confidence; she wanted me to witness the fact that King Henry still loved her, despite their recent lack of intimacy.

Her mood had changed from listless indifference to brisk intention. 'Call the steward, Mette,' she said. 'I want to hear the arrangements for my lord's arrival. And bring my sunset gown – the one I wore for my wedding. I will wear it to greet the king today.'

All afternoon, from the window of her chamber, Catherine watched the western sky and it had hardly begun to acquire the first pink tinge of sunset, when a trumpet sounded from the battlements of the keep. She scrambled to her feet, excited and agitated.

'They have sighted the king's procession. Quick, Mette! Bring my mantle. I must be waiting for him when he rides in.'

The sunset gown was so called because it was made of dark-blue, filmy gauze embroidered with tiny gold fleurs-de-lys and was worn over a cloth-of-silver kirtle with a wide gold lace hem. When Catherine lifted the skirt to walk, the lace beneath gleamed like the setting sun against a darkening sky. It had been made by my son-in-law, the tailor Jacques, and she had worn it for her wedding to King Henry in the city of Troyes the previous June. It was the first time she had put it on it since that day and it was Catherine's intention that he should recognise it and understand the significance of her choice.

As the king and his retinue clattered over the causeway and through the fortified gatehouse, Catherine took her place at the top of the sweeping stone stairway that led up to the great hall.

Long shadows had formed across the flagging of the inner court and the sky was a fiery orange, causing the approaching horsemen to shield their eyes from its glare. King Henry was in the van and did not wait for a squire to rush forward to take the reins before flinging himself from his horse and taking the steps two at a time to reach Catherine's side. Heedless of the numerous observers, he first kissed her hand and then drew her to him and kissed her on the lips, clasping his arms hungrily around her as he did so. It was by no means a gentle or decorous salute and, when he eventually pulled back from it, there was a broad smile on his own lips.

'Catherine my queen, my beautiful bride! I have galloped hard and eagerly to greet you!'

Her cheeks pink with shy pleasure, Catherine sank into a formal obeisance, as all of us around her had already done at the king's approach. 'You are well come, your grace,' she said, tilting her head up to return his smile and expose the long, white column of her throat, where a pulse beat visibly, revealing her own heightened emotions. 'I too have waited eagerly for you.'

He pulled her quickly to her feet and putting his arm around her shoulders led her through the porch into the great hall. 'Then let us waste no time, my lady. I have much to show you.'

'But you must take refreshment, my lord,' she protested. 'You have ridden hard.'

The king shook his head. 'It is no distance from Warwick and they gave me food and drink there. No – let my men rest and eat, I have other plans for you and me. We have not much time before darkness falls.'

Inside the hall the king took me by surprise, addressing me directly. 'Always nearby, Madame Lanière,' he remarked with a smile. 'Has the queen a warm cloak?' He felt the velvet of the formal mantle Catherine wore and pulled a face. 'This mantle is not suitable for our purpose. Be sure I recognise the gown however. We will do it justice, I promise you.'

Quite what he meant by that I hesitated to guess, but I bobbed my knee and hurried away to fetch the cloak. 'And bring one for yourself, Madame,' the king called after me. 'A queen cannot do without her handmaid. Meet us at the Water Gate.'

I felt my own heart racing as I hurried to do his bidding wondering, as Catherine must have been, what surprise he had planned for her. I had to seek directions to the Water Gate because, like her, I was as yet unfamiliar with the castle lay-out but I found it quite close to the privy apartments, directly opposite a tunnel leading from the kitchens to a steeply sloping court behind the great hall undercroft. I guessed that supplies for the kitchen were brought by boat across the lake and carried via this route into the cellars. Passing through the gate I found steps leading down to a stone quay and a sailing boat moored alongside. I recognised it as the one we had seen approaching the castle the previous night.

King Henry was already handing Catherine carefully down into the boat. She was shivering and I hastily passed her fur-lined cloak to the king who leaped into the boat, sat down beside her and wrapped her swiftly in its folds. 'You were just in time, Madame,' he said, his teeth gleaming in the dying rays of the sun. 'I think my lady's blood was about to freeze.'

'But now I am warm, my lord,' Catherine murmured softly, 'and intrigued to know where you are abducting me to at this darkling hour.'

King Henry did not answer her question, but put his arm around her and she snuggled down into his embrace, a smile lighting her face. He pulled the capacious hood of the cloak over her ears and over the gold nets and circlet which held her hair in place. 'These are regally elegant,' he said, tugging lightly at the nets, 'but they will not keep you warm in the lake breezes. Cast off, boatman, and jump aboard, Robin.' This last was addressed to the young squire who was holding the prow of the boat fast against the quay.

Catherine sat up in alarm. 'And Mette. Do not forget Mette, my lord!'

The squire grinned and gave me his hand to steady me as I stepped aboard. There was a narrow plank seat set in front of the mast and, unbalanced, I sat down rather heavily, rocking the boat. 'Your Mette is certainly aboard now, Catherine!' cried the king with what I considered unnecessary mirth.

The boat nosed out into the lake, pushing the water aside like wrinkled black silk as the red sail filled and flapped in the light breeze, driving us south-east around the castle mound and towards the opposite shore. Little was visible there except the silhouette of an uneven line of trees standing out against the pearly grey sky. Having no fur-lined cloak or lover's embrace to warm me, I thought a little enviously of the household, sitting down to their hot meal in the great hall and wondered what awaited us in the dark forest ahead. Behind me a murmured conversation was taking place between Catherine and the king, but the words were too indistinct to make out and anyway I assumed they were private. Suddenly I felt terribly lonely, marooned on that black lake with no idea where I was going and glumly certain that I would be the last to be rescued if a sudden storm blew up and threw us all into the water.

I should have had more faith in King Henry's generalship. There was nothing random about this twilight escapade. Within a few minutes we rounded a low headland and there before us, set against the trees, stood a small castle with crenellated towers, a moat and a drawbridge and torches blazing spluttering greetings from the gatehouse walls.

'Welcome to the Pleasance,' said King Henry to Catherine. 'This is my surprise for my beloved queen.'

Catherine was enchanted. I could hear it in her voice.

'It is beautiful! It reminds me of the Vallon Vert.'

'I thought it would,' the king responded, sounding pleased. 'Like our pavilion there, the Pleasance is timber, painted to look like stone. I had it built soon after I came to the throne. I wanted a place to retreat to.' The boat grounded on a gently sloping shingle beach and Robin jumped over the side to keep it steady. 'Come, there are fires to warm you and a meal has been prepared.'

The king followed his squire over the side and took Catherine in his arms to carry her to the shore. I tutted in disapproval as the train of her bridal gown trailed in the water but she was heedless, as well she might be, snug in the arms of her royal spouse. Clambering down the length of the boat, I was glad to see that it was possible to jump down onto the beach without getting my feet wet, for no one was offering to carry me.

Catherine was right when she said the place reminded her of the Vallon Vert. That had been her name for the little green valley where King Henry had had wooden pavilions built for himself and Catherine and for her parents, the King and Queen of France, to live in during the siege of Melun. It had been high summer and while they were staying in that cool oasis of shade, she and King Henry had discovered that real love might be possible between them.

Those summer pavilions had been little more than wooden

tents, but The Pleasance was a more solid construction, designed as a miniature version of Kenilworth with glazed windows and graceful oriels giving views over the lake. King Henry told Catherine that, in the days before his marriage, he had used it to entertain his close friends, hunting in the surrounding forest and feasting in the hall. I assumed that these feasts had not been for men only, but no details were forthcoming. There was certainly plenty of space for amorous adventures. On a quick inspection of the facilities, I discovered several privy chambers in the towers behind the hall but for this romantic interlude, alone with his young queen, the king had ordered a large tester bed set up in the great hall, where the two of them could spend a few days alone together without interruption or distraction.

'And no siege guns thundering away on the other side of the hill!' Catherine pointed out to me with joy when the king had gone to check arrangements with the small band of castle servants seconded to The Pleasance. 'Oh, Mette, is this not perfect? I had no idea that Henry was planning this idyll for us, which makes it so much the better!'

'And look, Mademoiselle,' I said, laying my hands on a harp which stood in the shadows beside the carved mantle-hood, beyond the reach of the fire's heat.

'A harp!' she cried, dancing across the room to run her fingers over the strings, filling the air with a rush of liquid notes. 'It must have been Henry's mother's, do you not think?'

'What must have been my mother's?' The king strode back into the room and I hastened to melt into the shadows as he came up behind Catherine. 'Oh, the harp – yes. She was always making music with some instrument or other. She taught me my first chords when I was three. She loved to sing to us.' He put his arms around Catherine's waist and pulled her to him so that her head lay back on his shoulder. 'Come, let us eat. I am famished!'

'But I thought you said you ate with the Earl of Warwick,' Catherine protested.

'I said I ate at Warwick,' agreed the king, 'but the earl was not there and the fare was bread and pottage.' He shuddered. 'It filled my belly but offended my senses. Here the cooks have prepared mussels and crayfish, with melted cheese.' He glanced over his shoulder at me, knowing exactly where I was. 'Mette can serve us and Robin will play and sing. He is not as accomplished as Owen Tudor, but he will do.'

The squire had followed King Henry into the hall and picked up the harp with a hasty bow before carrying it off. His head soon appeared above the balustrade of a small minstrel's gallery on top of the screen and a series of notes wafted down to us as he bent to tune the instrument.

King Henry led Catherine towards the fire, where a pile of cushions had been heaped beside the hearth. 'Where will Owen be now?' asked Catherine as she sank down onto the soft couch. 'Have you any idea?'

Owen Tudor was a Welsh archer whom the king had heard playing around a campfire at the siege of Melun and, being impressed with his music, had invited to entertain at the pavilion in the Vallon Vert. All who heard him agreed that he had great skill on the strings and a voice that could vibrate the senses. After the siege ended, King Henry had persuaded Owen's captain, Sir Walter Hungerford, to allow the archer to join the royal household temporarily, but when the king and Catherine set out for England Sir Walter had requested the archer's return to his troop, convincing King Henry that it was foolish to waste a good soldier on domestic duties when there were military objectives to accomplish.

'Hungerford's troop has joined my brother of Clarence, besieging strongholds on the Loire,' Henry replied, lowering himself down beside Catherine. He pulled at a cushion so that he could prop himself on his elbow to look at her and she blushed under his intense gaze. 'Young Edmund Beaufort is there too. Clarence is determined to break the hold of the Pretender in the south.'

I hoped the king would not pursue this subject as it entered territory painful to Catherine's ears, namely the war between her husband and her brother Charles, whom the English called 'The Pretender'. It was less than two months since Catherine had discarded into the sea a letter from Charles denouncing her for marrying the enemy and declaring her a traitor to France. It was a painful topic for me as well, because my young son Luc was a huntsman in her brother's entourage and had been the carrier of the letter. The war which King Henry pursued so relentlessly had opened a raw wound in all French lives, which had not healed since the Battle of Agincourt – England's glory and France's catastrophe.

Fortunately he changed the subject to less contentious ground. 'Kenilworth holds many memories for me. This was where I was healed after I was wounded in the cheek at Shrewsbury. I was brought here with the arrowhead still embedded in the bone of my jaw and a surgeon called Bradmore pulled it out with a special tool he had made.'

I could see that Catherine's stomach turned over just as mine had at this story. 'Oh, but my dearest lord, that must have been exquisite agony,' she cried, her hand reaching out to touch his scarred cheek. 'How did you stand the pain?'

'I knew I had to,' he replied simply. 'They strapped me down to prevent me moving and I could not cry out because that would have jolted the tool, so I prayed inside my head as loudly as I could. They told me afterwards that I should have died, but God did not permit it. I spent three months here recuperating – the wound was cleansed daily with local honey and my flesh healed in the good air of Kenilworth. Ever since then, I have believed that God intends me to lead England into a great future.'

At this point a small procession of servants emerged from the screen passage at the far end of the hall bearing dishes of various shapes and sizes, followed by a pair of pages with bowls and napkins. The dishes were set down on a buffet and a small table and two chairs were arranged at a suitable distance from the fire, ready for the meal. I hurried to spread a clean linen cloth and cut trenchers from a manchet loaf as the servants departed, leaving the pages kneeling beside the chairs, their bowls ready for hand-washing. I shook my head, took the bowls and napkins and shooed them away, frowning fiercely at the smirks and knowing glances which they cast in the direction of the lovers on the cushions. Rippling harp music began to drift down from the minstrel's gallery.

All this while Catherine and King Henry had carried on talking in undertones, heads close together. I gave a discreet cough to attract their attention.

Catherine dragged her gaze from the king's and shot me a glance of mild irritation. 'I can feel the breeze of your ears flapping, Mette,' she complained. 'I hope you will keep a curb on your mouth.'

'Of course, Madame,' I responded, hurt at the very suggestion that I might repeat anything I heard from my position of trust and hoping she had only mentioned it in order to satisfy the king's concern for discretion. 'Would your graces care to eat while the food is hot?'

'Indeed we would!' King Henry rose immediately to his feet and bent to assist Catherine to rise. In the firelight she looked ethereally beautiful in her shimmering night-sky gown, her cheeks rosy with love and warmth. My heart lurched at the sight of her, much as it had eighteen years before when I had pledged my life to the service of the tiny peach-skinned cherub who had been given to me to nurture. If she inspired this emotion in me, what must the king feel when he looked at her?

'My heart wishes to feast only on the sight of you, fair Kate,' he said as he bent to kiss her lovingly, 'but my belly clamours for more solid fare. Luckily, your Mette has the chairs arranged so that I may satisfy both needs at once.'

When they were seated across the corner of the table, Catherine said shyly, 'Mette knows how I have yearned to be close to you again, my dearest lord. It has been weeks and I have been churlish for the lack of you.'

Precedence ruled that the king be offered the basin first and he gave me a rueful smile as he dipped his fingers in the water. 'I cannot imagine my beautiful Kate being churlish, Mette. Tell me what she means.'

Handing him the napkin to dry his hands, I jogged the basin and a little water spilled over my apron. Brushing it off gave me a moment to gather my thoughts for a response. 'I am sure I do not know, your grace,' I said, retrieving the napkin from him. 'Churlish is not a word I would associate with Madame. But I do know that she refused to be shown Kenilworth castle by anyone but you.'

King Henry turned to Catherine, raising an enquiring eyebrow. 'Is that true?' he asked.

I turned to offer the basin to Catherine. Her face wore a slightly mulish expression and I thought she was going to chastise me, but eventually she gave a direct answer to the king's question. 'Yes, it is true and it is because you once told me that this is where you discovered love – the love of your mother and your brother Thomas.'

I could not see King Henry's face because I was dealing again with the bowl and napkin but his voice sounded gruff. 'We were always happy here at Kenilworth when our mother was alive,' he acknowledged. 'But my younger brothers and sisters cannot remember her as vividly as Thomas and I. She made this place a playground and every corner of it contains memories of her presence.'

King Henry leaned over to take Catherine's hand. 'I learned my military skills on the Welsh border, but it was here that my mother taught me to love music and books and poetry and all the things that raise men above the animals. In recent years I have been too busy fighting to enjoy the finer things of life, until God blessed me with a beautiful wife as my companion. I too have missed you and missed sharing your bed, my sweet love, but I thought it best to let your body recover after our great disappointment. I believe that my mother died from giving birth too young and too often. My sister Philippa was her eighth child in ten years and she was worn out. She died of exhaustion at the age of twenty-four. I hold you too dear, my Catherine, to allow anything similar to happen to you.'

At this point I thought it tactful to move away from the table. I may be accused of undue prurience, but I was as anxious as they that normal marital relations should be resumed and the essential heir conceived as soon as possible. At the same time, I needed to preserve my close relationship with Catherine because while King Henry would doubtless be off on campaign as soon as a pregnancy was established, I was the one he would hold responsible for nurturing it to a successful conclusion. It was obvious that they both fervently desired each other – you could feel the sexual urgency crackling between them – but while Catherine's desire for him was artless and emotional, his desire for her was controlled and dynastic – or so I thought . . .

I took a seat in the shadows beside the fireplace hood where I could not see or be seen by the two diners, but it was not long before I leaped up again in response to a loud bellow from the king.

'Guillaumette! Where are you when we need you? Come and unlace this tiresome gown!'

The sunset gown was beautiful to behold, but needed the services of a maid to release the wearer from its clutches. I hurried to perform the task, pulling the gold laces from their hooks as quickly as I could while the squire Robin took the narrow stair down from the minstrel's gallery two steps at a time to come to the aid of the king. Nothing was said but the king and Catherine never took their eyes off each other as we undressed them and when they were both reduced to their chemises, King Henry gathered his queen in his arms and almost threw her onto the embroidered silk cover of the great tester bed. The squire and I had scarcely managed to give them the privacy of the crimson curtains before we heard the urgent sounds of passionate love-making. We exchanged wry glances and while he hastened to set a reviving flagon of wine and accompanying cups on a side table, I retired to the hearth to stoke up the fire. As I stirred the embers and sent sparks flying with fresh logs, I could not suppress a gurgle of mirth, picturing my incendiary task as a metaphor for what was taking place only yards away behind the drawn bed-curtains. A few days and nights of this, I thought with an indulgent smile, and England would soon have its longed-for heir.

6

For three days and nights, the king and queen scarcely left the confines of the hall with its blazing fire and accommodating bed. Soon after dawn on the first morning, I took it upon myself to commandeer the boat and boatman to take me across the lake to fetch fresh clothes and other necessities for Catherine and we returned with a priest and the clerk, Walter Vintner, his scrip full of letters and documents for King Henry's attention. Fragrant new loaves from the castle bake-house, milk and cheese from the dairy and a large basket of fruit and vegetables had also been loaded on board, an indication that the king would not be leaving imminently, and who could blame him?

During the return journey, being privy to the royal itinerary, young Walter proved a fruitful source of information. 'The king intends to visit Coventry and Leicester while he is at Kenilworth and the queen is to go with him. They will stay on here until after Easter and then they are to make a progress through the northern shires. I hope you will not suffering unduly from all that riding, Madame.' A mischievous grin crossed the young clerk's face.

I shot him an indignant glare. 'It is not I who bears the strain, Master Walter, it is my stalwart mare. Perhaps on your return to the castle you might be kind enough to check that Genevieve is well tended in the stables.'

'No need, Madame. I went there last night to check my own cob and met Lady Joan Beaufort, who told me she had been speaking to the stable master about all the queen's horses, so I think you may be reassured on that score.'

I was impressed. 'I will tell the queen that her youngest maid of honour shows great initiative. Although I am afraid it may only confirm her opinion that Lady Joan cares too much for horses.'

Walter made an appreciative noise. 'She is a beauty though, is she not, Madame? Many a young squire would be happy to loosen her girths!'

I glanced at the priest's back, straight and prim on the forward thwart and wondered if he had heard the last remark. 'Whoa Master Vintner!' I murmured reprovingly. 'Lady Joan is the king's cousin and destined for a great match. You had best keep your eyes down if you value your position!'

He had the grace to look a little sheepish. 'I was just saying . . . I do not aspire to a high-born love, I assure you. However, if I did, I would pick Lady Joan over that Eleanor Cobham. She is another beauty right enough, but I reckon she would be a handful – and I do not mean in a buxom way!'

I decided there and then that it was time Master Vintner found himself a wife and wondered if he had a sweetheart at home in London. A position like his in the royal household did not lend itself to a steady domestic life and I knew that many of the courtiers in the king's retinue made use of the whores who were allowed to follow at the back of the train if they submitted themselves to the court physicians for regular health checks. My curiosity did not extend to questioning Walter on this matter however.

The royal couple were still abed when we returned, giving

66

time for breakfast to be prepared and warm water to be brought for washing. After dressing quickly, the king spent half an hour with his clerk in an adjoining chamber while Catherine stood before the fire in a dreamy reverie, allowing me to dress her in a simple kirtle and warm fur-lined over-dress of the sort the English called a côte-hardie; a very French name for a garment which I had never seen worn in Paris, at least not by a woman. I had acquired it for Catherine in London, thinking it a practical style for informal wear.

It was not until she was fully clothed that she even noticed her apparel but then she commented on it. 'Is this new, Mette? I have not seen it before.'

'Yes, Mademoiselle. It is an English style. A little old-fashioned, perhaps, but I thought it suitable.'

She fingered the fine cornflower-blue wool. 'It is a pretty colour but why now, particularly?'

I gave a casual shrug. 'You may notice that it has no lacing at the back.'

A sly glance showed me that she was digesting the significance of this remark. Then an irrepressible giggle burst forth, which soon developed into a lusty laugh. 'Oh, Mette, you are a rogue!' she cried when she could speak. 'Sometimes I think you forget that I am a queen.'

'Only when you do yourself, Mademoiselle,' I assured her. 'Which is when you are happy – as you were last night, unless I am very much mistaken?'

'No, Mette, you are not mistaken,' she admitted twisting to and fro, trying to find a fastening in the loose garment which skimmed the hips and had characteristically wide arm-holes. 'But I will be even happier when I discover how I get out of this.'

I moved forward to unfasten the plaited silk girdle around her hips. 'Undo this and just lift it over your head,' I explained. 'Or get your lover to do it for you,' I added with a twinkle.

She gave me a reproachful look. 'My husband, Mette,' she corrected primly. 'King Henry is my husband.'

I assumed a suitably contrite expression. 'Forgive me, Mademoiselle. Last night I mistook him for your lover and I hope to do so again tonight.'

I could see her wrestling with herself, undecided whether to chastise me or to concur. I hoped she would soon discover an ability to be both queen and coquette.

She and her lover-king settled into a relaxed companionship which lasted until Easter. It was interrupted by an official two-day visit to Coventry, when they were fêted and entertained and Catherine's beauty and charm loosened the purse-strings of the rich merchant guilds so that the king's campaign coffers were much replenished as a result. They returned to the Pleasance and a few more days of private indulgence before taking up residence in the formality of the castle to celebrate the feast of Easter with the rest of the court.

When we finally left Kenilworth, the royal household took up a nomad existence, heading north and riding a minimum of twenty miles a day. King Henry was an impatient traveller and tended to push the timetable to the limit. An overnight stay would always include an official dinner with opportunities either for fund-raising and recruitment or a visit to a chapel or shrine. By the time we reached York, a hundred and twenty miles north of Kenilworth, we had visited ten cold, grey shire towns and monasteries and March was well behind us.

Catherine was tired and, sensing this, King Henry suggested that she stay in York and rest while he fulfilled his vow to visit the famous shrines of two northern saints, St John of Bridlington and St John of Beverley. Since the many pilgrims to such locally popular shrines greatly enriched their attendant abbeys and priories, he also took the opportunity to obtain further financial support. Religious houses were a fruitful source of campaign funds because farmland that did not have enough men to work it quickly became unproductive and shrewd abbots preferred to offer the king substantial loans rather than provide rustic recruits for the campaign army.

In York we lodged at the house of the Dean of the Minster, and Catherine spent time praying in the beautiful cathedral-church. Meanwhile King Henry completed his pilgrimage a shaken man, having received disastrous news on the return journey from Bridlington. He maintained a calm façade in public and during the evening meal in the dean's presence, but his outward shell cracked as soon as the door closed behind them in the bed chamber.

He sank to his knees at the queen's feet, burying his face in the folds of her her skirt, like a little boy seeking comfort from his mother. 'Oh, Catherine, God has sent me a grievous trial. My beloved brother, Thomas, is dead, killed in a battle at Easter-tide.'

With a cry of horror she sank to her knees before him, taking his face in her hands. 'My dearest lord, this is dreadful news. How – when – did you find out?' Her own blue eyes blurred with tears and she called in an anguished voice, 'Mette, bring wine! My lord needs strength.'

I hurriedly poured two cups of the strong Bordeaux wine provided by the dean's cellarer. Catherine had persuaded King Henry back to his feet and they sat down together on a cushioned bench beside the chamber fire. Their hands shook as they took the cups.

'A courier met me on the road with a dispatch,' the king explained.

Catherine gasped with dismay. 'Then the duchess does not yet know? Poor lady! She loved your brother so dearly.'

Henry nodded slowly and sorrowfully. 'Yes, theirs was a love match like no other. It was a forbidden marriage, but our father was eventually won over. How am I going to tell her? She will be devastated. We should send for her before she learns the news from any other lips but ours. Perhaps Mette would bring her here?'

'Ah yes, Mette, would you go please?' Catherine endorsed his request, adding, 'And bring Lady Joan also. Poor girl.'

'Yes, Madame.' I dipped my knee before hurrying to perform the unwelcome task. The Duchess of Clarence and Lady Joan were lodged with their entourage in a house nearby and had taken their evening meal there. When I relayed the king's summons, they responded immediately, donning warm cloaks against the cold night.

The duchess was understandably curious, but I parried her queries about the reason for the summons, struggling to hide my knowledge that she was only moments from despair. I had brought a lantern and we were able to pick our way quickly across the flagstones of the Minster court without mishap. I thought it best to admit her and her daughter to the royal chamber and then retire. Despite their high status, this was above all a family bereavement and the terrible news should surely be broken in private. After only a few moments, I heard the duchess's long and heart-rending cry of grief and made the sign of the cross.

I was full of admiration for Margaret of Clarence during the ensuing days as the royal progress followed the spine of

England south to Windsor. It seemed it was not the custom here, as it was in France, for everyone and everything to be plunged into black mourning at the death of a prominent person; besides, no thought was given to protracted obsequies because the king was preoccupied with planning his new campaign which was now more imperative than ever. Masses were sung in the Minster for the Duke of Clarence's soul and, when we set out from York, his duchess rode beside the queen as usual, sitting straight-backed and proud on her beautiful, high-stepping horse and Lady Joan rode close to her mother's side, not among the other ladies-in-waiting as she had done hitherto.

It transpired that the Duke of Clarence had not been the only death at the disastrous Battle of Beaugé. Two other royal knights had been killed and there had been prisoners taken, among them, to add to the duchess's burden of misery, her two sons John, Earl of Somerset and Edmund Beaufort, the young squire who had acted as a special messenger between Catherine and the king during their so-called 'siege-honeymoon' which followed their wedding in France.

During the second day of our long journey south, King Henry singled the duchess out for a long horseback discussion and I was surprised when, at the same time, Lady Joan sidled her horse up to mine. Long bouts of crying had left the girl's normally smooth-skinned face rather blotched and puffy and my heart went out to her.

'May I speak with you privately, Madame Lanière?' she asked in French.

'Of course, Mademoiselle,' I replied, happy to use my own language for once. I kicked Genevieve to move out to the side of the column where we should not be overheard. 'How are you

71

and your lady mother? It must be hard riding out in public at such a time of great sadness.'

She shook her head. 'Oh no, I am glad to be on a horse and out in the air,' she said. 'Much better than being cooped up indoors with nothing to think of but the death of my stepfather and the captivity of my two brothers. I just wish I knew how they were, I believe they are injured.'

'Surely the king will get word soon about their circumstances,' I suggested, wondering why she had sought me out.

'He and my mother are talking about raising the ransoms at this very moment. Of course, Edmund's will not be too onerous for he is only a young squire, but John's will be crippling, an earl's ransom, even though he is not yet knighted. My mother will have to leave the queen and go to our estates in order to raise the necessary funds. That is why I wanted to speak to you.' She gave me a rather watery smile. 'I wondered if you would put in a good word for me with the queen because I really do not wish to accompany my mother on a long trek around Kent and Somerset, but nor do I want to hurt her feelings by refusing to go with her.' She looked a little guilty as she said this, but persisted eagerly. 'I would hate to lose my place in the queen's household and I am sure you can persuade her grace to ask my mother to let me stay on. On the way south we are to pick up my little sister who has been staying with my aunt and Margot will keep my mother company much better than I could. They have not seen each other for nearly a year and she is much more accomplished than I am. I am afraid my boyish ways rather annoy our mother, now more so than ever.' She opened her huge speedwell-blue eyes wide in earnest supplication. 'Please say you will help me, Madame Lanière!'

I have to confess that, despite the sad circumstances, it was a pleasant feeling to be at the receiving end of a plea from a member of the nobility. It would certainly not have happened in the French court, where I had been a servant of low birth. In England, where I was a courtier, few people were aware of this and Lady Joan, whether aware or not, was only interested in exploiting my influence with Catherine.

I smiled at her, a beautiful girl, so different from the style-obsessed demoiselles of the French court. 'I cannot guarantee success, Mademoiselle, but I will take your part with the queen on one condition,' I said. 'You must assure me that you do not wish to remain at court in order to pursue some unsuitable romance with a young and ill-bred squire. Your lady mother has been very kind to me and I would not like to do her a disservice by inadvertently bringing her distress, especially at this time of her profound grief.'

Lady Joan looked crestfallen. 'I am sorry that you would even think that of me, Madame,' she said indignantly. 'I am the one female among the queen's ladies who would rather chase a deer than dawdle in a pleasure garden. Did you not hear that I gave one stupid squire a thick lip for his wandering hands during a galliard?' She gave me a sidelong glance – a flash of bright blue filtered through thick, dark lashes. 'I do not know who I will marry, but I do know that it will not be a booby such as that.'

I detected a rather endearing touch of the convent schoolgirl in Lady Joan's pugnacious prudery, very similar to the queen's.

'I have poured my heart out to my horse over the past two days. She is the most loyal of creatures, aren't you, Artemis?'

She leaned forward and scratched her pretty dappled mare fondly between the ears. The horse responded with a flick of those ears and a little sideways swerve, which almost sent her into the path of a well-lathered horse galloping past us ridden by a man in royal livery. Lady Joan clung to the saddle like a limpet, calming her startled mare with a steadying hand and giving a little cry of excitement.

'That might be a dispatch from France! I must go and see. Au revoir, Madame – and thank you!'

I watched her horse dance away on dainty hooves, following the messenger's sweating courser, and wondered what Lady Joan's real reason was for wanting to stay at court.

7

We French have always believed St George to be an Anatolian knight-errant who, among other chivalrous acts, fought crusades in the Holy Land, slew a dragon in Cyrenia and was finally executed there for refusing to deny his Christian faith, but the English placed his feats in a whole variety of other places, most of which were located within a few days' ride of Windsor. Rather than being a Mediterranean martyr, in English eyes St George was a local hero, greatly honoured for pursuing and killing a dragon which had terrorised the maidens of numerous English villages. King Edward III had named his new palace at Windsor St George's Hall and his great-grandson had given the saint much of the credit for his Agincourt victory. King Henry had planned a tournament to celebrate the Feast of St George on the twenty-third of April, a week after arriving back at Windsor. Knights from all over England, those who were not involved in the French campaign, had been invited to take part and began riding in the middle of the month but a downpour had turned the tourney ground to a quagmire. The event had therefore been postponed until the first of May. Like the king's recent pilgrimage around England's shrines, the tournament had a hidden agenda.

'With the borders relatively peaceful, most knights will surely be glad of the chance to flex their fighting muscles and it will be a good opportunity to recruit more lances for France,' King Henry observed to his brother Humphrey one morning as they prepared for arms practice together.

The Duke of Gloucester had ridden in the previous night, full of his usual flamboyance and self-assurance. 'I am still short of knights ordinary for my contingent,' he admitted. 'I will tell my captains to keep an eye out for likely recruits.'

The two brothers were standing outside the barrier surrounding the area of hard sand where knights and men at arms practised their fighting skills. Squires worked busily around them, buckling on various pieces of armour. Part of the reason for arms practice was to maintain fighting fitness, so heavy plate and mail was worn to give their muscles a proper work-out.

After the downpour, spring had re-asserted itself and Catherine had asked the king for a chance to watch him at practice. She had brought her ladies with her to spectate and their fashionable gowns made bright splashes of colour against the grey walls of the castle. I noticed several of the bolder young ladies, particularly Joanna Coucy, casting eloquent sidelong glances in Gloucester's direction. A bachelor prince who was so closely related to the reigning monarch was inevitably going to attract female attention, although Humphrey affected to ignore their sly scrutiny, restricting his attention to Catherine.

'Since I am supporting my brother in France on this campaign, Madame, you may be sure that your lord will be in safe hands.'

It had already been announced that during King Henry's next campaign, Humphrey and his brother John of Bedford would swap their roles as king's lieutenants in England and France, but I could see that Catherine was not enormously impressed with Humphrey's flagrant boast.

'If your hands prove as safe as his were when he defended you against all comers after you were felled at Agincourt, my lord of Gloucester, that will indeed be great reassurance.' Noticing his flush of irritation at her reference to the king's famous battlefield rescue of his youngest brother, she was unable to suppress a twitch of her lips before turning to her husband with an eager query, 'Where will be the best place to view your swordplay, my lord? I so look forward to watching you hone your legendary skills.'

Clearly riled at being put in his place by a woman, Gloucester cut in with a glacial smile, 'So you like to see men sweat, do you, Madame? Or perhaps it is blood you relish? If so, I fear you will be disappointed. We spar only with wooden swords – see!' His squire had just placed the practice sword in his hand and he thrust it towards Catherine, making her jump back.

King Henry rounded on his brother furiously. 'How dare you, sir! A knight never shows the point of his sword to a lady, let alone a queen, as well you know. You will apologise at once or consider yourself on a charge of treason!'

With a shaky laugh, Humphrey hastily drew back his weapon. 'Steady, brother. It was only a play thrust, I meant no harm.' Nevertheless, seeing the king's fierce expression, his bow to Catherine was so abasingly deep, he almost kissed his own kneecap. 'I humbly beg your grace's pardon if I startled you.'

This was not enough for King Henry, who abruptly shoved his brother in the back, making him stumble to the ground. 'On your knees, villain! Apologise on your knees!' he ordered. 'You have offended the queen, not merely startled her. I should make you eat dust.'

Humphrey shot an astonished glance at Henry, as if expecting him to break suddenly into a laugh, before realising that he was fiercely in earnest and swivelling back to fall on his knees before Catherine. All bluster apparently gone, he bent forward to gather a handful of dirt from the ground which he held out to her and said, 'On my knees I abjectly crave your grace's forgiveness. If you so desire, I will indeed eat the dust from beneath your feet.'

Catherine's intense look of gratitude to the king surprised me and the determination of her riposte to the duke was equally unexpected. It was also delivered in French, which gave it added fluency and authority. 'I crave dust as little as I crave blood or sweat, my lord Gloucester. But I demand and I will have the respect due to the wife of your king; so I will pardon your sword thrust, but I will not forgive any repeat of the disrespectful thrust of your original remarks.'

Humphrey was taken aback. Expecting only a formal acknowledgement of his insincere grovel, he was more than a little shocked by her robust rebuttal of his veiled insinuation that she might have an unnatural lust for blood and sweat, so it was a somewhat sullen Gloucester who rose, frowning, to his feet, backed away and followed his brother across the sand towards the row of pells at one end of the practice ground. I detected more than a trace of venom in the violent blows he immediately began to inflict on the quilted padding of the stout pell-post, a far cry from King Henry's deft thrusts and lunges.

I noticed Walter Vintner approaching from the palace with an impressive-looking missive in his hand. He bent his knee to Catherine. 'This has just come for the king, your grace; it is from the Duchess of Hainault and I believe his grace will want to consider its contents with all speed.'

Like all the king's official correspondence, the seal had been broken and the letter read by his chief clerk so Catherine was able to scan its contents. It was written in Latin, the universal diplomatic language of Europe.

'It is from Jacqueline, Mette,' she confided, moving nearer to me so that her voice did not carry to the rest of the spectators. 'Jacqueline of Hainault, who was married to my poor brother Jean, if you remember. Her father died soon after Jean did and left her heir to the territories of Hainault and Holland. Then I believe she married her cousin the Duke of Brabant, although it seems not willingly.' Her brow creased with concern as she read on. 'Now she is in terrible trouble and asking for our help.' She nodded at Walter dismissively. 'You are right, Master Clerk; his grace will want to deal with this immediately. I will see that he gets it.'

We moved to the seating area where Catherine perused the letter more closely.

Nearly an hour passed before the king and Gloucester abandoned their energetic assaults on the pells and wandered across to the barrier to take refreshment. Their faces were glistening with sweat and both men hastily removed the heavy gauntlets they had been wearing in order to grasp the cup of the wine their squires poured for them. Catherine immediately approached the king and drew him aside to read the letter, while the duke took the opportunity to stroll over to the spectator stand where Catherine's ladies still sat. He rapidly had the three Joannas giggling at some light-hearted remark, but his dallying was interrupted when King Henry strolled up and thrust the letter into his brother's hands.

'You had better read this, Humphrey,' he said. 'The Duchess of Hainault and Brabant is a lady in distress. You may have met her in Flanders when you stood hostage for the Duke of Burgundy during our peace talks in Calais four years ago.'

Humphrey pondered this suggestion but shook his head. 'No, although I did hear talk of the new dauphin's beautiful wife. Would that be the same lady?'

'Yes, but she was not dauphiness for long, as Prince Jean died soon after that and she married the Duke of Brabant. Not a successful union it seems. Anyway, she is in Calais now and asks permission to come to England. Awkward though it may be in view of her close relationship with our ally Philippe of Burgundy, I do not see how we can refuse. Greeting her is a job for the Lord Warden of the Cinq Ports but, although we must regard her as an honoured guest, I would not advise carrying her ashore in one of your infamous chair-litters. This lady is reputed to need careful handling.'

Catherine protested at this. 'I think that is a little unkind, my lord. Her husband is a violent brute and the Burgundians have invaded her territory. She deserves our sympathy.'

Ignoring this outburst, Humphrey returned his attention to the letter, but King Henry gave Catherine a quizzical look. 'Another way of looking at it may be that she has run away from her husband and abandoned her people. Not something any prince worth his honour would do.'

'But she is not a prince,' Catherine insisted. 'She is a princess who has been forced into marriage with a half-wit cousin by the Duke of Burgundy on the basis that there will be no offspring to inherit either of their territories, meaning that in due course he can add them to his own. That is manipulation of the ugliest kind and Burgundy should surely not be allowed to get away with it. Jacqueline is connected to every royal house in Europe and might have been Queen of France, if my brother Jean had not died before his time. She deserves our help.'

King Henry forced a placatory smile, clearly unwilling to

enter into a public debate on the subject. 'I understand that you have sympathy for your former sister-in-law, Catherine, and with that in mind I will agree to let her come to England, even though it will undoubtedly annoy Philippe of Burgundy who, I am sure I do not need to remind you, is our greatest ally against the forces of the Pretender. Now, let us drop the subject.'

Catherine allowed him to take her hand and lead her back to her seat on the dais, but from where I stood I could see a mutinous expression that the king did not see. King Henry immediately went to speak to his brother, who was again surrounded by a giggling gaggle of young ladies.

'Well may you practise your charm, Humphrey,' I heard the king remark in a tone too low for Catherine's hearing. 'You may soon need all you can muster. I will send a courier to Calais today and I suspect that Duchess Jacqueline will waste no time in taking ship for Dover. If you take the highway tomorrow, you should be there in time to greet her and bring her back to Windsor for the tournament. You do not want to miss that!'

Following the talk about the Duchess of Hainault's letter, Catherine became unusually quiet for the rest of our stay at the practice ground. She waited to reveal the reason for this until we were in her bedchamber with no men present, preparing her for dinner in the great hall.

'Why should a woman have no say in her own future, even when she is the ruler of her own country?' she asked indignantly as Agnes and I removed her fur-lined heuque and began to unlace the warm woollen kirtle beneath. Sensing that the question was rhetorical, we exchanged quizzical glances, but remained silent, expecting further enlightenment. Being the maid of honour on duty, Lady Joan busied herself in the queen's jewellery chest, selecting the pieces to be worn and sensibly keeping her counsel.

'If we show the slightest sign of exercising any power, even power that is legally ours, we are instantly considered to be difficult or, as my lord puts it, to "need careful handling".' Catherine glanced round at the three of us, still busy at our tasks. 'Not one of you speaks, but you all know what I mean. Joan, has your mother never complained of such things?'

Lady Joan looked up from the jewel casket, her cheeks hot. 'Not in my hearing, your grace,' she said diplomatically.

Catherine shrugged and sat down on her dressing stool. Agnes moved in to arrange her hair more elaborately for the formal headdress she would wear with her elegant ground-sweeping gown. I had not yet noticed any of the court ladies copying Catherine's French fashions, but it could be only a matter of time before there was a rash of steeple hats and houppelandes.

Agnes began to twist handfuls of Catherine's hair into ropes, pinning them to the crown of her head. 'Have you ever met the Duchess of Hainault, Madame?'

'No.' Catherine shook her head, tugging against the tress her attendant was arranging. 'Ouch, be careful, Agnes! Well, I was at her wedding when she married my brother Jean, but we were all children then and I do not remember her except as a bride in the cathedral at Compiègne. Charles met her later, when she was the dauphiness, and said she was very beautiful but heiresses are always beautiful to men, are they not?'

'Will she live here at the English court now?' Lady Joan laid a collar of Lancastrian SS gold links set with diamonds on the dressing chest, ready to drape around Catherine's shoulders. 'After she arrives, I mean.'

'We shall have to see if we like her,' Catherine responded.

'She may not fit in with our merry little band. You are happy that you stayed with me, are you not, Joan? Or do you miss your mother?'

This double question flustered Lady Joan. 'Oh yes – I mean no. Well, I miss my lady mother, of course, but I am very happy that you managed to persuade her to let me remain in your service, Madame.'

'That is good because it was not easy. And of course King James is here for the occasion of his being knighted by the king. Does that please you also?'

This abrupt change of topic seemed to turn Lady Joan's cheeks a deeper shade of pink. 'King James, Madame?'

I frowned, striving to fathom where this conversation was going.

With a teasing smile Catherine pursued her theme. 'He spoke to me of you yesterday, Joan. He said he had watched you from a window, playing bowls in the garden, and thought you the most beautiful creature he had ever seen. I received the impression, however, that he actually knows you rather better than merely as a vision of loveliness viewed from afar. Would I be right?'

Both Agnes and I were by now wide-eyed with astonishment. This suggestion of a liaison between Lady Joan and the King of Scotland came as a complete surprise; then I remembered Joan's plea for my intervention with Catherine on her behalf. Suddenly I understood the real reason why she had been so anxious to stay at court.

I felt quite sorry for her in the circumstances. Clearly her lover, if he was that, had spoken to the queen of his interest without forewarning Joan. Tongue-tied and deeply embarrassed, she was unable to think of anything to say.

Catherine took pity on her. 'Well, since you do not deny it, I must suppose that the two of you are at least acquainted. And whilst King James is obviously very enamoured, he spoke most honourably and delicately about you. He writes poetry, did you know that? Well, of course you do. Really, Joan, there is no need to look so crestfallen. You have not committed any crime and not even your high-minded mother could object to such an acquaintance. King James has asked me to take his part in marriage discussions with your mother and the king, but first I would like to know whether you would be willing. Consent is still required by the Church, however; many marriages are somehow forced on unwilling and unfortunate noblewomen like Duchess Jacqueline.'

By now Lady Joan had dissolved into tears, and it was impossible to tell if they were tears of relief or remorse. I was about to rush to her side and put my arm around her, but Catherine beat me to it, pulling her hair from Agnes's grip and abandoning her dressing stool to take the tearful girl's hands and lead her to a window-seat where they subsided together. Wordlessly I handed Catherine a kerchief taken from my sleeve and she gently mopped Lady Joan's eyes.

'I am sorry, little Joan. I took you by surprise and clearly King James has raised the question of marriage without your knowledge. Men do that, I am afraid, especially kings, I find. They tend not to understand that women have feelings and wishes of their own and should be consulted. But do not cry. There really is no need. You are lucky if you have attracted the love of someone you might be permitted to love in return. If you wish, I will speak to your mother on your behalf when she returns to court. Meanwhile, I think you may continue your friendship with King James, always remembering that he is still a king without a kingdom and may never be in a position to marry if he is not restored to his throne. Besides, you know that he will be going with King Henry to France before too long, so perhaps it would be wise not to get too attached.'

'H— he has promised to write to me f-from France, Madame,' confessed the sniffling girl. 'I did not wish to deter him. I am told that men going to war often need someone to write home to.'

'Ah – the sweet innocence of the child!' Catherine handed Lady Joan the kerchief, casting a playful smile at me as she did so.

I raised an eyebrow in return, thinking that she was not so far from being a child herself.

'I am sure he will write charming and lyrical letters and you will treasure them.' Catherine stood up, her tone suddenly brisk. 'Now, I must finish dressing or there will be scores of people waiting for their dinner and I shall be chastised by King Henry for keeping them all waiting. You see – even queens live under orders.'

I shrugged my shoulders and gave her a smile of sympathy. At eighteen she had thought marriage and a crown would give her freedom to exercise her own will and was fast discovering otherwise.

8

Early next morning I had thought the queen was still abed, asleep, when Agnes came rushing into the robe room, her face a mask of fear. 'Quickly, Mette, come quickly! The queen is hurt!'

Catherine was very pale, propped up on cushions in a chair in the presence chamber, where she had been carried by the Master at Arms, a sturdy soldier who had heard Lady Joan's cry for help as she clattered into the stable yard at a hectic canter. It seemed that the horse-mad lady-in-waiting had been persuaded to assist Catherine in taking a secret dawn ride in the Windsor deer-park, which had come to grief when the queen had been knocked from her horse by a low branch. King Henry had been sent for, but had not yet arrived because at sunrise he had crossed the river to inspect the latest Thames navigation works. He must have missed Catherine and Joan sneaking out of the royal stables by minutes.

'I am perfectly all right. Do not cluck like a mother hen, Mette!'

Catherine was right, I was fussing around her in trepidation, feeling her brow and propping her feet on a stool. 'Well your grace, if you would care to tell me exactly what happened, I might be able to help,' I fretted. 'Should we send for a physician, I wonder?'

I would have liked to give her a more thorough examination, but was very conscious that we were not alone. Several high-ranking courtiers had interrupted their breakfast to offer help and were hovering anxiously in the background.

'My back hurts a little, that is all. I was knocked clean off my horse!' Catherine's indignation had increased in proportion to the number of people she could see in the room. 'Blessed Marie, Mette, send all these spectators away! There is nothing for them to see.'

She had dropped her voice to a hiss, but it still carried to every ear in the room and most of the courtiers began to drift away, muttering to each other.

'Truly, Mette, I am not badly hurt, just shamefaced because I am entirely to blame for my bruises. I wanted to gallop, to be free!' She winced as she shifted on the cushions. 'I daresay the king will scold me thoroughly.'

'Certainly he will and with some justification!' King Henry heard her words as he strode through the door. The small gathering of remaining courtiers dipped their knees as he passed. Frowning fiercely, he bent over his wife and kissed her cheek, placing one hand on her forehead in concern. 'I am happy to see that my worst fears appear groundless. I had dreaded to find broken bones at least. Please tell me there are none.'

Catherine's expression was that of a small girl found with her fingers in the sweetmeats. It was only with a visible effort that she met his gaze, shaking her head. 'No, my liege, none. I am sorry you were brought back from your business unnecessarily.'

King Henry continued to stand over her, like a tutor over an unruly student. 'I heard that you fell from your horse in the park. What in Heaven's name made you ride out without even a groom, Catherine?' Turning to me, he demanded, 'Did you not notice she had left her bed, Madame Lanière?'

So flustered was I by this sudden verbal thrust that I neglected to make any deferential move, simply staring dumbstruck at the king before dragging a garbled response from my frozen brain. 'Er, no, your grace. That is – I usually rouse the queen soon after first light but I had not yet entered the bedchamber.'

'Oh do not blame Mette, my liege! Do not blame anyone but me, it was my idea!' cried Catherine. 'I am not a child to be watched every moment of the day and night. I simply wanted to go for a ride with my lady-in-waiting without everyone else knowing where I was. Now let us have an end to this and allow me to retire to my chamber and lick my wounds!'

At this she kicked away the stool and rose gingerly from her chair, allowing me to support her in a painful progress towards the door. There were dirt-marks on her skirt, but I was relieved to see no sign of blood. She stopped halfway across the room to speak to Lady Joan, who stood shifting from one foot to the other, biting her lip and looking guilty. Dishevelled and also splattered with mud and dirt, it was clear that it must have been Lady Joan who had been persuaded to tack up the horses for this dawn escapade. Catherine put her hand on the girl's shoulder and turned to face the two kings.

'And no one is to lay any blame at Joan's door. It was entirely my idea and she was kind enough to make it possible for me that is all. I confess that the result of our adventure is a disappointment for myself, but Joan is a skilled and daring horsewoman and I, for one, am proud of her.' She aimed a look of encouragement at her maid of honour and made a wobbly curtsey to the king. 'Have I your permission to retire, my liege?' She gave him a tremulous smile, which I swear no red-blooded man could have resisted and his sternness visibly melted under its beam.

'I will come soon to see how you are faring,' he said, his eyes still anxious.

On closer inspection, I found Catherine's injuries to be just as she had claimed; bruises, both of body and pride, exacerbated by a few sharp twinges in her back. However, I noticed that she had become alarmingly pale and encouraged her to return to bed. She did not need much persuading. Uneasily I wondered if there might be more to her pallor than simply the after-effects of hitting the ground at speed. The bed was still rumpled from when she had abandoned it before dawn and, as I pulled the bedclothes straight ready for her to climb in, I posed the question foremost in my mind.

'You have not asked me for a napkin lately, Mademoiselle,' I remarked, crossing my fingers among the sheets. 'Should I be drawing any conclusions from this?'

There was a pause. 'Perhaps,' she admitted in a very small voice. 'To be honest, Mette, I do not dare to look.'

I felt my stomach lurch. Dressing herself for her clandestine excursion, she had only managed to pull a woollen kirtle and her fur-lined heuque over her chemise and so far I had only removed the heuque.

'Do you mean you might be pregnant?' I gulped, instinctively crossing myself.

Catherine nodded, tears beginning to trickle down her cheeks. 'Or I may have been – before I fell off the horse. I realise now I have been very stupid, Mette. I was angry yesterday, the men were being so . . . so male! I wanted to show them that we women are just as spirited as they are; not difficult and "hard to handle", as they put it.'

Her white face worried me, but I thought it a good sign that she had made no mention of stomach pains and, when I removed her kirtle, I was heartily relieved to find an unblemished chemise beneath. 'All is well,' I declared gratefully, 'so far anyway.' I had to tell her because she had covered her own eyes for fear of what mine might see.

'Are you sure, Mette?' she asked, dropping her hands but still unable to allow herself to believe it. 'I confess that I have a pain in my back and I feared the worst.'

'Then you must rest immediately, Mademoiselle,' I said briskly, dumping the kirtle and moving to pull back the bedclothes. 'You must keep your feet up for a day and more, until we know if there is definitely to be a child.' I forced a consoling smile, although I was suddenly very angry with her. She and King Henry had prayed for an heir at every shrine on their progress through the country and yet with one foolhardy action she had risked destroying any new life that might be growing inside her. I now pondered whether I should immediately inform King Henry of the situation.

In the event it was a decision I did not have to make because the king arrived almost as soon as Catherine was between the sheets and once he had satisfied himself about her general condition he asked a very direct question.

'It is nearly six weeks since we came together at Kenilworth, Catherine, and I have not been kept from your bed by any female effusions. Is it possible that you are pregnant?'

When Catherine confessed that it was possible, he was torn between praise and reproach, elated and exasperated at the same time.

'I do not know what to say,' he admitted, somehow managing to smile and frown at the same time. 'Glory be to God it is wonderful news! But we must pray that no damage has been done by your impulsive action today. I want you to promise that you will take the greatest possible care from now on. I cannot believe that you have risked the safety of our son and heir.'

His pacing brought him to the bedside where he gazed down at her with stern admonition. 'I have been forgetting that you have still not reached your majority and possess all the head-strong recklessness of youth. To a certain extent, I blame myself for the danger in which you have placed our son, but it must never happen again. I want to be sure you understand that. I need to know if I can trust you, Catherine,' he added earnestly.

'I promise to take more care in future, my liege,' she said solemnly, 'but I stress that I am not yet certain that I am with child. I beg you to wait before making any announcement. Remember what happened last time.' She reached out and took his hand, pressing it fervently to her lips. 'And I beg you to remember, my dearest lord, that any child we have might just as easily be a girl as a boy.'

King Henry gave her a pitying look. 'Believe me, madam, there is no question of this baby being a girl. God has promised me an heir and I have fulfilled all His requirements to deserve one. You must not harbour another thought that our first child could be female for that will weaken our son's strength and sense of purpose. Never forget that you are carrying a king, Catherine. We are building a dynasty, you and I.'

His messianic expression brooked no denial and Catherine subsided into the pillows, her face paler than ever. I hastened to intervene, moving forward from the shadows.

'Forgive me your grace, but the queen has had a bad shock and needs to rest quietly,' I said hesitantly, anxious not to stir his wrath further.

To my relief he nodded and bent to stroke his wife's brow in tender farewell. 'Yes, rest, Catherine. I will send to hear how you are this afternoon. Take care of our son.' He stepped away from the bed and beckoned me to approach him. 'Keep a close watch on her, Mette. This time there must be no mistakes.'

A sudden late snow storm laid a slippery cover over the ground and the tournament in celebration of St George had to be postponed once again. The conditions also delayed the arrival at Windsor of the Duchess of Hainault. She and the Duke of Gloucester were forced to wait out the storm at Eltham palace.

'This weather might well make Duchess Jacqueline regret her decision to come to England,' Catherine remarked wistfully, trapped indoors with her ladies embroidering an altar cloth when she would have preferred to be playing bowls in the palace gardens. 'There will be blossom in the orchards at the Hôtel de St Pol by now. Do you not sometimes long for France, Mette?'

Since I was doing my best to repair a delicate Valenciennes lace trimming on one of her gowns and wishing I had my daughter Alys's skill with the needle, her question brought a sudden tear to my eye. 'Oh yes indeed, Mademoiselle, quite often; especially when something reminds me of Alys and little Catrine.'

A meaningful glance passed between us at the mention of my infant granddaughter. There had been no announcement of Catherine's pregnancy yet, but with every passing day we became more certain that there was a child on the way. What I now recognised as King Henry's rather calculated romancing of his young bride at Kenilworth had reaped its reward and those passionate days spent in the Pleasance had born fruit. If all went well England would have its heir by Christmas.

'If it is a boy, of course,' Catherine reminded me tartly when I mentioned this calculation in private. She was smarting from the king's abrupt abandonment of her bed the moment he thought she was with child and also from his total denial of any prospect of it being a girl. Poor Catherine; she never quite knew where she was with her enigmatic husband. One day he was the charming lover, another the conquering hero and at present, unable to be either of these, he had transformed into God-fearing King Henry and was closeted with the clergy composing a new set of rules for English Benedictine monks, whom the Pope had accused of losing sight of their vows of work and prayer and, above all, of chastity. Catherine was discovering that she had married a chameleon.

'But when the snow melts, suddenly spring will be here,' said Lady Joan brightly. Perhaps as a result of her burgeoning romance with the Scottish king, the Beaufort girl was fast becoming the twinkling star of the queen's troop of ladies, always ready with a cheerful remark or a distracting riddle. 'The sun will shine and the flowers will bloom and the world will be a beautiful place.'

'Oh thank you, Lady Goody Sugar-plum,' I heard Joanna Coucy mutter. 'And we can all kiss a May-frog and find he turns into a king.'

Coucy's remark had not reached the ears of either Lady Joan or Catherine, but I shot her a fierce glare so she knew I had heard. I sighed and bent over the infuriating frill of torn lace, thinking that we could all do with some timely distraction.

We did not have long to wait.

9

As soon as the unseasonal blanket of snow had melted, the Duke of Gloucester rode into Windsor with the Duchess of Hainault and, to the surprise of Catherine and her ladies, her sole female attendant was none other than Eleanor Cobham.

The king and queen received Duchess Jacqueline with due ceremony in St George's great hall and we all had a good look at her as she swept down the room on Gloucester's arm, looking to my eyes nothing like a damsel in distress. She was tall and statuesque with milky skin and red-blonde hair dressed in plaited 'horns', capped with a headdress of exquisite wired Valenciennes lace. Seeing this and her magnificent and unsullied gown of dark-green broadcloth trimmed with sable, I concluded that she had prevailed upon Gloucester to make a halt somewhere in Windsor so that all evidence of the journey could be removed from her person. Jacqueline of Hainault knew the value of first impressions.

When the initial greetings were over, she was invited to take the place of honour beside the king at the high table and a splendid welcome feast was served. However controversial Jacqueline's departure from mainland Europe may have been, it was made evident to all that she was an honoured guest at the English court.

During the meal Eleanor Cobham was seated among

Catherine's ladies at a lower trestle and we were able to quiz her about her new patron. 'It was a complete surprise when his grace's messenger arrived with the invitation to serve the duchess,' she confessed coyly, 'especially as my family had moved from Sterborough to Hever, so he was obliged to battle the blizzard to seek me out. Fortunately, Hever is only a day's ride from Eltham.'

'Goodness, did you ride there in the snow?' enquired Lady Joan admiringly. 'Even in daylight, it must have been a cold and slippery journey.'

'A little cold,' acknowledged Eleanor, 'and of course we had nothing but saddlebags, so this is my only gown.' She made a deprecatory gesture at her serviceable grey tunic and blue côte-hardie, serviceable for riding hard over snowy roads, but lacking any of the style and colour of court costume. 'However, the duchess has promised me five marks to buy cloth for new gowns as soon as we are settled.'

'Five marks!' I echoed, impressed. 'The duchess's purse is well-lined. I thought she had been forced to flee Hainault with barely the clothes on her back.'

Eleanor frowned. 'Yes, she did, it was a daring escape from all accounts. But she assures me she will receive funds from the king until such time as she regains her own treasury. I hope there are some good tailors about the court.'

'The queen does not think so,' Lady Joan remarked. 'She is sending Madame Lanière to London as soon as the roads dry out, to recruit tailors and mercers. Is that not so, Madame?'

'More or less,' I admitted, although since my mission was quickly to acquire some looser gowns to accommodate Catherine's soon-to-be-swelling belly, I could have done without it being generally known yet. 'But if I can persuade a number of

London craftsmen to come to Windsor, it will be some time before they arrive. Meanwhile, perhaps you may be able to borrow a gown. Several of the queen's young ladies are more or less your size.'

Eleanor favoured me with an innocent-seeming smile, but I caught a calculating glint in those violet eyes of hers. 'Or perhaps the queen herself has some old gowns she no longer wears?' she suggested. 'You would know that, would you not, Madame?'

I immediately had a vision of Eleanor preening herself in one of Catherine's Parisian creations and revelling in the jealous glances of the queen's own maids of honour. 'I would,' I confirmed, 'and I can tell you that all her surplus gowns were left in France, to be distributed to charities in Rouen where the terrible siege left people destitute. Incidentally,' I added casually, 'does the duchess know you are not yet fourteen? Is she happy to be responsible for one so young among the schemers and lechers of the court?'

Eleanor's ingratiating smile faded and was replaced by a smug and steady stare. 'Actually I was born on the feast of St Richard of Chichester, a saint my mother particularly reveres. And so on the 4th day of April I became fourteen.'

'Congratulations, Damoiselle. But, even so, you are not old enough to know the difference between a gentleman and a serpent masquerading as a gentleman – and there are plenty of such bejewelled serpents who are not instantly recognisable, not until you find yourself alone with them in a dark corner. Do you take my meaning?'

'Oh yes, Madame,' she responded seriously, 'and I assure you that any man lucky enough to find himself in a dark corner with me will be there at my invitation and extremely rich, titled and unmarried!' She broke into a gay little laugh. 'I am joking,

Madame!' she hastened to add, seeing my astonishment. 'No, the Duchess of Hainault will have in me a diligent and discreet companion. I was merely pointing out that young ladies come to court not only to serve our noble patrons, but also to find a rich and landed husband. I assure you the duchess completely understands the importance of making powerful connections.' She glanced slyly up at the high table where, with smiles and elegant hand gestures, Jacqueline was adroitly managing to draw the attention of both the king and his brother. Catherine was also leaning forward to listen to their conversation, temporarily ignoring King James who sat on her other side.

Meanwhile I was assessing the impression Eleanor had made on me, admitting astonishment that a girl of such tender years should already have developed this hard-nosed attitude towards her own assets. Where were the wild, romantic notions that filled the minds of most girls of her age and which caused their guardians such worry and heartache? If Eleanor Cobham was to be believed, at just fourteen she already had high ambitions and a very clear idea of how to achieve them.

Joanna Belknap had eagerly taken over Eleanor's attention with questions about the intriguing stranger and she was not alone in her curiosity. Jacqueline of Hainault had sparked a new fascination in the court.

Eleanor spoke candidly of her new mistress. 'I have only known her a short time, but she is a lady who knows what she wants and tells you in no uncertain terms. I think she may have rubbed a lot of important people up the wrong way in Brabant, which is why she has come to England. She has even run away from her mother, you know.'

'Her mother is the sister of the previous Duke of Burgundy, Jean the Fearless; the one who was killed on the bridge at

Montereau,' I observed darkly. Even pronouncing the name of Catherine's 'devil Duke' sent a shiver down my spine. I could not help wondering if his sister might be tainted with the same evil nature, even towards her own daughter. It was not that long since I had risked my life and that of my son and daughter to save Catherine from his vile abuse.

Eleanor shrugged. 'I do not know about that, but I think she is lonely. She was delighted to receive me when I arrived at Eltham, saying it was several weeks since she had had any female companionship, and I must say her clothes were in a terrible state. It took me a whole day and the help of his grace of Gloucester's body squire to make that green gown presentable again. The sooner she acquires some menial servants the better, as far as I am concerned. My nails are ruined.'

She laid a pair of dainty little hands on the cloth to prove her point, but they did not look particularly work-worn to me. These days, at court, I kept my own hands hidden as much as possible because there was no disguising the evidence of their years of physical toil.

Eleanor continued cheerfully, 'Indeed, from what I know of her grace's intentions, the establishment of her household is precisely what she will be discussing with the king at this moment.'

She was right and very successful that discussion proved to be, for by nightfall the Duchess of Hainault and Eleanor were installed in a suite of guest chambers beside the queen's and planning how to spend the allowance of a hundred pounds a month granted to Jacqueline from the Royal Exchequer, a very considerable amount of money. The immediate problem of the ladies' lack of apparel was solved with the loan of a gown to the duchess from Catherine's wardrobe and one to her lady in waiting from a generous Lady Joan, which was just as well because the delayed tournament, when everyone would be sporting their finest apparel, had been rescheduled for two days' time.

It was intriguing to watch Catherine and Jacqueline quickly establish a close relationship, for since they were both princesses of European courts they had a great deal in common, not least the fact that they had once been sisters-in-law. At the time of her birth, Catherine's brother Jean had shared the royal nursery at the Hôtel de St Pol in Paris with their older siblings Louis and Michele and, for nearly four years, I had tended them all, as well as, when he came along, their younger brother Charles. I remembered Jean as a tough, pugnacious little boy who had constantly scrapped with his brother Louis and shown scant interest in any form of learning other than how to fight. At the age of seven, together with Louis and Michele, he had been more or less abducted by the Duke of Burgundy; Louis and Michele he had betrothed to his own children and Jean to his niece Jacqueline, after which the young prince of France had gone to live with her family and become a stranger to his own.

'I barely remember Jean,' Catherine admitted on Jacqueline's first visit to her solar. 'I was three when my brothers left and I can only recall Jean teasing me about my imaginary playmates. He would call me Lame-Brain.'

'Oh that was Jean all right,' laughed Jacqueline. 'He had absolutely no imagination. He had no time for anything that did not have a military purpose. If he saw me reading a book he would snatch it out of my hands and throw it across the room. "Books are for nuns," he would shout. "They make you dull. Come and play chess with me." He was good at chess and later became quite a strategist. Wherever we went he would assess the lie of the land and devise imaginary battle plans. If he had lived he would have made a good general.' Her face fell as she said this. 'France could have done with a dauphin capable of fighting a war.'

'Yes, we could,' agreed Catherine thoughtfully. 'That is why Henry is now the Heir of France rather than Charles.' A brief silence fell between them while she made a few token stitches in her embroidery, which had otherwise lain abandoned on her lap. Then she added, 'This may sound an impertinent question, Madame, but did you become fond of Jean?'

Jacqueline gave her a keen glance. 'No, not really, he was not *sympathique*, as you know. But we understood each other. That was the advantage of growing up together. Moreover he was more interested in knightly pursuits than those of the bedchamber and so he was more like my brother than my husband. In truth I mourned him as a brother when he died.'

'His death must have been a terrible shock. He was only eighteen, was he not? It certainly it took us all by surprise in Paris. It was so sudden. Did he suffer greatly?'

A shadow seemed to cross the duchess's face. 'Yes he did. There was some bubo or tumour in his ear and it pressed on his brain they said. I sat with him while the doctors tried to relieve the pain with the most terrible treatments, which he fought against like a madman. In short he screamed and groaned until he was utterly exhausted and then he fell back dead. It was truly horrible.' She sat back white-faced at the memory, which still obviously haunted her.

'But it does not sound as if he was poisoned, as some people suggested,' Catherine said gently. 'Did the doctors suspect any foul play?'

Jacqueline shook her head. 'No, not at the time, although some of our courtiers spread rumours about witchcraft or sorcery, but no names were ever spoken.'

'There were rumours like that when Louis died, but I was always certain that he drank himself to death. And now there is only Charles left, the last of our mother's five sons.' Catherine dropped her voice and glanced around at her ladies, most of whom were quietly squabbling over embroidery silks in a far corner. 'But we do not speak of him outside this room, especially since his forces killed my lord the king's brother. You met Charles once though, did you not?'

Jacqueline gave a brief laugh. 'Yes. Charles came to try and persuade his brother to kiss his father's hand, but Jean would not go to Paris. Actually Charles did not try very hard to make him. They discovered that they both hated their mother – your mother – and did not trust her. Jean declared openly that she said one thing and did another.'

'Well, he was right there,' observed Catherine dryly. 'Yet he trusted Jean the Fearless, which I find incomprehensible.'

Jacqueline visibly shuddered. 'It was. I think she admired his ruthlessness. Your brother would have been a ruthless ruler too, if he had lived. At least he had all his wits, unlike my brute of a cousin of Brabant, whom I was forced to marry after your brother died. That marriage was Jean the Fearless's doing, too. I was drugged and dragged to the altar.' Her full lips were pressed together into a thin line and the next words were forced through her teeth. 'Jean of Burgundy was a man of whom it is impossible to speak well, even though he is dead.'

I quickly rolled my eyes at Catherine in silent warning, but she was discreet in her response, sensibly giving no hint of her own extreme and justified abhorrence of the murdered duke.

'How much you have suffered,' she said sympathetically. 'Life in Brabant must have been unbearable if you were forced to flee in terror – even from your own mother.'

'They all conspire to take my lands,' insisted Jacqueline bitterly. 'My mother, my uncle and my cousin all blatantly seek the expansion of Burgundy's territories. I am without friends save for his grace, your husband. King Henry is the only man of power to embrace my cause. I am eternally grateful to him and the Duke of Gloucester.'

'Yes, you and Humphrey have had time to become well acquainted, being snowed up together as you were, and he brought his little protégée to your notice too.' She cast a glance at Eleanor, who sat a little removed from the other young ladies across the chamber. 'She is something of a beauty your new companion, is she not?'

The duchess laughed happily. 'Oh yes – and quite delightful; so accomplished for her age and very bright. Of course I will seek other attendants too, but I know already that she will be of particular help to me.'

Even though she sat apart from the conversation, Eleanor must have been listening intently to hear what was said about her for I saw her lips twitch in a secret, self-satisfied smile. Suddenly I felt a surge of relief that she had entered service with the duchess and would therefore presumably no longer be in line to join Catherine's household. Beautiful though she was, with all the lustre of youth, there was something deeply troubling about Eleanor Cobham.

By the time the herald trumpets sounded, the St George's Day tournament had been delayed by two weeks. It was well into May when the Knights of the Garter attended their solemn re-dedication service in the castle chapel before donning their burnished armour and parading on horseback around the Upper Court acknowledging the cheers of a large crowd of courtiers and any townsfolk who could wangle an entry by bribery or civic rank. King Henry led the parade, followed by the Duke of Gloucester and the ten other distinguished members of the order of Knights of the Garter who were not fighting in France, were indisposed or had died in the last year. In view of these restrictions it seemed a good turnout.

It was the first time I had ever had a grandstand view of a tournament. The royal box had been erected in front of St George's Hall and lavishly decorated with banners and spring flowers. Queen Catherine sat enthroned between her new friend Jacqueline of Hainault and Henry Beaufort, Bishop of Winchester, while I sat at the back among her ladies, pinching myself and wondering whether, nineteen years ago, my mother could ever have envisaged me in this position when she hired me out, red-eyed from the loss of my stillborn son, to be a wet-nurse to the Queen of France's new baby girl. 'It is a good opportunity, Mette,' she had said encouragingly. 'It will be hard at first, but who knows where it could lead?' I stroked the fine cloth of my sleek slate-blue worsted gown and concluded that even in her wildest dreams she could not have conjured this eventuality.

King Henry was to open the tourney with a formal tilt against his brother, but before they rode to their respective ends of the lists, a trumpeter blew a loud blast and Windsor Herald called the crowd to attention in a sonorous, carrying voice.

'Your Graces, My Lords, Ladies and Knights of the Garter, and all the king's subjects here present, pray silence for joyful news. Our most puissant King Henry, the greatest knight in Christendom, and his fair Queen Catherine have commanded me to announce that an heir to the thrones of England and France is expected during Advent. And so, God willing, at Christmastide, England and France will celebrate the coming of both the Christ-child and a newborn prince. God save the king and God save Queen Catherine!'

Another trumpet flourish resounded at the end of the herald's announcement and cheers swelled from among the crowds in the stands. The tilt ground was not a vast arena and the enclosing walls of the castle seemed to shake with the shouts of joy and celebration. Then the bells began to ring, first from the Curfew Tower in the Lower Ward, from which the carillon was taken up by all the church bells in the town of Windsor. Vibrations seemed to shake the clear blue arc of the spring sky and speech became impossible against the tumult of echoing chimes. In the royal box we all burst into spontaneous applause and Catherine stood to acknowledge the enthusiastic greetings that were offered from every side. Blushing prettily, she reached into the floral display before her and plucked an early red rose bud from the garland, leaning over the rail to proffer it to King Henry, whose charger pranced impatiently, agitated by the bells, stirring the sand with its hooves. Controlling his horse with one hand, the king reached over to take the bloom from his wife with a broad smile of pleasure, kissed its tightly curled petals and tucked it into the shoulder joint of his glinting suit of armour, where it nodded jauntily. The red rose was a badge of Lancaster and the king's delighted smile acknowledged her subtle intention to mark the budding of a new flower of the Lancastrian tree.

The previous day King Henry had announced the appointment of four new Knights of the Garter, including his standard bearer Sir Louis Robsart and the Earl Marshall, Sir Thomas Mowbray, who both now entered the arena on foot bearing spurs and a sword and escorting King James of Scotland modestly dressed in a white jupon, black hose and red shoes. King Henry's intention was to personally confer the accolade of knighthood on his fellow monarch prior to allowing emissaries at last to enter into negotiations over the Scottish king's ransom from his prolonged captivity in England. Catherine had expressed a wish to see this ceremony and so it had been decided that it should be performed at the start of the tournament.

Out of interest I kept one eye on Lady Joan as her professed suitor crossed the sand; predictably her eyes were bright with excitement. Meanwhile Joanna Coucy made an accurate but to my mind unnecessary observation.

'He is somewhat old to be receiving a knighthood, is he not? I thought twenty-one was the usual age. The King of Scots must be all of twenty-five or six. It does not say much for his fighting skills if he has had to wait until now to be dubbed.'

Lady Joan rounded on her fellow lady-in-waiting with an indignant glare. 'He has not exactly had an upbringing of the usual kind!' she exclaimed. 'How would you like to be held for ransom for fifteen years? The old king refused to let him have instruction in the use of arms in case he employed them against Englishmen. He only started his training for knighthood under King Henry, who seems to think he has succeeded, even if you do not!'

Joanna Coucy glared back. 'Well! You are very quick to defend him, Joan! I wonder why?'

'Hush,' I cautioned, leaning from behind to push my face between them with a frown. 'King James at least deserves your attention at this important moment in his life.'

Lady Joan turned back instantly to watch the proceedings, but Joanna Coucy continued to stare at me balefully. 'Your title is Keeper of the Queen's Robes, Madame Lanière, not Keeper of the Queen's Damsels. What makes you think you have any authority over me?'

Hiding my angry reaction I said quietly and with a pleasant smile, 'Seniority,' and put my finger against my lips. As I averted my gaze to the lists I could not help noticing that the Duchess of Hainault had turned in her chair to watch and listen to this exchange. Her eyes were narrowed, as if she pondered a question of profound significance.

A silk carpet had been laid on the sand of the tourney ground and King James was now kneeling before King Henry, who had dismounted and taken the great two-handed sword of Edward the Confessor from his Leopard Herald. Stepping forward he raised the heavy weapon and delivered the accolade of knighthood by three firm taps on the royal squire's shoulders. 'James Stewart soyez chevalier – be you knight!' he declared in a loud, clear voice. 'Be true to God and guard your honour.'

After a solemn pause, King James rose and the two monarchs kissed each other on the cheek in brotherly acknowledgement, while each of the Scot's two distinguished sponsors knelt to buckle a polished spur around his ankles. When the sword of knighthood, safe in its scabbard, had been slung from his knightly girdle, they then took him by the arms and turned him to face his fellow knights gathered at the Herald's Gate, whereupon they put up a rousing cheer which was echoed by King Henry and the Duke of Gloucester, who was still mounted at the far end of the lists. Beside me Lady Joan clapped excitedly, tears of admiration glinting in her eyes.

10

Genevieve flicked her ears irritably and drops of water flew off to join the misty drizzle that seemed to penetrate every seam of our clothing. It was a whole day's ride from Windsor to London and within half an hour of setting out, we were wet through to the skin. I had been looking forward to this trip with Walter Vintner as an opportunity to escape the restrictive confines of the castle and breathe the fresh air of the countryside, but I had reckoned without the English weather. After the late snow and thaw, the road was still fetlock deep in mud. We tried as much as possible to avoid the boggiest stretches by riding on the verges, but they were soft also and Genevieve was as miserable as I was, slipping and sliding and pecking so that I was hard put to stay in the saddle. Riding single file with our hoods pulled well down over our heads, it was a morose journey, and no pleasant conversation was possible. It was not until we stopped to rest the horses and restore ourselves at a tavern in Hounslow that there was any opportunity for communication.

'Normally I would expect to make it as far as Chiswick by midday at this time of year,' Walter grumbled. 'The Swan Inn there always has a hearty welcome for us since it buys wine from our family vintry.' He looked around the crowded low-beamed room where we sat crammed into a corner, unable to get near enough to the fire to dry our sodden clothes. 'This place is run by a mean-spirited bunch of monks from the local priory and their trademark is weak ale and tasteless pottage. And look at that fire, not enough heat to dry a kerchief.'

'At least the roof is not leaking,' I observed with a wry smile. 'We will not get any wetter for the time being. And we look so poor and bedraggled that no one will try to overcharge us.'

Walter gave me a lop-sided grin. 'I did not think there could be a bright side but you found one. That is the mark of a good travelling companion.'

'Thank you, kind sir,' I smiled back. 'I am just happy to be out of the rain for a while.'

'Perhaps when we set out again it will have stopped,' suggested Walter.

'Ah – optimism!' I cried. 'You see, you too are a good travelling companion.'

The pot boy brought us ale and, as Walter had predicted, it was weak but not sour and the pottage, when it came, was actually quite tasty, well-seasoned and laced with herbs and scraps of meat. It served its purpose, which was to warm us up and fortify us for another long ride. Providing the horses had been as satisfactorily cared for, all should be well and, to our delight, when we stepped out into the stable yard the rain had stopped and a watery sun stood high in the sky.

'Now we might reach London before curfew,' said Walter, taking Genevieve's reins from the ostler and helping me to mount. 'It pays to be optimistic.'

At last able to ride with my hood back, I settled in the saddle and began to look around me. We were travelling east on the Great Western Road out of London and a steady procession of traffic came against us. Mule-carts and hand-carts, many of them empty, were returning to the vegetable gardens and poultry farms of the Thames valley having sold their loads of roots, onions, chickens, ducks, geese and eggs in the city markets. Well-guarded strings of laden pack-horses plodded steadily at the start of their journey to the ports of Bristol and Exeter and the occasional sound of a horn heralded a knight or nobleman with his posse of retainers, bidding us to clear the road to give him passage. We passed through a series of villages until the road once more met the River Thames at Chiswick and became even more crowded as the spires and towers of Westminster grew clearer in our sights.

We skirted the palace and abbey to the north and it was very slow going on the stretch between there and the London wall, but the sun had dried us out and I was comfortable enough to be fascinated by the sights. This loop of the Thames was, like the stretch of the Seine between the Grand Pont and the Hôtel de St Pol in Paris, the chosen location for the city residences of a number of nobles and bishops, close to both the merchant hub and the centre of royal power that was the palace of Westminster. These mansions were well-protected by high walls and gatehouses, but often the gates were open and it was possible to catch a glimpse of the busy courtyards within, noisy with the clatter of horses hooves and the shouts of servants and varlets bustling through doors and arches.

'This road will take us to the Ludgate,' Walter shouted above the rattle of iron-bound wheels on a passing cart. 'Let us hope there is not too much of a queue.'

'Why, when is the curfew?' I yelled back.

'Not until after the Compline bell, so we should get through before dark. Then it is not far to Tun Lane.'

Walter had very kindly invited me to stay at his family house on the edge of the Vintry, the wharf area on the river where wine cargoes were unloaded and stored in warehouses.

'Shall I meet your father?' I asked with interest. 'Is he in London?'

'I believe so. He usually lets me know if he is travelling to France.'

'And will your aunt be there? The one your sisters wish was not?'

He gave me a worried look. 'Yes, but I hope you will not make any mention of that,' he said. 'I probably should not have told you.'

I smiled reassuringly. 'I promise I will be the soul of discretion. It is extremely kind of you to offer me lodging. I hope your aunt will not be put out by it.'

He looked as if the thought had never occurred to him. 'I cannot think why she should. We have plenty of room. Anyway, you can have my chamber if there is any problem and I will sleep in the hall with the servants. It would not be the first time.'

I did not pursue the subject, but nevertheless felt a stab of misgiving. His original description of his aunt had not encouraged me to think that she was an easy-going woman and I feared my arrival might rouse her ire.

'Well, I will be very grateful not to have to take a room in a strange inn,' I said. 'The prospect does not appeal to me.' Catherine had suggested I seek lodging at Westminster Palace, but I suspected that when the royals were not in residence such a place would be cold and eerie and, anyway, I wanted to be closer to the shops and workshops in the city.

We waited less than half an hour in the queue to pass through the wall and immediately began to plod up a hill on a narrow roadway lined with tightly packed half-timbered houses whose overhanging gables almost grazed our heads, obscuring the setting sun and trapping the acrid odour stirred by our horses' hooves. Behind us the Compline bell began to ring from a nearby abbey, tucked into the corner formed where the London wall dipped down to the river bank.

'Blackfriars Abbey,' Walter revealed. 'Of the Dominican order. Their bell denotes the start of curfew. We only just made it through the gate.'

At my request we had been speaking English all day. I was getting more fluent and needed the practice. I had discovered that learning the language led me to understand the English character better and it was becoming clear to me that although many of them were descended from Normans, they displayed very different characteristics from their continental cousins. I found them more phlegmatic, less quick to anger and generally more straightforward in their attitude to life.

Walter leaned from his saddle to speak above the clanging sound of another bell which began to ring out from a large building silhouetted at the top of the hill. 'That is St Paul's,' he said, 'the greatest church in London. In the churchyard you'll see a big cross where many a famous sermon has been preached. Crowds block the street to hear them, especially in times of trouble.'

When we reached the elevated churchyard it was just possible to see over the patchwork of tiled rooftops down to the river Thames, its brown and turgid waters transformed by the reflected sunset into a golden highway dotted with boats and ships. London seemed smaller than Paris, crammed tightly within its walls and, judging by the miasma of smells that assailed our nostrils, afflicted with the same city problems; waste, ordure and disease. It also radiated all the excitement and opportunity that resulted when people massed together in the right location for trade, industry and creativity.

We had stopped to let our horses draw breath after the climb and to allow me to admire the view. Walter was eager to share his pride in his native city, 'The river looks magical in this light, does it not? The Vintry is this side of London Bridge,' he said, indicating the higgledy-piggledy line of buildings on the many-arched bridge I remembered crossing the day before Catherine's coronation. 'Our house is in Tun Lane, off Cordwainer Street. Ten minutes' ride. I hope supper will be ready!'

When we reached the Vintner house it was already shuttered against the night, but the street gate quickly opened in response to Walter's rat-tat-a-tat-tat coded knock. A grizzled servant emerged first from a narrow passage at the side of the house and took our horses, while seconds later down some steps at the main entrance tumbled two young girls, laughing and exclaiming as they came.

'Walter! Walter! It's you at last!'

Light spilled out a welcome from lamps burning in the inner porch and Walter returned the enthusiastic embraces of the two whom I assumed to be his sisters before shushing them and ushering me up the steps towards the warmth of the interior.

'Now calm down and show your manners to my guest,' he admonished gently. 'This is Madame Lanière, who is Keeper of the Robes to Queen Catherine and deserves your greatest courtesy. Madame, may I present my sisters? This is Anne, the eldest and this hoyden is Mildred, although we call her Mildy because she does not deserve such a saintly name.'

I received the solemn curtsies of the two girls with a grave nod. 'I am enchanted to meet you,' I said in French and saw that they understood immediately. Some of the education Walter had received had clearly also been afforded his sisters. They were very like him, blue-eyed, open-faced and handsome rather than pretty, dressed plainly in brown woollen kirtles and practical unbleached linen aprons, their hair hidden under neat white coifs.

'I hope you have not eaten all the supper,' their brother said, pulling them aside to allow me to mount the inner stair to the first floor. 'Madame Lanière and I are very hungry. We have been riding all day.'

'We have not started,' Anne revealed. 'Father is here. He came back from the Temple only an hour ago.'

So far there had been no mention of the aunt, but when we entered the hall at the top of the stairs a lady was waiting at the hearth who was obviously she. Walter introduced her as Mistress Elizabeth Cope. My first impression was of a strict disciplinarian; a wimpled lady with a thin face and dark features, unrelieved by the grey and black of her widow's weeds. She greeted me civilly but without warmth, and I felt instantly that there was no joy in her. However she made no comment about me being an unexpected guest and an extra place was soon being laid at a table set before a good fire, which gave me hope of a clean and comfortable bed later.

'We have very few visitors, Madame Lanière, so I hope you will not find our hospitality wanting,' Mistress Cope remarked in her surprisingly deep voice. 'Try as we might, our standards are hardly likely to measure up to those of the royal household.'

'I have sometimes found the greatest of palaces draughty and cold, Madame,' I replied in hesitant English. 'Courts are not always lodged comfortably.'

She did not respond to that, hardly seeming to have heard because a door opened in the inner wall of the hall to admit a well-set man in a fur-trimmed black gown and a lawyer's coif that hardly seemed able to contain his thatch of springy silver-threaded brown hair. The atmosphere of stiff formality instantly lifted. Master Geoffrey Vintner was about as similar to his sister as wine is to vinegar. Where she was narrow, he was broad, where her brow was furrowed, his was smile-lined and where she looked coldly down her nose, his good-natured expression burst through a full set of dark, gingery whiskers. If I had nursed a stereotyped image of a stern, pompous lawyer, it was instantly expunged by the presence of this pleasant, warm-spirited man.

When Walter introduced me, his reaction was genuinely cordial. 'It is a privilege to welcome you to our house, Madame,' he declared in perfect French. 'I am honoured to have a member of the queen's household under my roof.'

I returned his smile and his bow in equal measure, surprised to find myself wishing that I had been able to remove the dirt and dishevelment of the road before meeting him. He must have read my mind for he immediately called for warm water and ushered me to a place at the table nearest to the fire. 'Come, Madame, let me take your cloak. Sit down and my maid will bring the bowl and towel for you to wash your hands. Walter, you should have offered Madame Lanière these comforts as soon as she crossed the threshold. Where are your manners, boy?'

I saw Walter's cheeks flush with embarrassment and felt bound to spring to his defence. 'Truly sir, there has not been time and Walter has been the most attentive escort all day. He does not deserve a word of criticism.'

Meanwhile, Mistress Cope and the two girls arranged themselves around the table and a maid in a bleached apron and coif brought the hand basin, offering it to me carefully so that it did not spill. As I made use of the water and towel, Walter gave his father details of our journey while the two girls tried not to stare at me as they absorbed every detail of my appearance.

'I believe you have come to London on the queen's business, Madame?' enquired Master Vintner, regarding me as intently as his daughters. 'Are you at liberty to reveal what that business is? Perhaps I can be of assistance to you.'

I smiled. 'That is a kind offer, sir, but I think it unlikely that a professional man like yourself would have much business with craftsmen skilled in ladies apparel. Queen Catherine has sent me to visit certain recommended tailors and merciers – I think you call them haberdashers? – in order to refresh and replenish her wardrobe. Walter has promised to guide me to the quarters in the city where these are to be found.'

The lawyer looked surprised. 'Really? You amaze me. I had no inkling that my son was familiar with the haunts of fashionable ladies. Walter, were you neglecting your studies all that time I was paying for your education at the Inns of Court?'

Once again poor Walter went bright pink. 'No indeed, Father, but I do know the way to Threadneedle Street. When I last looked, that was the location of the Tailors' Hall, where I believe all masters of that craft in London are registered.'

'Ah yes, I see,' nodded his father. 'So you will take Madame Lanière there tomorrow.'

'And may I ask how long you intend staying in the city?' Mistress Cope's enquiry was couched in such a way as to indicate that she hoped it would not be too many days, an inference that was not lost on her brother.

'Elizabeth, Madame Lanière is welcome to stay as long as the queen's business keeps her here,' Master Vintner said firmly. 'And tomorrow I think you might acquire a good haunch of beef to roast for our dinner and I will ensure that there is some fine Bordeaux wine to go with it.' He cast a disapproving glance at the dish of cold mutton pie which the serving woman had placed on the table alongside a loaf of day-old maslin bread and a hunk of hard cheese. 'Is there none of that onion tart left to go with this pie?' he asked. 'There was plenty left last night as I recall.' He leaned in my direction to ask confidingly, 'I expect you like a good slice of onion tart as much as I do, Madame?'

'Perhaps not quite as much,' I responded with a smile. 'But I do care for a slice of roasted beef.'

'The onion tart was eaten for our midday meal, brother,' Mistress Cope interjected.

'I did not have any,' Mildy piped up, speaking for the first time.

I cast a swift glance at Mistress Cope and saw her pale cheeks colour slightly. It occurred to me that the remains of the onion tart had been hers and hers alone, but she did not look plump enough to be hoarding food for her own consumption.

'You do not like onion tart, Mildred!' the dame told her niece acidly. 'And young ladies should hold their tongues at table unless invited to speak.'

'I would like to ask you girls where you learned such excellent French,' I intervened, changing the subject.

'Our mother taught us,' answered Anne proudly. 'And she taught us to read as well.'

'And Latin, have you learned any Latin?'

'No. Our father speaks Latin but he says it is not necessary for females.' Anne looked a little crestfallen, as if she would have been keen to study the language that opened the door to so much learning. 'Do you know it, Madame?'

I shook my head. 'No, and I am only just learning English so you are well ahead of me, being fluent two languages already. In France not many women even learn to read.'

'That is the case here in England as well,' said Master Vintner. 'My wife was an exception and wished her daughters to be educated to a certain degree. My sister does not read, do you, Elizabeth?'

Mistress Cope sniffed. 'I have never felt the need,' she said stonily. 'Running a household requires other skills.'

I cut a piece of mutton pie with my knife and bit into it. The meat inside had not been stewed long enough and was tough and stringy. I swallowed it with the help of a sip of the wine Master Vintner had poured and decided to make do with bread and cheese. I noticed Walter and his father both chewing mightily and pondered how much skill it took to hire a cook who could cook or find a pie shop that could make pies.

However, when I was shown to my chamber later I found it clean and well furnished with a jug of water for washing and a night pot for my convenience. I decided that what Mistress Cope lacked in the kitchen, she made up for in the bedchamber, then smiled at my own thought, glad that I had not voiced it aloud and in company. Then, exhausted after my journey, I snuggled gratefully beneath the covers and blushed to think that I had even conjured a single thought about any bedtime activity other than sleep.

11

O n waking the next day, my first thought was for Genevieve. Guilt stabbed me as I realised that I had seen my beloved mare led away down an alley and had not given any further thought to her welfare. However, during our evening meal my two saddlebags had been delivered to my chamber and I had been able to shake out my best blue Flanders wool gown and hang it on a convenient clothes pole to allow the creases to fall out. I intended to wear it in the evening for Master Vintner's promised feast. Meanwhile, I washed my face in the water provided, gave my travel-stained russet riding kirtle a good brush to remove the worst of the mud splashes and donned it once more before hurrying downstairs to find the stable.

In daylight the house in Tun Lane was revealed to be one in a row of substantial town houses constructed on a frame of strong, dark oak beams filled in with lime-washed lath and plaster, similar to hundreds I had seen in the towns we had passed through on the court's progress around England. It was larger than most, boasting four windows on each side of the two gabled upper floors and was roofed with slate tiles which, considering the danger of fire in cramped city streets, I thought a vast improvement on the straw and thatch used in poorer neighbourhoods. An intriguing series of pargetted designs relieved the rectangles of plasterwork on the first floor overhang, the beams framing images of twining vines laden with fruit, a ship loaded with barrels and capering youths and girls treading huge vats of harvested grapes. There was no mistaking that this house had once belonged to a wine merchant, even if it now housed a lawyer's family.

The narrow tunnel down which the horses had been led the previous night opened on to a rear courtyard surrounded by outhouses, one of which I rather hoped might be a privy. A stable boy was busy tipping a barrow-load of soiled straw onto a muckheap in the corner of the yard and I asked him to show me where Genevieve was. On the way past a feed-barrel I grabbed a handful of oats and enjoyed my mare's little whicker of recognition before she snuffled them off my outstretched palm. She was comfortably settled in a stall beside Walter's cob and looked none the worse for the previous day's long trek. Following the advice of the horse-loving Lady Joan, I felt her legs carefully and was happy to find no sign of heat. I reckoned a day's rest would do her no harm however.

Having found and made use of the privy, I took a quick tour around the rest of the yard, discovering that the ground floor of the house was given over to a chamber of business where two legal clerks were already busy penning entries in large leather-bound ledgers under the sharp gaze of their employer, Master Geoffrey Vintner. As I passed the open door that led directly into the yard, he called my name.

'Madame Lanière, good morrow to you! I trust I find you well rested.' He came out to meet me, his amiable face wreathed in smiles. I found myself wondering if this genial man could really be a forceful interrogative lawyer, then I remembered that he was also a diplomat, where I imagined that cordiality was a definite advantage.

I returned his bow with a bob. 'Thank you, Master Vintner, I slept well. Your house is very comfortable.'

'I am glad you think so and it is close enough to the wine warehouses for me to keep an eye on the legal side of our family business. My older brothers are the wine merchants, but I am of some use to them. May I escort you up to the hall to break your fast?'

'Thank you. I have been checking on my mare but, of course, it was unnecessary. Your stable is as well set up as your house.'

We entered the back door and climbed the narrow stairway from the front lobby. In the hall the table had been pushed to one end of the room and bread and jugs of ale were laid out on the cloth. There was evidence that we were not the first there but whoever had already eaten had also left. We took a bowl each and some bread to a small table by the hearth. Someone had stirred the fire back to life and a cauldron of pottage stood on a trivet keeping warm. The lawyer ladled some into my bowl.

'My sister may not be good at mutton pie, but she does make decent pottage,' he said, eyes twinkling. 'She has breakfasted early and gone off to seek the makings of a good beef dinner and she has taken the girls to carry her baskets.' He filled his own bowl and sat down opposite me, adding confidentially, 'I am fortunate that she agreed to come and care for my daughters after their mother died. Elizabeth has a brusque manner but a good heart. I can trust her to do the best for the girls.'

'I am sure you can,' I said, breaking some bread to dip in the pottage and deciding it would be tactful to change the subject. 'Your son tells me you travel frequently to France. Is that on wine business?' I knew it was not but did not want to make trouble for Walter if he had told me too much of his father's affairs.

Geoffrey Vintner pursed his lips. 'Partly,' he concurred. 'But because of my knowledge of both French and English law, I am sometimes employed on missions for the king; a glorified messenger really between the English court and the governing councils of Paris and Rouen. Do you have family in France?'

I suddenly found the bread hard to swallow as a lump came to my throat, a problem which had started to occur more frequently lately as I struggled to come to terms with the extended separation from my children. I tried to clear it and spoke hoarsely as a result.

'Yes I do but, sadly, they eat from different plates. My son is a huntsman in the dauphin's household – I am sorry, I mean the Pretender of course . . .' I blushed and rushed on, 'and my daughter is married to a Parisian tailor and so now lives under English rule. She has a little girl, my granddaughter.'

Master Vintner ignored the dauphin/Pretender slip in favour of blatant flattery. 'Saint's bones! You are a grandmother? Impossible!'

I felt my cheeks burn even hotter and inwardly scolded myself for foolishness. 'It is only too possible, sir,' I said, avoiding his teasing gaze. 'You might be a grandparent yourself if your son were a daughter.'

He thought about that for a moment. 'Ah yes, I see what you mean. I find it difficult to contemplate the fact that my daughters are nearly of an age to take husbands. Am I the only father who hates that thought?'

I gave a small laugh. 'That depends on the husbands they take. Fortunately mine chose well.'

He frowned. 'Chose?' he echoed. 'You mean she chose her own husband? What was her father doing?'

My cheeks had cooled now and I gave him a direct look.

'Sadly I lost my husband after the Battle of Agincourt. He was as much a casualty of that disaster as the Duke of York, even if he was not a nobleman.'

'A disaster you call it?' He kept his expression neutral. 'Well I suppose for many thousands of your countrymen it was just that. Did he fight in the battle?'

I laid down my horn spoon to clasp my hands tightly in my lap. I did not wish to begin a detailed description of Jean-Michel's miserable and unnecessary death. 'No, he was a charettier. He drove supplies for the royal army. Although I serve the queen, I am not of noble stock, sir.'

Master Vintner struck his knee with the palm of his hand and laughed. 'No more are my son and I, Madame, and yet we serve the king. These are changing times, are they not?'

I resumed my meal and we ate in silence for a few moments. 'Where is Walter?' I asked at length. 'I do not imagine he is a lay-abed.'

'No, no. I have sent him about his own business. He has gone to buy quills and paper. If you will permit me, I will escort you to the Tailors Hall myself. As it happens, I have done legal work for the guild and I think my introduction may ensure you more solicitous attention than my young son's.' He paused, observing me humbly. 'I hope this arrangement does not offend you.'

In fact I found myself unexpectedly pleased by his offer but I restricted my response to a brief smile and a nod of appreciation. 'Not at all, sir,' I said. 'It is very generous of you to spare the time.'

On Master Vintner's advice I strapped pattens onto my shoes for the walk to Threadneedle Street and I was glad I had. The muckrakers may have been out at dawn, but the gutters in the lane had already received new and generous dumps of household waste and the main thoroughfares were liberally scattered with fresh droppings from travellers' horses and the wild pigs that still apparently roamed the streets and gardens. London's fifty thousand citizens had to eat and drink and pursue their livelihoods and so they also had to live with the side effects. Although the pattens made walking clumsy, at least they kept my feet and my skirt off the ground and my escort was kind enough to offer me his arm over the worst parts.

It was not far to the Tailors Hall and, on the way, we passed numerous workshops of crafts I would need to explore later; haberdashers, drapers, cordwainers, hatters, glovers and hosiers. London might be only half the size of Paris, but there seemed to be no lack of the skills necessary to maintain Queen Catherine's reputation for setting the style, even when she began to change shape from her usual willow-wand slimness. The only question lay in whether there was a tailor who would be able to satisfy her demand for the new and avant-garde. My son-in-law Jacques had proved exactly the young and daring innovator she had wanted and I needed to find his equal in the lanes off Threadneedle Street.

By coincidence, while we waited in the dim oak-panelled hall for a meeting with the grand master of the guild, we witnessed an argument between a tailor and his wife which stirred my interest. For a guild freeman, which he clearly was, the tailor was a relatively young man; in his mid-twenties I would have guessed, his wife about the same, and their conversation centred on a subject which, in view of my own daughter's position; working in Paris with her husband, was of particular interest to me.

'Whatever happens, you are not to become excited and start shouting.'

These were the first words I heard as we drew near to the couple, who were among several groups and individuals standing around the long room. The young tailor was addressing his wife, who was already red-faced with suppressed irritation.

'It will not help your cause and nor will it help mine, which is more important,' he added.

'It is unjust!' she seethed, her voice vibrating with passionate indignation, 'My work is lauded in the guild when it carries your name and yet I am not permitted to sell it as my own. I do not know how you can take all the credit when you know it is I who do the work.'

'It is our business, Meg, and we are making our reputation,' he insisted, keeping his tone deliberate and hushed. 'When we married, you were happy just to have an outlet for your designs. Do not forget that you would have had no opportunity at all without the backing of my name.'

'But it is not your name that actually does the designs, cuts the patterns and sews the seams, it is me! How would you like to have someone else receive all the praise and money for your singular endeavours?'

'I would not stand for it, but I am a man and that is the way things are and you will not change it by shouting at the grand master like a Billingsgate fishwife!'

She looked mutinous, but simmered down enough to keep her thought process logical. 'Perhaps the answer is for me to stop work and then we will see if our business makes any money!' she muttered.

'You can stop work when you fulfil your marriage contract and produce the children to staff our workshop,' retorted the man with what I surmised was unkindness born of disappointment. 'Until then, let us turn our attention to the more urgent business of how we are going to answer the guild's accusations of over-pricing.'

She sniffed loudly, her resentment simmering. 'We demand the highest prices because our gowns are of the highest quality. I will insist that fact until the moon turns blue.'

At this point a clerk nudged my companion's elbow and asked us to follow him to the grand master's chamber. As we traversed the hall, I asked the clerk if he knew the name of the couple we had been standing next to. He glanced back and smiled with instant recognition. 'Ah yes, goodwife,' he said, embarrassingly mistaking us for a married couple, 'that is Master Anthony and his wife. Their designs are presently in great demand by London's richest and noblest and, because of that, they think they can break the guild's price tariffs. They are in dispute with the Chapter.'

'And with each other,' I murmured and made a mental note of the name Anthony, but I had more interest in the mistress than the master. A female tailor with a reputation for style might be just what Catherine needed in the months leading up to her confinement.

On my return to the house in Tun Lane, the smell of roasting beef assailed my nostrils like a benediction. After introducing me to the Grand Master Tailor my host had left me to attend to his own business, leaving strict instructions for me to meet Walter by the Cheapside fountain at the Vespers bell.

'I have told my son to escort you home because London is a safe city in daylight,' he had advised, 'but as darkness falls a good woman risks being mistaken for one of her less reputable sisters. Besides, you might lose your way and I do not wish you to miss any part of the meal my sister is preparing for us this evening!'

Elizabeth Cope was indeed a great deal better at roasting beef than preparing mutton pie and her prowess had also lightened her mood. It was a cheerful party that gathered around the long table in the hall as night fell. The smoky oil lamps of the previous evening had been replaced by beeswax candles in polished pewter candlesticks and there was manchet bread cut into thick slices as trenchers to soak up the delicious juices of the meat. Best of all there was a leek and oyster pudding as an accompaniment. Master Vintner clearly wished no expense to be spared in demonstrating to the queen's keeper of robes what a fine household he kept.

He was also assiduous in asking after my success in the workshops of the Cheape and Threadneedle Street, so I delivered a brief account of my meetings with various tailors and the orders I had placed in a number of shops where accessories were made. I kept it short because I did not want to reveal too much before arrangements were finalised with those craftsmen I had patronised. Orders such as these could make or break reputations and when news of the queen's favour spread, I wanted it to be accurate.

'And did you make contact with Master Anthony in the course of your activities?' my host enquired, rather to my surprise. I had not realised that he had heard my exchange with the clerk at the Tailors' Hall.

'I called at his workshop, but the apprentice told me his master was still at the Tailors' Hall,' I admitted. I did not add that I had gone back there later and spoken to Mistress Anthony, nor reveal anything of the conversation I had had with her. The results of that interview might become known later – or they might not.

Mildy, who had been jiggling about on her chair, could contain herself no longer. 'Did you buy any pretty things for the queen, Madame?' she asked excitedly. 'Any ribbons or lace or jewellery? And if you did, may we see them?'

I smiled at her. She endeared herself to me; as curious as a kitten and twice as irrepressible. At her age I should have been as eager for them as she was, had I ever had the chance even to look at such fripperies. 'Mostly I ordered drawings and designs to collect tomorrow, but I do have some samples to take back to her grace. You are welcome to see them later if you wish. Tell me though, what did you get up to today? I felt like a slug-a-bed for you were up and out before I broke my fast.'

Mildy's brow creased under the turned-back brim of her white linen coif. 'Oh yes, we rise early and today we went to market with Aunt to carry baskets. We had to get there soon after dawn in order to catch the best produce, that is what our aunt said.'

'And so it is and so we did,' interjected Mistress Cope, 'as I think is proved by the quality of the beef we are eating.'

'Indeed it is!' echoed her brother heartily, raising his glass. 'Let us drink a toast to the king and queen and the roast beef of England. Long may they grace our land!'

Mistress Cope spluttered and I caught my host's eye, fighting to suppress a chuckle at his somewhat subversive conjunction of royalty and bullocks.

'And now a toast to our guest,' he added, drawing instant colour to my cheeks. 'May this not be the last time she honours my house with her presence.'

Later that evening, when the girls had exclaimed over the few gee-gaws I had purchased for Catherine and been chivvied up

127

to bed by their aunt, my host and I sat conversing by the hall fire with the last of the flagon of Gascon wine and I asked him the question I had been pondering ever since I learned of his regular trips to France.

'I wonder, Master Vintner, if I were to write a letter to my daughter Alys in Paris, whether you would be kind enough to take it to her on your next visit? It would be wonderful to be able to tell her all my news and perhaps there might be an opportunity for her to write a reply while you are in the city.'

Master Vintner did not hesitate for a second. 'With great pleasure, Madame,' he said. 'As a matter of fact, I will be making the journey very soon, on one of the ships that will carry the king's relief troops. I believe they will sail at the end of the month so I should be in Paris in early June.'

'Ah, the best time of year,' I said enviously. 'I will write the letter tomorrow and give you clear directions to her house. It is very kind of you to do me this favour.'

'It is no favour, I assure you,' he responded, 'for it will give me the pleasure of hoping for another visit from you so that I can tell you how your daughter fares and of course describe the progress of your little granddaughter. And perhaps one day there will be an opportunity for me to accompany you in person to Paris to see them for yourself.'

I gazed at him, speechless, asking myself how many times this man's warmth had brought a lump to my throat during the brief hours of our acquaintance. This last offer had taken me completely by surprise. To him it appeared to be the most natural and logical idea, but to me it suddenly seemed like an offer from heaven and I was overwhelmed by a longing to accept immediately, which merely served to tell me how much

I had been suppressing my heartfelt wish to see my family again. But I knew of course that it was impossible, at least until after Catherine was safely delivered of her baby, for I had promised faithfully to see her through the momentous process of presenting England and France with their crucially important heir.

After several seconds I managed to deliver what I hoped was a serene smile and say, 'What a kind and thoughtful offer, Master Vintner, but I hope you will not think me ungrateful if I turn it down, at least for the foreseeable future. You see, perhaps the news has not reached London yet, but the queen is *enceinte* and as you can imagine it will be a long time before I am able to leave her for more than a few days. I have been with her more or less since she was born and I will be with her when she brings her own child into the world. I would not be human if I absented myself from that event.'

He nodded solemnly. 'Indeed you would not. I had heard the good news of the queen's happy condition and of course I should have realised that there was no question of you leaving England at this time. But please remember that the offer is always open.' He leaned forward and poured a last drop of wine into my cup before emptying the flagon into his own. 'Let us drink to the health of the queen,' he said. 'May God give her an easy confinement and a healthy babe in the cradle, be it boy or girl.'

We drank and I inwardly blessed him for being among the few men in England who would not have prayed exclusively for a son for the king.

His eyes twinkled in a way in a way with which I had now grown familiar as he added earnestly, 'And I hope you will not think it untoward if I suggest that in private at least we abandon formality and call each other by our baptismal names. Mine is Geoffrey.'

I set down my cup and nodded contentedly. 'And mine is Guillaumette, but that is my serving name. My friends call me Mette.'

'Then, if you permit it, I shall call you Mette.'

12

I stayed one more night at the House of the Vines and spent the daylight hours completing my business in the craft workshops of Cheapside. Fortunately the weather was kinder on our return journey and we arrived back at Windsor well before sunset, dry and contented. However, comfortable though it was, my chamber in the queen's apartment felt dull and lonely after the cheerful bustle of the house in Tun Lane and when I presented myself in the queen's solar after the evening meal, my welcome was disappointing. Deep in intimate conversation with the Duchess of Hainault, Catherine displayed little interest in my arrival and did not enquire whether my trip had been successful.

When I made my curtsy at the door, 'Goodness, Mette, have you returned already?' was all she said, before resuming her tête-à-tête. For a moment I thought I heard her mother speaking and felt a jolt of dismay. She had addressed me in English and her broken accent reminded me of Queen Isabeau's fractured French.

Fortunately Agnes, Lady Joan and Joannas Belknap and Troutbeck greeted me enthusiastically, Joanna Coucy being the exception as I had come to expect, and I spent a pleasant hour describing the sights of London and the new styles and fabrics I had seen in the warehouses and workshops I had visited. None of them asked where I had lodged during my visit and so I did not tell them about the house in Tun Lane or the friendliness of its inhabitants. When Catherine showed signs of retiring, I hurried through to her bedchamber as usual only to find Eleanor Cobham already there preparing a herbal mixture in a pestle and heating a kettle of water over the fire. She smiled at me brightly.

'There you are, Madame Lanière,' she said impatiently, as if I were a junior lady-in-waiting reporting late for duty. 'I am preparing a tisane for the queen. It is one that I have made for the duchess and it was she who recommended it as a night-time posset. Are their graces coming now?'

'The queen is coming,' I said. 'Perhaps you should hurry along to the duchess's bedchamber.'

'Oh no,' Eleanor responded. 'They will take the tisane together before they retire, but the queen's new confessor will come to say the Angelus with them first.'

I frowned. 'A new confessor,' I echoed. 'Who is that?'

'Maître Boyers.' I noted a triumphant gleam in Eleanor's eyes, doubtless sparked by the fact that she was able to tell me something pertaining to Catherine that I did not know. 'The king appointed him to the queen's household as a parting gift when he left for Winchester. Was it not a great kindness? He said the priest would bring the queen God's comfort during her pregnancy.'

'Has the king left for France already?' I asked faintly, marvelling at how much had occurred during the four days I had been away.

'No, he has gone to attend to business with Bishop Beaufort in Winchester and will return before he takes ship. The Duke of Gloucester is still at Windsor, however. Ah, here is Maître Jean.'

A tall, thin tonsured man in the white habit and black cloak of a Dominican had entered the room and paused uncertainly on the threshold. 'The queen told me to come to the oratory,' he said apologetically. 'She and the duchess are on their way.'

'God's greeting, Maître,' I said, approaching the priest and making a small bob. 'I am Guillaumette Lanière, the queen's Keeper of Robes. Eleanor here tells me that you have been appointed her confessor. May I offer my congratulations?'

Maître Boyers made me a small bow over clasped hands. His thin face and frame gave him an aesthetic look, but his smile was warm and friendly. 'I have heard about you, Madame,' he said. 'The king tells me that you guard the queen's physical well-being whilst I am to attend to the spiritual. Would that be a fair summary?'

'I have served the queen with all my heart and soul for many years,' I said. 'But she certainly craves spiritual guidance from the right person. If the king has chosen you, you must be that person.'

'As well as studying theology at Oxford, I am a member of the Dominican Priory of St John there, the Blackfriars. My lord, the king, thought that since her grace was educated by Dominican nuns in France, she might be receptive to spiritual guidance from one of our order.'

I was about to remark on the king's thoughtfulness when the door was thrown open to the swish of silken skirts. My knee touched the floor and I expected Catherine to raise and greet me as she usually did, but behind her came Jacqueline of Hainault and they both swept past me without a glance in order to acknowledge the priest. The three then immediately disappeared into the little oratory off the bedchamber and the door closed behind them.

Still kneeling, I felt my stomach twist into a hard knot of distress and my mind flew back to when Catherine had returned to Paris after ten years of convent schooling and I mistook another young lady for her. Bonne of Armagnac had been the newly appointed and high-nosed mademoiselle whom I had wrongly assumed must be Catherine and her disdainful attitude towards me, a mere servant, had led me to believe that my beloved nursling had no memory of one who had loved her like a mother. The crippling sense of worthlessness which had assailed me then resurfaced at this moment with astonishing force, making me realise that Catherine still had an over-whelming power over my emotions.

I got to my feet and saw that Eleanor Cobham was watching me closely, her lips curved in a half smile. She could not have failed to notice the tears in my eyes, but made no comment. I turned away and busied myself preparing the great bed for Catherine's repose. As I smoothed the lavender-scented sheets and arranged the monogrammed pillows, my mind was a blur of bewilderment at Catherine's apparent and sudden change of attitude. I thought I knew what, or rather who had caused it and I fretted over the possible consequences.

Then I caught sight of the smug look on Eleanor's face as she poured boiling water onto the mixture she had prepared in the mortar. I do not think I am normally vindictive, but my fingers itched to scratch those creamy, perfect cheeks. A strange, bitter-sweet aroma filled the room and twitched at my heightened senses.

'What is in your tisane? The smell is curious,' I said, emerging from behind the heavy hangings of the bed.

Steam rose from the stone mortar as she stirred its contents, a frown of secretive intensity on her face. For a few moments I thought she was not going to answer, but then she straightened and her expression cleared. 'There are fresh mayweed flowers, angelica and all-heal and I have added some elderberry syrup for sweetness. It is a family recipe. There is an excellent herb garden in the lower ward of the castle, near the Curfew Tower. I will show you if you like.'

I nodded. 'Thank you. All-heal and mayweed are not names I am familiar with. What are their properties?'

'Their Latin names are valeriana and chamomilla. They are both good for inducing gentle sleep and the elderberry syrup is a tonic for calming nerves. I thought they would all benefit the queen in her present condition.'

'Ah yes, I know valerian and camomile of course, and the properties of elderberries. You have studied herbs, then?'

'My mother learned from her mother,' Eleanor revealed, 'and she has taught me all she knows. She is a Culpepper. Her family have always used herbs extensively.'

'May I see?' She moved aside and I peered at the contents of the mortar, which looked slightly sinister with blackened leaves and wilted flowers swirling around in a dark liquid. 'I have heard that knowledge of herbs has sometimes led to people – women in particular – being held in suspicion by those who have no such understanding. Has your mother experienced any such reaction?'

'Not at all, Madame.' For once the ready smile was not in evidence as Eleanor abruptly picked up the mortar. 'I will strain this before it is drunk and you will see how pretty the liquid looks when cooled in a silver cup. The queen took some before retiring last night and was full of praise for its effects this morning.'

I watched as she deftly strained the drink into a flagon, taking care to keep the trailing sleeve of her new houppelande out of the way. Then I recognised the gown as one of Catherine's and felt a surge of indignation. In my absence Eleanor Cobham had achieved what I had flatly denied her – the loan of an item from the queen's wardrobe. I noticed that she had also somehow acquired Catherine's two gold hanaps from the strongbox, the key of which I had entrusted to Agnes during my trip to London. Of course there was nothing to stop Catherine telling Agnes to bring the cups from the strongbox, but I had the uncanny feeling that Eleanor had somehow made herself seem sufficiently trustworthy to acquire the key personally. She would not have done so while I held it and I made a mental note to get it back that very night.

Within minutes, the door of the oratory opened and Catherine and the duchess emerged, followed by Maître Boyers. The two ladies took seats at either side of the hearth and Eleanor prettily presented her tisane, pouring it into the two gold cups in a tempting stream of luminous, dark-pink liquid. A faint curl of aromatic steam wafted from the surface of each drink.

'Mmm,' Catherine took a cautious sip and then another, more liberal one. 'It is just the right temperature and as delicious as before. Mette, have you tried Eleanor's tisane? It is very good. I have never slept so well as I did last night.'

I stepped forward, going on one knee between the two fireside chairs. 'I have not tasted it no, your grace, but it smells effective. It is the valerian, I expect.'

'Oh, there are more things in it than that!' the queen exclaimed. 'Eleanor, give Mette a taste, but only a sip, mind. Otherwise she might not wake up in time to bring me my morning posset.'

So I was brought a dribble of tisane in the bottom of a horn cup while I stayed on my knees before the hearth. It was the first time I could ever remember Catherine failing to signal me to rise. Meanwhile Eleanor remained on her feet and her smug smile was back. Somehow she had made my meagre sip of tisane cold. It tasted to me of gall.

With remarkable speed Jacqueline of Hainault had become Catherine's new best friend. She had never really enjoyed such a friendship before and I understood how welcome it must be for her to have a companion of her own rank and age. Hard though it was for me to take, I suppose it was inevitable that our unusual mother-daughter relationship should suffer. I was still the one she wanted to perform all the most intimate services, but during my short stay in London I had been supplanted as her special confidante. Moreover, because the king was no longer at Windsor, his presence as chief male advisor and protector had been taken by the Duke of Gloucester and, unlike King Henry, neither he nor Jacqueline of Hainault saw any reason to hold me in high esteem.

I received my first intimation of this the next morning when I entered Catherine's chamber and placed her usual hot posset beside the bed. She must have been lying awake for some time because, when I drew back the curtains, she immediately sat up against the pillows, snatched her chamber robe from me and pulled it around her shoulders.

After exchanging the usual morning greetings, she cupped her hands around the posset cup as if to take courage from its warmth and said in an unnaturally formal manner, 'I would prefer it if you did not attend my afternoon salons in future, Mette.'

I took a moment to absorb the full meaning of her words. Ever since she had become Queen of England and, at least in matters of personal choice her own mistress, she had treated me in exactly the same way as she treated her ladies-in-waiting – in other words as one of her close companions. Now, for some reason, there was apparently to be a change in that situation.

'Of course I will do whatever you wish, Mademoiselle, but may I know the reason for this request?' I said, straightening up from my task of stirring up the fire in the hearth. Spring was well underway but these early May mornings were chilly still.

Catherine shifted a little under the covers. 'The Duchess of Hainault noticed your presence and asked me why I included a servant in my social circle. It is the old problem, Mette. She has been brought up in one of the most rigidly structured courts in Europe and she says she cannot talk freely when there is someone present who does not conform to the noble code of honour. Unfortunately the Duke of Gloucester encourages her in this attitude, so if I am to have their companionship I must ensure their ease in my company. I am sure that in due course I shall manage to change their opinions, but not while you are within earshot I am afraid.'

I felt more angry than hurt and found I could not hide my indignation. 'Is King Henry aware of his brother's viewpoint, I wonder? He himself seems to favour those who are intelligent and industrious rather than necessarily from the top branches of the tree.'

Catherine frowned and took a sip of her posset before replying. 'I do not wish to have a debate with you about this, Mette. Please accede to my request and let us leave it at that, otherwise there is a danger that we will fall out over the matter.'

'Yes, your grace,' I muttered rebelliously. 'May I at least ask if there have been any other changes during my absence? For instance now that you have a confessor, will you be going to the chapel to hear Mass as before, or will Maître Boyers be saying it in your oratory before you break your fast? I may not have prepared the correct garb for your morning activities.'

'Maître Boyers will come to my chamber at the Tierce bell and so will the duchess,' Catherine replied impatiently. 'We will hear Mass together and then break our fast in my solar. Does that answer your question?'

I dropped a humble curtsey, anxious not to offend any further. 'Indeed, your grace. I will fetch your clothes immediately and your ladies to help you dress.'

She nodded. 'Thank you. Oh, Mette,' she called as I hurried to the door, 'Agnes will serve us at breakfast. I am sure you have much work to catch up on after your trip to London. You may come later to give me your report on your activities there. The duchess will be interested too, for she needs a good tailor.'

So the duchess needs my advice, I fumed as I took myself off, but she cannot tolerate my presence.

While I was selecting suitable attire for the queen's morning activities, I speculated how I might withhold my advice from Duchess Jacqueline without revealing my reasons, but in the event I resisted the temptation. There was no escaping the fact that I had no choice in the matter. I was lucky to have my position at court and I must dance to the rhythm of the one who called the tune. I might not like it, but I had to bear it.

The first thing I noticed when I was at last summoned to reveal the results of my research in the workshops of London, was that there was a chamberlain keeping the door of her salon, a task I had habitually performed in the past. Although

139

Catherine seemed pleased with what I had achieved, my arrangements met with criticism from her grace of Hainault.

'I would hesitate to use the services of an unregistered seamstress, however well her designs have been received by the Tailor's Guild,' she observed. 'Are you sure you wish to patronise this Mistress Anthony, Catherine?'

'Well Mette does know my taste in such matters,' Catherine responded in what I thought an unnecessarily apologetic tone. 'And I must admit I think I would prefer a female to be fitting my gowns while I am with child. It sounds as if she has some very good ideas about putting lacing at the sides of the kirtle and drawing the attention away from the waistline to the hemline with embroidery on the under-skirt. Jacques did that for my wedding gown, did he not, Mette? And it was very successful. But then he was always ahead of his time, your son-in-law.'

'He would be pleased that you think so, your grace,' I said, slightly mollified by her championing of both my arrangements and my family. 'May I suggest that if her grace the duchess is unhappy about using a female tailor, she might commission a trial gown from Mistress Anthony's husband, who is a registered master tailor? They will both be coming to Windsor next week, as will a chosen collection of craftsmen. There will be quite a number of them showing their wares in the great hall.'

Jacqueline pouted again. 'We do not want to find ourselves wearing the same fabrics as a courtier's wife,' she complained. 'The queen and I must have first and exclusive pick of all the goods before they display them in public.'

Short of locking the visiting craftsmen up until the royal ladies had inspected their wares, I did not see how I was to achieve this, but I decided to tackle the problem when it arose.

The craftsmen I had approached had seemed very keen to come to Windsor and try their luck at the queen's new court, but they had all stipulated that they would need at least a week to arrange transport and protection for themselves. The roads were clear at this time of year, but their goods were precious and even in the relatively prosperous and well-populated countryside between London and Windsor there were tracts of land that were known to harbour bandits and outlaws.

I made an effort to bow deferentially to the duchess. 'That goes without saying, Madame. I will ensure that each and every master craftsman is aware of your exclusive priority – after the queen, of course.'

Catherine giggled at her new friend. 'Oh I do not think we will come to blows over a girdle or a pair of gloves, will we? After all, your need is greater than mine, Jacqueline. Although I must admit that I am rather looking forward to buying some pretty things. It seems a long time since I did.'

At that moment the Duke of Gloucester was announced by the chamberlain and made his approach with a low bow to both ladies. In deference to the milder season he had dispensed with a gown of any kind and wore a splendid padded doublet of lavishly embroidered green brocade over part-coloured hose in black and crimson. On his head he wore a draped black chaperon set off with an eye-catching, enamelled brooch depicting a boar's head, his personal emblem. The tight fit of his hose over his thighs and his gold S-link Lancastrian belt accentuated the snake-like motion of his hips as he moved. He cannot have been unaware that the duchess was mightily impressed.

'You are welcome to join us, your grace,' Catherine said, 'although our conversation may not be to your liking. We were discussing fashion.'

'Judging by his present garb, I would say that fashion and my lord of Gloucester are hardly strangers,' put in the duchess, an arch smile dimpling her porcelain cheeks. 'I cannot imagine you wearing that doublet, my lord, when you ride out on campaign.'

Gloucester preened himself, stroking the gleaming fabric of his sleeve. 'I hoped it would meet with your approval, Madame. Why else would I have worn it?'

Catherine's glance swivelled from the duke to the duchess and a frown creased her brow. Then she caught sight of me, standing in the shadow of the gold-fringed canopy over her chair and her frown deepened. 'Are you still here, Mette? Thank you, you may leave us.'

'Yes your grace.' I bent my knee briefly and backed away.

But I had not reached the door before the Duke of Gloucester said clearly, 'What was that woman doing here? No sooner is she back at court than she is eavesdropping again!'

I heard Catherine respond rather indignantly, 'Mette was telling us what she had organised . . .' but I did not hear the rest because the chamberlain closed the door on me.

I was incensed because a chamberlain was permitted to remain in Catherine's salon while I was not. I asked myself why the high-nosed duchess and the self-satisfied duke could ignore his presence when apparently they could not tolerate mine – and the answer came instantly: they were fearful of my influence. But they had not stopped to consider their own security. I was only too aware of what happened when servants got together in passages and anterooms and I knew that no subject broached in Catherine's circle now would remain confidential with lose-tongued chamberlains keeping the door.

When my anger had cooled, I gave thought to another matter

of interest; the nature of the relationship between the Duke of Gloucester and the Duchess of Hainault. I am good at detecting smouldering embers and I definitely felt a glow forming between those two. After all, they had spent several unscheduled days snowed up together at Eltham Palace and they struck me as birds of a similar feather – handsome, hubristic and arrogant. It was not that I cared whether passion had flared between them – they deserved each other in my opinion – I was just grateful that Humphrey of Gloucester would soon be joining the king on the campaign in France, which might leave Jacqueline of Hainault less confidant and less likely to throw her weight around. I told myself that I merely had to bide my time.

13

The letter came to the queen as she was dressing one morning in early June. Catherine had been enjoying trying out some of the new trappings and accessories acquired from the London craftsmen, showing them off to Jacqueline and, for once, not signalling me to make myself scarce in the duchess's presence, perhaps because Eleanor and Agnes were also there, helping with the boxes and wrappings. The letter was written in the king's own hand and delivered by one of his squires to the ever-present chamberlain, but I took it firmly from his hand outside the queen's bedchamber, pleased for once to be able to close the door on him rather than the other way round and hating myself for relishing such a petty triumph.

Catherine was twisting and turning before the Venetian looking-glass the king had sent her before their betrothal, which had happily survived the journey from France, trying to gauge the effect of a beautiful new jewelled girdle. 'I really think you should have this, Jacqueline,' she suggested, sighing a little. 'I do like it, but it requires a slender waistline and mine is soon to be that no more.'

The duchess's pale-blue eyes gleamed and I knew the costly girdle would be around her waist within hours, but she demurred punctiliously, 'At least you should wear it until the baby shows,' she said. 'It would look well with the bronze and blue silk you ordered from your lady tailor.'

Catherine unhooked the girdle and held it up to admire the pretty topaz-studded braiding threaded through the gold links. 'You are right, but by the time that gown is here my waist will not be.' She patted her stomach and held the belt out to Jacqueline. 'It is yours. Consider it a gift from the next King of England.'

The duchess murmured profuse thanks and bent to fasten the belt around her own waist as I stepped up to Catherine with the letter. 'This has come from the king, your grace,' I said, taking care to curtsy deeply.

She took the letter and gazed intently at it. 'This is in his own hand! He has even written the address.'

'We will leave you to read it in peace, Madame,' I suggested as she broke the seal and opened the folded sheet of paper. It contained only a short message.

'No, wait.' She glanced at the writing and raised one hand. 'The king is on his way to Windsor and will be here shortly. He wishes to speak to me privately.'

I looked expectantly at the duchess, but she showed no sign of leaving. 'Would you like me to attend to your hair before I go, Madame?' I asked, thinking that Catherine appeared troubled at the content of the letter. 'You will want to look your best to receive the king.'

She moved to sit down on her dressing stool, her gait clumsy as if her legs might give way beneath her. 'Yes, thank you, Mette,' she acquiesced distractedly. 'I would – I do. Here.' She thrust the letter at me and put both hands over her face.

I noticed immediately that the letter was in French and deduced that she wanted me to read it so I perused it quickly, turning its contents away from the duchess's prying eyes. Half of my mind wondered why Jacqueline did not rush to comfort her friend rather than make such an obvious effort to read over my shoulder.

—§§—

My sweet Catherine,

In two days we take ship for France, God and the wind permitting. I will be with you before Sext today to bid you farewell. There is also a grave matter to discuss so I would see you alone, save of course for Mette who I know is privy to the secrets of your heart and guards them with her life.

I ride within the hour.

Henry R

Written this Seventh day of June, 1421 at Odiham Castle.

—§§—

'Are you ill, Catherine?' I heard the duchess say, having at last noticed that her friend looked pale. 'Is it the babe?'

Catherine straightened up and shook her head. 'No. It was the realisation that my lord comes to take his leave. I am foolish, for I have known he would take ship any day now.' She stood up and clasped Jacqueline's hands. 'The girdle looks well on you, as I knew it would. Now I must finish dressing and so must you. I am sure his grace will want to bid you farewell also. I will send word when he is departing.'

It was a gentle but obvious dismissal, and Jacqueline was not too thick-skinned to take the hint. However she did not quit the queen's chamber without aiming a long and enquiring look in my direction, to which Catherine hastily responded. 'No, Mette is to stay. She has to help me with my hair and, besides, the king has asked particularly that she be here when he comes.'

I tried not to let them see that I registered the exchange of disdainful glances between the duchess and Eleanor as they both curtsied to Catherine and made their exit, closely followed by Agnes. The room seemed suddenly very empty. I crossed to Catherine's seat and handed the letter back to her.

'Now, Mademoiselle, tell me what it is in there that has made you suddenly so pale and faint?' I asked gently.

'You have read it, Mette,' she replied, staring down at the closely scrawled missive. 'What can this "grave matter" be that he wishes to discuss? Have I done something wrong?'

I went on my knees by her stool and saw the tears glistening on her eyelashes. It was a surprise to see her suddenly look so frightened when she had recently appeared happy and confident in her new friendship with the duchess, despite the absence of King Henry and his imminent departure for France.

'No, Mademoiselle. Why should you think it is anything you have done? The king probably wants to advise you of any problems that may require your attention while he is away.'

'Yes, but the Duke of Bedford will be here to handle all that. Perhaps Charles is trying to foment trouble in England and the king thinks I am involved. Perhaps he no longer trusts me. Suddenly I feel terribly fearful, Mette.'

'It is the child, Mademoiselle. Many mothers-to-be feel like that, especially the first time. It is a great responsibility you have, to bring that babe safely into the world. But I am sure you have nothing to fear from the king and believe me you are not alone. I will always be here.'

She looked up at me sorrowfully. 'I know, Mette, and I am grateful, but you do not understand. I may be the Queen of England but the English have no love for us French. When the king is far away, who will defend me against prejudice and false accusation? I have learned that the last French Queen of England, my lord's stepmother Jeanne of Navarre, was accused of witch-craft and lives under restriction somewhere. She never comes to court and no one talks of her. She is powerless and friendless and cannot even return to her own country. And it would be the same for me if the king were to turn against me. I know you think I am weak not to defend you against the Duchess of Hainault and the Duke of Gloucester, but you see I need their support. It is important that people know I have powerful friends at court.'

'Which people, Mademoiselle? Whom do you fear?' I was worried that she might be losing her grip on reality, remembering with deep concern her father's mental frailty, locked for months at a time in his almost deserted palace.

However, she seemed suddenly to throw off her apprehension, straightening up and shrugging her shoulders. 'There is no one in particular. I daresay I have been studying too much English history in order to try and understand my new country. Take no notice. Let us enjoy our brief time alone together, Mette, for it happens too infrequently these days. What shall I wear to greet my husband cheerfully?'

King Henry arrived just as I had finished pinning a gossamer veil over Catherine's carefully arranged hair. The day was growing warm and we had chosen a loose yellow silk houpp-pelande over a pretty blue tunic with a collar of lustrous river pearls. Henry stopped short at the doorway, relishing her fresh beauty as she sank to her knees before him.

'My sweet Catherine! You are a sight to quench the desert thirst of Araby!' he exclaimed, his face wreathed in smiles. The scar on his left cheek stood out white against the weathered tan on the rest of his exposed skin and his crimson doublet, scattered with white Lancastrian swans, was dusty from the road. He took both her hands, raised her and enfolded her in his arms, pressing his lips to hers. All evidence of Catherine's earlier misgivings had vanished and I turned away, swallowing a rush of emotion at the passion of their kiss.

'How am I going to leave you when all my being cries out to have you with me in the field, as we were at Melun?' King Henry's outburst would have seemed melodramatic, had it not been expressed with such genuine feeling. Despite my sense of intrusion, I found my eyes drawn back to them and he was gazing down into her upturned face as if he would have her image burned into his memory.

'You must know that I wish with all my heart I could be there with you, my dearest lord, but the fruit of our love comes between us. We can never regret the advent of the child we have made together.'

'No indeed, and it is that very subject I wish to talk to you about before I leave.' He led her to a cushioned bench where they could both sit close together. 'I want you to hear this too, Mette, because I rely on you to remind Catherine of it when her time comes.'

'What is it, my lord? What have I done?' All Catherine's previous anxiety seemed to flare again.

The king smiled and shook his head like a father reassuring a child. 'You have done nothing, my love. But I want you to promise me something. I am troubled by a prediction shown to me in an astrologer's almanac. I wish you not to have the babe at Windsor, Catherine. The stars do not bode well for the birth of a king within these walls.'

Catherine frowned deeply. 'I have never before known you to set much store by astrologers, my liege. It is my brother, Charles, who consults them at every turn and little good it has done him. Besides, I like it here at Windsor. It has kept English kings and queens safe for centuries. There can be nothing unlucky about so impregnable a fortress. I feel safe here.'

But King Henry was adamant. 'The warning is clear. The astrologer writes: Of all that Henry of Monmouth gain, Naught will to Henry of Windsor remain. I have fought hard to win back territory that should be ours, Catherine. I do not want it all to be for naught. Arrangements are being made for your lying-in at Sheen.'

'I have never been to Sheen,' Catherine protested. 'I am comfortable here and the air is fresh and clean.'

'And so it is at Sheen for it is also on the River Thames. It is not so far away, a palace with a pleasure garden, elegant and beautiful – more like your French chateaux; not a vast military stronghold like Windsor. I am having it refurbished and the royal apartments will be ready by the autumn. Promise me you will go there for the birth.' He paused, looking for me and raised his voice when he could not see me. 'Mette! Mette, where are you?'

I had retreated to a corner behind the great curtained bed, still within earshot but wishing to let them feel their conversation private; however I emerged at his call and bent my knee. 'Here, your grace.'

'I am relying on you to ensure that the queen goes to Sheen

for the birth of our son, Mette. When do you estimate that will be?'

I cleared my throat nervously. 'These things are never certain, sire, as you know, but it should be in December, probably before Christmas.'

'I dearly wish I could be here for it, but there is much still to be done in France.' He turned back to Catherine. 'You will write to me from time to time, will you not, my queen? I shall await your letters as eagerly as any lovelorn squire.'

Catherine rose from the bench. 'Of course I will write. My lord does not need to ask, but I must also be sure that you are well protected.' She reached out to where the neck of his chemise showed above his doublet and felt there for the chain he always wore. Pulling out the gold reliquary she had given him as a wedding gift she put her lips to it, muttering a little prayer. 'There,' she said. 'I have begged Sweet Jesu to keep you safe while you wear the thorn from his crown. You must promise me never to take it off.'

King Henry took the reliquary from her and kissed it himself. 'I swear. And may Christ's holy mother keep you and our child safe.' Their eyes locked for several seconds and I rose with the intention of disappearing from sight once more, but the king saw me move and swung round. 'Mette, I charge you also to send regular reports on her grace's progress. Now we will break our fast here together. Will you organise that for us? And get a message to my captain to have the men and horses ready immediately afterwards. We must be in Dover by tomorrow.'

For nearly an hour it was as if we were back in the Pleasance at Kenilworth as I served them bread and ale and cold meats and they sat at table together looking so longingly at one another that had King Henry not sworn a solemn oath of abstinence for fear of harming the baby, I believe they would have thrown themselves onto the big bed for a passionate farewell embrace. The official parting, performed in the Upper Court under a brilliant azure sky and the curious gaze of many, seemed sadly formal compared to the ardour of that meal.

The leaves were beginning to turn when news came from Sheen Palace that the refurbishment work had been completed on the royal apartments. I thought Catherine would immediately begin plans to move there but, to my surprise, several weeks went by and she made no mention of it. To be fair, although there was no doubt that she was pregnant, her belly was not yet massively swollen and, disguised by the flowing houppelande gowns which she made every effort to ensure remained the fashion, many people might not have guessed her condition. With most of King Henry's closest friends and courtiers at his side in France and his brother John, Duke of Bedford, residing mostly at Westminster where the Regency Council sat, Catherine's court at Windsor was cosy and intimate, consisting of herself and Jacqueline and their small band of ladies, occasionally boosted by visiting nobles and their wives. All summer she had been happy and relaxed, and there was every reason to think that the pregnancy was progressing perfectly normally.

With the lovesick Lady Joan urging her on, Catherine busied herself particularly over the matter of the Scottish king's ransom and to that end cultivated the help of King Henry's half-uncle Bishop Beaufort, who had been instrumental in getting negotiations started during a diplomatic mission over the northern border earlier in the year. Spurred on by the advantageous prospect of having his niece as Queen of Scotland, the wily bishop had also managed to secure agreement from King Henry to support a marriage between Lady Joan and King James, provided the recently knighted young king proved helpful in securing the capitulation of certain French strongholds, which had been garrisoned by troops of Scottish mercenaries. Understandably therefore, of all the ladies Joan proved the most ardent collector of news from the French campaign, growing more jubilant every time word came that another town or castle had surrendered to the English. For her part Catherine remained passively neutral about such matters, neither celebrating King Henry's victories nor crowing over the dauphin-pretender's defeats. I often wondered what her true thoughts were as King Henry secured one victory after another over her brother, systematically pursuing his revenge for the death of his brother Thomas of Clarence, but she gave no indication of them and showed me no encouragement to ask.

Meanwhile, Lady Joan's mother, Margaret of Clarence, had been successful in arranging a ransom for at least one of her two Beaufort sons, taken prisoner during the terrible English defeat at Beaugé, the battle which had robbed her of her husband. Edmund Beaufort arrived in Windsor in early November to the great joy of his mother and Lady Joan and the delight of Catherine, who had grown fond of him during her siege honeymoon.

'Captivity has changed you, Edmund,' she observed as he knelt before her in the Windsor great hall. 'You have become a man.'

She received him in front of the assembled household and those of us who had last seen him a year ago in France were struck as she was by the change in him. Then he had been a callow youth, smooth-cheeked and quick to blush. Now he was taller and broader and carried himself like the confident soldier he was, even after six months of imprisonment.

'I hope so, your grace,' he said with a wry smile. 'I have

certainly done things and seen sights to inspire maturity. I hope you will not be offended if I say that you have altered considerably as well, Madame.'

Edmund's mother, standing beside him, shot him a disapproving glance, but Catherine laughed. 'That remark demonstrates the change in you,' she observed. 'When you were a young squire, bringing me messages from the king, you would have blushed at the sight of my condition and made no mention of it.'

'And now I salute it and congratulate you for it, your grace.' He bowed enthusiastically. 'It is a blessed state and one that the people of two kingdoms joyfully celebrate.'

'Thank you, Edmund, and we should both congratulate your lady mother for so quickly realising the funds for your ransom and achieving your release.' She turned to the dowager duchess with sympathetic concern. 'Tell me, Madame, what news is there of Edmund's brother, my lord of Somerset? Is he still in France?'

It transpired that the heavy sum demanded in ransom for the release of John Beaufort had proved more difficult and he still languished as a prisoner of the Duke of Alençon, likely to remain captive while hostilities raged in that duchy between the forces of King Henry and the dauphin.

Margaret of Clarence remained optimistic, however. 'The king has generously agreed to exchange a French nobleman of similar rank for John's release, should one such be taken captive. So far that situation has not arisen.'

'But the Duke of Orleans is a prisoner in England still,' Catherine observed. 'Could this not be an opportunity to end his captivity also?' There was an awkward silence which caused her brow to crease in a puzzled frown. 'Is there some problem?' she asked.

The duchess exchanged meaningful glances with her son and then mutely bowed her head. Edmund cleared his throat and addressed the queen apologetically. 'There is no question of that, Madame. Six years ago, after the battle of Agincourt, it was decreed that the Duke of Orleans should not be ransomed until he and all of France recognise King Henry's legitimate claim to the French throne.'

Catherine pursed her lips and nodded slowly. 'Ah, I see. Well, in that case we shall all have to pray for a swift resolution to hostilities across the Sleeve.' Her solemn expression brightened into a smile. 'But we can celebrate your return to England at least. Tonight I decree that there will be feasting and music and I hope you will entertain me, Edmund, by dancing with all my young ladies!'

During that evening's festivities I noticed Catherine growing progressively more pale and quiet until I eventually plucked up courage to suggest that she retire. To my surprise she agreed and, as I helped her wearily to bed, I nearly broached the subject of the move to Sheen but decided to leave it to the morning when she might be more amenable. This turned out to be a mistake, for by morning she felt rested and cheerful and dismissed the idea airily.

'No, no, Mette. There is plenty of time for that. Life will be unutterably boring at Sheen. Once we have moved there, people will think I cannot be disturbed. There will be no visitors. I am not ready yet for confinement. We will wait here at Windsor until nearer the time.'

14

Walter Vintner had gone to France in the king's train, but to my delight a letter was delivered to me from my daughter Alys, brought from Paris by Walter's father and from London to Windsor in the royal courier's bag. It came with an additional note from Geoffrey Vintner himself, but I was so eager to read the one in my daughter's hand that I put his aside and broke the seal on the other, tears springing to my eyes when I unfolded the paper and instantly recognised Alys's neat, looped script, tightly packed into every inch of the page.

—ξξ—

Warmest greetings to my best beloved Maman,

How clever of you to arrange your own courier service and with such a cultivated and charming messenger! But how I wish you could have come with Master Vintner. It is nearly a year now since we were together and I am desolate to tell you that I think little Catrine can no longer remember her fond Grandemère, although of course I speak of you every day. She is such a pretty little maid with her glossy dark-brown curls and constant dimpled smiles. I do not think she can be anything like me but takes after her Pépé, as she calls him. Jacques adores her, as you can imagine, and is thrilled, as I hope you will be that I am expecting another babe in the spring of next year. Maître Vintner indicated that he offered to escort you across the Sleeve once you have fulfilled your duty to Queen Catherine in her confinement, so perhaps we may hope to see you in Paris within the year and to introduce you to another grandchild?

Everything here goes well, although without an active royal court in the city there is little call for fashionable garb and Jacques has to be content with making gowns for the merchants and guild-masters and their wives, which he does very successfully. However I am sure that he misses introducing new designs and fabrics as he did for Queen Catherine.

I wonder if the queen ever speaks of her little god-daughter. Please tell her that we are thinking of her and praying for the safe delivery of her child. She must be fervently hoping that it will be a son to inherit the thrones of France and England. I am glad I do not have to worry whether my baby is a boy or a girl, although I think Jacques would like a son to follow him in his craft. My dearest wish would be to have you, Ma, to help me when the child comes, as you did for Catrine's birth. I truly believe I would have died then if it had not been for you but they say that the second time is easier, do they not? The queen is fortunate indeed to have you at her side.

I kiss and embrace you and then kneel for your blessing as a good daughter should. May St Margaret protect us all and bring a happy conclusion to our labours.

Your loving daughter
Alys

Written at La Ruelle du Louvre, Paris, this day Sunday the Sixth of November 1421

—§§—

I scanned the letter half a dozen times and had to wipe my tears after every reading. The more I read it, the more I heard the note of desperate longing in Alys's words. I felt a terrible stab of guilt. I do not know if I saved their lives, but it is true I had done my utmost to bring a difficult birth to a happy end when little Catrine was born. I had employed my instinct and every bit of folklore I could muster, including rubbing Alys's belly with a jasper stone to bring the baby out. And now all I could do for her second labour was pray that it would, as so often happened, be easier.

Geoffrey Vintner's covering letter confirmed my suspicions about Alys's true feelings.

—§§—

To my esteemed friend Madame Guillaumette Lanière, greetings,

I write to tell you that I visited your daughter while I was in Paris and delivered your letter. As you see, she immediately wrote a reply.

I found her well and your granddaughter Catrine a delightful little girl who called me M'sieur Vin-vin, which I think I prefer to my real name! She entertained me by showing me her 'poupée', a wooden doll wearing a beautiful robe her mother had made. What fine stitching was in that gown!

Unfortunately your son-in-law, the tailor, was not at the

*house but away taking a commission from a new customer,
so I did not meet him. However, judging by the amount of
visible work in progress he has no shortage of orders and
your daughter assured me that they were making a good
living. She was kind enough to serve me a drink of good wine
and some delicious Parisian wafers while we spoke of you
and your son Luc, of whom she regrets she has not seen or
heard during the past year. She asked me if I ever visited the
Pretender's court and I was sorry to disappoint her by
answering in the negative.*

*Alys is only a year or so older than my Anne and yet
apparently so much more capable. No doubt a credit to your
upbringing. She does, of course, miss you fearfully, I will not
be disingenuous on that account.*

*I think it very likely that I will be undertaking another
journey to France early next year and would be honoured to
have your company, should you find it possible to lay aside
your duty to the queen. Meanwhile I remain your respectful
friend,*

   Geoffrey Vintner

*Written at the House of the Vines, London, this day the
12th of November 1421*

—§§—

I was tempted to sit down there and then and write to accept
Master Vintner's kind offer, without even consulting Catherine
about it and over the next weeks I wished many times that I
had. It only became more difficult to broach the subject as the
tension between us increased, for Catherine resolutely refused

to pack up and retire to Sheen for her confinement. Initially I did not blame her because I considered childbirth practice among the English nobility to be unnecessarily draconian, insisting that an expectant mother retreat into a closed room a month before the expected date of the birth.

'Look at me, Mette,' she protested vehemently, 'I am hardly waddling like a duck! There is plenty of time to take up a life of tedium and waiting. I shall go mad sitting in one room all that time. It is less than a day's journey downriver to Sheen and you can send servants on ahead to make sure that everything is made ready. I do not need to take to the barge until mid-December.'

We were walking in the garden outside St George's Hall, adjacent to the royal apartments, taking advantage of a burst of weak sunshine that had broken through the persistent autumn mist. I sighed, cast my gaze about for eavesdroppers and, lowering my voice to a whisper, responded as forcefully as I could. 'We cannot be sure of that, Mademoiselle. You were with the king from the middle of March. God may have blessed your union at the earliest possible moment. You know what the king said about not having the child at Windsor. I beg you to leave before the end of November.'

But she would not be tied down. 'I feel fine. Do not fuss, Mette. I promise to leave in plenty of time. It is my Saint's Day next week and Jacqueline has organised some special enter- tainment, including a new fool who has a reputation for being very rude and extremely funny. I do not want to miss that.'

Jacqueline! That name grated on my brain like a cartwheel on gravel. The Duchess of Hainault had insinuated herself into Catherine's life with the same effect as bindweed twining through woodland – elegant, ubiquitous and impossible to get rid of. I had no personal reason to dislike her, except that she had a very obvious disdain for me, equally without a personal reason since she did not know me. Unfortunately Catherine and the duchess were together almost constantly and it was very difficult to serve two ladies, one of whom did not recognise my existence, while the other coolly ignored me, as I had been warned she was obliged to. Then there was Eleanor Cobham to contend with, the artful, dark foil for Jacqueline's fair Nordic beauty, who followed her around like a hare-hound masquerading as a lap-dog, nimble-brained, shrewd and always looking for ways to please her mistress, frequently by undermining me. It was not a year since Eleanor had been presented and rejected by Catherine as one of her ladies in waiting and yet she had now contrived to spend more time in the queen's company than I did. When I had welcomed her recruitment by the duchess, I had not realised that it was tantamount to her being employed in the queen's household after all. Had it not been for the faithful Agnes, on whom we all relied, those months of Catherine's pregnancy would have been purgatory for me.

A midwife had been appointed for the birth, one Mistress Bet Scorer who had been recommended by Margaret of Clarence and came from a village called Eye, not far from the palace of Westminster. In mid-November an escort was sent for her protection and she travelled to Windsor with her husband and a young couple from the same village, William and Margery Jourdemayne. Once they had seen their wives settled in the royal household, the two men returned home to their farm work. Mistress Scorer was a plump, practical soul, a veteran of a hundred births, who examined Catherine respectfully but thoroughly and took care not to frighten her with too many details of the skills she had to offer. Her assistant, Margery, was a handsome, sturdy young woman of about Catherine's age who had been some years with Mrs Scorer learning the science of midwifery. It quickly became evident that she was of more than average yeoman intelligence and Eleanor started to favour her company, showing her the Windsor herb garden and comparing and exchanging knowledge of cures and remedies.

My campaign to get Catherine to travel to Sheen was not aided when, towards the end of November, Eleanor announced loudly in the queen's hearing that she hoped the household would not leave Windsor until she and Margery had completed their work with the plants in the castle herb garden to prepare fresh salves and potions to ease and assist the queen's confinement. I decided to speak to Mistress Scorer privately with a view to acquiring an ally over the move to Sheen, but she did not prove instrumental.

'The baby is small yet,' she told me matter-of-factly. 'I think it will not be born until Christmas. If the queen wishes to stay here until Margery has completed her remedies, I will not gainsay her. It would be better in my opinion if she had the baby here at Windsor anyway.'

Since it had been a private matter between the king and Catherine, I did not wish to reveal his grace's prohibition of a Windsor birth and so I had no argument to present for an imminent move. Instead I decided to seek reassurance from the midwife on another matter that had been worrying me.

'Are you familiar with the recipes Mistress Jourdemayne and Damoiselle Cobham are preparing for the queen?' I asked her. 'We need assurances that they will not be in any way harmful to her grace or the baby.'

The midwife looked seriously offended. 'Margery Jourdemayne has been apprenticed to me for four years now and she is very skilled in the use of herbs and simples, Madame,' she protested.

'She has been studying under a renowned apothecary in Westminster and, young though she is, there can be few who excel her in knowledge and expertise, especially in balms for use in childbirth. Ask the dowager duchess if you do not believe me.'

I hastened to assure her that I did indeed believe her, but made a mental note to check with Margaret of Clarence anyway. As for the move to Sheen, Catherine announced that same day that she would be happy for arrangements to be made to travel there after the feast of St Nicholas but not before, because she wished to preside over the distribution of presents to children on the holy day of their patron saint, which fell on the sixth of December. I bit my tongue and hoped for the best.

On the fifth of December her pains began. It was a mild day for the season and she had taken a walk with the Duchess of Hainault around Queen Philippa's garden, laid out for King Henry's great grandmother on a flat area of ground behind St George's Hall where the curtain wall sheltered a pretty enclosure of paths, low evergreen hedges and ornamental flowering bushes. While Catherine walked and talked intimately with her royal friend, I had hung back discreetly, but I noticed that she was not moving with her usual grace and occasionally her hand strayed to her back, which she rubbed distractedly. On their return to the queen's solar, she took her usual chair but fretfully demanded that more cushions be provided.

'Are you feeling pains, Madame?' I asked. 'Shall I fetch Mistress Scorer?'

'No, no, Mette, do not fuss. I am just a bit stiff. Heaven knows I am carrying enough extra weight around. Just do as I ask and fetch the cushions – today if possible!'

Such sarcasm was not typical of her, even when in the company of the duchess, who often treated servants with sharp impatience. So while I was collecting the requested cushions I also sent a page to find the midwife. Prudently, these days Mistress Scorer was never far away. When I returned and began to arrange the cushions in order to give her more support, she suddenly drew a sharp breath and grimaced.

'Oh – oh! What was that? Did you poke me?' Catherine's voice was harsh and accusatory.

Hastily I drew my hand back. 'No, your grace.' I was conscious that the duchess shot me an irritated scowl but ignored it. 'Why? Did you feel something?'

I was not unduly concerned, believing as I always had that this first week of December was a much more likely delivery date than Christmastide, which the midwife had predicted, but Catherine went into a panic and stood up, casting the cushions to the floor.

'Mette, Mette! I must leave now!' she exclaimed. 'I promised the king I would not deliver my baby at Windsor. Order the barges. How long will it take to get downriver to Sheen?'

'Oh no, your grace! If your pains have started, you cannot travel now, not even by barge.'

For once it was not me telling Catherine what she could and could not do; it was the midwife. Mistress Scorer had answered my summons with impressive speed and bent her knee at the door before hurrying to the queen's side.

'It will distress the child and the babe needs all its strength to make its way into the world. No, we will prepare your chamber for delivery and meanwhile you must rest. Margery will provide hyssop water to soothe the cramps and you must drink an infusion of camomile to calm you.'

'But it cannot have started; it is too early!' cried Catherine. 'I promised the king that I would not have the baby at Windsor. He read of some prophecy which predicts ill fortune if his son is born here. You said the birth would not be until Christmas.'

'Babies come when they will, honoured lady,' said the midwife soothingly. 'The babe is small, but that means it will be easier to deliver. Now, pray do as I say and rest. All will be well.'

As another pain seized her, Catherine grabbed at my hand, clenching it until the bones crunched audibly and staring at me in alarm. 'Ah! It hurts, Mette. It hurts!'

'Yes, Mademoiselle, it is not easy. That is why we call it labour.' I was not going to tell her that the pain she felt now was only a fraction of what was to come. 'Come, we have laid cushions on this bench and in no time we will have prepared your bed. Your confessor has been called and very soon he will be here to pray with you. Prayer always calms you.'

I noticed that the Duchess of Hainault remained rooted to her chair, her expression one of alarm, even distaste. She seemed unwilling or simply unable to offer any sympathy or encouragement to her friend in these circumstances. I knew that Catherine had asked her to be godmother and sponsor to the child and to witness the birth, but I rather wondered if she was up to the task. For once Eleanor was not with us, away in the workshop she had set up with Margery to prepare their herbal lotions.

When he arrived, it was obvious that Maître Boyers was equally perturbed by the prospect of entering a room where a woman had begun the process of giving birth and hovered in the doorway wringing his hands. I bustled up to him, smiling reassuringly. 'All is well, Maître Jean. Things are at a very early stage, but we will not be moving to Sheen. Her grace would like to hear Mass and receive the comfort of the host before she retires to her confinement. She asks that you go with her into the oratory.'

By this time Catherine had grown more accustomed to the strength and rhythm of the pains, which were still only coming at extended intervals, so she felt confident about hearing the Mass and feeling the reassuring touch of the holy wafer on her tongue, without frightening the priest by delivering the baby while kneeling on the prie Dieu. Lady Joan accompanied her to the oratory and I went to fetch supplies of napkins, sheets and soft linen waste for mopping, in readiness for the birth. A messenger was sent to the wife of a local baron who had agreed to wean her own child in preparation for becoming the royal baby's first wet nurse. Catherine had declared that she wished to feed the baby herself, but her wishes had been silenced by loud protests from both Jacqueline of Hainault and Margaret of Clarence. In England as in France, a queen simply did not put her child to her own breast.

A few hours later, there was no great sign of progress and Catherine became fretful and restless. 'It is too hot!' she complained, throwing off the bedcovers. 'Why do the windows have to be shuttered and the fire made to burn so fiercely? I know it is winter, but I am stifled.'

'We must shield the baby from bad humours,' explained Mistress Scorer placidly, wringing out a pad of linen waste in a bowl of lavender water. 'Here,' she handed it to me. 'Bathe her grace's face and neck with this. And is there no one who can sing or read to the queen while she labours? Some of my high-born ladies have poetry read to distract them. I have heard wonderful poems by someone called Geoffrey Chaucer, all about pilgrims on the road to Canterbury.'

Margaret of Clarence was in close attendance and made a disapproving noise. 'Oh no, the queen would not like to hear those. They are too earthy and besides they are in English, and very coarse English too. I do not think her grace would understand them. But I could certainly read to her – from the Gospels perhaps or St Augustine's Confessions.'

Bet Scorer made a sour face, clearly not impressed with the duchess's choice of literary distraction. Catherine lay bathed in sweat, panting as another pain gripped her and I moved in to wield the lavender-scented linen pad, wiping it gently over her brow and neck. We had long ago undressed her and she wore only a damp chemise, its ribbons tangled and wet.

'That is lovely and cool, Mette,' she said when the pain had passed. 'I would like a drink.'

'I will bring some watered wine, Mademoiselle,' I murmured, smiling fondly. In the crisis of childbirth our relationship had reverted to its mother–daughter origins. 'I will fetch a fresh chemise also, you will be more comfortable.'

She nodded. 'Yes, Mette, please do. Will it be very much longer, do you think?'

I looked at Mistress Scorer, who shrugged and moved her hands slowly apart to indicate a considerable interval of time. Fortunately Catherine could not see her, but I knew anyway that her real trial had barely begun and I prevaricated. 'In a few hours, Mademoiselle, when your babe is in your arms, you will not remember how long it took to arrive.'

Catherine scowled at me and shook her head. 'Not "it", Mette, "he",' she said. 'How long he took to arrive.'

As if calling it male could change its sex at this late stage, I thought, but I said, 'Of course,' crossing my fingers as I went to the door. 'I will fetch that drink.'

With the shutters closed, we lost all track of time and in due course Catherine lost all awareness of how long her body had been wracked by the progressively more violent contractions of her womb. Whereas at first she had made little sound, eventually she began to cry out with each new onslaught and then, clutching at my hands and staring at me with wide, agonised eyes, she began to beg for it to be over. Time and again I wiped her sweat-beaded brow and whispered soothing words into her ear, resolutely quashing my own surges of alarm in order to show her only calmness and compassion.

'All is going well, dear Mademoiselle,' I crooned again and again. 'Soon, very soon, it will be over and you will be a mother.'

'Of a son, Mette, of a son. The mother of a son,' she repeated through cracked lips, as if simply by saying it over and over again she could make it so. Cracked lips, I thought. Where were all those balms and potions? I raked the room with my eyes, spied Margery whispering in a corner with Eleanor and impatiently beckoned her across. However it seemed the much-vaunted emollients were meant only for the actual delivery, not for the comfort of the poor labouring mother. Making no secret of my irritation at hearing this, I asked Agnes to find some of Catherine's cosmetic lip lotion in her toilette chest.

We had been informed by this time that Bishop Beaufort had arrived from Winchester and waited in the great hall with the Royal Steward, the Lord Chamberlain and a posse of heralds and couriers who would convey news of the birth to Westminster and on to the king in France. I was interested to note that, unlike the French court which insisted on certain officials actually witnessing a royal birth, the English tradition restricted the birthing chamber to women only, although I had asked Maître

Boyers to stay near at hand in the ante room, just in case. I vividly recalled the tragic stillbirth of my own first child and his subsequent burial in unhallowed ground for lack of instant baptism. I knew only too well that there was always a danger in childbirth that either mother or child or both might need the urgent services of a priest.

The midwife kept making secret examinations under the covers and nodding with satisfaction until at last the labour began to show signs of reaching a conclusion. Instead of moaning and writhing, Catherine seemed to acquire renewed strength, pulling herself up on the pillows and shouting at us in French and there were plenty of people to shout at. Apart from myself, Agnes and the two midwives, the room now contained the Duchess of Hainault and the Dowager Duchess of Clarence, all the ladies-in-waiting and several tiring women, scurrying in and out with fresh logs and pails of warm water.

'Mother of God! What are you all doing standing around?' Hoarse though her voice was, the queen conveyed her message unequivocally. 'A prince strives to be born and you all do nothing but stand and gawp at us like idiots? Jesu protect us. Mette – tell them all to go away. You will help me as you always have, and Agnes, where is Agnes? Ah the pain! Blessed Marie save me, I can take no more.' Suddenly she hurled the covers back and tried clumsily to scramble off the bed in some desperate attempt to escape the unrelenting spasms. I rushed to catch her in my arms and stop her falling to the floor, holding her fast and rocking her like the only mother she knew and all the while I glared wildly over her shoulder at Bet Scorer who was placidly arranging the tools of her trade on a cloth-covered table nearby; a sharp silver knife, a strip of clean linen and a round silver bowl.

'Always silver for a royal birth,' she declared, favouring us with a gap-toothed smile. 'All is well, your grace, do not fear. It will not be long now. Mothers often shout a good deal just before the babe arrives and sometimes in much worse language than Master Chaucer's.' A coarse chuckle bubbled from her lips and she turned to beckon to her assistant who hovered at a respectful distance. 'Bring those salves of yours now, Margery. It is time to ease the baby's way.'

Catherine suddenly caught a glimpse of the knife and screamed afresh. 'No! Dear God no! Blessed St Margaret save me from the knife! Mette, do not let them cut me!'

Margery approached the bed and punctiliously dropped a curtsy. 'The knife is to cut the cord, your grace. Have no fear, Mistress Scorer is very skilled. She will not touch you or the baby with it.' She showed the queen the earthenware bowl of fragrant balm she held carefully in both hands. 'And this will make it easier for the child to push his way out. He will slip into the world like an eel through a pipe. He is ready to come now and you must use all your strength to help him on his way. Rejoice, my lady, for you are about to give birth to England's next king.'

Whether it was the confident way she assumed that the child would be male, the invigorating aroma of the pale-green balm she waved enticingly under Catherine's nose, or the calm, reassuring tone of her lilting country voice, Margery's words seemed to settle Catherine's panic so that she relaxed against me and allowed me to place her gently back against the pillows which Agnes hastily plumped into a heap.

'Where are the witnesses?' Mistress Scorer enquired, turning to gaze around the now-empty room. 'Do we not need official witnesses at a royal birth?'

Agnes and I exchanged glances as we stripped back the heavy covers of the bed to allow the midwife freedom to perform the delivery. 'She is right,' whispered Agnes, dumping a heavy quilt on the floor. 'The royal ladies have retired at the queen's bidding, but they should be here; should I fetch them back?'

I nodded, turning away from the bed where Catherine had reluctantly settled back against the pillows, cooler now that only a fresh linen sheet covered the mound of her belly. 'Yes, fetch them,' I whispered, 'and warn Maître Boyers. Her confessor should be near at hand, just in case.'

I need not have whispered, for by now Catherine had retreated into a world where only she and the midwives and the new life within her held any significance. Bet Scorer lifted the lower end of the sheet and Margery began applying her salve, all the while holding a muttered conversation, the gist of which I caught as I stood behind them, soaking another pad to wipe Catherine's brow.

'I can see the head, Mistress, but there seems to be something shiny all around it, like a halo,' Margery was saying, bent over Catherine with a note of awe in her hushed voice. 'Jesu, what can it be?'

Bet Scorer peered over her shoulder and made the sign of the cross. 'It is the Veil!' she murmured breathlessly. 'I thought it possible since the waters had not broken. The babe will be born behind the Veil. It is the sign of a very special birth. I have seen it only once before.'

I was greatly relieved to see that Catherine appeared oblivious to the midwife's words.

'The old saying goes that a child born with the birth-caul still intact is blessed with spiritual gifts; a healer or a mystic, but priests say it is the work of the devil so we will say nothing of it, Margery, do you understand?' She too cast a glance at Catherine, whose face was congested with the effort of the next big push. Even so, the midwife's next hasty instructions to her assistant were issued in the same cautious whisper. 'When the head emerges fully, I will break through the caul to let the child breathe and, God willing, there will be no harm done. Do not show the babe to anyone until you have completely removed it. This is just a normal birth, remember that.'

Margery nodded. 'I will remember, but I will also never forget, for the child's face seen through the Veil is a truly wondrous sight.' She left the end of the bed then and moved up to speak to Catherine, leaning close to speak in the same low, persuasive tone she had used earlier. 'You can work as hard as you like now, your grace. All is well and in moments your son will be born.'

Catching sight of me, Mistress Scorer beckoned me closer and said softly, 'Have plenty of that linen waste ready, Madame. The waters are about to break and there will be a flood.'

While I stood ready but alarmed, hands full of the absorbent linen, I stared at the translucent caul which covered the emerging baby's face. I could see why it was called a Veil, for it bore an eerie resemblance to the fine gauze used in ladies' headdresses. In the flickering candlelight the gently moving liquid-filled bubble glowed around the crown of the baby's head and looked, as Margery had said, wondrously like a halo. 'It is a miracle,' I breathed. 'Like an angel being born.'

The midwife smiled grimly. 'Indeed,' she nodded. 'But if you value your life you will keep your mouth shut about it – for ever.' She spoke in a low, conversational tone, but her words chilled my blood. 'We must be very careful now, Madame. As I break the caul, you must place those soft pads on either side of the mouth to prevent the fluid rushing down the baby's throat when it breathes. Pray that the first breath will come quickly and cleanly. Above all, we do not want the child to choke.'

I did as she told me, whispering an earnest prayer to St Margaret and the midwife gently stroked the liquid under the caul away from the baby's mouth and broke through the delicate mucus skin with her fingernail. Fluid gushed out and I hastily wiped it clear of the babe's small mouth with the absorbent linen. As the translucent caul slipped back, the baby took its first gasp, only a few tiny bubbles of fluid frothing around its lips.

'God be thanked,' I murmured. At Margery's urging, Catherine made one final effort and the rest of the child's body slipped into my waiting hands. Bet swiftly tied the cord and sliced cleanly through it with her silver knife, then Margery was beside me with a big, soft napkin and we carried the little body reverently and laid it carefully on the midwife's table, ready to wipe the rest of the mucus clear. Freed of the caul, the skin glowed pink and smooth against the snowy white linen, unblemished by the usual marks of childbirth, and the baby uttered small, healthy whimpers.

'A boy, your grace,' I said with difficulty but Catherine did not hear me.

'Is it a boy, Mette?' she called fretfully from her pillows, her voice hoarse from her enormous effort as Bet drew the sheet down to cover her while they waited for the afterbirth.

'God is good,' breathed Agnes, who had been waiting at the table, unaware of our recent agitation. She made the sign of the cross. 'Beautiful!'

This answered the queen. 'But I know it is a boy,' she said joyously. 'Show them, Mette! Show everyone the new Heir of England!'

Solemnly I carried the baby across the room and watched the Duchess of Hainault, pale and wide-eyed, take one long look at the naked infant and nod acknowledgement of her witness before turning into Eleanor Cobham's arms and fainting clean away. The Dowager Duchess of Clarence, herself the mother of six, was more circumspect in her reaction; bowing her head in acknowledgement she crossed herself and smiled.

Out of the corner of my eye, I saw Bet swiftly scoop the birth remains into the silver bowl, which she covered with a cloth. Later, I found the bowl empty. I know now that I should have wondered why it was empty and should have enquired where the caul and the afterbirth had gone, but at the time Bet and Margery took charge of washing and wrapping the baby while I sponged Catherine clean and found her a fresh chemise to wear. When she was once more lying back against the pillows, I took the baby to her. The room settled into a hushed silence and I felt a surge of love and relief as I laid the precious bundle in her arms, my face wreathed in smiles.

'It is a male child, your grace, just as you prayed for and predicted. May God and His Holy Mother be praised. Here is your perfect prince.'

15

I thought that the closeness I had enjoyed with Catherine during her delivery might have reminded her how much history we shared and reinforced the importance of our ties of love and loyalty. However, as soon as she was recovered from the physical strain of giving birth and had enjoyed a good night's sleep, she immediately asked for the Duchess of Hainault and, within minutes, Jacqueline was back at Catherine's bedside, passing on all the praise and acclamation of the court. Before she arrived, Catherine suggested in a tone that brooked no argument that I should go and get some rest, thus ensuring that I was not present during the duchess's visit. Agnes told me later that Eleanor also frequented the bedchamber as the bearer of a constant stream of tonic drinks and herbal restoratives which she had been busy preparing with the duchess's encouragement and the help of the midwife's assistant, Margery Jourdemayne. I was not called to the bedchamber again until the following morning. Catherine floated on a cloud of elation and approbation, but I felt a terrible sense of anticlimax, berating myself for remaining loyally at the queen's side until her first child should be born, when I could have been in Paris assisting my own daughter as she prepared for the birth of her second.

The lowest point came two days after the birth when I

prepared the baby for his baptism. From the vaults of the Treasury I had acquired the royal christening robe, a tiny and exquisite gown of the finest white silk embroidered with swans and antelopes and other emblems of Lancastrian heraldry. It had been worn by King Henry and all his brothers and there was a new white silk chrism cap to cover the head of the baby once he had been anointed with the holy oil. Catherine had embroidered the cap herself with pearl beads and little crowns and it would be given to the Church a few days after the christening ceremony in gratitude for the little boy's purification. Although he had not yet been given a name, it was generally accepted that he would be called Henry after his father and grandfather. Of course Catherine would not be attending the baptism because she would not be churched and purified herself until a month after the delivery so, as the nominated godmother, the Duchess of Hainault would carry the child to the castle chapel at the head of a procession which would, by tradition, include the midwives and ladies who had officiated or been present at the birth. I naturally expected to be part of it.

When I took the baby from the nursery to the queen's bedchamber to show him to her, robed in his finery, the duchess was already there arrayed in her most splendid apparel, ready to take her pivotal role in the ceremony. Catherine was sitting by the fire looking remarkably cheerful and it did my heart glad to see it.

'I am so happy to see you already up from your bed, your grace,' I said, bending my knee as far as I could without endangering the baby in my arms. 'Here is your beautiful son, ready for his baptism.'

Catherine took the child from me and tenderly kissed his forehead. 'Thank you, Mette, he looks wonderful. You are obviously so in love with him yourself that you did not come to me this morning. I missed you.'

I gave her a stricken look and shot a questioning glance at her companion. 'I did come, your grace, but the duchess was already here and told me that I was not wanted.'

A small frown creased Catherine's brow. 'Did she? There must have been a misunderstanding. What I told her was that I did not want you to attend the baptism. It is only for the godparents and clergy and members of the court.'

She must have seen my disbelief in the effort I had to make to speak. 'Is that so, Madame? Shall I inform the midwives of this? They are expecting to attend, according to tradition, as was I.'

She shook her head impatiently. 'No, Mette. Of course they are to attend. It is their prerogative. But the same does not apply to you and I wish you to remain here.' She turned to the duchess and held out the baby. 'Take him, Jacqueline. I charge you to carry him into the arms of Holy Mother Church and bring him safely back to me.'

'Of course I will, Catherine; you need have no fear of that.' Jacqueline stepped forward to take the child and I was gratified to hear him set up a wail of protest the minute he left his mother's arms. The duchess hurriedly headed for the door, trying to shush the baby as she went and Eleanor Cobham fell into step in her wake, giving me a pitying glance as she passed. One by one the other ladies-in-waiting followed on behind.

My despondency must have shown, for Catherine said, 'Do not look so sour-faced, Mette. I need you here to bind my breasts while the others are away. You did not warn me of the pain involved in not suckling one's child.'

A surge of indignation swamped me as I recalled holding the

177

infant Princess Catherine to my full breast and how good it had felt to give her suck. What had happened, I wondered, to the bond of love that had flowered between us during that process? I could no longer detect any sign of it in Catherine and I could feel the remnants of it congealing like an icicle in my heart.

I decided to take up Geoffrey Vintner's offer to escort me to Paris. He had sent a message to say that, winds permitting, he was due to sail from Dover at the beginning of March and so, screwing up my courage, I asked Catherine for leave of absence. We met in the nursery after breakfast and I stood beside her as she scooped Prince Henry out of the carved and gilded cradle to which the wet-nurse had returned him after his morning feed. The dangerous first two months of life were over and he was now a plump and healthy baby showing every promise of growing into a healthy prince.

Her reaction to my request was instant and violent. She clutched little Henry to her breast and turned on me furiously.

'But you promised to stay with me, Mette! You said I could always rely on you.'

I stood in shocked silence, my heart pounding and my thoughts an incoherent jumble. I could think of nothing to say in reply to her outburst so I lowered my gaze and wrung my hands in agitation, waiting for the storm to pass.

The baby whimpered at being held so tightly and Catherine loosened her grip, bent to give him a soothing kiss and then lifted tear-filled eyes to mine. 'I know now that the strongest claim on a mother's heart should be from her own flesh and blood, so I suppose I must accept that you wish to leave me for your daughter.'

'It will not be for ever, Mademoiselle. When Alys is safely

delivered and has returned to her full strength, I will come back. You have my word on that.'

I had never seen Catherine's sapphire gaze harden as it did then. It made my blood chill and I heard her next remarks through a pounding in my ears. 'But can I still trust your word, Mette? And should you assume that I will call you back?' She turned away from me, smiling fondly at her little boy and rocking him gently. 'There are others who love me now, you see; others on whom I can rely.'

What could I say? Apart from an intense desire to see my family and be with Alys at the birth of her child, the prospect of some respite from the irritation caused me by Catherine's relationship with Jacqueline was a factor in my decision to go to Paris. It was clear that the duchess had managed to bring Catherine round to her way of thinking. During the days leading up to my departure, the queen preserved a glacial manner in my company and our encounters were awkward and uncomfortable.

As far as I know, the king had maintained a perfect silence on the subject of the location of the birth, and had reproached no one for breaking the promise that it would take place at Sheen. The splendour of the occasion and the health of the heir were seen as an obvious refutation of any ill omen whatever.

I had come to recognise that with the birth of a son, Catherine now felt herself invincible and had assumed the sense of superiority and sovereign contempt for everyone of inferior rank that seemed to afflict most occupants of a throne. I hoped and prayed that it might be temporary and that in due course she would recover her natural grace and compassion, but I left court with a heavy heart and received no fond farewell.

After such a depressing departure I should have known that the journey to Paris would be far from smooth. The good ship

Hilda Maria had appeared a sturdy enough cog when viewed from the quayside at Dover but, having sailed out of harbour in benign weather, halfway across the Sleeve the wind turned to the north-east and anxious crew-members began racing up the rigging to reduce the sails. Before they could complete the task, black clouds swamped the sky and a squall came screaming in off the North Sea, picking up the ship as if it was Queen Mab's nutshell, lifting and twisting and hurling it about on waves that were suddenly thirty-feet high. How those sailors clung to the spars I will never know. I kept expecting bodies to hurtle down onto the bucking deck as wave after wave heaved us skywards then raced away ahead, leaving us lurching drunkenly back into the trough before the next one came up from behind and tipped the bow sickeningly forwards once more. The *Hilda Maria* was not so much running before the wind as lumbering from moving mountain to moving mountain, clinging desperately to their slippery slopes as the procession of rolling giants tried their best to shake her off. Unfortunately, although the sky had darkened, it could not hide our perilous situation from us and the sea, once merely green and choppy, now appeared as a series of black, luminous-crested monsters, surging straight from the gates of hell.

With commendable forethought, Geoffrey Vintner had reserved us places in one of the cabins under the aft-castle but when we boarded we found it so crammed with travellers that I begged him to remain outside with me where the air at least smelled of salt and fish rather than stale sweat and vomit. As a result, when the storm hit we were caught in the open belly of the ship, unable to take shelter because the violent tossing of the deck made moving more than a step in any direction a life-threatening action. The bulk of the cargo was bales of raw wool being shipped to Flanders, so we stayed where we were, huddled down between them on a pile of tarpaulins, which should have been protecting the cargo, but had not been deployed before the storm hit. At least we were able to pull one over ourselves as some protection against the driving rain and the regular dousings from waves breaking over the gunwales. In the violent, whistling wind conversation was impossible; words were snatched away almost before they were uttered, but in my shuddering terror I felt Geoffrey's arms wrap around me like the hug of a friendly bear and I clung to him in return, eyes tight shut, moaning and whimpering to myself and sending prayers to God and his Holy Mother, St Nicholas, St Elmo and St Christopher; in fact to any relevant saint I could dredge up from my shamefully scant knowledge of who might intercede on our behalf. All I received by way of an answer was an explosive cracking sound followed by rending and creaking as the foremast came crashing down and lodged against the lowest spar of the mainmast, leaving its tattered sail and snapped stays whipping dangerously about in the wind. Unbeknown to us, in that moment of terror, it was this event which may have been our salvation because the ship had been too heavily rigged for the sudden change in conditions and we had been in danger of being pushed under the waves instead of over them.

At the height of my fear I began to believe the storm was some sort of retaliation for my having had the temerity to leave Catherine's side. In the moan and mayhem of the storm, I thought I could hear her voice reproaching me in the petulant tone I had noticed so frequently in recent weeks.

After two long hours, the storm abated as quickly as it had arrived and the movement of the ship diminished to an undulating motion which, although less frightening, proved embarrassingly nauseating. Suddenly I was forced to tear myself from Geoffrey's protective embrace, stagger to my feet and throw myself at the leeward rail, abruptly donating the contents of my stomach to the still-rolling waves. When I recovered enough to drag myself back to our shelter, Geoffrey had managed to release a wineskin from his baggage bundle and silently offered it to me. I took a gulp of the sweet wine and swirled it round my mouth to rid it of the foul taste of sickness. Having handed the skin back, I immediately began trying to adjust my bedraggled wimple, guessing I must look as damp and dishevelled as an alehouse pot-washer. Certainly, Geoffrey's hat and coif were crumpled and dripping disasters. However, like the ship, although battered and torn, we were still miraculously afloat, an outcome which had seemed impossible only an hour before. Despite my bruises and *mal de mer*, was profoundly grateful to be breathing and not swirling lifelessly in that evil black sea, staring upwards out of sightless eyes. I caught Geoffrey's amused glance and smiled ruefully back, recalling the comfort of his closeness during the darkest moments of the storm and nursing a certain secret pleasure at the memory of his embrace.

The ship had narrowly avoided being blown by the storm onto the deadly rocks of Cap Griz Nez, and it took the *Hilda Maria* the rest of the day to struggle back against the wind to Calais, with relieved sailors manning the oars in shifts and singing shanties lustily in gratitude for their delivery from drowning. With a face like one of the thunderclouds we had recently endured, the captain prowled around the hold, muttering and cursing at the harm inflicted on the precious bales of wool. Of the human cargo it was a toss of the dice which of us had fared the worst storm-damage, those who had weathered it outside or the whey-faced individuals who staggered out of the fetid castle cabins at either end of the ship. Personally I considered clothes saturated by sea-water preferable to the cloying stench of sickness that clung to the cabin travellers, who clutched the ship's superstructure and gulped fresh air like prisoners released from a dungeon.

A brisk March breeze kept the skies clear for the next week, luckily. It nipped at our faces, but at least it meant that the sun shone on our journey to Paris. I had left Genevieve at Windsor and we were to rely on hired mounts, which Geoffrey had acquired in Calais, arranging for us to join a party of merchants who were also headed for Paris. On the road he regaled me with comparisons between our travelling companions and the characters portrayed by the famous Geoffrey Chaucer in his *Canterbury Tales*, revealing at the same time his interesting connection with the poet's son.

'I have travelled on several missions to France with Thomas Chaucer. His father served the last king and Thomas has done even better for himself. He is the present Speaker of the House of Commons and was one of the negotiators for the king's marriage to Queen Catherine. That was when I first met him.'

'You negotiated the queen's marriage?'

My astonishment must have showed in my face, for my companion laughed heartily. 'Well, I was one lawyer among many, a whole team of them. My job was to put the agreements into legal Latin for the clerks to copy, but Sir Thomas was one of the front-line diplomats. I am surprised you have not met him at court, he is officially the king's butler, but he is very busy elsewhere and I think he mostly pays substitutes to serve for him in the post.'

'Sir Thomas? He has been knighted then?'

'Oh yes, and fought at the Battle of Agincourt. You do not

have to be born into the gentry any more, as you yourself know. Geoffrey Chaucer's father was a vintner just like mine and yet his granddaughter Alice has married the Earl of Salisbury. Mind you, she is a very beautiful woman.'

'What are you saying? That beauty and poetry are the passports to advancement?'

He laughed. 'So it would seem – and being called Geoffrey obviously helps as well!'

'Aha! So will you be marrying your daughters to earls?'

'Perhaps I will, with the help of my well-connected friends!'

Having temporarily abandoned the lawyer's coif and hat so battered by the storm, Geoffrey now sported a blue chaperon with a jaunty feather in it and to indicate who he meant by his 'well-connected friends', he swept it from his head to make me an extravagant bow, causing his horse to shy and spoil the effect as he dropped it in the mud. Watching him retrieve it and clamber back onto his horse inspired in me a rush of amused affection.

I was still chuckling as he spurred nearer and put his mouth close to my freshly wimple-covered ear. 'You know, Mette, when you laugh you become a girl again. You should do it more often.'

I tried to straighten my face and failed. 'And catch myself an earl you mean!'

'I would not put it past you. Nothing daunts you, does it?'

My smile vanished. 'On the contrary,' I said. 'Jacqueline of Hainault utterly defeats me.'

My heartfelt comment steered the conversation onto the subject of the duchess and it seemed that Geoffrey's diplomatic work kept him well informed on activities at many courts and councils of Europe.

'Duchess Jacqueline has a reputation for being one of the

more vainglorious notables of our time,' he observed, 'but then she has also been dealt a tricky hand. Being caught between a manipulative mother and a moronic husband cannot be an easy path to tread.'

I pursed my lips. 'I am sorry for her unfortunate situation but I have to say that England seems a random choice for her to make as a safe haven and I wish she had not latched on to my kind and compassionate mistress as her bosom friend.'

'I think you will find it is no random choice. Having fled from her so-called protectors – I mean her acquisitive cousin the Duke of Burgundy and her grasping uncle, the Bishop of Liège – she needed to find a knight in shining armour and where better to look than in the court of the hero of Agincourt, who just happens to have two unmarried and powerful brothers?' He cocked one quizzically curling eyebrow. 'Do you follow my line of thought?'

I frowned and chewed my lip. 'But she remains married to the Duke of Brabant, however mentally unstable he may be. How does she hope to snare the support of an English prince without being able to offer him the enticement of her territories of Hainault and Holland as a reward?'

Geoffrey's expression became guarded. He muttered, 'Well, you know, marriages can be annulled.'

When we reached Paris, Geoffrey insisted on escorting me all the way to Alys's house and even fished out a small cask of wine from the panniers of our packhorse to present to my daughter and son-in-law Jacques. So a pleasant hour was spent distracting them from their work while we tapped the cask and celebrated our family reunion. It was such a joy to find Alys looking bonny and blooming as her time fast approached, and my heart did cartwheels when I saw little Catrine, now a sturdy toddler of two with a mass of bright-brown curls and a good deal to say for herself in her piping little voice. Geoffrey was enchanted by her and engaged her in a solemn conversation concerning her painted wooden doll. I caught Alys glancing from me to him as if she could barely contain her curiosity about what was his place in my life.

When Geoffrey left to take up his lodging at the Louvre, he promised to make a return visit after his work for the Council of Regency was completed and before his departure to England. Alys suggested that, if he gave us due notice of his coming, he might like to join us for a meal.

'If it is not during my confinement, of course,' she added shyly. 'Ma and I might be a bit busy then.'

Geoffrey thanked her heartily. 'I shall keep in close touch and make sure to avoid such a crucial time,' he added. 'May Our Lady give you and your baby a speedy and safe delivery.'

After he rode off up the lane, leading the pack-horse, I had to endure much ribbing from my daughter on the subject of Geoffrey Vintner.

Only ten days later, Alys was brought to bed and her second confinement was as uncomplicated as her first had been fraught with danger. The midwife scarcely earned her fee as another daughter was born and swiftly baptised Louise after Jacques' mother, who had died in a coqueluche epidemic four years previously, when that terrible fever had swept across France claiming many thousands of victims. This was one baptism where I could play my rightful part and I was pleased to see how many of Jacques' clients and fellow tailors and their wives attended, which showed how well he and Alys had settled into their Paris community. I had delivered the purse which Queen Catherine had entrusted to me for her little god-daughter and now I added one of my own for the new arrival.

'I am sorry we have not named the child for you, Ma,' said Alys when I tucked the purse under her pillow after the baptism, which of course she had not attended. 'Jacques was very keen to commemorate his mother and, strictly speaking, it was his turn to name the baby. I promise we will call the next one after you.'

'It might be a boy,' I pointed out with a smile.

'Well then, we shall call him Guillaume.'

I crossed myself. 'Perhaps we should not make assumptions that there will be another,' I said. 'Just thank God for the safe delivery of this one and pray for good health to you both.'

Alys frowned. 'It is not your usual habit to be cautious, Ma. I do not think I like it.'

'It was the storm at sea,' I confessed. 'It made me realise that we should never take our lives for granted. We must thank God for what we have and not always expect Him to give us more.'

Alys shivered. 'Well, speaking personally, I hope for a few more years yet and I dearly hope a good many more for you, too, especially if that nice man Geoffrey Vintner is involved. Have you heard from him, Ma?'

I chided myself for blushing, but found I could not help it. 'Yes, I sent him a note to tell him that your baby had arrived and I received a letter today saying that he would be leaving France next week.'

'Well you had better send one back and tell him to come on Sunday for dinner. You will have to cook it yourself, Ma, because I will not be churched by then.'

My infuriating blush persisted. 'Actually, he asked me if I would like to visit the Louvre. He realised that it might not be convenient to dine here, but he says he will call to say goodbye to you and Catrine before he leaves.'

I had not told Alys of the coldness that had developed between me and Catherine, just as I did not show her the letter I gave to Geoffrey to carry to England on his return. I wrote it in a spirit of reconciliation, but I did not hold out great hope of success.

—§§—

To Her Grace Queen Catherine of England from Madame Guillaumette Lanière,

Loving and humble greetings from your loyal servant,

I am writing to tell you that I am safely arrived in Paris and that Alys has given birth to another daughter who has been baptised Louise. She had an easy confinement and this time I am glad to say we had no need of your jasper ring.

Alys and Jacques have established a good business in Paris and your god-daughter Catrine is thriving and looking prettier than ever. As you know she is two years old now and talks all the time that she is not asleep! If only you could see her I am sure she would make you laugh and she would love to play with Prince Henry and share her toys with him. I hope he is well and also thriving. I pray for you both every day and hope that you may be able to find time to send word to me of his progress and of your own health and well-being. I delivered your very generous gift to Catrine, for which Alys and Jacques send you heartfelt thanks.

As we agreed, I will stay here until Alys has been churched and is completely recovered from the birth and then, with your permission, I will make arrangements to return to England and to your service.

I remain your humble servant and ever-loving friend,
Guillaumette (Mette)

Written at Paris this fifteenth day of March 1422

—ξξ—

16

To Madame Guillaumette Lanière from Master Geoffrey Vintner,

Esteemed and trusted friend,

I write to you having heard the news that the queen will soon leave for France and therefore I assume you will not be returning to England as you hitherto intended.

Perhaps this is fortunate as I would have been unable to act as your escort owing to matters here at home which keep me in London; matters on which I admit I would have greatly appreciated your womanly counsel, as they concern my daughter Ann, who has presented me with a conundrum regarding a relationship with one of my legal apprentices which I neither condone nor approve. However I shall endeavour to tackle it without your help, in what I fear will be a somewhat inadequate fatherly fashion.

Owing to the queen's maternal concern for her young son, I think it unlikely that she will remain in France permanently and so, although I would readily understand if you decided to remain with your delightful family in Paris, I may hope that in due course you will be returning with her to England.

*Whatever your plans I entreat you to stay in touch as I
remain your good and sincere friend,*
   Geoffrey

*Written at the House of the Vines, Tun Lane, London on
the 7th day of May 1422.*

—ξξ—

Pleasant though I found the personal elements in this letter, the
part that concerned Catherine caused my heart to flutter painfully in my chest. That the queen was coming to France was no
surprise since King Henry would be unable to return to England,
being heavily engaged laying siege to the city and castle of Meaux,
less than forty miles east of Paris, but the manner of learning
the news shook me. Why had Catherine not sent me word herself
that she was coming? It was true that we had not parted on
good terms, but I could not believe that our differences meant
she did not want to see me back in her service; not after all we
had been through together and all we meant to each other.

The courier who had brought Geoffrey's letter had kindly said
that he would return later in the day to fetch my reply, so I sat
down immediately to compose one. I could not bring myself to
admit any estrangement from Catherine, so I thanked Geoffrey
for his letter and agreed that the imminent arrival of the queen
meant that I would not be returning to England for the time being.
I added that I hoped there was no serious problem concerning
his daughter Anne, but that I was sure his fatherly wisdom would
handle things more than adequately. Then I told myself firmly that
I must wait and see whether Catherine made any contact.

The following week Paris buzzed with the news that the city of Meaux had finally opened its gates to the English besiegers. For five months the dauphin's garrison had held out against all that King Henry's guns could hurl at them and market gossip had spread terrible accounts of disease and casualties on both sides but, once again, King Henry's military strategy and patience had succeeded, greatly assisted by the dauphin's failure to send adequate relief to the beleaguered defenders. Monastery infirmaries all over the Île de France began to receive streams of sick soldiers and citizens, most of them suffering from a devastating flux which shrank the flesh from their bones. Even King Henry himself was reported to be afflicted by it and, after receiving the constable's surrender, had retired to the royal castle of Vincennes to recuperate.

As the days went by, I became more and more distressed that I received no word from Catherine, although we learned that she had arrived in France and was travelling straight from Calais to Chateau Vincennes to meet the king. As she did not come through Paris, there was no opportunity for me to present myself or to deliver a letter. I had to content myself with what news I could glean on my regular trips to market. Then, in early June, I was filled with nervous excitement when I learned that King Henry and Queen Catherine were expected to make a ceremonial entry into Paris and set up court at the Louvre.

I stood amongst a crowd of strangers struggling to get a view of the royal couple as their procession passed through the city streets. Alys and I chose to watch from near the Châtelet, keeping our eyes averted from the gibbets where the latest condemned prisoners hung, and by skilfully employing our elbows managed to force our way to a position directly behind the line of marshals who kept the thoroughfare clear. I craned my neck over their crossed pikes, just in time to catch sight of the richly embroidered banners borne by the phalanx of knights in full panoply that preceded the royal couple. And there, suddenly, waving and smiling with regal finesse, was my Catherine, straight-backed and beautiful on a white horse, wearing a jewelled crown and a voluminous mantle of deep-blue velvet, scattered with gold fleurs-de-lys and trimmed with white ermine, which almost swept the ground behind her horse's rump. Beside her rode King Henry, also crowned in gold and wearing the familiar scarlet and blue royal doublet quartered with English lions and French lilies. He was waving and occasionally flashing his crowd-pleasing smile, but I was shocked at the change in his physique. When he had left England, he had been broad-shouldered and muscular, as a knight of his skill and reputation should be. Now his fine apparel seemed to hang off his frame like the rags of a scarecrow and his face was gaunt, the scarred cheek more prominent than ever. He still appeared to ride his horse with panache, but he did not look like a man who would have the strength to couch a lance.

When I got home I immediately put pen to paper, but I did not write to Catherine. Instead I wrote to Agnes de Blagny and told her that I had watched the king and queen ride into Paris and asked if she would broach the subject of my recall to Catherine. Then I picked little Louise out of her crib, tied her in my shawl and called out to Alys, who was in the workshop, that I was taking her for a breath of fresh air. It was only a short walk to the great gatehouse of the Louvre where I handed the letter into the guardroom and hoped that it would be swiftly delivered to the queen's apartments.

The next morning I was delighted to receive a visit from Agnes herself. We embraced warmly and were soon sipping a cup of cool buttermilk under a shady apple tree in Alys's small garden. As usual Agnes was looking trim and neat in a gown of dark-blue linen, relieved only by a handsome gold cross, her head covered in a wired white veil. I reflected that although it was more than seven years since she and Catherine had abandoned their life of books and prayer at Poissy Abbey, Agnes had never left the convent entirely behind.

'The queen is well,' she said in response to my immediate enquiry, 'but gravely worried about the king. He is ravaged by siege fever and cannot seem to shake it off.'

'Even from among the crowds I noticed the change in him. What do his doctors say?'

'That he will mend with rest and a plain diet and they prescribe some foul potion for him.' Agnes smiled. 'He does not take it willingly, or as often as he should probably.'

'And I do not suppose he rests at all,' I remarked dryly. 'I do not think he ever could. What does Catherine do about it?'

Agnes shrugged. 'What can she do, except pester him to rest and try to make him take his medicine? Apparently he does not sleep well and she has suggested that he should call Owen Tudor back from his troop to play for him. Do you remember Owen, the archer musician who used to play for them before they left for England?'

'Of course I remember him. His music was sublime. And will the king summon him?'

'He has promised to make a request to the captain of his troop, Sir Walter Hungerford, who is due in Paris soon, I believe.'

At this point I decided to take the plunge and ask her if she had spoken with the queen on the subject of my return.

'Yes I did,' Agnes said hesitantly. 'The queen says she does not wish to come between you and your family, so she will not ask you.'

I peered at Agnes under beetled brows. 'You are sure it is my family she is concerned about and not the opinion of the Duchess of Hainault?'

Agnes lowered her voice, as if fearful of being overheard. 'The duchess remains in England, fearful of being abducted by the Duke of Burgundy if she crossed the Sleeve. At least now the rest of us no longer have to suffer the scheming of the ambitious Eleanor. However, I know that her grace of Hainault made it clear to Catherine more than once that she did not approve of you having a court position. She managed to persuade her that, in his absence, her court should represent the king's power and her own royal status.'

I sighed. 'Appearances matter to Catherine. She is trying to act like a queen and her grace of Hainault has become her adviser.'

Despite my best efforts to conceal them, tears must have glistened on my eyelashes. Agnes laid a consoling hand on my arm. 'I certainly miss you and I truly believe she misses you too. But, Mette, has it not crossed your mind that you deserve a pension? Why do you not come to the Louvre and put it to her?'

'You mean approach her as a petitioner? Uninvited? Oh no, I could not do that. It would seem like begging and there is never any point in begging for friendship, even from a queen. If she needs me, she will call and I will come, whether the Duchess of Hainault likes it or not.'

Agnes did not stay long after that and when she left I found myself envying her return to the bustle and activity of the court. Greatly though I loved my family, I had to admit that living and working in a royal household had satisfied a craving for being at the centre of things, existing on a rather grander scale than that of bourgeois Paris.

Agnes came again to visit towards the end of July, but brought no summons to the queen's side. She did not immediately reveal the purpose of her visit, but talked of events at court she knew I would appreciate.

The good news was that the Welsh archer Owen Tudor had arrived in the train of Sir Walter Hungerford and was appointed to play his harp whenever King Henry summoned him.

'He comes every evening when the king retires and, let me tell you, he has caused quite a stir among the Joannas. I had forgotten how handsome he is. He draws female glances like a lodestone.'

'Yours included?' I enquired, tongue in cheek. I had never known pious Agnes to cast a glance at any man.

She gave me a reproachful look. 'No, but his playing is of great comfort to King Henry. No other harpist has been able to relieve the king's stress the way Owen's music does,' Agnes told me. 'Catherine is delighted with the improvement in his grace's health, but she is not so pleased when he talks of returning to the fray. Apparently taking advantage of King Henry's illness, the dauphin's forces have laid siege to the town of Cône, which is on the upper Loire, right on Burgundy's doorstep. The garrison there is small and badly supplied and the captain sent word that it could not hold out beyond the middle of August. Catherine urged his grace to let Duke Philippe handle it, but the king told her that the duke is too far away in Flanders and that by leading a force to Cône himself he will show the Pretender that reports of his illness are exaggerated. At the same time he has ordered Catherine to accompany her parents to

196

Senlis, where it will be cooler and better for her father's malady. King Charles has never fared well in the heat, as you know.'

'I do not suppose Catherine is happy about that,' I observed dryly.

'You are right. I accompanied her when she visited Queen Isabeau recently at the Hôtel de St Pol and her mother did not stop complaining that she was poorly attended and not afforded the respect due to the Queen of France. It is true she was rather dishevelled compared with the old days, but she wanted to talk of nothing else. Catherine wanted to visit her father, but when she made the request Queen Isabeau only said she had not seen King Charles for weeks. Catherine became very angry and was told her father was unwell and not receiving visitors and that was the end of it. Catherine has little time for her mother these days.'

'I am surprised she has agreed to go to Senlis with her.'

Agnes shrugged. 'She does not want to defy King Henry in his present state of health. She has begged him not to go to Cône and he has refused. There is really nothing more she can do.'

As usual Paris sizzled in the high summer and I fully understood why the royals had retreated from its heat and stench. In La Ruelle du Louvre, the narrow street of shops where Alys and Jacques lived, the air seemed barely breathable. At first we all worried about the health of baby Louise, but as long as she could lie in the shady garden in the minimum of clothes, like her older sister Catrine, she seemed unaffected by the temperature. As for myself, I sweated and fretted and tried to hide it from Alys.

Then, in late August, a courier in royal livery appeared unexpectedly at the workshop door asking for me. The letter he carried bore Catherine's royal seal but was not addressed in her own writing. When I opened it, concealed inside the official-looking paper was a brief note scratched roughly in her hand.

'Mette, I need you. In the name of Our Blessed Lady, come! Catherine.'

When I had absorbed the content of the note, the courier said, 'I was ordered to bring an extra horse, Madame. I think you are expected to ride back with me.'

I stood and stared at the man for several seconds. 'Wait here,' I said and turned to walk back through the house without speaking to Jacques or Alys who were stitching busily inside. In the garden I scanned the brief note over and over, trying to interpret the meaning behind its terse message. In one way it read like a desperate cry for help; one that surely could not be ignored. Alternatively it could be seen as a peremptory summons from a disciple of the Duchess of Hainault; one which was expected to be obeyed without question. Anyone who had a heart would respond instantly to the first; anyone with any pride would resent the second. I had to decide whether to listen to my heart or my pride.

17

W hen it came to Catherine, I had always let my heart rule
my head.

We rode as fast as I could manage on a somewhat capricious
mare, but it was dusk before we clattered under the portcullis
of the royal castle at Senlis, an ancient and sturdy fortress
with many battlemented towers and, within its curtain wall,
a palace of more recent construction with elegant mullioned
windows and steep slate roofs. From one of its turrets flew
the French and English royal standards, and at the foot of
the stair leading to the main entrance a groom took the reins
of my horse and helped me to dismount. Stamping the stiff-
ness from my legs, I asked him to have my saddlebags delivered
to Queen Catherine's apartments and wearily climbed the
steps.

When she came to collect me at the guardroom, Agnes's
expression was a mixture of relief and bafflement. 'I am delighted
you are here,' she said, 'but what made you come?'

When I told her about Catherine's ambiguous note, she
frowned fiercely. 'I did not know she had sent it. She is very
restless at present and her mood changes every minute.'

'Has she heard from the king since he left?' I asked as we
climbed an interior stairway.

'Once or twice – but nothing for several days. She is obviously very anxious and hardly eats a thing. Then yesterday a letter came from Sir Walter Hungerford. It must be that which caused her to send for you. She did not show it to me, but she has been up and down from her prie dieu ever since.'

We passed down a panelled passageway unchallenged by two sets of guards, then Agnes nodded at the liveried chamberlains who opened the doors to the queen's apartment. On entering I began to sink into a deep curtsey, but was forestalled by Catherine, who flew to embrace me.

'Oh, Mette, I am so glad you have come!' The small coterie of ladies-in-waiting had risen in surprise at the queen's impulsive greeting. Glancing at them, Catherine said, 'Please leave us, all of you. I want to talk to Madame Lanière alone.' When Agnes showed signs of hesitation she added, 'You too please, Agnes. I will call you in a short while.'

I was obviously expected, for she led me to a seat at a table where food and wine had been placed in readiness. 'You must have refreshment after your ride, Mette – please eat, drink.'

She took the chair opposite, poured wine into a cup, then waited in silence for the ladies to depart, her eyes disconcert-ingly fixed on my face. Gratefully I drank some wine, took a small piece of pie and bit into it. She was right; having ridden all day on a bread and cheese breakfast, I was thirsty and hungry. Not until the door closed did she speak, trip-ping over her tongue in a rush of words, her eyes fixed on my face.

'Oh, Mette, I have realised that I cannot trust anyone but you! I am so sorry not to have replied to your letter. I know I have ignored you shamefully and I beg you to forgive me.'

Suddenly registering her bony wrists and sharp cheekbones, I felt a jolt of alarm. I had not seen her look so haggard since the dreadful days before her marriage when Jean, Duke of Burgundy, had threatened to ruin her life.

'Mademoiselle, there is nothing to forgive,' I hastened to assure her, abandoning the pie. 'I have always said I would give my life for you or live it without you if that would serve you better. What is it that troubles you so much it makes you ill? For I can see that you are.'

She shook her head. 'No, not ill but worried sick, frightened and – pregnant. Yes, pregnant, Mette, but not like the last time. This child drains all the strength from me and makes me vomit every morsel I eat. I need your advice about that, but it is not why I called you here. It concerns my lord the king.' She clasped her hands together as if in desperate prayer, the knuckles showing white. 'He is ill, Mette, so ill. Oh I know he has put it out that he has recovered and is fit enough to lead his army, but in truth he is not. When I first saw him in June I thought he was likely to die; especially when I discovered that the reliquary containing the Sacred Thorn I gave him at our wedding had been lost in a skirmish at Meaux and with it his protection against disease and sorcery. I feared the worst then, but his health did improve when he rested at Vincennes for a few weeks.' She smiled; a bleak, tired smile which seemed to pierce my heart. 'Improved enough to get me with child at least.'

'God be praised, Mademoiselle. That is a blessing, surely?'

The wan smile came again. 'It should be, of course, and I pray constantly for the grace to call it that but, at present, I see it only as a blight because it prevents me from going to Henry. Look.' She reached into her sleeve and pulled a letter from a concealed pocket. 'I received this yesterday.'

I took the letter from her and unfolded it. It was from Sir Walter Hungerford, King Henry's most respected captain and advisor.

To her grace the Lady Catherine of France, Queen of England,

Honoured and gracious Lady,

It is with deep concern and a troubled mind that I write to tell you that the king has been carried grievously ill to the castle of Vincennes and has summoned all available counsellors and members of his household to his side.

After leaving you at Senlis, he rode courageously and in growing discomfort at the head of his army for three days until we reached Corbeil, when he was no longer able to remain in the saddle. Seeing his pain and prostration, I and his closest friends and companions prevailed upon him to turn back and brought him to Chateau Vincennes by barge and litter.

The king has not given instructions to summon you because I think he wishes to spare you anguish, but his physicians are extremely concerned about his condition and I consider it proper that your grace should be informed. Rest assured that priests are with the doctors at the king's side and everything possible is being done to bring him comfort both in body and in spirit.

I am, Madame, your most true and humble servant,
Walter Hungerford (Knight of the Garter)

Written this day, Monday the 27th of August 1422 at Chateau Vincennes.

I lowered the letter, my thoughts and emotions in turmoil. King Henry was dying. When it took hold, siege fever could be a fatal malady, purging the body constantly with a bloody flux which robbed its host of all strength and dignity. The proud and magnificent victor of Agincourt and Heir of France was on his deathbed and his suffering must be exacerbated by the knowledge that his son, the heir to all his great achievements, was not even nine months old.

Tears spilled from Catherine's bloodshot eyes. 'Henry knows I am pregnant, that is why he does not summon me and why he made me come here to Senlis. No one else knows and I feel so unwell that I fear I may miscarry anyway. What should I do, Mette? I yearn with all my being to go to him, but is not my first duty to the child?'

I let the letter drop from my shaking fingers. Her dilemma was an agonising one. 'Oh, Mademoiselle, what can I say? It is a terrible decision to make.'

'If I do not go, the world will ask why I was not there and if I go and lose the child, I will not bring Henry comfort but instead a terrible loss. I am already filled with remorse that I did not go to Sheen in time for young Henry's birth. My lord has not reproached me, but because I defied the prophecy I feel I am responsible for his recent misfortunes.'

Her eyes sought mine in desperation. 'Perhaps if I travelled in a litter I might bring him the solace he needs without harming the child . . .' Her voice broke on the words.

'Have you confided in no one else, Mademoiselle? Do any of your ladies know of your condition?'

I asked the question in the faint hope that I might share

the responsibility of commenting on such a critical situation.

'No, Mette. They think I am unwell in my stomach. I only tell you because I know I can trust you and I have often called to mind your advice from my first pregnancy. What do you think? Will the child come to harm if I make the journey to Vincennes in a litter?'

I hesitated, recalling that Prince Henry had been a healthy baby despite his mother's tumble from a horse whilst carrying him.

'If your heart is set on going, Mademoiselle, perhaps you are prepared to risk a mishap?'

There was a long silence as Catherine struggled to make a decision that she alone could make.

At dawn the following day, Queen Isabeau's horse litter was drawn up outside the entrance to the royal apartments and surrounded by royal guards mounted and waiting as an escort. As we descended the steps, I glanced anxiously at Catherine. In the gathering light she looked deathly pale but determined, head held high, the line of her jaw a sharp silhouette.

Neither of us had enjoyed much sleep and nor had Agnes, who rode her mount close by. She had been invited to join us the night before and once she was fully informed of both the urgency of the journey and the risk involved, we three had talked into the small hours as we righted wrongs and made plans.

Once Catherine was securely seated in the well-cushioned litter, I took the seat opposite and waved at a worried-looking Agnes to signal the procession to move off. With a rest-stop planned at the abbey of St Denis, at our slow and steady pace we were unlikely to reach Chateau Vincennes much before dusk, but our fervent hope was that Henry would survive the day. We had covered only a few miles however when I noticed Catherine's face suddenly go as pale as bleached linen and she clutched at her stomach.

'Holy Marie, Mette, I should not have come!' she cried.

Abandoning all niceties, I lifted her skirts to be confronted with a dreadful sight. Her chemise and kirtle were already soaked in blood.

'Turn around!' I thrust my head out of the litter door. 'Turn around now! We must go back.'

All the way back to Senlis, I held Catherine as she lay crying with pain and misery, and I cursed the evil demons that had brought her to this state. It seemed that not only was King Henry on the brink of death, but his queen had jeopardised her own life trying to reach his bedside. My vision of death stalking them both did not fall far short of the mark. As the queen miscarried their child and almost died from loss of blood, the soul of Henry the Fifth of England was slipping away from his disease-ravaged body in the King's Chamber at the castle of Vincennes. The last day of August 1422 proved a fatal one for King Henry, his potential offspring and very nearly for his queen.

It was Windsor Herald who brought the dreadful news of the king's death and Catherine struggled from her bed, white and shaking, to receive it. She was far too weak and distressed to do more than murmur an almost incoherent acknowledgement and after the herald left she collapsed back into bed. We had managed to pull her through the miscarriage, but the added grief of Henry's death rendered her completely prostrate in body and mind. However, the following day a more familiar courier arrived from Vincennes bearing another letter from Sir Walter Hungerford and in his saddlebag, his harp.

When I opened the door of Catherine's chamber in answer to his hesitant knock, I did not immediately recognise him. His handsome face was drawn and grey, a mirror of Catherine's, and he was clad all in black, adding to the sombre nature of his appearance. Although it was not a year since I had last seen him, he looked several years older, still broad-shouldered and slim-hipped but his curly chestnut hair had been given a military clip and his dark-brown eyes were deep-shadowed, witnesses to recent sorrow. I stepped from the room.

'Master Tudor! I am sorry I did not at first know you. The queen is refusing all visitors.'

He bowed his head apologetically. 'I am sure she is, Madame. I have a royal warrant, so the guards let me pass this far. Sir Walter sent me with a letter for her grace. He thought my music might bring her some solace but chiefly he thought she would need someone familiar and trustworthy to carry information between Senlis and Vincennes. There will be many arrangements to put in train for the king's obsequies.'

'That was very kind and considerate of Sir Walter,' I replied. 'Of course the queen's first thought was to go to Vincennes herself, but in truth she has not been well and grief has prostrated her.'

The young squire seemed relieved to hear this. 'To be honest, Madame, at present Chateau Vincennes is not a place for a queen in mourning. When a king dies there is much to be done. The castle is overrun with captains and counsellors, clerks and couriers running in all directions.'

'Yet you seem to have managed to acquire black clothes,

Master Tudor,' I said, appraising his neat and new-looking attire which, together with his pallor, made him look like a soldier in scholar's clothing. 'That cannot have been easy at a time of such frenzy.'

He shrugged. 'The heralds and pursuivants always have a supply of black clothes for delivering news of battle casualties and I scrounged some from their store. I could not sully the queen's quarters with the dirt of a troop camp. Will you take the letter to her now?' He pulled a folded and sealed missive from the purse on his belt.

I took it from him. There was a tray of wine and wafers on a side table in the ante-room where we stood and I gestured towards it. 'Wait here and take refreshment if you please. Her grace might wish to speak to you.'

Catherine's chamber was shuttered and shadowy, lit only by a few candles scattered about. I brought one to the bed and bent over her with the letter. She was wide awake, her eyes huge and red-rimmed. When I had helped her to sit up, I broke the seal of the letter at her bidding and handed it to her.

'It was carried by Owen Tudor, Mademoiselle. He has brought his harp in case music might bring you solace. I believe he played for the king at Vincennes.'

There was a crackle of paper as Catherine unfolded the letter. 'I do not wish to see anyone, Mette. I told you.'

'Perhaps if the door was open he could play in the ante-room. Shall I at least ask him to fetch his harp?'

I put the candle down beside her so that she could see but she did not respond to my suggestion, seemingly absorbed in the contents of the letter. I took silence to mean consent and left her to read it.

When I returned, the letter lay on the coverlet beside her

and she was staring into space but she turned to look at me as I approached. 'Henry knew he was dying,' she said dully. 'He gave detailed instructions for what was to be arranged for the regency after his death and for the education and care of his son. But, Mette, it seems he said almost nothing about me.'

She shivered and I took up a shawl to cover her shoulders but she went on directly 'The king's body is to be embalmed and an effigy of him is being made that will lie on his coffin. Sir Walter tells me the funeral procession from Vinciennes will move slowly through France to Calais and I am invited to join it at St Denis in two weeks' time. I am to follow at what he calls "a suitable distance".' Her voice broke at the words 'a suitable distance' and no wonder!

She dissolved into deep, heart-rending sobs and I went to cover her shoulders with the shawl and take her in my arms. For a long time she wept for a marriage and a man whose true nature she was only now beginning to understand. From outside the chamber door in a haunting elegy came the ripple of harp music.

The grand funeral cortège wound through the Île de France and Normandy to Calais; King Henry's final farewell to the territories he had conquered. As instructed, Catherine joined the cortège at the abbey of St Denis and, in the basilica where so many of her relatives and ancestors were buried, she had her first opportunity to pray and weep over the coffin of her dead husband. How desperately she must have longed to seek solace from the warm and living presence of the little son she had been obliged to leave in England and how much the separation must have added to her grief.

Agnes and I attended her vigil, watching as she knelt beside the catafalque, her black widow's weeds drooping shapelessly off her bony frame like mourning flags on a windless day. At only twenty years old she was a dowager queen stranded between kingdoms, without husband, father or brother to champion her cause. It was a lonely and precarious position.

The effigy of King Henry that was laid on top of his massive lead-lined and gilded coffin was fashioned from boiled and tooled leather, crowned with gold and adorned with the mantle of sovereignty, but in my eyes it was a grotesque puppet which made a mockery of the magnificent and forceful man that had been Henry of Monmouth. The features of the face were painted in garish colours, the hair was coarse and kinky like the fibres of a frayed rope and the expression was that of a peevish merchant, not a proud and glorious king who had been admired and fêted throughout Europe; by whom I myself had been both frightened and, fascinated. And, of course, there was no sign of the iconic scar which had disfigured his face and shaped his character. However Catherine appeared not to notice these failings and kept touching the effigy as if it were the man himself and this her last contact with the husband she had waited five years to marry and lived with for only a few short months.

For days on end, as the cortège wound its way through the war-torn countryside, it rained, almost as if the heavens were weeping for the conqueror of the land he was passing through. But, much to everyone's relief, a mile or so before we reached Pontoise the rain stopped and the sun came out. Steam began to rise from the long column of horses and riders and a courier galloped up to the Duke of Burgundy who rode at its head. Without drawing rein Duke Philippe perused the letter handed to him, but it was not until the cortège had entered the town and the catafalque was being lifted off its car that the duke approached Catherine as she emerged, dazed and blinking, from her litter.

'I regret to tell you that I have received terrible news from Ghent,' he said, taking her arm supportively. 'My beloved duchess, your sister Michele, is dead. There was an outbreak of sweating sickness and she succumbed quite suddenly and unexpectedly. I am shocked and saddened almost beyond words. I cannot believe that God has taken such a good and beautiful person.'

Catherine stared at him dumbstruck, the small triangle of her face almost as pale as the widow's barbe which she now wore to hide her chin and throat. For several seconds she seemed to gasp for breath then she uttered a keening cry and crossed herself. 'Ah sweet Jesu, death truly stalks us. You are right, my lord, Michele was a good person but it seems the good are beloved of the angels whilst you and I stumble on under an earthly pall of misery.'

Together, in respectful silence, they watched the royal bier with its bizarre effigy carried slowly into the church of St Eustace under a richly embroidered canopy borne by the leading citizens of Pontoise. The duke bowed his head in salute. 'I admired Henry enormously,' he said. 'He was a man of great faith, an implacable enemy and a staunch ally. In some ways I think he and Michele were quite similar; conscientious, loyal and God-fearing. I believe they will both be safely gathered into Heaven's grace.' He bent to give Catherine a brotherly kiss on the cheek. 'I must bid you farewell, sister,' he said. 'I need to make a start for Flanders while the light lasts. I know you think your future looks bleak at present but, for Henry's sake, I will always be your friend, should you need me. May God give you strength.'

As he strode off to remount his horse, I rushed forward to support Catherine, who looked as if she might sink to the ground. 'Oh, Mette, he is right,' she murmured faintly. 'If I am to give due honour to my lord and support to my son, I need God's strength now as I have never needed it before.'

18

When the cortège reached Rouen, King Henry lay in state for several weeks, giving time for the new barons of Normandy to pay homage to the monarch who had rewarded them for their part in his campaigns by granting them title to the estates of dead or dispossessed French nobles.

Owen Tudor had ridden in the escort of five hundred men at arms who had followed the king's coffin but, after leaving Senlis, Catherine had not asked him to play for her again. However, during her vigil beside the catafalque in Rouen, she sent for him to come in the evenings, after the long queue of citizens had gone. Apart from quietly thanking him each time, nothing passed between them except, after several days, a small purse of coin which she placed beside his harp as she left.

Owen sought me out to ask if this 'payment' meant she no longer wished him to come. 'I fear she does not like my music after all,' he said, his deep-brown eyes troubled.

I hastened to reassure him. 'On the contrary, Master Tudor, I think she appreciates it greatly. She merely feels that you deserve some recompense for the time you have already spent playing. Please do not stop coming.'

He slung his harp over his shoulder, safely packed away in

its leather bag. 'When I played for the king it was often to lull him to sleep and judging by the weariness I see in the queen's eyes she, too, needs help in that way.' I noticed the blood rush to Owen's cheeks as he said this and guessed that his awe of King Henry had also inspired a young man's fascination with his queen, to the extent that the very planes and shadows of her face were imprinted on his mind. His lilting Welsh voice trailed away as he added hesitantly, 'Perhaps I could play outside her chamber door again . . .?'

'It is an idea, certainly.' His shy concern for Catherine induced in me a similar benevolence towards him and I had another sudden thought. 'Have you eaten, Master Tudor? You are probably missing your evening meal by coming here. Let me arrange some refreshment for you.'

He shifted from one foot to another, fiddling with the strap of the bag. 'I usually find some scraps left when I return to troop headquarters. We are billeted in a barn on abbey land outside the walls.'

I waved my hands in dismay. 'Oh no, Master Tudor, that will not do. I should have asked sooner. Come with me. I think we can do rather better than scraps.'

While Catherine nibbled listlessly at a meagre meal with her ladies in the great hall of the bishop's palace, I sat with Owen Tudor in a small chamber off the kitchen as he consumed a large bowl of pottage enriched with venison and several slices cut from a manchet loaf. 'Bishops dine much better than bowmen,' he grinned, dipping the delectable white bread in the meaty soup. 'I have not touched white bread nor eaten venison since leaving Wales.'

'And where did you dine so royally in Wales?' I enquired. Deer-meat was the prerogative of the hunting classes, which meant that it was generally restricted to the tables of monarchs, bishops and barons.

'In the wild lands of the Welsh mountains, deer are not guarded as closely as they are in England and France. My godfather hunted them even when he was a hunted outlaw himself.'

My eyes widened. 'And who is your godfather?' I asked.

His expression darkened and he made the sign of the cross. 'Not is – was – for he is dead, God rest his soul. The great Welsh freedom fighter Owen Glendower was my mother's uncle.'

It was a name that had been infamous across Europe twenty years ago. Owen Glendower had led a Welsh rebel force over the English border to try and win back the principality from the English crown. Around the fire in their honeymoon camp at the siege of Melun, King Henry had told Catherine stories of this battle in which, as a young prince, he had received the arrow wound which had scarred his cheek and nearly killed him; an incident that had also given him a deep respect for the power and accuracy of Welsh archers.

'Glendower tried to unite the Welsh people, like his ancestor Llewellyn the Great had done two hundred years before. He failed, but he was a great man for all that. And because the people loved him, they did not betray him to the English. Officially he was an outlaw, but he lived on his manors in the wild lands of the Welsh border for years after the war and he took me into his household and taught me everything – reading, writing, swordplay, archery, manners and, best of all, music and poetry. Everything I am, I owe to him.'

'And was it his death that caused you to join King Henry's French expedition?'

Owen shook his head. 'No. Glendower sent me away. I was fifteen when he arranged for me to join Sir Walter Hungerford's troop. He said he wanted me to learn battle-craft under a great leader, but he was already ill and I believe he did not want me to watch him die. So instead I fought at Agincourt and later watched King Henry die. Ironic, is it not?' I waited as he took another spoonful of the venison pottage and presently continued. 'And here is another irony. King Henry and I are both descended from Llewellyn the Great; he through his mother and I through my father.'

My reaction to this statement was laced with a touch of sarcasm. 'No! Are you telling me that you are the rightful Prince of Wales, Master Tudor?'

Owen gave me an impish look. 'My claim is as good as his was anyway, for we are both descended from daughters of Llewellyn, although admittedly his six-times-great grand-mother, Gladwys ap Llewellyn, was my five-times-great grandmother Anghared's elder sister – if you are still with me.'

Now I had to laugh. 'Well, we are all descended from Adam and Eve, Master Tudor, are we not?'

To his credit he shared my mirth, but only briefly. 'That is what I thought and more or less what I said when my godfather drew my bloodline, but he roared at me in anger, "The blood of Welsh princes flows in your veins, Owen – never, never forget that!"' The young archer's sculpted jaw jutted proudly and he shrugged. 'So I do not.'

I relayed the gist of this conversation to Catherine while she prepared for bed and was rewarded with a wisp of a smile. 'I wonder if Henry knew that he and his squire were related, however remotely?' In the mirror glass and the dim light of the bishop's chamber her face, dominated by her sunken cheeks

215

and framed by the unforgiving widow's barbe and wimple, reminded me agonisingly of a skull. Then, as happened so often when she thought of the dead king, tears misted her blue eyes. 'I think he might have told me if he did, for it would have amused him.'

'Master Tudor wondered whether you might be having trouble sleeping. He suggested he might play outside your chamber door again.'

'That was a kind offer. I will think on it. Will he come to the cathedral tomorrow?'

'He will come wherever and whenever you summon him, Madame.'

She folded her hands, staring down at the great ancestral betrothal ring Henry had given her. 'It is good to know that I have such unconditional support.'

At that moment there was a knock on the door. A page entered, dropping to one knee. 'Despite the late hour his grace the Duke of Bedford begs an audience, your grace,' he said.

Catherine frowned and straightened her back. 'Place another chair beside the fire, Mette,' she told me, adding to the page, 'and tell his grace I will see him.'

Like all the members of the funeral cortège, John, Duke of Bedford was dressed entirely in black, except for the Lancastrian S-link collar of mourning silver he wore around his shoulders. He bowed low, unsmiling, over Catherine's hand and kissed her cheek briefly, before obeying her silent gesture and seating himself in the cushioned chair across the hearth. Swarthier of complexion than his older brother King Henry had been, there was already a scattering of grey in his thick dark hair and responsibility had drawn deeper lines on his brow than on that of his younger brother, Humphrey of Gloucester.

'I regret that I have more sad news for you,' he said sorrowfully.

I had not thought that Catherine could become any paler, but somehow her white face blanched further and in a strangled whisper she pleaded, 'Not little Henry, please God not my son . . .'

He hastened to relieve her distress. 'No, no, Madame. The young king is well as far as I know. It is your father, King Charles. News has just come from Paris that he died yesterday. The herald said that he fell asleep at night and never woke in the morning. Such a peaceful death is granted to very few.'

Catherine's hand flicked over her face and breast in the sign of the cross. 'God rest his soul,' she said faintly, adding in a clearer voice and almost without emotion. 'In truth he has been dying for years. Every time he slipped into madness he emerged a little less alive than he had been before. His was a tragic life.'

'And it brought tragedy to his country,' observed Bedford, nodding. 'Had he been a strong ruler like his father, he would not have lost control of his nobles. Henry would never have invaded if he had been confronted by a united France.'

'Do you really believe that, my lord?' Catherine looked surprised. 'Well, you may be right. My father was a peace-lover. He tried to placate and only succeeded in antagonising. And my mother was no help to him. Sometimes I think his madness was a retreat – a cloak to hide his sense of failure.'

'Yet I have heard him called Charles the Well-Beloved,' responded Bedford. 'There will be those who greatly mourn his passing.'

'Myself among them. How sad that only four of his children still live and three of them will not be able to attend his funeral. Jeanne cannot leave Brittany, I must bury my husband and Charles remains an enemy. Perhaps my sister, Abbess Marie, may emerge from Poissy to attend his obsequies. I hope he will be buried with due honour.'

'I shall see to that,' Bedford announced. 'Regrettably I must leave my brother's cortège now. It is imperative that I go immediately to Paris to secure the throne for your son. Young Henry must be declared King of France as well as England.'

'Poor babe,' murmured Catherine, 'so young and with such a burden to bear.'

'He will not be alone. His father made strict provision in his will for his care and guidance and he will have many able men to help him rule.'

She leaned forward earnestly. 'But you are the one Henry trusted most. So do not stay too long in France, my lord. My son will need you particularly.'

Bedford looked doubtful. 'I regret that I may not be in England for some time. Philippe of Burgundy has refused to take the French regency, saying he is too much affected by his wife's death. I must lead the council in Paris therefore.'

'But who will take charge in England?' asked Catherine anxiously.

'Henry's will names our brother Humphrey as protector of the realm, unless the regency council rules otherwise.'

'Who will be on the council?'

'Warwick, Exeter, Beaufort, Hungerford – there are many who are worthy.'

'And me? Is there a place for the king's mother on such a council?'

Bedford looked astonished at this suggestion, almost as if she had blasphemed. 'I do not know. Henry made no mention of it. The English have long memories and Isabella, the last French queen regent, was far from popular.' He was almost squirming in his seat as he said this.

'In France we have had several strong queen regents,' Catherine pointed out. 'My mother was regent for my father on and off for years.'

Bedford's unease appeared to increase and he coughed apologetically. 'Forgive me, Madame, but not with any great success and, as you may be aware, there is no great love for French ways in England.'

Catherine sighed. 'Or for the French themselves, I think. Ah well, we shall see. First we must bury two dead kings. How strange it is that they should die so close together.'

'I believe it is a tragedy for both our countries that my brother did not live to inherit your father's throne. We cannot know how it will play out.' Bedford stood up. 'Forgive me, Madame, but I must take my leave. I wish to ride as far as Mantes before dark.'

Catherine also stood and gave him her hand. 'Farewell then, my lord. I shall pray that we see you soon in England for I feel we shall have need of your wisdom and statesmanship.'

The following evening, Owen Tudor came to play in the cathedral as usual and when she left the coffin's side Catherine spoke briefly to him. I was not close enough to hear what was said but I noticed that Owen slipped off his stool to his knees at her approach and remained humbly kneeling until she left. Passing quite nearby as I followed Catherine out of the cathedral, I saw a slight smile twitch at his lips and heard him begin to hum a little tune under his breath as he pulled the leather carrying-bag over his harp.

Later she asked me to arrange a place for the harper in the ante-room outside the bishop's bedchamber, which the prelate had vacated in her favour. From then on Owen played Catherine to sleep every night. For a while his presence caused a flutter among the impressionable young ladies of her household, but Owen was scrupulous in his behaviour towards them as they passed to and from the bedchamber. Not by so much as a glance or a smile did he display any interest, even in the wondrously pretty Lady Joan Beaufort, although to be fair her twinkling glances tended to be reserved for her royal suitor, King James of Scotland, who was among the cortège followers.

Being much the same age as Catherine, Owen tended to regard me as a mother figure, a safe companion whose friendship would not involve him in awkward situations. So when his harp music had lulled Catherine to sleep we would often drink a cup of wine together while the brazier in the anteroom died down. He told me stories of the home and family he had left ten years before, his war-scattered brothers and sisters and his dead parents. Seven years spent campaigning in France had not blunted his love of his homeland and his descriptions of the Welsh landscape were so vivid and evocative that I felt as if I had personally visited the Isle of Anglesey where he had spent his early years.

'When you cross to it by boat, it is like arriving in a magic world. All around are rolling hills and the sea constantly beats at the shore with an eternal music. They call it the Lovers' Isle because it is so green and lush.'

'Is that the only reason, Master Tudor, or could it have something to do with the warmth of its people?' I asked, smiling.

He gazed at me solemnly. 'If poetry and music and beauty combine to feed love then yes, Madame, we are a people rich in love, but regrettably these days not rich in freedom.'

'Because of your godfather's rebellion?'

He frowned, deep creases marring his handsome features. 'No. Glendower failed to win Wales back for us, but we have suffered under an English yoke ever since the first King Edward stamped his iron-shod foot on us. We live in the shadow of Beaumaris Castle and the injustice of English rule.'

'And yet you fought under the English banner at Agincourt.'

He shrugged. 'King Henry was born in Monmouth. Although he was the King of England, he had an admiration for the Welsh people. He will be mourned on both sides of the border.'

The crossing to Dover at the end of October was mercifully uneventful, but the onward progress of the cortège was slow, stopping two days in Canterbury for a solemn requiem mass and plodding on over four more days to another lengthy and solemn requiem mass at St Paul's in London. As the end of the journey drew nearer, Catherine fretted at the pace of travel but every town and village we passed through wanted to pay homage to the hero of Agincourt, so that the halts were many and frequent, culminating in a sombre welcome at Blackheath from the mayor, sheriffs, aldermen and guildsmen of London, who escorted King Henry's body into the City of London. Catherine's cold and miserable overnight stay in the Tower was in stark contrast to her visit there less than two years earlier, when she had prepared with awe and anticipation for her coronation.

'All I want to do is ride to Windsor and take my son in my arms!' she cried as she crept into bed that night with no harp music to comfort her, for Owen had been asked to play at the funeral in Westminster Abbey the following day and had ridden ahead to prepare. 'My poor little fatherless boy who must bear the weight of two kingdoms on his tiny shoulders. What a heavy burden Henry has left him and what a cheerless future he has left to me!'

To receive the body of Henry of Monmouth, the monks of Westminster had prepared a resting place of the greatest honour, between the Lady Chapel and the shrine of St Edward the Confessor. Standing beside the yawning hole in the church floor, Catherine appeared swamped by the magnificence of the ceremonial. She was surrounded by bishops and barons doing honour to their king in their most glorious copes and mantles, while she retained the deep mourning she had worn ever since hearing of his death. From my viewpoint in the choir-loft she looked like a small black mayfly lost among a crowd of multicoloured dragonflies.

Afterwards she wept in my arms. 'I gazed down on that massive coffin, so grand and ornate and embellished with gold leaf, and I could not believe that Henry was in there. I feel he must still be alive somewhere, assembling another army, raising another siege, determined to win back what he considers to be his by divine right. England grieves for a symbol, a warrior and a king; only I grieve for a man, Mette, a unique and individual spirit who was possessed of a spark of passion. Now I have no husband, no father and no brother – for although he lives, Charles is as dead to me as Henry – and I have no country. I can never return to France, England does not want me and yet I cannot leave my son. Until he grows into manhood, truly I am alone.'

As I tried to comfort her, I almost felt we were back in the old nursery at the Hôtel de St Pol in Paris, on the day

222

her two-year-old brother Charles had been forcibly removed on the Duke of Burgundy's orders, to be reared in the household of his godfather the Duke of Berry. For one night Catherine and I had been left together before she was carried off to the nuns at Poissy Abbey and we had both been in despair at the prospect of separation. That time I had been forced to bid her farewell, but I knew I could never do so now. She might be Dowager Queen of England and a Daughter of France, but today those titles and honours meant nothing. When it came to loving and being loved, I was all she had left.

PART TWO

The Secret Years
(1427–1435)

19

fter King Henry's demise and the long, mournful weeks
behind the funeral cortège, coupled with the deaths of her
sister and father, all Catherine had wanted to do was be a mother
to her baby son. She had therefore willingly allowed her household to be joined to that of the little boy who was to be raised
as King of England and France. She shared his chaplains, his
steward and his treasurer, his masters of Household, horse and
wardrobe, his clerks, his cooks, his cleaners, his pages, his laundry,
his horses, his stables and his couriers but, most importantly,
she lived close to his nursery, was able to visit him daily and
wherever he went she went too, even when, sitting on her knee
at the tender age of two, he had officially opened Parliament
from the throne in the great hall at Westminster. The queen's
own household was relatively small and consisted only of her
confessor, her secretary, her ladies-in-waiting, a pair of seam-
stresses, a clutch of tiring women, four chamberlains, four pages
and myself, still nominally the keeper of the queen's robes,
although now that she wore only sober, dark gowns with little
jewellery and her constant headdress was a widow's barbe and
wimple, I had become more the chief companion and counsellor
and less the robe mistress.

Two days after the little king's sixth birthday, Queen Catherine
called the members of her household together in her presence

chamber at Windsor Castle. There were only twenty of us; no great number for a royal lady. As she waited for us to settle, Catherine sat slim and still in her usual place, a throne-like armchair on a dais, tented in bright-blue gold-tasselled silk, patterned with fleurs-de-lys. She liked to display the French royal symbol and her nationality became even more obvious the moment she opened her mouth. Her mastery of English was good, but her accent was terrible, probably on purpose, for she was immensely proud that her royal blood had brought her son the crown of France and always encouraged him to converse with her in French. Successfully ruling half of France from Paris and still determined to fight on for the other half, the English scornfully labelled her brother Charles de Valois 'the Pretender', but he styled himself King of France. Catherine never spoke of her brother but, although she fiercely defended her son's claim, I suspected that she still wrestled with her conscience over who should really wear the French crown.

Her expression when she addressed us was as sober as her gown. 'I have brought you all together because I want to be the first to tell you of some changes at court which will affect my household,' she said, pausing to take a sip from her cup of watered wine. I think we all held our breath, wondering what was to come.

'As you know, on the king's birthday each year there is a meeting of the regency council to assess his progress and plan his future and, as a result of this year's deliberations, it has been decided that it is time my son quitted the nursery and began serious preparation for his role as our king.' I could see her struggling to keep her composure, swallowing frequently as if the words caught in her throat. 'The debilitating illness of the Duke of Exeter means that the Earl of Warwick is now to take sole responsibility for the king's care and governance. New tutors are to be appointed. In short, his household is to be considerably altered and is no longer to be linked with mine.'

Loud murmuring broke out among the assembled group and Catherine summoned a falsely cheerful smile. 'The change was inevitable and anyway is not immediate. There will be the usual round of Christmas and New Year celebrations here at Windsor, but soon after Twelfth Night I shall be leaving to take up a separate residence. Exactly where that will be has yet to be decided, but any of you who would rather stay with the king or seek positions in another household have time to make arrangements. Obviously since I am to live apart from the king, there will be some additional appointments made within my own household and some of you may be asked to step into different roles. Please be assured that no one needs to find themselves without a livelihood.'

Her pause to let her announcement sink in was met with a buzz of murmured comments from around the room. Sighing, she gazed deliberately from one to another, as if to memorise their faces. 'It is hard to take in, I know, but you have all played your part in ensuring the health and welfare of the king through his tender years and I warmly thank you for it. Now my ladies will remain here as usual and the rest of you may go back to your duties.'

As the others trooped out, murmuring together with the skilled inaudibility peculiar to courtiers and servants, I studied Catherine's face and considered the implications of the momentous news she had so calmly imparted. Behind her mask of control I knew that she must be devastated by the council's ruling. It would almost completely cut her out of her son's life, handing his rearing and education over to virtual strangers and

229

placing her, his mother, on the periphery of his existence, like an elderly aunt or a distant cousin. The lords of the council had effectively told her that she was surplus to requirements, no longer needed, almost an embarrassment in the king's life. Without warning or consultation they were taking little Henry over.

The inner circle of the dowager queen's companions had changed somewhat since the late king's death. When Catherine retreated to Windsor following the funeral obsequies, she had been hurt and astonished to learn that during her absence the Duchess of Hainault had quitted Windsor and taken up residence at the Duke of Gloucester's castle of Hadleigh on the Thames estuary. As the infant king's godmother, Jacqueline had promised to keep a close eye on Henry's nursery during Catherine's absence in France and the bereaved queen was furious that the capricious duchess had abandoned her charge to pursue Humphrey of Gloucester, the man she hoped would regain her lands in the Low Countries.

Jacqueline had not attended King Henry's funeral and it was not until after the official period of mourning ended that she had reappeared at court, triumphant as the new Duchess of Gloucester, her marriage to the Duke of Brabant having been conveniently annulled by a compliant pope. Catherine had received her politely and invited her to visit her godson, but after they left the nursery she had rounded on Jacqueline angrily, asking if she realised how seriously her marriage to Humphrey threatened the little king's French throne.

'Even on his deathbed my lamented lord urged his brothers to do nothing that might undermine England's alliance with Burgundy,' Catherine protested. 'Only two years ago you accepted King Henry's help and money from the English crown and yet you and Humphrey ignored his dying wishes and the clearly expressed opposition of Duke Philippe. It is only due to the diplomatic skills of my lord of Bedford that the alliance has held.'

It was not in Jacqueline's nature to accept a rebuke without retaliation. 'Well Bedford acquired himself a well-endowed wife in the process,' she retorted. 'By all accounts he and Philippe's sister Anne are now inseparable. It has turned out to be a love match, they say.' There was scorn in her voice, as if love between members of the nobility was somehow distasteful.

'At least they married in public, in the same church in Troyes where Henry and I were married and with the blessing of their families and peers, not secretly in some remote and crumbling castle without the support of kith or kin.' Catherine's disappointment in her erstwhile friend was bitter. 'Gloucester has always hankered after power. An English dukedom is not enough for him; he wants dominion over his own territories – your territories, Jacqueline.'

'Well, if he can get them back for me, he is welcome to it,' retorted the spirited duchess before subsiding into a more placatory attitude. 'You have not visited my lord Gloucester's castle of Hadleigh, Catherine, but when you do I think you will find it neither remote nor crumbling. It is a lively place, Catherine, a substantial stronghold which guards the north bank of the Thames, protecting London. I am hoping that your grace will consent to visit us soon and do us the honour of standing godmother to the child we expect early next year.'

I could see from her startled look that Catherine's feelings were torn. Joy for her erstwhile friend's expectations tussled with the tug of loyalty to her late husband's wishes and an increasing dislike for his grasping and manipulative youngest brother. 'I am delighted, of course, that God has blessed your union, Jacqueline, but I cannot make such a commitment without referring to the council of regency.'

The duchess smiled. 'Of course, and since my lord holds sway in the council, I am sure it will quickly endorse your sponsorship and we can look forward to further cementing our close relationship.'

Doubt flickered over Catherine's face at this confident prediction but, in the event, no commitment was needed, for sadly the duchess's baby son was premature and stillborn. This did nothing to halt Gloucester's territorial ambitions however, and as soon as his new wife had recovered from this personal and dynastic tragedy she was persuaded to accompany him and a substantial army to Hainault in an attempt to win back control over her inheritance. But on the Flemish border to the duchy they found that the Duke of Burgundy, predictably furious, had massed a force capable of defending it against any such incursion, causing the fearful citizens of Hainault to inform Jacqueline that whereas she was welcome in her duchy, her new husband and his army of retainers was not. Such obduracy infuriated and frustrated Humphrey and within a year he was back in England, having abandoned his wife to face the might of Burgundy alone. In a matter of months Hainault, Holland and Brabant were annexed and Jacqueline was in Duke Philippe's power, under close confinement. Also there was a new pope in Rome and Burgundy had persuaded the Vatican to rescind the annulment of her marriage to the Duke of Brabant, making her union with Gloucester invalid. Far from being chastened by the experience, Humphrey now appeared to have washed his hands of Jacqueline altogether.

So, too, it seemed had Eleanor Cobham, who had travelled

to Hainault in the service of the Duchess of Gloucester, but returned to England with the duke and it was not long before she sought an audience with the dowager queen at Windsor. It was by then nearly three years since I had last seen her, before I left to be with Alys for her second confinement in Paris, and while the intervening years had turned Catherine into a widow in black weeds, they had transformed Eleanor from an adolescent nymph into a young woman of quite breathtaking beauty. For her appearance before the Queen Dowager, she had arrayed herself in a headdress sparkling with amythysts and a sumptuous gown of indigo damask which drew instant attention to her celebrated violet eyes and porcelain complexion. I immediately wondered where she had acquired the money to fund such a striking ensemble.

'I regret that I was not able to remain with the Duchess of Gloucester owing to the animosity of the Hainault court,' she said, after being granted a seat beside Catherine. 'But it has been brought to my notice, your grace, that Joanna Coucy has recently left your service to get married and so I am presuming there is now a place in your household for another lady-in-waiting. You were gracious enough to indicate to the Duke of Gloucester when he introduced me previously that you would consider me as a future candidate.'

Catherine did not immediately reply, coolly meeting the demanding gaze of the younger woman until Eleanor was forced to look away in some confusion. Then Catherine spoke in a tone of guarded sympathy. 'I have heard that your mother recently died, Damoiselle, for which I am truly sorry. May God rest her soul. Had she still been alive, I am sure she would have advised you that it is not customary for a queen to be directly approached for an appointment to her service. Should a post become vacant, an intermediary will suggest a candidate and thus both parties are saved the embarrassment of any face to face refusal. However, since you have chosen not to follow customary court procedure, I cannot save you that embarrassment. Regrettably I am unable to offer you a place because the departure of Joanna Coucy has by chance allowed me to achieve the reduction in my household that the council recently demanded of me, so I will not be appointing a replacement. I do hope you understand.'

Eleanor Cobham had a cat-like habit of narrowing her eyes when she was angry and never was a look more feline than that which flashed across her face at that moment. There was intense resentment in it, an emotion swiftly disguised but unmissable for its brief duration. This was the second time Catherine had refused her a place at court and she clearly regarded it as a snub, unlikely to be forgiven or forgotten.

Less than a month later, Windsor and Westminster had been set buzzing with the scandalous news that the Duke of Gloucester had taken a mistress and flagrantly installed her as the chatelaine of Hadleigh Castle. Her name was Eleanor Cobham.

Catherine had been almost incandescent with anger. 'Not only has Gloucester humiliated and disparaged Jacqueline of Hainault, he has now made it more than clear that he expected me to provide his paramour with a place in my household in order to enable him to conduct a relationship with her under the noses of the king's court! Now I am doubly glad that I did not include Damoiselle Cobham among my intimate companions. She and Gloucester have both rendered themselves utterly graceless in my eyes.'

More regrettable to us all than Joanna Coucy's departure had been that of the loveable and exuberant Joan Beaufort. Before the late king's death, arrangements had been finalised for the ransom and return of his royal hostage, King James, to Scotland and a marriage between him and Lady Joan approved. Their wedding at the beautiful church of St Mary Overy in Southwark, with feasting at Bishop Beaufort's nearby episcopal palace, was the first opportunity for celebration and merrymaking after the extended period of mourning for the dead king. Immediately afterwards, the newlyweds left for their restored northern kingdom. It cannot have been an easy throne-coming for the couple, but I must admit it pleased me greatly that the pretty girl who had once removed a stone so skilfully from my mare's hoof now wore a crown. After nearly four years of marriage, Queen Joan of Scotland was already the mother of two daughters and presumably praying for a son. I had no doubt that she provided invaluable and practical advice to her royal spouse and was a hands-on mother to her children.

After telling her staff that she was no longer to be a part of young Henry's life and once she was alone with her ladies in her bedchamber, Catherine announced that she would cease to wear the barbe, the uniform of widowhood. 'Now that my son is to be taken from me, I do not see that it has any meaning. I am only twenty-six and I am not a nun; why should I hide my throat from view? Agnes, you may take it off!'

Agnes de Blagny, quiet and obliging as ever, hastened to remove the offending neck-curtain and its accompanying wimple from her mistress's head. Freed from its tight frame, Catherine's appearance of nun-like severity was returned to a familiar luminous beauty. Joanna Belknap fetched a comb, released the long pale-gold hair from its knot at the nape of her neck and began to braid it.

'You should marry again, Madame,' said Agnes sympathetically. 'You might have more children.'

Catherine pursed her lips doubtfully. 'Hmm. I think the council would consider that a contentious issue.'

'I do not see why,' protested Agnes.

'The man I marry would become the king's step-father. That is a position of some power.'

'I had not thought of that,' Agnes confessed. 'But they cannot require you to remain single and celibate against your wishes.'

'They can do anything!' Catherine put scornful stress on 'they'. 'It would be a different matter if I were on the council of regency. Then I might be able to influence proceedings.'

This was a sore point. A month after her husband's burial, she had spent a humiliating afternoon arguing her case for a place on the council, but the assembled lords had unanimously and unhesitatingly rejected her claim, as if she had suggested placing a viper in their midst. Her only consolation was that they had also refused to make Humphrey of Gloucester regent, appointing him only protector of the realm, which curtailed his powers and angered him considerably.

'Do you have anyone in mind as a candidate for your hand, Madame?' I asked curiously. I had not noticed her favouring one particular lord over another. 'Perhaps you are looking abroad?'

This suggestion inspired a vehement shake of the head. 'No, no, Mette. I would not leave England while my son is here! Besides, English people distrust foreigners, have you not noticed?'

Joanna Belknap brought a coronet and veil and began to fit them around the braids now coiled at Catherine's temples, commenting indignantly, 'Not all English people, your grace!'

'Very well, Belknap, I agree that there are some exceptions, but you cannot deny that many of the laws of England restrict what foreigners can and cannot do. For instance Owen Tudor told me that Welsh people are not allowed to brew ale or bake bread, even within their own borders. The English have the monopoly of these essential commodities and can therefore wilfully overcharge for the basic necessities of life. My lord's father enforced that law after the Welsh rebellion.'

'That is true, Madame,' nodded Belknap, 'and marriage between the Welsh and the English is forbidden except by special licence, which carries with it a substantial fine and loss of status for the English partner.'

'Master Tudor believes that the English hate the Welsh even more than the French, despite the crucial role their archers play in France,' Catherine remarked with a hollow laugh. 'Prejudice is not logical.'

However, despite being Welsh, Owen Tudor had played his harp rhapsodically at King Henry's funeral and had been appointed a Squire of the Chamber to the baby king. In recent months he had taken particular pride in teaching young Henry the rudiments both of archery and music, but he was chiefly responsible for administering and organising the guard on both the king's and the queen mother's apartments, so we frequently encountered him on our daily visits to the nursery. At Catherine's suggestion and with the encouragement of the young king's elderly uncle and official guardian, the Duke of Exeter, Owen had also arranged frequent excursions and games in the gardens and parkland around Windsor castle with other young children chosen from among courtiers' families. He had come to be regarded as someone who could be relied on to devise activities and amusements and occasionally administer discipline in a kind and constructive way. I know that Catherine believed that, for a little boy otherwise surrounded by female nursemaids and governesses, such a young, strong and masculine presence in his life was of great value. Now that a whole posse of male tutors and custodians had been officially appointed for the king in Owen's stead, I was not surprised to learn that Catherine had taken steps to retain the services of someone whom she had found to be utterly reliable.

'As a matter of fact, today Owen Tudor has been appointed my new master of the wardrobe,' Catherine announced, a hint of glee in her voice, 'which may give the grey-beards on the council something to splutter about at their next meeting but, happily, they have no jurisdiction over appointments to my new staff.

'Master Tudor will take responsibility for the business side of the household, working with my treasurer and receiver-general, who have yet to be appointed. All the domestic servants will report to him and he will supervise my dower manors which, as you know are scattered around the country. He is to set out tomorrow to inspect the various residences at my disposal so that arrangements can be made to prepare one for our occupation. He will also be responsible for our security. We will need our own detachment of guards. It is a heavy burden he assumes, but I am sure he will be diligent and thorough in his undertakings.'

I was delighted for Owen. At twenty-seven this new post represented a timely promotion for him and would release him from daily duties which had sometimes been more akin to those of a children's nurse rather than a courtier. Of course running the dowager queen's household would take him away from the king's favour, but all real opportunity and influence had long ago gravitated to Westminster, where the chief crown officials and council members kept their households and somehow I did not see the archer-musician flourishing in the field of politics and diplomacy. If he did not want to go back to fighting the French wars, then a job that made him effectively the dowager queen's right-hand man should suit him well. I did not encounter him before he left to begin his tour of inspection, but I imagined Master Tudor was in buoyant mood.

'I have come to say farewell, my lady mother.' The king's treble voice held a slight tremor but by no other sign did the boy betray any emotion. At six years old the young Henry already displayed some of his father's ability to disguise his feelings; a useful attribute in a king, I thought, but a sad skill to practice on your mother. He was a solemn boy, tall for his age with a pale, oval face that reminded me a little of Catherine's brother Charles, perhaps because of the Valois set of his nose, already long (too long some might say) and straight, which might suit the man he would become better than the boy he now was. His shoulders were square and he held himself erect, but there was always a dreamy look in his eyes, as if his mind was not completely focussed, away somewhere in a dream or a prayer. Even at such a tender age he was of a markedly religious bent and would often have to be called away from his prie dieu to attend lessons.

Queen Catherine sat, calm and smiling, in a crimson-draped chair. The parting was taking place in the king's presence chamber because Catherine's goods and furnishings had already been packed into barges to be transported by river to Hertford Castle, where it had now been decided she would start her new life. 'I hope you have enjoyed the festive holiday, Henry,' she said. They addressed each other in French because she was determined he should speak it as his mother tongue but, of course, he also spoke English and was already learning Latin.

'Oh yes. I think the choir here at Windsor very fine and the Christmas services were beautiful, but I did not much like all the japes and jests at the Twelfth Night feast.' He climbed into the throne-like chair on the dais beside his mother's and sat there awkwardly, legs dangling. He wore a scarlet sable-trimmed doublet and soft draped black hat and his curious speckled eyes roamed the faces of the assembled courtiers as if seeking evidence that they agreed with his observations.

With an instinctive motherly gesture Catherine reached out to arrange his short mantle for him, receiving a frown of annoyance for her pains, which she ignored. 'Indeed?' Her brows rose in enquiry. 'What did you not like about them?'

On Twelfth Night there had been the usual merrymaking, with a Lord of Misrule chosen by lottery from among the squires and pages of the household. The youth who drew the black bean from among the white ones in the closed bag took charge of the entertainment, with carte blanche to call on anyone or anything that might supply amusement for the revellers. His first act had been to demand that the king swap places with him so that he could rule the feast from the throne and as Henry good-naturedly made his way down the hall to the lower trestles he had been presented with a scroll on which a poem was inscribed that he was ordered to read. Luckily it had not been bawdy, but it had been scurrilous, making irreverent mention of the Bishop of London's substantial paunch and the various bodily shortcomings of other clerics, and it had quickly become obvious that the pious young king was not comfortable reading it. However his blushes and mumblings had only increased the raucous laughter from the assembled diners, so that the new 'king' of the banquet had yelled for him to speak up. At a Twelfth Night feast even the King of England had to dance to the tune of the Lord of Misrule.

'I do not think the king's grace should be made to insult a

bishop of the Church,' Henry had declared loudly so that everyone should hear. 'I do not mind a joke, but such rudeness as was in that poem is an offence to Our Lord and His hierarchy.'

Catherine smiled sympathetically. 'Yes, I agree that it was a bit naughty, but that is the point of misrule, is it not? We must all learn to accept a joke against ourselves otherwise we become puffed up with too much pride.'

Henry sniffed. 'When I am really king I shall abolish misrule,' he said primly.

Some thought the young king's piety excessive and believed that his love of prayer and Church ritual prevented him developing other important skills, such as military prowess. Among them was the Earl of Warwick, who had noticed his unwillingness to play with wooden swords and shields and his preference for music and bible stories.

'There are too many women around him,' Warwick had reportedly complained to the council of regency during the debate on the king's future. 'Women make a man weak. King Henry should be starting to train for knighthood.'

Catherine turned now to the earl, who stood protectively within earshot of his new charge. 'I urge you to take very good care of my son, my lord of Warwick. I know that in the absence of his own father there can be no better man to teach him knightly skills, but I beg you to remember that one day he will be married and his queen will require him to have at least some knowledge and understanding of the gentle arts.'

The earl bowed punctiliously. The charming gallant, who had been so instrumental in bringing about Catherine's marriage to the young king's father, had not lost any of his diplomatic tact. 'My own son is not yet two, your grace, but I assure you that yours will receive all the training in social graces that I deem essential for my heir. I can offer no more to the son of my old friend and comrade in arms, whose memory we both hold so dear.'

Catherine gave him a brief smile. Her admiration for Richard of Warwick, once that of a star-struck young girl for a celebrated and handsome chevalier, was now tempered by the high-handed way he had usurped parental control over her son. 'I will hold you to that, my lord,' she said. 'I trust that you will care for him as if I were hovering at your shoulder, watching your every move.'

As she spoke, the town bells began to ring for Tierce. The days were short and it was already full light. We would need to start for Hertford if we were to reach it by dark. The Earl of Warwick coughed loudly into his hand.

Catherine looked at him sharply. 'You are impatient, my lord. Impatient to send me from my son's side, but he will not forget his mother, of that you may be sure.' She turned back to her son and kissed his soft, childish cheek. His bottom lip was now visibly trembling. 'You must hold that kiss in your heart, Henry, for I think you will not have another until we meet again at Easter.'

Under the archway of the main entrance to St George's Hall the king knelt before his mother for her blessing, baring his bright auburn head for the touch of her hand. She managed to keep her voice steady as she called for God's blessing and protection on her little son, then she took a deep breath, wrapped her sable-lined riding cloak around her shoulders and descended the steps to where the earl himself waited to hold her stirrup while she mounted her palfrey. An escort of a hundred royal guards would accompany her to Hertford Castle, where Owen Tudor had been sent ahead to prepare the royal palace for the young dowager queen's life of retirement.

From the steps the little king gave a slow, sad wave, but with brimming eyes fixed on her horse's ears Catherine did not see it. The warm breath of horses and riders condensed to steam in the chill January air, clouding us in a faint mist as we trotted under the Norman gatehouse and past the Round Tower, riding out to a new and unknown future.

20

The biggest drawback to Hertford Castle was that once inside the gates it was difficult to see anything of the surrounding countryside, unless you climbed up to the battlements on the high curtain wall. The great hall, the chapel and all the living quarters were clustered together around a central court and were built long and low so that they nestled under the parapets, shutting off all sight of the outside world except to those soldiers who kept watch from the towers. It produced the same sense of confinement as a convent, when all activity is enclosed in stone and incense robs the air of freshness. In a small inner court there was a formal garden, but it was laid out in straight lines with pebble paths and little hedges and, despite being open to the sky, proved nearly as restrictive as the gloomy stairways and passages of the royal apartments. It was no wonder that Catherine quickly established a daily habit of riding out into the well-tended hunting park outside the walls.

The two remaining Joannas accompanied her on these excursions, along with a detachment of guards and frequently Owen Tudor and Walter Vintner, who had been recruited as her chief clerk. This was an appointment which had delighted me because I maintained a close correspondence with his father, Geoffrey, who had spent several years in Rouen attached to the new Council of Normandy, where he had legally secured many land titles and estates which had been granted to English knights and nobles as a reward for their efforts in the campaign that had won the territory back from the French crown. Much of the dowager queen's business was conducted during these rides, when Owen and Catherine would discuss arrangements and problems and Walter would take notes in order to write letters and keep records afterwards.

I often joined the rides also, because I liked to exercise Genevieve myself, being absurdly fond of my faithful and sturdy palfrey. However, on Shrove Tuesday, I had elected to remain in the castle to supervise arrangements for the traditional feast to mark the transition into Lent. It was a sin to allow good food to go to waste over the six weeks of fasting and so, as was the custom, before dusk we would all assemble together to eat and drink as much as we wished and the leftovers would be distributed to the poor of the surrounding villages, some of whom were already assembling in the outer bailey to await their share. So I was not among the excursion party who encountered a colourful cavalcade of knights and horsemen advancing unexpectedly on the castle from the south.

Alerted by a trumpet blast and a loud clanging of the bell on the watch-tower, Agnes and I rushed to the main courtyard where there was much scuttling and scurrying among the grooms and stable lads, because instead of only ten horses returning from the usual ride there were suddenly thirty or more clattering over the drawbridge and under the gatehouse. Leading the procession with Catherine was a splendidly accoutred knight wearing half armour and identified by a blue standard bearing scattered fleurs-de-lys slashed diagonally by a red and white bend. It was not a crest familiar to me, but Agnes recognised it.

'Those are the arms of the Counts of Mortain,' she murmured

in surprise, 'but is that not Edmund Beaufort, the Duchess of Clarence's son?'

It was indeed Edmund Beaufort, but a very much grander and more mature figure than the lanky squire we had last encountered at Windsor before the present king's birth. The men at arms in his retinue all wore the Beaufort portcullis on their shoulders, but they also bore the Mortain arms on their pike pennants. It was very obvious that Margaret of Clarence's youngest son had not only become a knight, but had also been granted tenure and title to a large part of Normandy. I wondered if Geoffrey Vintner might have drawn up the title deeds.

'He must now be the Count of Mortain,' marvelled Agnes, her eyes round with awe. 'Who would have imagined?'

'Not Catherine, I would wager,' I murmured, turning on my heel. 'I must go and warn the kitchen.'

No sooner had I briefed the cooks, than a message came for me to attend the queen and I hurried up from the kitchens to Catherine's private solar off the great hall. The hall itself, as I passed through, was crowded with soldiers, members of Edmund's retinue whose loud calls for refreshments had servants scurrying about with flagons of wine and pewter cups. Hertford was a sprawling castle, but our relatively small household was not sufficiently staffed to manage such a sudden influx.

When the chamberlain admitted me, I found Catherine and Edmund seated on either side of the hearth in her well-lit private chamber whose walls were hung with bright-coloured tapestries depicting scenes of English legend; an ancient king receiving the swords of a surrendering garrison on one, a queen begging the lives of hostages outside a besieged city on another. Hardly appropriate for a lady's solar, I considered, but Hertford

Castle had a colourful history, which Catherine was explaining to Edmund.

'Believe it or not, my ancestor King John of France was housed here as a prisoner of King Edward the Third; and thirty years ago it was where my eldest sister Isabelle came to live as the child-queen of King Richard,' she told him with a nervous laugh. 'Neither of them can have been very happy, I imagine.'

Edmund echoed her laugh, but on a merrier note. 'We shall have to try and cheer the place up,' he said. 'I am glad to have arrived before Lent so that we can have a proper celebration of our reunion. I have much to tell you of the situation in France.'

Catherine caught sight of me and beckoned me forward. 'That is why I summoned Madame Lanière. You remember her, do you not? She is still my beloved companion and loyal servant.'

Edmund acknowledged me with a smile and a nod of the head. 'I do indeed remember Mette. She once did me the honour of riding pillion behind me during my time as your squire.'

Disconcertingly I found myself blushing, remembering the days when I had been unable to ride my own horse and was obliged to undertake some excruciatingly uncomfortable and sometimes embarrassing journeys in Catherine's wake. I bent my knee dutifully to the count. 'I am glad to say that I ride my own horse these days, my lord,' I responded.

'I thought you would be interested in the progress of the war in France, Mette.' Catherine gestured towards a stool set behind and to one side of her. Its placement indicated my role – I was to listen but not participate. Catherine was acutely conscious of the need for a chaperone when entertaining male guests. As Queen Mother, any whiff of scandal that reached the ears of the regency council might prompt them to further restrict her access to the king.

Edmund cleared his throat. 'I think it safe to say that, at present, our English lions fly at their highest over France, Madame. My lord of Bedford and the Earl of Salisbury are even now drawing up plans to invest a siege of Orleans and once that city is taken, the whole of the south will open up to us.'

Catherine shifted a little uncomfortably in her chair. News of England's successes always indicated losses on her brother's part. 'Is that so? And will you be returning for that campaign, Edmund?'

'I will certainly be returning to France because my estates in Normandy require much attention, but whether I will take part in the siege I do not know. I have still to pursue the matter of my brother's ransom but, while the Duke of Orleans remains a prisoner in England, I cannot see him being released.'

'So that is what brought you back to England.' Catherine gave him one of her dazzling smiles. 'It is good to see you, but if you have won yourself such lands and honours I think you must be much in demand across the Sleeve.'

To the complete surprise of both of us, Edmund suddenly flung himself to his knees beside Catherine's chair. 'I came back for one very good reason, Madame,' he said breathlessly, 'to put an important proposition to you.' He took one of her hands in his and continued what sounded like a well-rehearsed speech. 'I will come straight to the point. My lady mother informs me that you may be of a mind to re-marry now that the king has a separate household. Would you think it presumptuous of me to ask whether you might consider a match with me? You know I have always held you in the highest esteem and I dare to think that a marriage with someone like myself might be exactly what you need.'

He looked only slightly sheepish as he hastened to boast his credentials. 'I am landed now, but not so greatly that I might be anything but a loyal subject of your son. I am also of the blood royal, though as a younger son not too close to the succession. Most importantly of all, I am young and vigorous and think you the most beautiful woman on earth. There – I can put it no plainer than that.'

He came to an abrupt halt and set her hand to his lips in an ardent salute before fixing her with an enquiring gaze. Catherine was staring at him in amazement and I suddenly realised that I had risen to my feet, perhaps with some crazy idea of curtailing excessive advances. Edmund's proposal had come out of the blue.

'I . . . I am honoured,' Catherine stuttered, nonplussed by this assured approach by a man whom she had scarcely had time to appreciate was no longer a boy to be teased and ordered about. 'I do not know what to say, Edmund. You have taken me completely by surprise.'

I sheepishly resumed my seat as Catherine shook her head in bewilderment. I could sense her regarding him differently, weighing him up as a lord and partner and found myself doing the same, studying his honest face and candid grey eyes, which were twinkling at her now, kindly and without guile. He looked confident, intelligent and capable. Perhaps Catherine might even find him attractive.

'Your suggestion is very interesting to me, Edmund,' she said gravely. 'I will give it the serious consideration it deserves.'

He sat back in his chair, suddenly relaxed and I guessed that his proposal had cost him more mental stress than he showed. 'I am glad,' he said. 'There is no great hurry for your answer, except my own impatience of course. I return to France next year and very much hope you will come with me as my countess.'

Catherine inclined her head in my direction. 'Pour some wine please, Mette, and we will drink to future possibilities.'

When I brought the two cups to them, they stood and raised them in a toast. The sudden change in their relationship hovered between them like a phantasm.

'There is just one more thing,' said Edmund suddenly, taking her cup and turning to place them both on a nearby table. Then, swinging round, he gathered her into his arms with gentle ardour and kissed her on the mouth. It was not a snatched kiss from an awkward admirer, but a long and businesslike statement of intent from a man of confidence and experience and she showed no inclination to repulse it. When their lips finally parted, he gazed intently down at her. 'It would not be a marriage of convenience, you know, Catherine.'

It was the first time he had ever used her name.

In France we call Shrove Tuesday Mardi Gras or Fat Tuesday, more apt in my opinion because although we were all shriven by the priest before sunset, the hours between that and midnight were given over to feasting and merry-making. On this occasion Catherine and Edmund sat side by side at the high table, sharing a cup and offering each other choice morsels of meats and sweetmeats. It was the first time since the death of her charismatic husband that I had witnessed her really come alive and it did my heart good to see it. With them sat the priest, Maître Boyers, Edmund's two knight-captains and the two Joannas, invited there to entertain the men. In the body of the hall the actions of the hostess and her principal guest caused plenty of nudging and winking among Edmund's louder and less courtly retainers and beside me Agnes expressed mild shock at her widowed friend's lively demeanour, as if two well-matched and unattached people were not allowed to flirt a little during a Fat Tuesday feast without bringing the wrath of God down upon their handsome coroneted heads.

Along with Agnes and me at the 'reward' table on the dais, a trestle set for Catherine's officials to one side of the high table, sat Owen Tudor, Walter Vintner and Thomas Roke, a young London lawyer who had been appointed her Receiver-General. At first Owen spoke little and kept his eyes firmly on his trencher, leading me to suspect that he too was surprised and not a little shocked by this sudden turn of events.

I sought to lighten Owen's mood by telling him the reason for it. 'Perhaps you should not spread this fact around generally, but the Count of Mortain has made a proposal of marriage to Queen Catherine,' I told him. 'It is very likely that they will marry quite soon and it does not look to me as if they should wait too long.'

Owen lifted his head and I noticed with surprise that his eyes were clouded with concern. 'She looks happy,' he said, 'and that worries me. Her grace has had enough heartbreak in her life. She does not need more.'

I frowned, suddenly wary. 'What do you mean? Do you know something about the count? Is he perhaps not free to marry?'

'No, no. Nothing like that. You are right. They would suit each other well, perhaps a little too well for some people.'

Thomas Roke leaned around my shoulder to address Owen. 'I take it you have heard the rumours on your travels, Master Tudor?'

I swivelled to look at him. He was a solid young man, ruddy-faced and broad-beamed, with the air of someone who would brook no opposition – a useful characteristic for a receiver-general whose job was to travel around Catherine's dower manors collecting rents and checking crops and tallies. He was actually

Walter's brother-in-law, having married his sister Anne several years ago, the eventual result of a secret love affair which had been the cause of some distress at the time to their father, my friend Geoffrey Vintner, with whom I still maintained an intermittent correspondence. Geoffrey had not approved of his legal apprentice courting his daughter, but once Thomas had qualified he had been persuaded to give his permission for the marriage to take place. The young lawyer had turned up at Hertford only a few days after Catherine's household had moved in, with impressive letters of recommendation and a courteous and obliging manner, which contrasted with his stolid appearance. Catherine had appointed him on three months trial and so far he had justified her trust in him. Now he was about to prove that he kept his ear to the ground and had a nose for political intrigue.

Owen sipped from his wine cup. 'Madame's retirement has been the subject of much discussion in the inns and taverns. It is hard to ignore it.'

Thomas nodded solemnly. 'And in London, particularly, many rumours are rife that she has been sent from court because her lewd behaviour was corrupting the young king.'

'What!' My cry of disbelief was so violent that I clapped a hand across my mouth to stem it, continuing in a muffled whisper. 'Are you telling me that people believe she is wanton? That she behaves lasciviously? When nothing could be further from the truth!'

Thomas regarded me with patient disparagement. 'Truth is never paramount in the minds of rumour-mongers, Madame. When it comes to spreading gossip about royals and nobles, they tell the stories that glean the most gleeful reactions. People love to think that their lords and masters – or lady in this case – are no better than they should be.'

'But who is starting these terrible rumours about Queen Catherine?' Agnes asked indignantly. 'And what exactly do they say?' We must have looked like a gaggle of gossips ourselves as we sat hunched over our trenchers, talking in urgent whispers and frequently stopping in mid-sentence so that passing servers and stewards should not hear.

Owen Tudor gave an awkward cough. 'If we tell you both, I do not want the story spreading to the other ladies, or more importantly to the queen herself. I do not wish her to think for a minute that I either believe it or condone the spreading of it.'

He looked so stricken at the thought of this that I hastened to reassure him. 'I promise I will not tell another soul,' I said, 'unless I discuss it with you first. For there may come a time when the queen needs to be told.'

Agnes echoed my assurances. 'I will never speak of what I do not believe either,' she said.

Owen pondered this for a moment then nodded sharply at Walter, who had so far sat silent and goggle-eyed at the turn the conversation had taken. 'The same goes for you, Master Clerk. Not a word.'

Walter inclined his head to indicate agreement as Thomas Roke glanced about for eavesdroppers before launching into his full account. 'You may know already that the Duke of Gloucester is very popular among the merchants and burgesses of London. He cultivates them because he knows they are a good source of finance for the French campaign. So if he wants to sow the seeds of a rumour that is where he does it, in the inns and exchanges of the Cheape. And that is where I first heard the gossip about Queen Catherine.'

'And what exactly did it say?' I asked. 'Was it just generally malicious or did it name names and make specific allegations?'

I felt sick at the thought that drunken men in seedy taverns had been bad-mouthing my sweet and unimpeachable lady. A similar thing had happened in Paris during the Terrors, but then the rumours were about her mother's rash expenditure and adulterous liaisons and they at least had more than a little grounding in truth. I seethed at the thought that without cause or justification, Catherine was being tarred with the same brush as Queen Isabeau.

'No, it did not name names, for that could have led to litigation. Instead there were scurrilous stories of banquets and entertainments at Windsor when the king had been compelled to watch naked tumblers and bawdy jesters and Queen Catherine had danced lewdly with knights and squires and wantonly exposed her hair and throat to open view.' I must have looked utterly horrified, for Master Roke gave an apologetic shrug and added, 'I am only relating what I heard, Madame. We all know that none of it is true.'

It was not, but I could see where the roots of it lay. Catherine's immediate reaction at being denied a role in her son's further upbringing had been to put aside the widow's barbe and wimple and wear her jewels and fashionable gowns at the Christmas festivities at Windsor. It did not take much exaggeration to turn golden hair braided into mesh nets and the absence of any neck covering into 'wanton exposure of the hair and throat'. But how a few Twelfth Night pranks had turned into 'naked tumbling and lewd dancing', I could not credit.

'You imply that these rumours originated in the Gloucester camp,' I persisted, 'but why should the Duke of Gloucester have any reason to smear the reputation of the Queen Mother, of all people?'

Owen Tudor scratched his head. 'That is what puzzles me.

Her grace has no power in the land, no influence in the regency council; so Gloucester can have no axe to grind with her.'

I said nothing, but I suspected we should not only be looking to the duke for a motive but perhaps also to the resentment of Eleanor Cobham, who had been twice rejected as a lady-in-waiting and had not been received by Catherine since becoming Gloucester's mistress. Then Master Roke gave me even more food for thought.

'While we are watching Queen Catherine enjoying the Count of Mortain's company and considering a proposal of marriage from him, we should not forget that there is much bad blood between Gloucester and the House of Beaufort.' Wielding his knife with relish, the stocky receiver-general stabbed a slice of fat pork and laid it carefully on his gravy-soaked trencher. 'It is only three years since the duke and Cardinal Beaufort almost caused a civil war over who held sway in the council. As she dallies with Edmund Beaufort, her grace may be unaware that the cardinal is very likely to be behind this apparently innocuous offer of marriage. A step-father to the king can only become more powerful as our young sovereign grows older and any step-brothers would bear the name of Beaufort. There is a great deal in a name.'

21

The following day I stood with Catherine as she bade farewell to the Count of Mortain, who was riding to London to take part in a grand procession to mark the recent elevation of his uncle, the immensely rich and powerful Henry Beaufort, Bishop of Winchester, to the College of Cardinals. It was an appointment which Henry the Fifth had blocked, for fear that his rich and powerful uncle would owe a greater allegiance to Rome than to the English crown; but now the wily Beaufort had managed to bring the council around to the idea of England having its own representative in the Vatican conclave and the cardinal's red hat was firmly on his head. Not a situation that met with the approval of the Duke of Gloucester.

On the steps of the great hall Edmund kissed her hand with genuine regret. 'I would not leave you so soon, Catherine, but Gloucester has consistently opposed the pope's offer of the cardinal's hat and may get his retainers to stir trouble among the London crowds. My uncle needs all the support he can muster. However, I will be back before Easter for your reply to my question.'

After Mass Catherine, Agnes and I wrapped ourselves in fur-lined cloaks against the chill February wind and walked in the frost-nipped garden in order to avoid being overheard. The offer of marriage was still not public knowledge.

'I wrote to the king today to ask his opinion,' Catherine revealed. 'Do you think Henry will approve of the match? I could not possibly go against his wishes.'

'It is a pity you could not tell him face to face, Madame,' observed Agnes. 'He is very young to understand your reasons for taking another husband.'

Catherine gave a shaky laugh. 'I am not sure I understand them myself, Agnes,' she said. 'But I pointed out to Henry that he might like to have brothers and sisters and that would be one good reason for my marrying.'

'Are you sure your letter will remain confidential?' I asked with concern, recalling the previous day's reward table conversation. 'Is not the king's correspondence vetted before he sees it?'

'Not letters from his mother, Mette!' Catherine was indignant at the very thought. 'I always put my personal seal on them. No, I do not believe my correspondence with Henry is vetted.'

I was far from confident about this myself, but merely asked, 'If the king approves, have you definitely decided to go ahead, Mademoiselle?'

We walked at least ten strides in silence before Catherine suddenly stopped and regarded at me candidly. 'Yes, Mette, I have. I cannot think of any nobleman in England I would rather marry than Edmund. Besides, I would have Margaret of Clarence as a mother-in-law and Queen Joan of Scotland as a sister. It is a family I would gladly join.'

'Not forgetting the cardinal,' I said under my breath as we resumed our walk.

Catherine was too sharp of hearing not to catch this remark. 'Why do you say that?' she demanded.

I was still mulling over Thomas Roke's revelations. 'No particular reason,' I said lightly, 'except I think it unlikely Lord

Edmund would have made a proposal of marriage without consulting the cardinal first. He is head of the Beaufort family, especially with the Earl of Somerset still a prisoner in France.'

'I see what you mean. Well that is all right. Cardinal Beaufort is a good man to have on your side. Look how he managed to get King James's throne back for him.'

It was true, I thought, she had little to fear from the Beaufort affinity, but should I warn her who her real enemies might be? At this early stage I decided against it.

To my delight, the following afternoon brought more new arrivals to Hertford Castle; Geoffrey Vintner and his two daughters Anne and Mildred, accompanied by a brace of hired men at arms. Ever since Master Roke had been appointed Receiver-General, it had been understood that his wife, Anne, would come to join him and might be found a role in Catherine's household, but the additional arrival of her father and sister was unexpected. I knew that Geoffrey and Mildred had recently returned to London from Rouen, but I had not yet had a chance to visit them.

'Apart from taking a letter to the king, Queen Catherine's courier also brought one to me,' Geoffrey explained when I found the Vintner family warming themselves at the fire in the great hall. 'Her grace requested that I visit her as soon as possible so of course I dropped everything to come and it seemed a good opportunity to bring Anne to join her husband. Nor was there any chance of leaving Mildy behind when the opportunity arose for an "adventure", as she put it. I hope that in a castle of this size there may be accommodation for all of us.'

I reassured him of this and smiled at the younger girl in her bright-green wool kirtle and darker green coney-lined cloak. Although it was some years since I had seen her, she did not seem to me to have changed greatly from the mischievous freckled imp I had first encountered at the house in Tun Lane. While her sister Anne, at twenty-one, had become a mature, almost matronly figure, Mildy was still small and vivacious, eager for new experiences and, at nineteen, as yet unwed. I knew that she had accompanied Geoffrey to Rouen to keep his house for him and in a letter to me from there he had expressed his pleasure that she showed no urgent desire to marry and his own reluctance to let her go. Owen Tudor appeared to have been expecting Geoffrey Vintner and, the household meal being over, had organised refreshments for him and his family, to which they duly settled around a small table by the hearth. Thomas Roke was not there to greet his wife because, being unaware of her imminent arrival, he had set out the previous day for one of Catherine's manors, some miles distant. Seating myself on the bench beside her, I could see that Anne was disappointed.

'I am afraid Master Roke is often away, Mistress Anne. It is in the nature of the job of receiver-general. However, he will no doubt be delighted to find you here on his return and, in the meantime, you can settle into your new home in the gatehouse. You must feel free to come to me if you have any problems or requests. When you have finished your meal, I will take you to meet the queen's ladies and I am sure Queen Catherine will also wish to make the acquaintance of her receiver-general's wife.'

Anne went quite pink at the idea of meeting Catherine. 'Oh, it would be an honour to meet the qu . . . I mean the dowager queen,' she stammered.

I laughed. 'Yes, it is a dreary title, especially for a young and beautiful woman. But she is a very proud mother to the king.'

'I can imagine. I pray to have a child soon myself.' She touched the little reliquary around her neck which I therefore assumed held some charm or amulet to assist fertility.

'The best thing for that is a husband in your bed,' I whispered with a wink and her blush deepened. Raising my voice I addressed her sister across the table. 'Did you have any adventures on the road from London, Mistress Mildy? We are told that all the outlaws have been cleared from the great north highway.'

Mildy pulled a face. 'We did not get a sight of one,' she said with obvious regret, 'even though father had hired guards to protect us.'

'Or perhaps because your careful father had hired guards,' Geoffrey amended. 'Although I am pleased to say there are now hefty fines for landowners if travellers are ambushed from their forests.'

'It takes all the excitement out of travelling,' complained Mildy.

'That is a silly thing to say,' Anne chastised her. 'Freedom to travel without fear is one of the signs of a well-ordered kingdom, Thomas says.'

'It is essential for his job and mine,' put in Owen Tudor, who had overheard the remark as he returned from informing Catherine of the Vintners' arrival. 'I am to take you to her grace as soon as you are refreshed and ready, Master Vintner,' he told Geoffrey, 'and Madame Lanière is requested to bring your daughters to her presently.'

I noticed with an inward smile that young Mildy fluttered her eyelashes rather prettily when Owen's gaze happened to light on her and in truth I could not blame her, for Catherine's master of the wardrobe was a sight to gladden the eye of any unmarried girl, and probably quite a number of married ones as well. Since he had played his harp for the dying king and then for his queen during the long funeral cortège, Owen had matured from a gauche young soldier with the face of a dark angel, into a handsome man of affairs who, instead of his battered archer's boiled-leather gambeson and boots, now sported the short fur-trimmed gowns, fine woollen hose and soft, artfully draped hats favoured by up-and-coming court officials. He still preferred to go clean-shaven and now wore his thick chestnut hair brushed to his shoulders, but the hours he continued to spend at the arms practice-ground had preserved his honed muscles and keen eye and even in the lofty halls of royal palaces he walked with the unconscious swagger of the trained warrior. Owen was quite accustomed to fielding the admiring glances of court damsels and frequently returned them with interest, as he did now with Mildy. He was certainly popular with the young ladies, but I had never heard any gossip about him taking advantage of them. It seemed he had a talent to amuse rather than abuse, and I had not heard of him making any long lasting relationships or fathering any by-blows. He was either principled or careful. During our occasional friendly chats I had not yet managed to discover which.

After settling Anne and Mildy into their gatehouse quarters and then conducting them to Catherine's solar, I spent the rest of the afternoon checking the castle stores, ensuring there were sufficient supplies of Lenten fish, cheese and vegetables available for the suddenly increased household. It was not until we were gathering for the evening meal in the great hall that I encountered Geoffrey Vintner again. He drew me into a window alcove so that we could speak privately.

'Queen Catherine has honoured me with a place at the high table tonight,' he revealed with a smile. 'It is not as flattering as it seems for there are no noble guests to take precedence, but nevertheless people will doubtless jump to conclusions. So you must be the first to know that I have agreed to act as her treasurer and legal adviser, and I feel certain that I have you to thank for her patronage.'

I beamed with pleasure, but could not resist commenting, 'Well, I may have made some mention of your smooth tongue and ready wit, but I think Walter probably has more to do with it than I. However, let me be the first to congratulate you and welcome you to the household. It is becoming quite a family affair, one way or another.'

'I have the feeling that is how Queen Catherine likes it,' Geoffrey observed. 'Once I had accepted the appointment, she also told me of the Count of Mortain's offer of marriage. What is your view of that?'

I frowned. 'On the surface it looks good – a suitable match in many ways and there is no doubt that she needs the protection marriage would afford.'

Geoffrey's lively blue eyes crinkled enquiringly. 'Do I detect a but?'

'Not on a personal level. Lord Edmund has admired Queen Catherine since he was a young squire and she likes him very well, so I am sure they would live together amicably. The "but" is that I am worried there may be objections from the council of regency. We hear much of the differences between the Gloucester and Beaufort affinities and this marriage proposal will undoubtedly kindle further argument. She would not want to find herself at the centre of a political row, especially if Gloucester does not play fair.'

Geoffrey gave a silent whistle and glanced quickly about for eavesdroppers. 'Dangerous words, Mette! What makes you think he may not?'

'Owen and Thomas were telling me about the rumours that have been spreading through London – that the queen mother has been banished from the king's side because she is wanton and lewd. Of course they are scurrilous and false!'

'I have heard them but ignored them. And they think they were started by Gloucester?' Geoffrey's voice had dropped to a whisper. 'Why would he do that?'

I shrugged. 'Because he wants to undermine her influence with the king, or because his mistress wants him to, or simply because he is a bully – who knows? What worries me is what else he will do when he hears about the Beaufort marriage proposal.'

Although Lenten meals were suitably frugal and soon over, there was no lack of evening entertainment at Hertford and Catherine encouraged her household to display any talents they possessed for the enjoyment of others. Professional mumming, acrobatics and comic capering were restricted to special celebrations outside Lent, but music and singing and story-telling were always welcome and, of course, Owen Tudor was frequently prevailed upon to play the harp. On this particular evening, when Catherine had no noble guests, the trestles were removed and the household gathered around the wide hearth below the dais. The flambeaux and candles at the far end of the hall were extinguished or moved so that a pool of light enveloped only the assembled company, at the centre of which Catherine sat, within range of the flickering fire but sheltered from its fiercest heat by the side-drapes of her canopied chair.

She was obviously in a merry mood for she clapped her hands for more wine to be poured and eagerly suggested that Owen should play for them first. 'Play something rousing, Master

Tudor,' she urged him, 'something to stir our senses and get us tapping our feet. What about those tunes you learned from the Spanish dancers when you were fighting in Anjou? We have not heard them in a long time.'

Owen went to fetch his harp and a page set a stool for him in the middle of the hall.

'Oh no, Owen, do not play so far away,' called Catherine. 'I love to hear the soundboard buzzing and see the strings vibrating. Come and sit here.' She indicated a prominent position directly in front of her chair and motioned to everyone to move their stools and benches into a closer circle. I positioned myself in my accustomed place, beside Catherine but set back a little so that the young ladies-in-waiting could arrange themselves around her chair.

'It is a fetching sight, is it not, the beautiful Queen Catherine surrounded by her damsels.' The voice in my ear was Geoffrey Vintner's. He had quietly moved to stand behind me with his back almost against the wall of the fireplace. Anne and Mildy sat on the other side of the circle on a bench with Walter between them.

'It is a pity she is no longer at the centre of a lively court, as by rights she should be,' I responded in a low voice. 'Fate has not dealt kindly with her. But your daughters look well among her retainers.' I did not know whether Catherine was considering the two girls as possible attendants, but I suspected that Geoffrey Vintner hoped she was. It would certainly do Mildy no harm in the marriage stakes if she was known to be a member of the Queen Mother's entourage.

At this point Owen stopped tuning his harp and placed his hands over the strings, ready to begin. The buzz of conversation halted and the company lapsed into expectant silence, all eyes on the squire who sat perched on his stool, the foot of the harp cradled on his knees, its curved neck resting on his shoulder. 'These dances are meant to be played on a gittern,' Owen said in his distinctive lilting voice, 'but I have adapted them to the small Welsh harp like this one that I play. I do not think the mad Spanish musician who taught them to me would approve, but he is not here, so – too bad.' He flashed one of his engaging smiles at the eager faces around him and plucked the first chord.

The tune started gently, on notes that rose and fell through a mellifluous motif, as if a pair of dancers was warming up, each following the other's moves, matching each flourish of the hand and each step of the foot on an ever-increasing beat until a pattern was established and the real revels could begin. There was a mesmerising, repetitive feel to the dance, the rhythm and pace building gradually, gaining confidence by minutes rather than seconds, so that it was some time before my foot started tapping.

As he played I watched Owen's expression; concentrated, intent and at the same time relaxed, his lips upturned in a smile of pure pleasure and his eyes unmoving, almost unblinking, never straying to his fingers on the strings, but entirely fixed in a concentrated gaze on Catherine's face. And hers were fixed on his; not avidly but dreamily, unconsciously, as if she was absorbing the message of the music not through her ears but through his eyes.

I hardly noticed the speed of the rhythm intensifying, but suddenly I found myself swaying to it and all around me people were reacting in their own way, some jigging, some flicking their fingers and those who were seated, tapping their knees. On his stool, Owen's body began to pulse forwards and backwards as his hands moved more and more energetically across the harpstrings and as the pace increased, so too did the beat, pounded out by his thumb on the short base string, faster and faster, forcing the player to rock forwards and backwards as he plucked out the tune on the longer strings.

Suddenly there was a loud crack and one leg of Owen's stool gave way, catapulting him onto his knees and almost into Catherine's lap. Yet the music never ceased. Somehow the harp went with him, wedged between his knees and his shoulder and he kept on playing, his eyes still fixed on Catherine's face. And because he continued to smile, she smiled back and began to laugh and soon everyone was smiling and laughing and clapping and tapping and the tune kept going faster and faster and higher and higher until it simply had nowhere to go and it ended with a plunging ripple down the strings to a loud, crashing, bass-chord finale.

Owen slumped sideways as if felled by the music and the harp toppled slowly over with him, causing Thomas to leap from his bench to rescue it. The broken stool lay upturned, its carved wooden leg splintered.

Catherine rose to bend over Owen. 'Are you all right, Master Tudor?' Her hand dropped automatically to the squire's shoulder. 'You never stopped playing! I do not know how you managed that. Are you sure you are not hurt?'

Owen suddenly seemed to realise where he was and scrambled hurriedly to his feet, his face turned away, eyes lowered in confusion. 'No, Madame – your grace – not at all. The stool gave way but somehow I could not stop. I am sorry. I hope my fall did not spoil your enjoyment of the music.' He was flustered now, his hand straying automatically to the shoulder where her hand had briefly lain.

Catherine straightened and stepped back, her composure also somewhat ruffled. 'Not at all, Master Tudor. Your playing was, as always, superb. Thank you.'

She returned to her chair and began to applaud, encouraging the rest of us to follow suit. Owen bowed and smiled in response, took his harp from Thomas with a nod of thanks and carried it to where light from a flambeau allowed him to inspect it for damage. The offending stool was removed from the scene and people settled back into their chosen places. Catherine called for another volunteer to entertain the company and during the discussion that ensued, Geoffrey came up behind me again, bending to murmur in my ear.

'Well, that was interesting, was it not? Have you been aware of vibrations between those two? And I do not mean the music.'

I turned enough to let him hear my muttered reply. 'I have not. And I do not believe they have either.'

I had once or twice considered the possibility that Owen had a secret crush on Catherine; that this might be the reason for his apparent lack of interest in finding a wife or even taking a mistress, but now I began to wonder if the boot could be on the other foot. Could Catherine's decision to marry Lord Edmund be a way of curing herself of amorous thoughts about someone else who would unquestionably be, as we French would put it, a *mésalliance*?

Catherine and Owen rode out together as usual the next morning and I made a point of going too. Was it coincidence, I asked myself, that their conversation about whether to increase the sheep flock at one of her Essex manors was conducted in a more stilted manner than usual and that she did not invite him to gallop with her down her favourite grassy woodland ride? Was she reacting against feelings aroused the previous evening? Then, chastising myself for indulging in idle speculation, I kicked Genevieve into a canter and put the idea firmly out of my head. If there were any unspoken feelings between the queen and Owen, surely it was all on his side. Catherine had made up her mind to marry Edmund Beaufort.

22

The watchman can hardly have had time to recognise the Duke of Gloucester's royal standard and boar's head badge before he and his retinue galloped over the castle drawbridge at such a hectic pace that splinters flew up from the planking. Clouds of condensed breath billowed from their coursers' flaring nostrils like steam from a row of kettles and afterwards the master of horse complained that most of them were so blown they were in danger of collapse.

His mount had barely skidded to a halt before the duke flung himself from the saddle and hailed Owen Tudor who happened to be striding across the courtyard from the practice ground, damp with perspiration from an hour at the pell-post. 'Hey, Tudor! Tell the queen dowager I want to see her now – and alone!'

I had been in the dairy giving instructions to the maids but, drawn outside by the commotion and made instantly aware of Gloucester's fury, I dodged around the mêlée of horses and hurried towards the private entrance to the royal apartments, from which I expected Catherine to emerge at any moment ready to start her morning ride. Unfortunately Gloucester spotted me and sprinted to intercept me as I reached the door at the foot of the access tower.

'Ah, Madame Lanière, off to warn your mistress of my arrival?

Let me save you the trouble.' He pushed me roughly aside and wrenched the door open, running straight into Catherine, who was already at the foot of the spiral stair within. 'Good day, your grace. I see you are free – excellent. I need to speak with you in private. Let me escort you back upstairs. Ladies, make yourselves scarce.'

The menacing tone of this last order precluded any misunderstanding and the two cowed Joannas pressed themselves against the wall as he brusquely shoved Catherine past them and back up the uneven steps. Taken by surprise, she protested loudly as she was forced to climb, stumbling over her skirts. I followed close behind the duke, determined that he should not succeed in being alone with her. However, as we neared the top I was foiled by his sudden and vicious backward kick which sent me flying down several treads and into an arrow-slit embrasure on the spiral where I managed to halt my descent, suffering only a few minor bruises, a broken fingernail and severe blow to my dignity. Unfortunately, before I could recover and scramble up to the top, I heard the slam of the queen's bedchamber door and the scrabble of the lock-peg being inserted from the inside. Whether anyone liked it or not, Gloucester was intent on having his private audience with Catherine and there was every sign that it would not be a pleasant social visit.

However, there was one feature of these apartments at Hertford of which I hoped the duke might be unaware. A latrine, built into the buttress supporting this particular part of the castle, was accessible via a passage from both the queen's bedchamber and the adjoining ante-room. Quickly tiptoeing through this room I took up a listening post in the latrine passage, hoping the duke would not realise the existence of a connecting door behind a hanging in the bedchamber, a door which I knew was unlocked because I had left it so after Catherine's toilette earlier that morning. Frightened of being overheard, I fought to control my heavy breathing for my heart was pounding, partly from the headlong climb but also due to my agitation about her safety. Bitter experience had taught me that some men classed as noble and chivalrous definitely were not and I very much feared that Humphrey of Gloucester was one of them. I considered his treatment of Jacqueline of Hainault reprehensible and if he was behind the scurrilous stories circulating about Catherine, then I feared his attitude towards her was equally contemptuous.

Pressing my ear to the door, I had barely begun to gather the gist of their conversation when I heard Owen Tudor creep up behind me. As the man in charge of the dowager queen's security, he must have made himself aware of every nook and cranny of the castle and finding the queen's bedchamber door locked against him, had instantly taken my own route through the deserted ante-room. I felt a profound sense of relief. Now, if a confrontation should be necessary, at least there were two of us to challenge the power of the duke. Owen did not speak, but bent close to the door to listen. In the narrow passage, the smell from the latrine mimicked our suspicions about the unwholesome nature of Gloucester's business at Hertford.

'What overblown sense of your own importance leads you to think that I wish to speak with you alone, my lord duke?' Catherine's voice was flint-hard. Her Valois temper had flared, but not enough for her to lose control.

'What wild stretch of your fevered female imagination led you to believe that you could even consider marrying Edmund Beaufort?' countered Gloucester, his tone thin as sour wine.

'Nothing as wild as the urges that link you to Eleanor Cobham, I would wager. If you are looking for a misalliance, you need look no further than your own. By contrast, the Earl of Mortain and I make a perfect match. What possible objection could there be?'

I thought I could hear Catherine's voice coming gradually nearer, as if she was edging towards the door behind which Owen and I stood. It occurred to me that perhaps she was hoping to make her escape. The sound of hasty booted footsteps followed, then a scuffle and a sharp cry.

'One word, Madame – Beaufort. The king's mother – marry a Beaufort? Not while I protect the realm!'

'Let – me – go!' Catherine's high-pitched, staccato protest was followed by a grunt of effort and a sudden squeal of pain from the duke.

I took a sharp intake of breath and made to open the door, but Owen raised his hand in warning.

Catherine gave a little crow of triumph. 'Hah! That will teach you not to lay hands on the king's mother! I trust you will not be fit to pleasure your paramour for several days.'

My eyes rolled in surprise and I saw Owen's mouth twitch. Gloucester's response emerged in short, agonised bursts.

'French bitch! But be sure that I will give her pleasure – which is more than you will get – from any man – ever again. I shall – see to that.'

'Empty words, my lord. A bully's threat which carries no substance. I shall marry whoever I choose – be he Beaufort, Beaumont or Beauchamp – and you cannot prevent me.'

There was a purposeful rustle of skirts and the noise of the lock being released on the bedchamber door. The hinges creaked. 'You have my permission to leave, my lord duke.' Catherine spat out this dismissal with venom and I could imagine her holding the open door, proudly defying him.

Gloucester made no move that was audible, but his speech sounded steadier than before. 'Mark my words Madame, Dowager, I will make it not only impossible for you to marry Edmund Beaufort, but impossible for you to marry at all. Then how will you quench the lust you hoped to slake in Beaufort's bed?'

In the pause which followed, I held my breath, wondering what Catherine's reaction to this malicious taunt would be.

She spoke slowly and clearly, as if to an imbecile. 'Lust is your bedfellow, my lord of Gloucester. Take it away with you, if you can walk.'

There was another pause, then Humphrey of Gloucester laughed – a deep-throated, salacious, sneering laugh of a kind I had heard only once before, when I had been raped by butchers during the Paris Terror; and it had the same effect on me now as it had then, fear and disgust turning my blood to ice and my limbs to jelly. I grabbed the wall for support and felt rather than saw Owen Tudor turn and hurry back down the dark passage. Meanwhile, Gloucester's laughter ceased and his scorn-filled voice took over. 'I laugh, sister, at the thought of you and Henry together, for you are all heat and hunger, which a man of his cold humours could never have satisfied. But I can, believe me. So – when you are no longer able to contain the fire between your legs, I will come and quench it for you. You will welcome me then, because there will be no husband for you; no marriage contract; no union of flesh with flesh. When I have finished, even your son will not want to know you. You will be nothing and nobody. Your future is blank.'

Suddenly Owen Tudor was to be heard arriving on the scene

as if unaware of its ugly drift. 'Forgive the interruption, your grace. The Duke of Gloucester asked me to inform you of his arrival, but I see he has pre-empted my task.'

As she responded, I could hear the depth of Catherine's relief at Owen's presence. 'The duke is just leaving, Master Tudor,' she said. 'Please see that he and his men are offered refreshment before they depart. They are scarcely welcome, but I would not wish to be accused of being inhospitable.'

At last I heard Gloucester stamp off to the other side of the room. 'What took you so long, Master Tudor? If this is an example of the speed with which your servants obey instructions, Madame, your household must run like a fat duck.'

It was Catherine's turn to laugh, a bitter chuckle. 'I see what my dear lord, your brother, meant when he lamented your lack of judgement, Humphrey. Fortunately I have never had cause to question Master Tudor's. He arrived at precisely the right moment. Now it is your time to leave.'

However Gloucester could not leave without one last, veiled insinuation. 'Farewell, Madame. Until our next meeting, when I predict I shall have no complaints about the warmth of your welcome.'

Gingerly I pulled open the passage door and peered around the concealing tapestry, only to see the furred edge of Gloucester's short gown disappearing from view. Catherine took one step back into the room before the blood suddenly drained from her face, her knees buckled and Owen just managed to catch her before she crumpled to the floor.

23

Paradoxically, Catherine recovered consciousness filled with renewed energy. She remembered nothing of being caught by Owen and laid carefully on her bed, but vividly recalled every word of Gloucester's threats and promises, which fuelled a fierce anger in her against at the evil intentions of yet another man of power.

'I was just a girl when the Duke of Burgundy defiled me, Mette. I am no longer a girl but a queen and I will not allow the ugly ambitions of any man to ruin my chance of happiness, even if he is the Protector of England. I shall write to Edmund at once, of course, but I will also write to those members of the council who have shown me kindness in the past. Perhaps between us we can spike Humphrey's malice.'

Couriers went out that day with letters to Lord Edmund and Cardinal Beaufort, to the Earl of Warwick, the recently ennobled Lord Hungerford, the Archbishop of Canterbury and Bishop William Grey of London. But of them all, only the bishop wrote a reply that offered anything other than platitudes and excuses. Even the cardinal, who Catherine thought Edmund would have consulted and might therefore prove a powerful ally, wrote to say that as the appointed papal legate to Hungary and Bohemia, he was leading a crusade against heretic Hussites and would be out of the country for the foreseeable future. The reason for this general lack of support became clear when Edmund made his second visit to Hertford a fortnight later, full of youthful indignation.

'I regret to say that we have fallen badly foul of Gloucester's spite,' he told Catherine, pacing about her solar in boots mud-splashed from his furious ride up the rain-sodden highway from London. 'He has drafted an act for the next parliament which forbids you, as queen dowager, to marry without the permission of the king or, prior to his majority, of the council of regency, and it specifies that any man who flouts this ruling will forfeit his land tenure and be subject to a heavy fine. Apparently Gloucester demanded an increase of his powers as Protector, which the council unanimously refused to grant. You can imagine his fury. In compensation they have agreed to back this heinous Marriage Act in parliament, and it will therefore be passed on the nod.'

Edmund's cheeks were flushed with mortification as he knelt at her feet and took her hand between both of his. 'But we need not be defeated, Catherine – your grace. It is only the law of England which forbids us to marry. I hold my lands and title in Normandy and there has been no such act there. We could cross to Mortain and marry.'

Catherine regarded him fondly, letting him kiss her hand in an attempt at earnest persuasion, but she shook her head. 'No, Edmund. I would not be the cause of any danger to you or any loss of the rewards you have earned for your faithful service to the crown. This marriage would jeopardise your future and that of your family. They might seize your brother's estates here in England and then what would finance his ransom? And there is no knowing whether a similar law might be passed in Normandy, making us paupers and total outcasts. Besides, I cannot contemplate going to Normandy and leaving my son in England, only to find myself barred from returning.' Gently she withdrew her hand from his clasp. 'You generously gave me time to consider my answer to your proposal. I have considered it and my answer, regretfully, is no.'

Edmund tried further persuasion, even attempting to embrace her, but she was adamant in her refusal. 'There will be another wife for you, Edmund. Your future will be brighter without me.' She tried to laugh, but her throat caught on the sound.

Edmund rose reluctantly, clasped his hands together and bowed in submission. 'Very well, it seems I must admit defeat. But I want you to know that there will always be a special place for you in my heart, Catherine. You are the first love of my life. If I can ever be of service, you have only to send word. I beg you to consider me your knight to command.'

Edmund swung round to address Agnes and me where we sat at a discreet distance, silent chaperones. 'I charge you two ladies to bear witness to this promise and to call me to her grace's side if ever she should need me, whether she orders it or not.'

I bowed my head in mute acquiescence, speculating at the same time how soon it would be before Edmund Beaufort found himself an alternative wife. I judged him to be a resilient man whose emotions did not run unfathomably deep, and who would ride with the tide of the times, just as he would ride out of Hertford Castle with his honour and pride intact.

For several days Catherine was downcast, saying little and obviously waging a battle with her inner demons. Marriage to Edmund had offered the chance of a purposeful life as the wife of an up-and-coming peer of the realm and the mother of more children. Now this future looked impossible, for no man of substance would sacrifice his family lands or his own fortune, even to become the stepfather of the king. To rub salt in the wound, the day after Edmund's visit she received the king's response to her explanatory letter to him. It was written in his own childish script, but manifestly the content had been dictated.

—§§—

To Her Grace the Dowager Queen Catherine from her son Henry, King of England and France,

My beloved lady mother,

After receiving your last letter with news of the Count of Mortain's offer of marriage, I have thought and prayed long and hard. As you suggest, if God were to be gracious enough to grant you children from such a marriage I would, of course, be bound to welcome them as my brothers or sisters. From our brief acquaintance I have personally found Edmund Beaufort of sound and sober character, but I am advised by my governor, the Earl of Warwick, and other wise counsellors that it would not be appropriate for my mother to take a new husband while I am still of an age to be influenced by the affinities and opinions of a stepfather. Therefore I cannot in all conscience recommend this marriage to the Council of Regency.

I dearly hope that we may soon meet together and that, meanwhile, God will keep you in good health as He does me.

I am, as always, your loving son,
Henricus Rex

Written at Windsor this day Monday the nineteenth of March 1428.

—§§—

Catherine did not usually show me her letters from her son but this time, after she had read it, she handed it to me without speaking. When she saw that I had absorbed its contents, she said, 'So you were right, Mette. They do vet my correspondence. I cannot even trust the words of my own son because they are not his.' Her hand went to her forehead where she rubbed at the fine lines which had not been there a month ago. 'Is there no one in the world of men whom I can trust?'

I passed back the letter and gazed at her with troubled eyes. 'It seems not, Mademoiselle.'

Suddenly she reached out to open the small gold-banded chest in which she kept her most recent correspondence. 'Perhaps you are wrong. There is one man who may be less full of self-interest than the rest. Where is that letter from Bishop Grey?'

She riffled through the box and brought out a letter bearing a large official-looking seal. It was longer than most of the replies sent by the other council members from whom she had sought help and it took her several minutes to re-read it.

'Like the others, Bishop Grey does not offer public support but he does make a kind suggestion. See here, Mette,' she pointed to a passage of the close script, 'he says that if I wish to retreat somewhere peaceful and private, I might like to consider staying at his episcopal palace of Hadham and he goes on to describe it and the manor around it in glowing terms, saying that it is a place where he has always found tranquillity and release from the world's iniquities. It is not a grand palace apparently, but he believes I could use it in conjunction with Hertford Castle as somewhere I might stay privately and discreetly, away from what he calls "the prying eyes of the court".' She paused, eyebrows raised. 'It might be an escape from castle walls at least. What do you think, Mette?'

'Like you, I am intrigued, Mademoiselle. Why do you not send Master Tudor to take a look at this manor and report his impressions?'

Catherine compressed her lips, considering this suggestion; then she flashed me a rather mischievous grin. 'I have a better idea,' she said. 'Hadham is less than ten miles from Hertford. It would be a pleasant ride. I think I will accompany Master Tudor so that I can judge for myself. And I would be glad if you would come with me, Mette, for two views are always better than one.'

I was pleased to see a bit of the old sparkle reignite in her eyes. 'I would be delighted to accompany you, Mademoiselle. When would you like to go?'

'As soon as the rain stops, Mette, and tell Master Tudor we will not require an escort. I want only companions I can trust, not those who might spy for others. Let us go incognito. You might ask Master Vintner if he would accompany you, for I know you find him good company. We could pretend to be two couples on a pilgrimage to the Shrine of St Edmund.'

I was pleased that Catherine approved of and trusted Geoffrey enough to include him in her secret expedition and although I knew he had pressing business calling him back to London, I found myself hoping that he would delay it long enough to join us. During the past few weeks, while he stayed at Hertford acquainting himself with the dowager queen's affairs, we had enjoyed each other's company, but we had not shared the light-hearted intimacy of the early days of our friendship. I wondered if he found the formality of the royal household rather daunting and hoped Catherine's spontaneous escapade might bring his cheerful good humour back to the surface.

'You realise, your grace, that we may find the manor house at Hadham quite uninhabitable,' said Owen as our foursome set out soon after dawn a few days later. 'We do not know how much use the bishop makes of it or whether he keeps servants there.'

Catherine's riposte rang out loudly in the crisp, frosty air. 'Firstly, Master Tudor, please do not address me as "your grace". We are supposed to be a pilgrim couple, remember. Catherine – or if you must be formal, Madame – would be more appropriate from now on. And secondly, this is supposed to be an adventure. It does not matter if the house is falling down. We will be back at Hertford before dark.'

Judging by her teasing tone, the awkwardness which had arisen between them after the broken stool episode was now forgotten, at least on her part. Owen, too, was relaxed enough to nod jauntily and raise his broad-brimmed pilgrim's hat. 'It shall be as you command . . . Madame Tudor. Perhaps I am permitted to say how fetching my goodwife looks today? That hood is quite the latest style!'

I had acquired suitable clothes for our disguises at a second-hand clothes stall in Hertford market and the hood I had found for Catherine was a mud-coloured homespun garment from the previous century, finished at the back with what I had been told was a liripipe, an extended tail tipped with a tuft of fur like that of a lion. Responding to Owen's mock flattery she pretended to simper girlishly, pulling it over her shoulder in one hand and twirling the tuft at him. 'Why thank you, kind sir. Do you not think it flatters the colour of my eyes?'

Unfortunately the whirling movement caught her mare's eye, causing her to shy in fright. Taken by surprise, Catherine's other hand lost its grip on the reins and she tipped sideways, grabbing desperately at the horse's mane to try and stay in the saddle, a movement which further spooked the skittish animal. Seeing her perilous position, Owen quickly kneed his horse in beside her and, putting his hands firmly on her rear, shoved her unceremoniously upright again. 'Take care, Madame,' he warned, catching up the reins and steadying the mare. 'You do not want to fall.'

Catherine had gone quite pink and flustered. Her skirt had flicked up and, seeing his gaze wandering to her exposed ankle, she swiftly adjusted it and arranged her grip on the reins. 'Thank you, Master Tudor. Once again, you come to my rescue. You are right, I do not want to fall. That will teach me not to be flippant.'

My steady little mare Genevieve had plodded on, unperturbed by the excitable behaviour of Catherine's palfrey, and I had noticed Owen's cheeks colour violently when his hands and eyes had made contact with parts of a lady's anatomy not usually made available to male appreciation. His embarrassment did not stop him fashioning a compliment, however.

'To liken your eyes to that sludge-coloured hood is not flippancy, it is sacrilege,' he declared roundly. 'They are to be compared to the blue of the Virgin's robe or the sea under a summer sun.'

His own brown-velvet eyes trapped hers in their gaze as he said this and I almost felt the bolt of recognition that seemed to flash between them, destroying in an instant their wall of

282

carefully constructed denial. I turned to look at Geoffrey riding beside me and I knew that he too had felt the force of that invisible thunderbolt. One of his bushy eyebrows had risen like a browsing caterpillar and he tested the air with an audible sniff. 'I would say that spring has suddenly sprung, would you not agree, Mette?'

I looked again at the couple riding ahead. There was nothing apparently different about them. They were silhouetted against a blazing dawn sky and studiously scanning the empty road ahead, but I noticed that their knees were now touching as they rode side by side.

I nodded in answer to Geoffrey's question. 'But there is also a saying that red sky in the morning carries a warning.'

He gave me a broad smile. 'Is that so? Well, I have the feeling that on this occasion it may not be heeded.'

We crossed the River Lea at Ware and for the rest of the journey followed a less-trodden trail along the secluded valley of the River Ash, through well-tended woodland and pastures already lush with fresh growth. Along the banks the attendant trees after which the river was named remained bare, but their branches were liberally speckled with crimson buds – latent promise of lush summer green. As the sun began to warm us, we rode in high spirits, enjoying the dappled shade and the starry clumps of primroses peeking through the grass. Birdsong filled the air and an occasional musical plop rose from the gurgling stream as a fish jumped or an otter dived. We skirted only one small village, dominated by its small timber-framed church and passed a few outlying farms, but otherwise there was little sign of human habitation. As the bishop had indicated, the valley of the Ash was a tranquil, serene place.

Our track approached the manor of Hadham between two

large strip fields, ploughed and sewn and already sprouting a haze of emerald shoots. Several men and women out hoeing the rows stopped work to stare at us and a couple of dogs rushed up barking, but were quickly called off. A scattered clutch of meagre one-roomed cottages with lath-fenced gardens were dotted along a path leading from these fields to a row of hedged orchards and, on higher ground, a stretch of common land where a herd of goats, bells jangling on their collars, could be seen browsing the whin. On the edge of the village we passed a sturdy water-mill with a large wheel straddling a leet cut to bypass a fast-moving stretch of the river but, obviously, the miller had nothing to grind that day; the wheel was still and the leet was dry. Chickens pecking in the road squawked and fluttered out of our way, scuttling across the village green as we admired an unexpectedly handsome flint-stone church with a crenellated bell-tower and an extensive churchyard. Beyond it, through a row of bare trees, we had our first sight of the manor house.

'Oh look, Mette, it is pretty!' Catherine turned in the saddle to smile at me.

Because it was one of their bishop's residences, it was called Hadham Palace by the diocese of London, but it was hardly of a size even to be called a mansion. Boasting only two stories and a floor of dormered attics, it surrounded three sides of a stone-flagged courtyard and was large enough to accommodate the bishop's chosen hunting companions, but definitely not large enough for his episcopal entourage. Perhaps that was why Bishop Grey had recommended it as a place of retreat. It was built on a framework of ancient-grained oak beams, filled in partly with flintstones and mortar and partly with mellow red bricks baked from local clay and laid in a miscellany of criss-cross patterns as if each mason had chosen one of his own. It gave the building a picturesque, quirky appearance that was endearing rather than stylish, presenting an impression that it had grown organically out of its surroundings. A series of small, leaded casements glinted in the upper dormers above the grander, mullioned windows on the two lower floors and the steep roofs were covered with mossy red tiles. A moat licked at the foundations of a brick wall surrounding the bailey, but both were probably a defence against the incursion of wildlife rather than any human foe, for the house was set in the bishop's extensive hunting park, where small herds of roe and fallow deer could be seen fleeing through the trees, away from the sound of our horses' hooves.

A drawbridge over the moat led us to confront a lowered portcullis, but again this was a defence against browsing animals more than people for it was quickly raised when Owen called out at the gatehouse and we trotted unchallenged into the court beyond. It occurred to me that the bishop must have warned his staff that the queen dowager's representatives might make a visit because a man in livery came out to meet us and said he was the bishop's seneschal. He looked a trifle puzzled by our unprepossessing garb, but he made no comment. Perhaps he assumed it was part of a Lenten vow. Owen did not engage him in conversation, but merely requested that we be given refreshments and allowed to wander at will around the house and grounds, requests that were readily granted.

There was no great hall with dais and screen at Hadham Manor, but there was a large central chamber with a substantial fireplace which served the same purpose, as a place for meeting and feasting, and from which a carved oak staircase led up to a long, windowed gallery linking the upper floors of the two accommodation wings. A hunting lodge would not have been used during Lent, especially by a bishop, and so all the bedchambers were dusty and musty, but there were sufficient of them to house the number of people Catherine would bring with her if she chose to come. The bishop's own suite of chambers, filling the ground floor of one of the wings, were all spacious and equipped with decorative stone fireplaces and highly polished furniture, including an imposing bed whose crimson tester was emblazoned with the crossed swords of the diocese of London.

'If I came here, I would bring some of my own fittings,' said Catherine, frowning. 'I am not sure I could sleep beneath the bishop's arms.'

Before we set off to inspect the domestic buildings, a meal was served to us in the central chamber by a pair of cheerful lads who looked very similar to the two who had taken the reins of our horses on our arrival. Rather mischievously, I asked one of them if they had also cooked the meal but he replied quite seriously that he had only chopped the vegetables for the pottage and that there was a cook in charge of roasting the fat tench that was also placed before us. I wondered what such a skilled cook did when the manor was unused for weeks on end, but by the time we ventured outside to the kitchens the fire had been banked up and there was no one there. Hadham Manor preserved an aura of sustained mystery, as if a magical interlude had been prepared by invisible hands especially for us.

Nor did further exploration burst this marvellous bubble, for when we had toured the kennel and the mews, also empty, and the stables which contained only our four horses and a couple more for the use of the seneschal, he came to suggest that we should take a walk through the gardens down to the river gate which he would open for us.

'When he is here my lord bishop goes daily to the river to

pray, your grace,' the man explained to Catherine. 'He says that is where he feels closest to God.'

The gardens were tidy, but lying mostly fallow, waiting for spring-sown seeds to sprout in freshly dug beds. As we strolled towards the river, we came across a series of fish-ponds which must have been the source of the main element of our excellent meal and there was an extensive herb garden which would prove interesting in a few more weeks when some of the frost-shrivelled plants had sent up shoots to reveal their identities. The more we wandered through the Hadham policies, the more I hoped that Catherine would opt to take up the bishop's offer. The place seemed to be working a spell on me. It struck me as a kind of Eden; a paradise where every Adam and Eve might live in fruitful harmony with the rest of creation. I yearned to see the park and gardens in the full panoply of their summer greenery.

When we came to the river this wish grew ever stronger. Large, gnarled willows leaned over sloping banks, dipping their bare branches into a broad pool above the mill where huge wooden sluice gates controlled the rush of water needed to turn the wheel. On the near side of this pool was an island, separated from the bank by a reed-fringed backwater spanned by an arched footbridge. It was a place that invited exploration and within minutes Catherine and Owen had crossed the bridge and disappeared into the osier tangle that grew around a coppice of hazel trees at its centre. Geoffrey and I watched them go and hung back, lingering on the grassy bank exchanging speculative glances. A pair of swans with a family of cygnets fossicked among the reeds for food and a few moorhens bobbed about on the calm water of the pool, but there was no sign of any other human life.

'This place works a kind of magic,' I remarked, lifting my

face to the warm sun. 'I can feel it pulling me in, but is it real or is it one of those fairy places that will vanish once it has us in its thrall?'

I could feel Geoffrey standing close behind me and he laid his hand gently on my shoulder. 'There are two kinds of magic,' he said, 'the good old-fashioned kind that comes from a pure, warm heart and the evil kind that is conjured by sorcerers from darkness. But I can feel no darkness here, can you, Mette?'

I turned within the shelter of his arm and his dear, kind face was very close to mine. 'No,' I said with a smile. 'I feel only lightness of heart.'

'I am glad, for I feel the same.'

His kiss was gentle, but there was passion in it that demanded a response and, to my surprise, I gave it readily. I had not been kissed with ardour since my husband Jean-Michel had disappeared from my life before the Battle of Agincourt and twelve years of unrecognised need suddenly surged through me like the spring sap rising all around us. I was forty-one and by now should surely have shrivelled with the frost of winter, but it seemed that, like the plants in the manor herb garden, I had not. Geoffrey's unexpected desire awakened in me a desire I had thought belonged only to the young.

Breathless, I drew back and stared at him, eyes full of unspoken questions of the kind not usually asked by matrons with plump cheeks and wimples.

He nodded. 'Oh yes. That Hadham magic you spoke of is working everywhere.' He stroked the side of my face with the back of his hand and his own face creased in a smile. 'I always knew there was a wild creature hiding behind that practical façade of yours, Mette. I cannot tell you how much I want to pull off that coif and run my fingers through your hair.'

I found myself laughing – or giggling might be a more accurate word for it, however undignified it sounds. 'You would find many streaks of silver, I am afraid.'

'Not would, Mette, will, if they be there at all. This kind of magic must be caught and treasured, particularly if it strikes in our autumn years. Soon, very soon, we will find a time and place and we will love each other until the winter turns our heads frosty white.' He took my hand, tucked it into the crook of his arm and we walked on together towards the footbridge. 'Do you think we dare venture over into youth's playground? Or might we find that they are behaving even less discreetly than we are and wish we had not interrupted?'

My mind was reeling from his frank expressions of love and need and I was at a loss for words to respond, so I pushed the thought of future possibilities away to concentrate on the present. 'I – I am not sure. Catherine has been headstrong in the past, but she is not wanton; far from it. The convent still guides her moral path. However I think I would rather not risk it.'

We turned away upstream towards the sluice, where we watched the water swirl and tumble over the lip into the pool in poignant imitation of my turbulent emotions.

24

Geoffrey was a diplomat in everything he did. I did not have to tell him that I was reticent about making our new intimacy public; he remained affable and courteous, as always, but managed to avoid appearing any more friendly towards me in front of the others than he had before, for which I was grateful. On the other hand, Catherine and Owen wandered back over the bridge looking awkward and self-conscious. I smiled inwardly, thinking that only young lovers in the first throes of discovered passion could imagine that the glow of their new-found ardour was not obvious to all. Theirs burned like a forest fire. I concluded that Geoffrey and I had no need to hide our own newfound feelings for each other because Owen and Catherine would not have noticed if Cupid's darts had been protruding from our foreheads, they were too enraptured by each other.

'I would not be surprised now if Catherine suggested that we stay here overnight,' I remarked to Geoffrey as we followed them back through the garden, trying not to laugh out loud as they made heroic efforts not to let their hands come into contact and failed miserably on several occasions. Nervous though I was of this rapidly developing romance, I had to admit that viewed dispassionately and without prejudice they made a well-matched couple for he had an archer's swift, light step and she walked with the confidence of a queen. They were both slim-hipped and lissom and held themselves erect with heads high on long, supple necks. Even in their drab, ill-fitting disguises they paraded like high-bred race-horses.

'I thought you said she was not wanton,' murmured Geoffrey, careful to ensure they did not hear.

'Nor is she,' I hissed back. 'But this place has a way of making one light-minded. You said you had felt it yourself.'

He cocked an eyebrow at me. 'I felt a lightness of heart rather than mind, but that was down to you, not the location.'

I found myself blushing, but pretended it was indignation. 'Well Catherine is sensitive to atmosphere even if you are not, and I believe Hadham will have exerted enough influence to make her want more of what she has found here.'

'And I believe it is the handsome Owen who is the main attraction and Hadham only a means to an end. But we shall see.'

He proved the more prescient, for Catherine made no mention of staying at the manor. Instead she asked the seneschal if he thought there was time for her to visit the church before leaving to ride back to Hertford. 'We do not want to be caught by the dusk but I would like to pray for a while in that beautiful church.'

The seneschal bowed. 'By all means, my lady.' He had obviously decided that whoever she was, she was no common female, regardless of her care-worn garb. 'It wants three hours until sunset. The church is always open but the priest is often in the fields at this time of day. If you like, I will go and find him.'

'That will not be necessary, thank you,' she replied, 'but

some light refreshment before we leave would be very welcome.'

We walked to the church of St Andrew, an unusually splendid place of worship for a small out-of-the-way manor, because after it had been selected by an early bishop of London as a retreat, he needed somewhere worthy of his standing in which to pray. Over the years generous donations to that end had been made by wealthy Londoners in return for indulgences to offset their sins. Many a Cheapside merchant must have hoped to reach heaven by contributing to the raising of St Andrew's flint-stone walls.

Catherine, with her ingrained reverence for the Church, was delighted by the wide nave with its fine arched bays and the soaring chancel with its beautiful stained glass east window and she went immediately to kneel at the bishop's prie dieu near the altar, but the rest of us were more drawn to the graphic paintings on the plastered walls of the side aisles. In the right-hand aisle brightly coloured pictures displayed the glories of paradise and the heavenly rewards offered to the righteous and in the left a dramatic mural in black, browns and reds showed the terrors of hell and the evil faces of the devil and his demons tormenting wrongdoers for all eternity. I lingered for some time over a crude depiction of an adulterous woman being torn from her lover's arms and dragged down to the flames by an ugly winged imp and I wondered what afterlife tortures awaited a middle-aged widow contemplating extramarital fleshly pleasures with a kindly widower.

'Queen Catherine has the better idea,' said Geoffrey quietly in my ear. 'She turns her back on such grim warnings and her face towards Christ's consolation.'

His humanity made me smile. 'That is because she believes the grim warnings,' I said, 'whereas I have my doubts.'

'Ah.' In the fold of my skirt his hand found mine and squeezed it. 'Then we can look forward to sharing heavenly doubts as well as earthly delights.'

The ride back to Hertford was a cheerful one for we were buoyed up by our own private exhilarations and so all the way along the quiet bank of the Ash we sang carols lustily, led by Owen whose strong tenor kept up a seemingly unending supply of verses while Catherine's light treble voice, my lower alto and Geoffrey's rousing baritone made quite a tuneful chorus.

Catherine rode beside me, not wishing to appear too intimate with Owen – or at least I assumed that was the reason. However when we were far enough ahead of the men to converse without being overheard she abruptly shattered my complacent belief that the new understanding between me and Geoffrey was still our secret.

'I saw you kissing Master Vintner, Mette,' she said suddenly. 'Is there something I should know?'

I hesitated, collecting my thoughts enough to summon an evasive reply. 'I might ask you the same question, Mademoiselle. We did not venture over the footbridge at the river for fear of interrupting something between you and Master Tudor.'

'Is that so?' She cast me a sidelong look. 'But I asked the question first. I thought you and Master Vintner were just friends.'

'We are friends,' I said, 'and have been so for some years as you know, albeit for some time at a distance. I wonder though whether a queen and a servant can even be friends, let alone anything more.'

She coloured violently under her drab hood, protesting, 'You and I are friends!'

'Yes we are, but not without attracting our share of slur and censure – and ours is only a friendship, not a love affair. You must be very careful, Mademoiselle.'

She would have flared up then, were it not for the two men riding a few yards behind us. As it was she set her jaw in a stubborn line and spoke through gritted teeth. 'We will talk about this later. I should not have touched on the subject of your kiss. I am sorry.'

I sought to lighten the mood with a mischievous smile. 'But I am not sorry – for the kiss I mean. In fact, if you want the truth, I rather enjoyed it.'

Her expression softened and she returned my smile. 'Did you, Mette? Did you indeed? Well, well.'

No more was said on the subject because at this point we had to manoeuvre into single file in order to negotiate an over-hanging tree and we rode the rest of the way in close formation. However I was grateful that she did not take long to seek an opportunity to continue the conversation because whatever opinions she held about my relationship with Geoffrey it was at least unexceptional, whereas I feared that an affair between the queen mother and a Welsh squire would attract the wrath of the world and, more seriously, its vengeance.

After Mass the following day, she asked me to bring our cloaks for warmth and steered me through the privy garden to the turf-seat in the centre, a bank of grass under an arch of rose briars affording a clear view of anyone approaching for twenty yards all around. Luckily the grass was dry and once we had settled ourselves, Catherine launched straight into the topic on both our minds.

'When I told you that I saw you kiss Master Vintner, I did not mean you to think that I disapproved, Mette,' she said. 'In fact I am glad if there is love between you, for you have been sadly lonely for too many years.'

'No more lonely than you, Mademoiselle. But nothing is settled between me and Geoffrey Vintner. I am far more concerned about what may have occurred between you and Master Tudor.'

She avoided my gaze, restless fingers smoothing the dagging on the sleeve of her gown. 'What do you imagine may have occurred, Mette?'

I took a deep breath. 'Let me put it this way. I imagine that a log shifted on sleeping embers and sparks flew, but I do not believe that any flames have leaped yet.'

Catherine's head remained down but after a short pause, a gurgling laugh rose in her throat. 'My goodness, Mette, how long did it take you to come up with that metaphor?'

Beguiled by her mirth I let my guard drop. 'Actually it was Geoffrey who came up with it. I thought it summed up the situation perfectly.'

Steely blue eyes were suddenly drilling into mine. 'You discussed my affairs with Master Vintner?'

There was no longer any point in being cautious. 'Of course I did, Mademoiselle. He is your treasurer and the only lawyer you can trust to give you accurate advice and not carry information straight to the council of regency.'

'But I have not given you permission to discuss my affairs with anyone! How do I know you are not carrying tales to the council? Someone is.'

I was flabbergasted. It had never occurred to me that she might accuse me of treachery. 'You honoured me yesterday by

295

asking for my company on a secret mission to visit Hadham and today you suggest I might be a spy for the council! There is no logic in that, Mademoiselle.'

Catherine shook her head as if to clear it and laid a hand on my arm. 'You are right. I am sorry, Mette. Of course you would not betray me, but however close you are to Master Vintner I would still rather you two had not discussed my relationship with Owen Tudor.'

'Is there a relationship with Owen Tudor? That is what I am anxious to know.'

'No, there is not. But yesterday he declared his love for me, a love which he says he has felt since the first time he played the harp for us in the Vallon Vert. That is eight years ago, Mette! He says he has loved me for all that time and I never knew.'

She turned to face me then, shifting on the grassy bank to take both my hands in hers, instantly establishing an intimacy between us that had not been there before. In my eyes she had hardly changed from the naïve thirteen-year-old girl who had been brought from her convent to the French court to be groomed as a bride for King Henry of England; luminously beautiful and educated in everything except how to handle the opposite sex. I thought by now she might have learned this art, but from what followed I realised she had not.

'Oh, Mette, I have been so blind. Perhaps I should have realised, but truly I did not. Not until I felt his hands on me, pushing me back into the saddle when I nearly fell. It seems ridiculous but it was like lightening striking through my body. Suddenly I knew that I matter to him: me – Catherine – I matter. He was not saving Queen Catherine, or the king's mother, or the highest lady in the land whom he is duty-bound to serve, but a woman he really cares about. I have never felt special to someone before, just for being me – not with Henry, not with Edmund and certainly not with that odious Guy de Mussy who turned out to be Burgundy's lackey. When Owen kissed me on the island later, I thought my body would melt!' She looked rapturous and distressed both at the same time and my heart went out to her. 'What should I do, Mette? It is such a wonderful, overwhelming feeling and I just want it to go on for ever. Tell me why I should deny myself this happiness when everything else that made me happy has been taken from me?'

Humphrey of Gloucester can have had no idea what a maelstrom he would create when he denied Catherine the chance to marry Edmund Beaufort. Had that union gone ahead, I thought, this situation would never have arisen because Catherine would have been content to follow her allotted path, making a marriage among her own kind which would doubtless have brought her all the satisfaction of rank and family that she had always been led to expect. And Owen Tudor would have remained silently in the shadows, loyally quelling his pangs of unrequited love as he had already done for so long. Now we were in unknown territory; passions had been unleashed that might have remained dormant and benign and the future looked uncertain and precarious, not just for Catherine but for all of us who loved and served her.

I shook my head, smiling ruefully. 'Oh, Mademoiselle! And you base all this on one shove and a few kisses?'

There were tears in her eyes now and I wanted to hug her. She was twenty-seven, but what did she know of love and affection?

'Yes, Mette, yes I do. And I know it is foolish. He wants me, Mette, just me – to be with me wherever and whenever he can. He does not expect anything from me. He does not ask for titles or honours or high office. He does not even mind if no one ever knows that we love each other!'

I did hug her then, like the daughter she practically was. All her life she had done what she was told, sometimes even when she was told to do it by evil men with wickedly selfish motives, and this was the first time I had seen her desperate to do something that the world and the Church and the law forbade her to do and do it just because it would make her happy. I hugged her because I desperately wanted her to be happy and yet I did not see how that happiness could ever come to be.

I had reckoned without her strong will and fierce determination. When we parted the tears had vanished. She had become practical. 'Now we have to devise a way to achieve this. Do you have any suggestions?'

I blinked, taken aback, then I blurted out, 'But it is impossible surely! How can you keep a liaison like that secret?'

Catherine scowled and shook her head. 'Oh no, Mette, not a liaison; I am going to marry Owen.'

'Marry him!' My exclamation came out like a squawk. 'You cannot! What about the Marriage Act?'

She snapped her fingers derisively. 'The Marriage Act – pah! They sent me a copy of that stupid act to frighten me. So I read it very carefully and there is one thing they forgot. No one with land and a title will marry me because of the forfeits, but Owen does not have any land or title to lose so he does not care. We need to find a trustworthy priest to marry us but

298

otherwise we will not tell anyone. The marriage will just be between us and God. That is all that matters.'

'All that matters to you, Mademoiselle, but to the rest of the world it will still look like a liaison. Even if the council do not find a way to end it, you will be branded a harlot and they will stop you seeing the king. And do not forget that Owen is Welsh. They may even declare the relationship treasonous. You would be risking Owen's life and even perhaps your own!'

'Only if they find out and they will not. We will disappear to Hadham and live there in secret. I will join the king for the Easter celebrations as planned and I will announce that afterwards I am going into retreat. That is what council members like the Duke of Gloucester want, is it not? – that I should disappear from the political scene. They do not care where or how, as long as I do not get in their way.'

'But can you disappear in Hadham? It is off the beaten track, that is true, but it is not in the wilderness. What if someone comes visiting – like the Bishop of London for instance? It is his manor after all.'

Catherine shrugged. 'Let him come. Let anyone come. Owen is my master of the wardrobe. That was a public appointment. Only my closest friends will know the truth. I can make this work, Mette, I know I can.'

'And what does Master Tudor say to this plan? Does he know he may be risking a charge of treason?'

She gave me a sheepish look. 'Well no, we have not discussed the future in that sort of detail. But he says he would die for me.' A note of defiance crept into her voice.

I snorted derisively. 'When a man says he would die for a

woman he generally does not mean he would literally give his life for her, Mademoiselle. It is a form of speech.'

'Not when Owen says it. He gave me his oath of fealty on his knees, just as a subject does to his king. He is my vassal in life and limb. Truly, Mette; you can ask him if you like. Better still, you can be there when I ask him to marry me and you can warn him he will be risking his life. He will not care, you will see.'

'I hesitate to suggest this, but would it not be better if Master Vintner were involved? He is a lawyer. At least he could give you his expert opinion on the legality of such a marriage.'

Catherine stood up and shook herself. 'Brr! I am getting cold sitting here and I want to go riding before dinner. I will think about your suggestion, Mette, and let you know my decision.'

Automatically I rose too. You did not sit when the queen stood, even when you had just hugged her like a mother. 'Do not leave it too long if you wish to take advantage of Master Vintner's legal advice, Mademoiselle. I happen to know that he has pressing business in London and will return there very soon.'

She shot me a sharp glance. 'Anyone's pressing business in law gives me particular cause for concern. The courts sit at Westminster, only a step away from where the council meets. But you tell me Master Vintner is loyal and I have to believe you. Come to me after my ride, Mette, while I prepare for dinner. We will talk again then.'

I would have liked to speak privately with Owen Tudor before that but there was no opportunity. Hitherto I had thought nothing of the fact that he invariably accompanied Catherine on her morning rides, but now I realised that those embers I had borrowed from Geoffrey's poetic analogy had been regularly stoked by these daily excursions and after Lord Edmund's suit failed had probably given Owen the courage to make his dramatic declaration. I dearly hoped that all the other inhabitants of Hertford Castle were equally unaware of where those rides had been leading, because if Catherine was serious about wanting her incongruous love-match to be kept secret, such mass ignorance would be essential.

25

I never admired Owen Tudor so much as I did that evening in the queen's presence chamber. The previous day, when he had declared his love for Catherine, he cannot have imagined being subjected to the kind of interrogation that Geoffrey put him through twenty-four hours later, yet he sat patient and still on his cushioned stool and laid his soul bare for us to scrutinise. When she agreed that Geoffrey should be present, I am sure Catherine cannot have expected him to probe quite as candidly as he did.

He started with his usual courtesy. 'With the permission of her grace I would like to ask you a few questions, Master Tudor. I assure you on my oath as a lawyer that nothing said within these walls will be repeated outside them.'

Catherine broke in hurriedly and with an apologetic look. 'They know what took place between us yesterday, Owen, but they are both on our side.'

The squire gave her a smile which spoke more eloquently than his words. 'I know that Madame Lanière will always be on your side, my queen, and I also know that she and Master Vintner are good friends. If you both trust him then I can trust him.'

Geoffrey nodded briskly, as if he had expected no less. 'First of all then perhaps you would tell us exactly what did take place between you and Queen Catherine yesterday?'

Preamble over – cut to the chase, I thought. I had not seen this professional side of my lawyer friend before.

Owen fielded a miniscule sign of assent from Catherine before saying simply, 'I told the queen that I loved her. That I have loved her ever since I first saw her in the light of the campfire at Melun.'

I was greatly affected by the way he spoke these words directly to Catherine, holding her gaze with his expressive brown eyes, as if what he was saying was meant only for her.

However, Geoffrey was not bamboozled by eloquent glances. 'Yet she was already married then and your queen. Now she is the mother of the king. What gave you the impression that her grace would even hear such a declaration from a servant of her household? Did it not occur to you that it was a trea-sonous insolence?'

Owen tore his eyes from Catherine's face and turned them indignantly on Geoffrey. 'Of course it occurred to me, which is why I did not say anything for nearly eight years. But suddenly the time seemed right.'

'Or, put it another way, Master Tudor. Suddenly you took advantage of a great lady in a state of distress over the terms of the Marriage Act. You thought you would strike while her guard was down.'

'No. NO!' For a moment Owen lost his calm but quickly regained it. 'I know nothing of a Marriage Act. My declaration was made on an impulse inspired by the beauty around us, the privacy and the intense emotion of the moment. Nothing else in the world concerned me. I wanted to show my queen that she was not unloved and unwanted as she seemed to think she was.' Once again he turned to look at Catherine and she held his gaze. 'I want to make her happy, that is all. Bring some peace and well-being to her heart to give her strength.'

'Or else you want to exploit her vulnerability to your own advantage.'

There was nothing affable about Geoffrey now, but Owen did not rise to his taunt. Instead he snatched off his soft chaperon and bowed his head, squashing the hat between his tense fingers. 'My queen is far above me and beyond me, I know that. She has the power of patronage, but I ask for no reward other than to see her smile as she used to in the valley camp when she first married the great King Henry.' He raised his head and there was anguish in his eyes. 'She deserves to be happy again, Master Vintner. You must agree with me surely.'

'We do not measure our lives in happiness, Master Tudor,' Geoffrey said sternly, 'even though we may like to. Her grace is the mother of the king, with a responsibility to set him an example. How would being loved by a squire of her household appear in the eyes of her son? Did you think of that when you made your selfish declaration?'

Catherine could stay silent no longer. 'Please, Master Vintner, stop! You are making something beautiful sound ugly and horrible. We are not here to put Owen on trial.'

I was relieved to see that Geoffrey was instantly contrite. 'I am sorry, your grace, but I consider it important to be sure that Master Tudor's intentions are good.' He spread his hands apologetically and sat back in his chair. 'Now I think we have established that.'

Catherine's copy of the vexatious Marriage Act lay on the table beside her. She picked it up and fiddled nervously with the official red ribbon that tied the scrolled document. In the tense pause that followed, colour gradually flooded her cheeks as she struggled for the right words. 'You cannot have seen this, Owen. It is the law which was passed by Parliament regarding my future. It is not very long. Would you read it please?'

He made no move to take the document from her. 'Regrettably my Latin is not good enough to read a legal document, Madame. Perhaps Master Vintner would list the main points for me.'

Owen listened intently to Geoffrey's expert summary of the act's stringent restrictions on the dowager queen's re-marriage. When it was finished, the squire took a deep breath and exhaled audibly, 'By all God's Holy Angels, there is not much joy in that!' His gaze swept the ceiling and he appeared to control his anger with great difficulty. 'Whoever was responsible for such malice certainly did not want you to be happy, my queen!'

His fervour drew a fond smile from Catherine. 'Just so, but you had to know what was in it because of what I am going to ask of you.' She placed the offensive act back on the table and paused, clasping her hands tightly together, steadying herself for what was to follow: 'This is not something I would normally ask in front of witnesses, but I think the circumstances require that I do.'

To the astonishment of all of us and to Owen's wonderment, she rose from her chair and sank gracefully to her knees before him. 'Yesterday, to my great joy, you told me you loved me. Then you knelt at my feet and gave me your oath of fealty. Now it is my turn. But I am a woman; honour and fealty are not enough for me if I am to have the happiness of returning your love. I need the blessing of the Church and the affirmation of the law. So, in full knowledge of what you have just heard and in the presence of witnesses, I am asking you, Owen Tudor, for love of me, if you will marry me.'

For the duration of a twenty heartbeats nobody said a word. Catherine looked steadily up at Owen, who returned her gaze with a bemused expression that was half awe and half disbelief. Gradually his hat with its jaunty green peacock's feather slipped from his fingers and fell to the floor.

Geoffrey cleared his throat. 'Before you answer, Master Tudor, I feel duty bound to remind you that in addition to the terms of the Marriage Act, there is the small matter of the ban on any marriage between an English citizen and a Welsh one and the possibility that marriage to the mother of the king may also be considered treasonous. You may wish to take time to consider your answer.'

Without breaking eye-contact with Catherine, Owen slid from his stool to his knees and took her hands in his. 'I do not need any time to consider. I would marry you if I was England's greatest earl, held half the kingdom and owned a chest full of gold, but all I have to offer is my harp and my bow. They are yours to command, my queen, and so am I. My answer is yes.'

Kneeling close together as they were, it only took moments for their arms to entwine like ivy round a tree trunk and their lips to join with such heedless passion that Geoffrey and I felt obliged to turn away. I returned the slow wink he gave me with a twitch of my lips and then, when reality eventually re-asserted its hold on the lovers, it was Geoffrey who found the right words.

'I hereby bear witness that this is a bargain well sealed! And now, with God's help, we must find a trustworthy priest who will perform the ceremony.'

Owen rose nimbly to his feet and helped Catherine to hers, gently kissing her hand before guiding her back to her chair. 'I do not think that will be easy, Master Vintner,' he said, resuming his own seat.

'There is Maître Boyers, my confessor,' Catherine suggested, her cheeks still flushed. 'He has served me loyally for many years.'

'And been well rewarded for it, Mademoiselle,' I pointed out. 'But he was appointed by the late king and is a court chaplain. If you want this to be a secret marriage, then perhaps you should take your vows before a priest who does not know either of you and use only your baptismal names.'

Catherine shifted her gaze from me to Geoffrey. 'Would that be legal, Master Vintner?'

He nodded. 'It would be legal and upheld by Rome, but it might not be accepted by the lords temporal and spiritual.'

'You mean the bishops and barons?' Catherine shrugged. 'Well that is no matter, as long as it is good and true in the sight of God and my loyal friends. As for the restriction on marriages between English and Welsh, I have never been declared an English citizen even though I married the English king. That law would not apply to a Welshman and a Frenchwoman, would it?'

Geoffrey inclined his head, giving the question due consideration. 'I do not see how it could, Madame,' he acknowledged.

'Then why should we not be married at Hadham?' she asked, taking us all by surprise once more. 'The seneschal said there was a priest but we did not meet him. So if I was to ask the bishop if I could stay at his manor anonymously and bring my own household and servants, there would be no one else there who knew who we were. We could be married just like any other inhabitant of Hadham by the local priest at that beautiful church.'

'You would ask the bishop to remove his own servants, including the seneschal?' It was Owen who spoke. 'Supposing that meant they were suddenly without a livelihood, my queen? We would not wish to be the cause of hardship to others.'

Such a consideration had clearly not occurred to Catherine, who looked slightly shocked. 'Oh! No. No, of course we would not. But the bishop is bound to be among the king's Easter guests at Windsor and I will make sure that he undertakes to find new positions for his servants.'

My gaze wandered from Owen to Catherine and back again. The light of love still glowed in his deep-brown eyes, but his jaw was set firm and I realised that, despite the difference in rank, theirs would not be a one-sided partnership.

26

Catherine and her entourage had travelled to Windsor in good time for Easter. In the shelter of the castle's high walls, the extensive herb garden in the lower ward already showed abundant spring growth and from the rows of newly planted seedlings it was evident that the king's gardeners and herbalists had been busy. Agnes and I had walked down the hill from St George's Hall, drawn outside partly by the warm April sunshine and partly to see if there were any camomile leaves available to lighten Catherine's winter-darkened hair. Now that she had abandoned the widow's barbe and wimple, her pale-gold tresses were once more on show under the nets and veils of her favoured headdresses and it pleased her that few English ladies could display hair of such a light colour. The Lenten days remaining, before the court displayed its best finery at the big Easter Sunday celebrations, left enough time for the welcome sunshine and some camomile rinses to lighten it even further.

As we entered the garden precincts, Agnes nudged me and pointed to the far end where a multi-coloured carpet of saffron crocus was flowering under a tree. Several kneeling gardeners were harvesting the full-blown blooms for their precious deep yellow stamens and nearby stood two women, one dressed in an elaborate fur-trimmed gown and eye-catching jewels and the other, who I recognised instantly, a plainly clad individual wearing a bleached apron and coif and carrying a basket.

Agnes turned to me, wide-eyed. 'Is that not Eleanor Cobham? Blessed Marie, all those gems sparkle enough to blind you!'

I squinted in the bright sunshine. 'You are right, it is Eleanor and she is definitely not hiding her light under a bushel. The other is Margery Jourdemayne,' I said. 'You remember, she was the assistant of the midwife at the king's birth. They seem to have their heads together over something.'

'As they did on that occasion as I recall – over some herbal concoction to ease the delivery. They have seen us so we are bound to approach.' Agnes acknowledged the languid beckoning finger aimed in our direction by Eleanor. 'We must remember that she is the Duchess of Gloucester now. A well-bent knee is required, Mette, or we may find ourselves badly out of her newly graced favour!'

'Mademoiselle de Blagny and Madame Lanière,' acknowledged Eleanor as we performed the necessary obeisance. She made no move to re-acquaint us with her low-born companion. 'If you are here, I take it that the queen mother has emerged from her retirement? I wonder why I have not yet seen her at court.'

I thought it prudent to leave the reply to Agnes since a knight's daughter outranks a baker's. 'Her grace arrived from Hertford only yesterday and dined privily with the king.'

'Privily?' queried Eleanor, elevating one of her fine dark eyebrows. 'I doubt that. The king is never without his tutors and counsellors.'

Agnes ignored this comment. 'Hence you would not yet have seen her, Madame. May I take this opportunity to congratulate you on your recent marriage? You must be happy to make a return to court yourself.'

As the Duke of Gloucester's mistress, Eleanor had been obliged to live for several years in relative obscurity, but since the new pope had invalidated Humphrey's marriage to Jacqueline of Hainault, he and Eleanor had been free to marry, an event which had been much disparaged behind their backs as a misalliance, but had satisfied court protocol. Any reference to the inglorious period of her enforced retirement must surely have riled the new duchess, but Eleanor showed no irritation since she had the gift of guile and her reappearance at Windsor for the king's Easter celebrations was beyond doubt her triumph.

'Oh I assure you that during a regal minority the throne is not the only seat of power and influence, Damoiselle. There are other courts and palaces to which the clever and ambitious flock.'

I could not resist putting in my pennyworth. 'Even at Hertford we heard that the Duke of Exeter was hardly cold in his grave before the masons moved in at Greenwich. His grace of Gloucester no doubt has extensive plans there, now that the palace is his.'

'It was sadly neglected by the old duke, but we intend to make it a centre of learning; a gathering place for intellectuals.' Eleanor stressed the collective pronoun. 'And I intend to extend my knowledge and cultivation of herbs, with the help of Mistress Jourdemayne here.'

Margery made a sketchy bob and smiled at me. 'I remember you well, Madame Lanière. You played a crucial role at the birth of the king.'

'As did you, Mistress Jourdemayne, and, God be thanked, his grace's health continues good.'

Eleanor did not allow attention to be diverted from her duke for long. 'As does the health of his kingdom under my lord's guidance,' she said. 'You will understand that my time is limited. I give you good day.'

With Margery Jourdemayne in tow and the heavy train of her gown rattling the pebbles of the path, she swept away. The gardeners turned to tug at their hoods as she passed; a salute she affected to ignore, maintaining a haughty expression that showed just how much she relished every ounce of the privilege her ambition had brought her. At twenty-one, she had achieved all that vanity could have hoped for.

'Our friend certainly learned a great deal from the Duchess of Hainault about playing the Grande Madame,' Agnes murmured under her breath, watching her go.

I responded with a grim smile, but my thoughts were on Eleanor's fascination with herbs, inherited from her Culpepper mother. I could not help wondering what kind of 'work' she and the even more skilled Margery Jourdemayne were engaged in together. I had always considered Eleanor to be shrewd and now that she was Duchess of Gloucester she was, more than ever, a force to be reckoned with. I hoped that while she was at Windsor, Catherine would manage to avoid seeing too much of the Gloucesters, for neither of them, it seemed to me, would make easy company for her.

Contact between them was of course unavoidable, and they were often together at court but never alone. On Easter Sunday, the day before we were due to leave, the royal party emerged from a glorious celebration Mass in the Windsor chapel with King Henry and his mother leading the procession out into bright spring sunshine, followed by the Duke and Duchess of Gloucester and the rest of the court. We were to walk up the hill for an Easter feast in St George's Hall and, knowing how much her son loved the sound of choral singing, Catherine had arranged for the St George's College choristers to reassemble in the Upper Ward to sing for the king beforehand – some light-hearted carols and motets specially chosen to be neither bawdy nor profane. However, as the procession approached the main keep, famously known as the Round Tower, the raucous noise of battle broke out as scores of knights, wearing French and English badges and yelling war-cries, came swarming from the base of the tower and around the dry ditch that surrounded it and began to stage a mock storming of the keep, orchestrated by the banging of drums and nackers simulating cannon-shots.

Initially the six-year-old king was terrified, glancing in alarm from his mother to his uncle, seeking reassurance that this was not some enemy force come to capture or kill him. Catherine, too, was fearful, clutching the little boy to her and casting about for the best place in which to take refuge. 'Merciful saints, are we under attack?' she cried. 'Gloucester, save the king!'

But the Duke of Gloucester was laughing and so was his duchess; laughing almost hysterically, as if the terror of the boy and his mother was the funniest thing they had seen in years. 'It is a surprise!' spluttered Gloucester, spreading his arms wide to show that he saw no reason to draw his sword or run for cover. 'An Easter surprise for my royal nephew! See, Henry, the English knights are storming the keep and will soon defeat the French garrison and take possession of the castle, just as your honoured father did so many times in Normandy and the Île de France before you were born.'

By now he had tugged the little king from his mother's skirts and flung his arm around the wide-eyed boy, guiding him to the low wall that guarded the steep drop into the ditch. 'Look, your grace, their swords are practice weapons like the ones they use for arms training and the bodies on the ground are only pretending to be dead. It is a play, a pageant staged for your entertainment. I thought you would enjoy it, Henry. Some of the "knights" are your friends, fellows who spar with you in the practice ground. Do you recognise them now?'

Henry gave a sheepish laugh. 'Oh yes. I thought it was a real fight.' He turned to smile at Catherine. 'It is all right now, my lady mother. Do not be frightened. It is only a play.'

Catherine was not smiling. She was intensely angry, her lips hardened into a thin line. 'Yes, so it is, my son, God be thanked. Though it would have been kind of your uncle to warn us, would it not, that he had planned this "entertainment" as he calls it? I do not think it right, my lord, that the king should have been frightened almost out of his skin.'

At this point Eleanor came to her new husband's defence, showing her teeth in a smile that did not reach her eyes. 'But then it would not have been a surprise, Madame, would it?' She went to place her hand on the little king's arm in a conciliatory gesture. 'I am sure that now you know it is done in fun you will enjoy it, will you not, your grace? Especially as the English are winning.'

King Henry began to look quite enthusiastic and he leaned on the wall to get a better view of the action, but Catherine was not so easily mollified. 'Perhaps the Duchess of Gloucester is not aware that it is lèse-majesté to touch the king without his express permission,' she said, 'otherwise I am sure she would not do it.' She waited until Eleanor had removed her hand, slowly, from her son's arm and then she bent down to speak in his ear. 'I have arranged for the choir to sing before the feast,

Henry. They have a new motet to perform for you. Shall we continue our walk to the Upper Ward and listen to them?'

'Or shall we stay and see our splendid English knights defeat the French Pretender's mercenaries?' suggested the duke with man-to-man cheerfulness, pointedly leaving his arm lying around the king's narrow shoulders. 'After all, it is only priests and women who prefer music to fighting.'

Henry looked up at Gloucester in puzzlement. 'Is it, uncle?' he asked innocently. 'I did not know that. My lady mother told me that my father liked music.'

Gloucester said airily, 'So he did, Henry, so he did – but he liked fighting better.' With his hand firmly on the boy's back, he eased his nephew nearer to the drawbridge that led to the tower entrance. 'See, the portcullis is rising. Our knights have entered the gate. Another French castle surrenders to English forces.' The sound of trumpets hailed this splendid 'victory'.

Henry clapped his hands with glee and shouted, 'Hurrah! Well done the knights of St George!' Then he turned to his mother, his face wreathed in smiles. 'Now we can go and hear the choir, my lady.'

'It is painful to me, Mette,' Catherine confided with a sigh when I brought her bedtime posset. 'I will never be allowed to share with my son the pleasures of the mind. Surely a king should be able to engage as much with poetry and music as war and strategy.'

'And yet according to his duchess, the Duke of Gloucester is a man of scholarly intellect, Mademoiselle.'

Catherine made a dismissive noise. 'Tcha! Eleanor's level of intellect is to dabble with herbs in order to fashion love potions. How else did she manage to snare Humphrey into marriage?'

'Well, now that she is a duchess she will have to watch out

for competition,' I remarked with a little wink. 'They say that if a man marries his mistress, it creates a vacancy.'

I was gratified then to see Catherine display a genuine burst of amusement. 'Oh, Mette,' she gasped. 'Thank goodness we can still laugh – and thank goodness we go back to Hadham and Owen tomorrow!'

27

Catherine's wedding to King Henry eight years before had involved a gilded litter borne by high-stepping white horses and an archbishop in a fabulously embroidered cope and mitre to preside over the ceremony at the church of St Jean au Marché in Troyes. By contrast, her wedding to Owen Tudor took place among a small group gathered at the studded oak door of St Andrew's church in Hadham. There were the bride and groom, a group of loyal friends and the grey-bearded village priest. Instead of liveried royal guards holding back a mob of excited citizens wildly cheering the royal bride and groom, there was a small group of curious locals murmuring amongst themselves in the churchyard as they watched two strangers make their marriage vows.

Agnes and I were the only people to have witnessed both ceremonies and I remarked to Agnes on the difference in Catherine's demeanour on the two occasions. In Troyes she had been a nervous girl, overawed by the charismatic king she was marrying and almost overwhelmed by the clamour and glamour of it all. Now she was a woman in love with the handsome man at her side, maturely beautiful in a simple wired veil and understated gown of blue flower-patterned linen. Not wishing to appear anything more than an esquire's wife, her only jewellery was a plain silver brooch set with a stone of polished crystal, given to her by her bridegroom on her wedding eve. Owen had brought it back from a trip he had made to her Anglesey dower manors and to visit his family while she was at Windsor over Easter.

To everyone's surprise he had also returned accompanied by two of his cousins, sturdy young men called John Meredith and Hywell Vychan, who he assured us were loyal and discreet companions from his youth with useful fighting and hunting skills. Catherine was too much in love with Owen to question the wisdom of bringing strangers into the tight-knit community of her household, but I had serious qualms about them. It occurred to me that two strapping young men might stir up trouble in the locality and misunderstandings could easily flare due to a general English mistrust of Welshmen and their own lack of fluency in the English tongue. I feared the worst and hoped for the best.

The village priest, Father Godric, was a man of Saxon origin as his name and appearance suggested, with deep roots in his native Hadham soil. Above his grizzled beard his cheeks were red-veined and weather-worn, evidence of his preference for taking God into the fields rather than spending his days in the shadowy precincts of the church. This reassured Catherine and Owen that there was little likelihood of him mixing with people of note, to whom he might speak of their wedding. When the bride and groom had made their vows and Owen had pushed a plain band of Welsh gold firmly onto Catherine's finger, Father Godric carefully pronounced their unfamiliar names in his rustic English.

'I hereby declare that Owen Tudor and Catherine de Valois have made vows of marriage in front of witnesses and are now regarded by the Church and the laws of England as man and wife. May God bless their union and let no one come between them.'

Although there was no sign that Catherine's name struck a chord with anyone in the crowd, common humanity caused a ragged cheer to rise from the churchyard when the newly joined couple kissed. A more subdued chorus of congratulation was to be heard from those of us gathered in the church porch but as we were trooping down the nave for the nuptial mass, Owen's cousins broke into a spontaneous hymn of praise, demonstrating that Owen was not the only Welshman blessed with the gift of song. Before the Mass began, the priest laboriously inscribed a record of the marriage in the battered parish book, making sure to ask the bride and groom how to spell their names as he did so.

Catherine's Hadham wedding breakfast was also a modest affair compared to her royal marriage feast. However, prior to the event, Owen and his cousins had enjoyed several days' hunting in the Hadham park, so that the tables groaned with an abundance of game of all kinds including venison, since Geoffrey had negotiated a contract with the bishop which included the right to take a number of deer. The dishes presented to the newlyweds were not grand, but the new cooks, hired in the town of Stortford five miles away, proved adept enough at roasting and grilling and the manor garden supplied plenty of salad vegetables to augment the store of roots still edible from last year's crops. There was even wedding mead, fermented from honey found in the bishop's cellars.

We made our own music. Owen played his harp a little, but during our impromptu concerts at Hertford we had discovered that Thomas Roke played the fiddle, while the newcomer, Hywell Vychan, proved to be quite an expert on the pipes.

When those two struck up a merry jig, we launched into the simplest kind of country carolling when everyone joined hands and danced around in a circle singing – and in this case of course we danced around Catherine and Owen, who swayed and swirled in each others' arms performing their own graceful wedding *pas de deux*. They looked happy and relaxed, laughing as if they had not a care in the world, even though, by making their wedding vows, they had defied the law of England and the might of parliament and the council of regency.

At Catherine's insistence there was no ceremonial bedding ritual; indeed she and Owen stayed to enjoy the music and dancing until the fire died and the lamps guttered and the whole company decided it was time to retire. Her costume was so simple that she hardly needed help with undressing, but she wanted me there as she prepared for bed because, as she said, 'You will remember how frightened and nervous I was when I married King Henry, so it is only right that you see how joyfully I approach my marriage bed with Owen.'

Her eyes sparkled as she discarded the filmy veil and coronet of spring flowers she had worn to be married. 'I believe this is the happiest day of my life, Mette! Perhaps I was not born to be a queen after all, but the wife of a simple soldier-man who loves me.'

It did my heart good to see her so blithe. 'May God bless your marriage bed, Mademoiselle,' I said wholeheartedly.

'I believe He will, Mette. I pray that He grants me and Owen a whole tribe of little Tudors! Who knows, one day the king may be glad to find that he has brothers and sisters to love and support him in his lonely task.'

I smiled and shook my head at her with matronly reproof. 'You should not tempt fate, Mademoiselle. I know you wish you had not had to marry without his grace's knowledge, but you must be careful for your own safety and even more so for Owen's. The marriage must remain a secret and so must any children who may be born as a result.'

But Catherine's happiness could not be tempered. 'Oh yes, I know. But I do not want to think of that now.' She reached up her hand and tore off the delicate silk nets which had secured her hair so that it tumbled down around her shoulders in a gleaming fall. 'I just want to think of loving my gorgeous, handsome Owen!'

Right on cue, Owen walked into the room dressed only in a robe and causing the blood to rush to my cheeks; his handsome face was creased in the widest possible smile as he went to Catherine. 'My truly ravishing queen!' he said.

I have to admit to a slight sense of shock at Catherine's reaction, for I had not fully realised until then how much this new love of hers had unfettered her reserve. She seemed to melt into his arms and he swept her up without effort, turning to call to me. 'Do not worry, Mette, I believe I can find my way around my queen's lacings and fastenings. God give you a very good night.'

Out of habit I bobbed a curtsy, even though Catherine was blissfully oblivious, and made a hasty exit. Unlike her first wedding night, this time I could go to my own bed confident that she would have no need of me.

Those first weeks at Hadham were an idyll for the newlyweds. May lived up to its reputation as the merry month, bringing almost unbroken sunshine and only the occasional shower to refresh the bursting buds. Blossom frothed on the fruit trees and in the hedgerows, bluebells carpeted the woods and bright yellow irises speckled the river's backwaters. It was an earthly paradise for two people who were discovering the delights of being released from a lifetime of restriction into a world of passionate freedom. They rode together in the vast hunting park, they roamed the river meadows picking wild flowers and weaving them into circlets and necklaces for each other and they spent hours in the butts giggling and laughing as Owen tried to teach Catherine the rudiments of archery. After she had struggled to haul the bowstring even halfway to her chin, she watched open-mouthed as his long-bow sent ten arrows crashing into the centre of the target before she could count to fifty. The rest of us went about our daily tasks, made cheerful by the constant presence of their happiness.

For a week or so I shared the mood of euphoria, but gradually the fever of spring began to work on me also and my thoughts turned to my own loving limbo. Geoffrey had attended the secret wedding at Hadham church and the subsequent marriage feast, but there were still unspoken thoughts and unfulfilled desires between us when he left for London at dawn the following day, leaving only the lingering promise of a few ardent kisses on my lips.

He left Mildy at Hadham, invited by Catherine into her inner circle now that the two remaining Joannas had returned to their families in the north. Theirs had been a sad parting, but one of mutual convenience. In all conscience Belknap and Troutbeck could not put their weddings off any longer and for her part Catherine was not confident of their ability to keep her marriage to Owen a secret. It was Mildy who stirred my thoughts about her father with an innocent question, posed

322

some days later as we foraged together for wild herbs in the river meadow beyond the bailey wall. 'Is there no love between you and my father after all, Mette?' she asked, dropping a bunch of pungent wild garlic into her basket.

I thought I detected disappointment in her voice and suddenly found myself rushing to reassure her. 'Oh yes, there is love but no loving relationship, if that is what you mean. Why? Would you like there to be?'

She replied without hesitation, her small freckled face uncharacteristically solemn. 'Well yes, I would. And so would Anne. We want him to be happy.'

I rubbed a young sorrel leaf between my fingers and sniffed its sharp, lemony scent. 'And you think I would make him happy?'

'Yes, I do. Has he not told you himself?'

'Not in so many words.'

Mildy tossed her copper curls. In the clement weather and the relaxed ambience of Hadham, she had left off her customary white coif and let her bright and luxuriant hair flow freely down her back and I cannot have been the only one to marvel at its arresting colour. 'For a lawyer who makes witnesses tremble, my father is remarkably shy when it comes to expressing emotion,' she said.

I pursed my lips in doubt. 'To be honest I think he has been distracted by the queen's situation and my own concern for her welfare.'

Mildy screwed up her face impatiently. 'Queen Catherine is oblivious to anything except Master Tudor at present, is she not? No one needs to worry about her.'

I laughed at her irreverence. 'Tell me – what is your opinion of their romance, Mistress Vintner?'

'I think they suit each other and she deserves some joy. Not that they give a fig for my opinion! And do not think to change the subject, Madame.' She refrained from wagging her finger at me, but the action was in her voice. 'We were talking of your romance with my father.'

I found myself blushing like a girl. 'I have not heard it called that.'

She threw up her hands in a gesture I found hard to interpret, then her gaze fell on something at her feet. 'Oh look, an omen!' Crouching down, she plucked at a creeping plant half hidden among the grasses and stood up to show me a dainty multiple flower-head, each tiny white-ish flower with a distinctive yellow dot on the lower petal. 'This is eyebright. You should make a concoction with it, Mette, and bathe your eyes. Then you, too, might see what is obvious to everyone else.'

I was too taken aback to ask what she meant, but I took the little flower-head from her and, embarrassed, changed the subject.

By coincidence, the following day Mildy's brother, Walter, rode into the manor house courtyard on his return from an errand to London for Catherine. He brought with him a letter for me. It was not long but it was very much to the point.

—§§—

From Master Geoffrey Vintner to Madame Guillaumette Lanière,

My dearly beloved Mette,
How much rather would I deliver the content of this letter personally, but sadly my work keeps me in London.

I have not forgotten however that there is a certain matter which remains unresolved between us and venture to suggest that now might be a good time for you to come to London to attend to it.

My son gives me to understand that our honoured lady is much occupied at present and unlikely to oppose a brief absence on your part, so I would beg you earnestly to consider a visit to Tun Lane. Walter will wait to accompany you here or else to bring your reply. I very much hope for the former.

Your faithful and devoted friend,
Geoffrey

Written at the House of the Vine, London, on this twelfth day of May, 1428.

—§§—

I managed to find a moment when Owen was away from the house organising a repair to the perimeter wall and approached Catherine as she was walking in the garden with Agnes. They were selecting salad leaves for the day's dinner, a mundane task the queen mother enjoyed now that there was a shortage of servants to perform them. At first, when I explained, she seemed agreeable to my request for leave of absence.

'You must go at once, of course, Mette, but what is it about, do you think?'

'I cannot say, Mademoiselle. He obviously does not want to go into details when the letter might fall into the wrong hands.'

'I hope he is not intending to involve you in any of his spying activities.'

'I think the need for discretion is due to circumstances here at Hadham, Mademoiselle, rather than anything concerning Geoffrey's diplomatic work.'

'Ah yes, you may be right. Well, do not stay away too long. I miss you when you are gone.'

My eyes widened. 'Even now, when you are – how shall I put it – so lovingly engaged?'

She shrugged and frowned. 'Yes, Mette, even now.' Then she said something that took me completely by surprise. 'You are not going to London in order to marry Master Vintner, are you?'

I gave a nervous laugh. 'That is not my intention, no. Why, would you object, Mademoiselle?'

The amount of thought she gave to this question made me uneasy. 'What possible objection could I have?' she responded at length. 'He is my trusted treasurer and you are my trusted friend. I need you both, just as I need Agnes here.' She took her friend's hand. 'Am I selfish to need you all around me?'

I noticed Agnes flush with pleasure and perhaps also with indignation that Catherine thought for a moment that she would leave her. My own thoughts were mixed. Undoubtedly there was an understanding between me and Geoffrey which might, if I let it, lead to a more passionate, loving relationship, but I saw my future as a straight choice, between marrying Geoffrey and remaining with Catherine. Of course there was another alternative but could I, at the ripe age of forty-two, embark on a no-strings, never-mind-the-consequences, love-affair? Was there anything left in me of the heedless girl who had romped in the hay with her stable-lad lover before

Catherine was born? Or was I now too mature for unwedded bliss?

Meanwhile, Catherine's question still remained to be answered; was she being selfish? It was a hard one. 'When the world has heartlessly tried to discard you, it cannot be considered selfish to want to keep those close who remain loyal companions, Mademoiselle,' I said. 'I will not leave your side for long.'

28

'Y ou seem very preoccupied, Mette.' Geoffrey and I were sharing a jug of wine in the hall at his London house late in the afternoon of the following day. 'Have you something on your mind?'

The house was quiet, only the sound of preparations for the evening meal permeated from beyond the hall screen where Geoffrey's faithful old servant Jem was tapping a new cask. On past visits I had been used to the sound of girls' voices floating down the stairs from the rooms above, exchanging snippets of conversation or singing the latest popular ditty picked up in the market place, plus the occasional flap of cloth as they folded linen or shook bedding. Now that both Anne and Mildy were employed in Catherine's household, the upstairs rooms were silent.

'Actually, I was thinking you must miss the girls.'

'Oh yes I do, very much. I may be too doting a father, but I have always enjoyed their company. However now they have an opportunity to broaden their horizons and so I must suffer a little loneliness.' He raised his glass to me with a rueful smile. I could tell that he had visited the barber's shop that morning because his cheeks were smooth but his linen coif and chemise looked rather rumpled and even frayed. I decided it was more than just loneliness he suffered due to the absence of women in his house.

'Queen Catherine is lucky to have their company,' I said, returning his salute. 'They are bright and amusing and full of ideas for her entertainment. The other day they organised a picnic and treasure hunt on the river bank and the whole household joined in. Mildy had painted faces on ducks' eggs and everyone had to find their own portraits. Some were good likenesses and some were caricatures. Several of them were really funny.'

'Not the queen's, I hope? Mildy can go too far sometimes.'

'No, the queen's was very pretty and she had dressed it with a jewelled headdress and veil. She is a clever girl your Mildy.' I took another sip of wine for courage before adding, 'I had a very interesting talk with her only recently.'

His bushy eyebrows rose gently. 'Indeed. May one ask what about?'

I hoped I had managed to control my impulse to blush. 'Yes. It was about what she rather sweetly called our "romance".'

The light was dim in the hall as evening approached; the candles had not yet been lit, but I was certain that his ruddy cheeks deepened in colour. 'Did she indeed? I told you she could go too far sometimes. What did you say to her?'

'I said I had never heard our friendship called that.' In the pause that followed, our eyes met. I took a deep breath. 'But I confess I liked the sound of it.'

He set his cup down on the table beside us and leaned forward so that his elbows rested on his knees. He was so close to me now I could see that his eyes were bright-grey irises flecked with brown, smile lines radiating from the outer corners. 'I am glad to hear that because I have been afraid that your regard for me might have cooled. There has been little opportunity for private conversation lately.'

'There has been little opportunity for anything private,' I said ruefully.

'You have spent too much of your life putting Queen Catherine first, Mette.' He reached out and took both of my hands in his. 'Now that she has settled on her future path, do you not think it might be time to choose your own?'

Suddenly Geoffrey was down on one knee before me, still clasping my hands in his and saying words I absurdly found quite startling. 'My beloved Guillaumette, would you do me the honour of becoming my wife?'

Although I had anticipated the question, when it came I still had no idea how to reply. Besides my heart was racing so fast it was impossible to form coherent thoughts. He must have taken my silence for tacit consent because he hurried on as if anxious to allay any fears I might have. 'At first I thought you would not marry for the queen's sake, but now we are both members of her household you do not need to leave her service. I do not expect you to live here permanently with me and I think you may be more comfortable sharing your chamber at Hadham as a married couple.' He grinned up at me, boyishly pleased with his analysis. 'If marriage is so important to your mistress, then I suspect it must be important to you. I do hope I am right, for I dearly want you to say yes.'

I shook my head in an effort to clear my mind and he must have thought I was going to say no, for his face crumpled into dejection and as it did so I knew immediately what I wanted to say but failed to express it plainly. 'Oh no, I mean no, do not think that my answer is no because it is not. I am not doing this very well but I have never received a proposal of marriage before. If you are sure, I would be honoured and delighted to be your wife, Geoffrey.'

At that he leaped to his feet like a man twenty years younger, pulled me to mine and then his arms were tight round me and I was enveloped in an embrace and subjected to a kiss which together took away all the breath I had managed to recover. It did not seem to take away his however.

'If I am sure – she says! Mette, my dear, my beloved, of course I am sure. I have long been sure. Probably ever since we survived the storm together on the *Hilda Maria*. I thought at the height of it that it would be a terrible shame that we might die and I would not have told you how I felt about you.'

I found myself laughing now. 'But that was years ago! Why have you never done so before this?'

He gave me a rueful grin. 'Something always seemed to get in the way. Your daughter needed you, then the king died and you could not desert the queen and then I had my own troubles with Anne and Thomas and did not want to burden you with that and then I had to work in Rouen for so long – oh all manner of things conspired to prevent it!'

He threw his arms around me again and this time we kissed like lovers, long and sweet and hot and I felt as if, instead of blood, warm honey was streaming through my body. It was a sensation I dimly remembered from kisses shared with my Jean-Michel, but I had forgotten how all-consuming it could be and how flustered a customarily sensible female could become.

When we parted I was trembling and Geoffrey was jubilant. 'You said yes, did you not, Mette? I am not dreaming, am I? We are to be married. We must celebrate. Where is Jem with that new wine and where is that wandering son of mine? Walter! Are you in the house?' He strode to the open door of the hall and leaned out, calling into the staircase beyond. 'Jem! Walter!'

After delivering me to Tun Lane, Walter had taken some quick refreshment and then gone off on business of his own, but he had obviously returned because he came leaping up the stairs from Geoffrey's legal chambers on the ground floor. When he heard the news he shyly kissed my cheek and said how very glad he was and then Jem brought a fresh jug of wine from the new barrel and some wafers and we all made a celebratory toast. I felt as if I had consumed the entire jug myself, so flushed was I with the excitement of the moment. I became elated and agitated at the same time; elated because of Geoffrey's obvious delight and agitated because I found it bewildering to be contemplating marriage after nearly thirteen years of celibacy.

We ate our supper in a continuing mood of celebration and I confess that, as the wine flowed, my agitation ebbed and my elation increased. It was pleasant to share a meal with two men whose company I enjoyed and find myself the centre of their attention and approbation. I had changed my travelling clothes for my formal gown of deep-green broadcloth, lined and trimmed with tawny sendal, a costume I had worn for Catherine's wedding and packed in one of Genevieve's saddlebags, just in case. It was somewhat crumpled from the journey, but during the evening, just as the wine soothed my unaccustomed jitters, its creases diminished. For such an intimate occasion I had left off my wimple, which normally covered my head and throat, and dressed my hair over my ears in a decorative silk net, fixed by a padded circlet of the tawny satin. My face undoubtedly bore the evidence of my years, but it was a matter of foolish pride that the streaks of grey were few in my still glossy brown locks and I hoped these were disguised by the lustrous net and the soft light of the candles. I had been gratified by the expression of undisguised admiration with which Geoffrey greeted me and throughout the meal I was aquiver with the secret and rather guilty physical pleasure his evident lustful longing aroused in me. I had thought these sensations long buried.

As the wine loosened Walter's tongue, he amused us with entertaining and sometimes scurrilous observations about the various members of the Hadham household. I was grateful that discretion prevented him including Catherine in his assessment, but agog to hear that he believed there was an attraction developing between Agnes de Blagny and Hywell Vychan.

'Hywell has taken to hanging around the dairy and stillroom where, as you know, Madame Mette, Agnes has assumed the job of supervising the new maids and often undertakes part of the preserving and cheese-making processes herself. Hywell is a quiet fellow who likes his own company as a rule, but lately he is often to be found lingering on one of the mounting blocks whittling a new chanter for his pipes or polishing his hauberk until Agnes emerges, when he just happens to make his way across the courtyard to intercept her. At first they just nodded a greeting, but now they can spend several minutes discussing such fascinating topics as the height of the sun and the quality of the day's cream for cheese-making.'

'These are crucial matters, Walter,' I protested, wagging an admonitory finger at the mocking tone in which he related these observations. 'Perhaps the two of them have more in common than you think.'

Walter's cheerful face registered exaggerated penitence. 'You may be right. Yesterday I heard them comparing the French and Welsh expressions for the sound of the cuckoo. Clearly the difference of their native languages is not hampering their friendship! At least they seemed to find the process amusing, for they were making strange giggling sounds.'

I felt a stab of guilt that I had not noticed this development and made a mental note to watch out for signs when I returned to Hadham. At which point I fell to thinking about how long I could stay away from the place and whether Geoffrey and I might be married before I returned. All of which brought me to contemplating whether we would wait for the sanction of marriage or anticipate it; a call which I suspected Geoffrey would say was mine to make.

In the event the decision was jointly made, or rather was not made at all but seemed naturally to happen. As we drained our cups and nibbled a final course of nuts and sweetmeats, we all became drowsy together and Geoffrey called Jem to remove the cloth and bank up the fire. The two costly wax candles which had lighted our celebration meal were burned down to a few inches.

'You take one, Walter,' said his father, 'and I will light Mette to her chamber with the other.'

Walter's raised eyebrow was met by Geoffrey with a terse jerk of the head in the direction of the door, which his son obeyed with a bow and a dutiful 'God give you both good night'. The remaining naked flame flickered enticingly, illuminating the mutely enquiring glance that passed between us. Geoffrey held the candlestick high as he took my arm and we kissed, briefly and lovingly. 'Come, Mette,' he said in a low voice, 'we have waited long enough.'

When I woke next morning, before I opened my eyes, I found myself thinking of Alys. To my astonishment, as the thought crossed my mind, I felt Geoffrey's hand brush my hair from my face and his voice whispered in my ear, 'After we are married, we could make a trip to Paris to visit your daughter if you like.'

I rolled over into his arms as if it was a completely natural thing for me to do and marvelled at the power of love to over-come inhibitions. There had been none the previous night as we helped each other undress and slid between the sheets, while on the chest beside the bed the candle had spluttered, sparking our own flame of passion.

I stroked his cheek and his stubble rasped against my fingers. 'How did you know I was thinking of Alys?'

He kissed my shoulder. 'It is an easy guess. Well, shall we go?'

'If you can spare the time, of course I would dearly love to. She has another child now, a boy whom I have never seen. And she wanted me to marry you from the beginning.'

'Did she? What a sensible girl she is. I have always thought so.' He drew back the bed curtain. 'The sun is up. Shall we break our fast and pay a visit to the priest?'

I watched him roll off the mattress and pull his chemise over his head.

'Surely we cannot marry today,' I protested, scrabbling at the clothes pole for my own.

He hauled up his braies and grinned at me. The skin of his belly was white and smooth and only a little paunched. For a man nearer fifty than forty, he was wearing well. 'It is surprising what can be done in a church if you have deep enough pockets. But we may have to wait a few days. Time enough for you to make a raid on Cheapside and Threadneedle Street.'

I stepped into my serviceable everyday brown serge and turned, inviting him to lace it at the back. 'Being a lawyer will you not want to draw up a marriage contract? After all you have not even enquired about my dower!'

He jerked hard on the laces, making me cannon back into him so that he could wrap his arms around me. 'I am already satisfied with what you bring to me,' he said, nosing my hair clear to press his lips to the hollow at the base of my neck. 'Do not tell me there is gold as well?'

I pulled away, turning to eye him over my shoulder. 'It does not behove a woman to reveal all she has to offer at once.'

He chuckled and reached for the laces again, completing the task as he declared, 'I will tease it out of you, Madame Mette, or else the law will have to take its course.'

I tossed my head and began to dig in the saddlebag for my hairbrush. Hoyden that I had become, I had not sought it the previous night because Geoffrey had been too eager to remove my headdress and sink his fingers into my hair. I watched his fascination grow as I brushed, extending the task longer than necessary to give him pleasure. 'Before you threaten me with the law, Master Vintner, had you not better introduce me to the priest?'

Geoffrey's parish church was dedicated to St Mildred, about whom I knew little except that Mildy was named for her and she was a nun who had been 'a comforter to all in affliction' according to the inscription carved over the chancel arch. Geoffrey translated the epigram for me from the Latin as we waited for the priest to finish hearing a confession and although we were far from being 'in affliction', he turned out to be a pleasant and accommodating cleric, not in the least put out by a marriage request from two people old enough to be grandparents.

'If I call the banns for three days in a row, we can slip it in before Pentecost,' he told us cheerfully, counting on his fingers. 'Will Friday suit you?'

Geoffrey bowed. 'Thank you. That will serve perfectly, Father. We shall make it noon if that is agreeable to you. Nothing grand; we will have a nuptial mass and St Mildred's will have the usual marriage fee, to which you may add this purse, if it please you.'

Thus, with an exchange of thanks and good wishes, we left St Mildred's a significantly richer church than when we arrived.

'And now we can visit your favourite tailors and have a new suit of clothes made for your wedding,' Geoffrey declared when we had stepped out into the May sunshine and were making our way towards Cheapside. 'I seem to remember that you and the queen favour a certain Master Anthony.'

I made a face. 'Actually it was his wife Meg whose designs we favoured, but I fear the queen's patronage may mean they are far too busy to fashion anything in the time available.'

'On the contrary, Walter called on them yesterday and they agreed that if we came this morning, they would measure up and start tonight. They seem to feel they owe their enormous success to a certain Keeper of the Queen's Robes.'

I stopped dead and stared at him, my head tilted in indignant enquiry. 'Yesterday? Walter spoke to them yesterday? Before you had even asked me a certain question?'

Respected lawyer though he was, Geoffrey had the grace to look sheepish. 'It was only a tentative enquiry,' he blustered. 'No assumptions were made.'

'I shall have words with Master Walter. It seems he knew more that I did about why he was bringing me to London.'

People began pushing past us with muttered oaths as we blocked the narrow thoroughfare and Geoffrey took my arm to move us along. 'A man has to consult his son about important family matters,' he said. 'And you may remember how happy Walter was with both his task and the result.'

I could not remain indignant for long, especially when my indignation was almost entirely pretence. 'I do,' I admitted. 'I have always thought Walter kind and obliging and now I know he is greatly to be trusted for he gave me no inkling of your intention. Your children are a credit to you, Geoffrey.'

'Thank you. And today, while you choose fabrics and trimmings, I will make arrangements to go to Paris. In favouring my children you must not neglect your own.'

Rays from the midday sun had found their way among the London rooftops to warm us as we stood in the porch at St Mildred's just before Sext on the appointed day. I watched with growing amazement as eight horses and riders clattered into the small square and up to the church steps. Leading the cavalcade were Catherine and Owen, followed by Agnes and Mildy, Anne and Thomas Roke and at the rear, John Meredith and Hywell Vychan. Ribbons and rosettes decked their horses' bridles and Owen and John had their musical instruments slung over their shoulders. All were dressed for a wedding, but Catherine had taken care to wear a veil and wimple in case any sharp-eyed Londoner should chance to recognise her.

'How could I miss your wedding, Mette?' she exclaimed as she swung down from the saddle. 'You have witnessed two of mine!'

I was so thrilled to see her I could scarcely speak. We exchanged a hug, laughing and crying at the same time, while Walter mustered several urchins off the street to hold the horses.

'How did you know when the wedding would be held?' I asked. 'We only arranged it four days ago.'

'Geoffrey sent a courier to Master Roke, asking him to bring his daughters and when I heard why they were going to London I just had to come too. But never mind that, let me look at you. By St Nicholas, dearest Mette, you look wonderful! People will accuse Master Vintner of cradle-snatching, having such a young-looking bride! Being in love certainly suits you.'

'I think you exaggerate, Mademoiselle, but if I do look well it is due to the cleverness of Meg Anthony. She has made me this gown and I have never liked one more. I think it surpasses even the work of my son-in-law Jaques.'

It was the fabric that was so special about the gown Mistress Anthony and her apprentices had made for me. It was a rich tabby silk, smooth and supple, in a gleaming golden brown which brought out the colour of my eyes and the skirt seemed to flow over my hips like ripe grain pouring from a sack. The sleeves were as long as the skirt, dagged and lined with nutmeg-brown satin and I wore it with a silver collar which Geoffrey had taken from his strong-box and said had belonged to his mother, and a gauze veil and padded circlet of the same tabby silk as the gown. It was the most beautiful and expensive ensemble I had ever owned and I felt like a queen trailing my train up the church steps to stand beside Geoffrey and make my vows, while all around us stood our friends and relations decked out as gaily as their four-hour ride from Hadham had allowed. No wonder a crowd of local people gathered in the square to watch.

Thomas had arranged for the boys to lead the horses to the stables of a nearby inn, and after the nuptial Mass we all walked in procession back to Tun Lane where Geoffrey's brothers had delivered a barrel of Gascon wine as a wedding gift and a roasted ox had been ordered from a local cookshop. We had thought there would be plenty to distribute to the poor after the feast but as it was, with the extra arrivals from Hadham, we were obliged to send out for more bread and purchase pies and pasties as alms instead. Everyone contributed something to the wedding entertainment; even Agnes and Hywell had prepared a sweet carol which they sang as a round in French and Welsh and eventually had us all joining in. I was pleased to see that Agnes seemed merrier than her usual retiring self and freely joined in the jokes and laughter, especially when her new swain was at her side. This time it was our turn to sway in the middle while the rest danced around us singing and holding hands.

'The only thing I wish,' I murmured in Geoffrey's ear, 'is that Alys and Luc were here. They would be so happy for me to be marrying you.'

'Well, if Saint Christopher grants us a safe passage, we should be seeing Alys within a fortnight,' Geoffrey whispered back. 'And perhaps she will have news of Luc.'

Our journey to Paris took even less than two weeks, and the crossing was as calm and pleasant as our trip on the *Hilda Maria* had been fraught with danger. I could not have expected Geoffrey to ignore the opportunity of combining a stay in Paris with some business for the regency council, which meant that we could lodge at the Louvre, rather than making Alys and Jacques feel obliged to vacate their marital bed in favour of their newly married parents and move in to sleep with their children, especially as Alys was still feeding her third child, a healthy-looking boy they had called Guillaume after me as she had promised. It was gratifying to find that every nook and cranny of spare space in their small house was filled with ells of fabric and piles of tailoring work-in-progress, so that once Alys had got over the euphoria of welcoming and congratulating us, she was not unhappy at this accommodation arrangement.

To add to the pleasure of spending time with my burgeoning Parisian family, there was also the delight of some news of my son Luc and even, heaven be praised, a letter, which Alys had received only a few weeks before our arrival.

'It came through the regency council's couriers, Ma,' Alys explained when she handed me the folded missive. 'Obviously he has found someone to write it for him so it is not very long but he is . . .' she halted suddenly, shaking her head. 'No, I will let you read it for yourself.'

It was the first time either of us had heard anything from Luc since we had all spent Christmas together shortly before I had crossed the Sleeve with England's new queen. Seven years without word of your son is a long time and I admit that I wept hot tears as I read the letter. The address was the best direction Luc could supply, but at least it had found her.

—ξξ—

To Madame Alys, wife to Master Jacques, Tailor of Troyes, in the street of tailors behind the Louvre,

Greetings Sister,
I hope this finds you well, and your husband and daughter also. No, I have not learned to write. Bertrand the Scribe pens this for me. I am in good health and continue to prosper, as does the cause of my lord King Charles. I am now the assistant to the head huntsman and in charge of the royal kennels. At present we are at Chinon. I believe that soon the king will be back in Paris and we may be reunited.

My master has looked kindly on me and given me his permission to marry. My new wife is called Elinor and is the head huntsman's daughter. We expect a child in the autumn. I wanted you to know that, God willing, your

daughter will have a cousin. I send you my best wishes and
wish that you would let our mother know of my new state.
I will endeavour to get word to you of the name and sex
of the child.

   Signed by your brother Luc
   His mark

—§§—

It was more a signature Luc had scrawled beneath the final two
words of script, remembered from the lessons I had managed
to give him before he found 'more important' things to do than
learn his letters, and beside it the ink-spluttered outline of a
dog's paw-print. It made me laugh through my tears.

29

Dust rose in clouds as I thwacked fiercely with a basketwork beater at a richly coloured tapestry. Hywell had rigged up a line for me in the courtyard, strung between the alehouse and the curtain wall; then he had carried the dusty hangings out of the bishop's bedchamber and piled them up in a heap over an empty hogshead barrel so that I could throw them over the line one by one and beat them. It was early March, the first time the weather had relaxed its winter grip enough to consider some spring cleaning and I was anxious to prepare the chamber for Catherine's lying-in. We had estimated that her baby would be born before Easter.

On my return from Paris the previous summer it had been no surprise when Catherine had confided that she thought she was *enceinte*. She and Owen had both been thrilled and excited about the prospect of a child, perfectly confident that they could easily keep the fact hidden from the rest of the world. 'And if anyone from the court should bother to come visiting afterwards, we can pretend the child is Anne's, or even yours, Mette, since you are both married women.'

I had to bite my lip to refrain from remonstrating with her for thoughtlessly even considering using my still sadly childless stepdaughter Anne Roke as a putative mother in order to preserve her secret and merely prayed that the necessity would never arise.

The biggest surprise had come when I discovered my own condition towards the end of that summer. I had just celebrated my forty-second birthday and had thought when I married Geoffrey that my childbearing days were behind me, but it seemed I was mistaken. He, however, was not only delighted but also confessed that he had secretly been hoping for it and strutted proudly about the chamber we now shared on his regular visits to Hadham.

I gave a derisive snort. 'That is all very well but what will you do with this autumn leaf of a child when its mother withers away under the strain of bearing it?'

He laughed, saying, 'Take another wife to look after it, of course. I have it all under control.' But his next words were more serious and conciliatory, 'Truly, Mette, I pray that you carry this child without mishap. You must take every care and not allow your concern for Queen Catherine to take precedence over yourself and our child. I fear the queen mother is apt to forget the difference in your ages.'

I recalled this conversation as I whacked away at the carpets. In fact I had fared well over the past six months and felt perfectly able to keep up my household duties. But Catherine had suffered a prolonged period of sickness and now, in the later stage of her pregnancy, she was plagued with persistent back pain. As I hefted another hanging over the line, I caught sight of her waddling across the bailey on Owen's arm, her swollen belly a very obvious burden. She was wearing a loose woollen smock and was wrapped for warmth in a thick peasant shawl, her hair tied in a kerchief rather like my own.

They stopped beside me and Owen helped her to perch on the step of a nearby mounting block. 'I do not think you should be doing that, Mette,' Catherine said with a worried frown. 'You will bring your baby early. Let one of the girls take over and come and sit with me in the sun.'

She patted the step beside her and I reluctantly abandoned my carpet beater and joined her. 'I will finish them later,' I said. 'I find the act of beating quite curative.'

Catherine laughed. 'It is rather too late to cure your condition now!'

'I mean that the exercise of wielding a beater cures the winter dismals. We spend so much time sitting around, do we not?'

Catherine shot a look at Owen who had picked up the carpet beater and was now trying it out on the next tapestry. 'That is what Owen says and why he spends so much time attacking the pell-post.' She coughed as dust clouded around us. 'Agh! Why do you not go to the practice ground, Owen, as you said you would?'

He stopped beating. 'Because I hesitate to leave you, cariad, when you are so near your time.'

I caught Catherine's eye and she laughed. 'Despite what I keep telling him, Owen truly believes that the baby will pop out the moment my pains begin and if he is not at my side at the time, he will miss the big event.'

Owen scowled at her teasing tone. 'I think no such thing, but I have caught you from a faint before and it is even more important that I do now, should the need arise.' He put down the beater. 'However, I will go and join Hywell and John at the butts if you will promise to stay with Mette and call for a strong arm when you wish to go back inside.'

Catherine acquiesced with a nod and reached up to stroke his leather-clad arm fondly as he departed. 'I wanted to speak with you privately, Mette,' she said as soon as he was out of earshot. 'I did not want to alarm Owen, but I believe my baby may be coming a little earlier than we thought.'

I looked at her sharply. Her pregnancy had rounded all her features for she had put on a great deal of weight, but I could see no anxiety in her face. 'What makes you think that, Mademoiselle?' I asked. Although our shared condition had rendered us even closer than mother and daughter, if such a thing were possible, I found it hard to address her any other way than by the title I had used since her girlhood. 'Your waters have not broken, have they?' I asked this although I did not know how she could have kept such an occurrence secret.

She shook her head. 'No, no. But there has been blood on my chemise – not a great deal and I do not think there is anything to be alarmed about. That is what happens, is it not, when the process begins? I was so alarmed when the king was born that I cannot remember much about it. But perhaps we should send word to the midwife.'

'There is time for that. First we will go inside and I will take a look.' I stood up, massaging my own stiff back, and as I did so the bell rang on the gatehouse, signalling an arrival from outside.

A look of alarm spread over Catherine's face. 'Who can that be? We are not expecting visitors. I do not want to be seen!'

She struggled to stand up and I pressed her to sit down again. 'Have no fear, Mademoiselle. Agnes is in the dairy. Wait here and I will fetch her to help you inside. Meanwhile I will tell the gatekeeper to hold whoever arrives for a few minutes.'

But it was too late. At first I was unconcerned when I saw a rider in royal courier livery trot under the gatehouse and into the courtyard, for couriers came once or twice a month with letters and documents for Catherine. I was fairly confident he

346

would not recognise her in her present garb, but nevertheless I stood in front to hide her from his sight as he swung down from the saddle and handed his reins to the stable lad who had run out at the sound of the bell. But when he turned to look around, my heart sank for despite the unaccustomed livery I instantly recognised his face, which broke into a smile as soon as he saw me. Lord Edmund Beaufort, Earl of Mortain, began striding across the courtyard towards us.

'There is trouble, Mademoiselle,' I warned. 'Lord Edmund is here.'

Force of habit made me step aside and bend my knee as he approached and I do not know who flushed the deeper red as he and Catherine set eyes on one another. Certainly, for several seconds, neither of them could speak; then she held out a shaking hand to him.

'My lord Edmund, you are well come – but an unexpected visitor. We do not receive many these days.'

Recovering his manners, he went down on one knee before her and kissed her hand. 'Catherine – your grace – forgive me for intruding. The Bishop of London told me in confidence of your whereabouts so I borrowed this livery to come undetected. I wanted to ensure that you were well situated.'

Catherine laughed. 'As you see, I am blooming! But I would rather that, too, went undetected. Please rise, Edmund. I would offer you a seat but there is only this mounting block.' As he stood, she held out her hand again. 'Actually you could lend me your arm, for Mette and I were about to go into the house. We can talk inside and I will attempt to satisfy your understandable curiosity.'

Placing his calloused sword-hand under her elbow, the young earl helped her to her feet. 'I do not believe I have any right to curiosity,' I heard him say as I followed them across the court-yard, watching anxiously for any further signs of Catherine's imminent labour. So far she seemed to be relatively unaffected, or else she was disguising her pain very effectively.

At that moment Owen Tudor, no doubt alerted by the sound of the bell, came striding swiftly into view through a sally gate in the curtain wall, beyond which lay the practice ground. I veered off to intercept him and explain who the visitor was.

He was not in a mood for delay, however, and brushed me aside. 'I do not care if it is the pope, Mette; I am not having her upset.' Then, giving me no chance to warn him that Catherine may be in labour, he hurried to catch her up.

Breaking into a run, I was just close enough to hear his tight-lipped greeting to Edmund; 'God give you good day, my lord Mortain. Let me relieve you of my wife's arm.'

Taken aback, Edmund's jaw dropped and he released his hold on Catherine, who smiled at Owen and laid a gentle hand on his cheek. 'There is no need to worry, Owen,' she said, visibly grateful for the supporting arm he immediately wrapped around her waist. 'Lord Edmund will understand when I explain. But first I must sit down.'

As she staggered a little, Owen swept her up and carried her swiftly into the house, leaving me to follow with Lord Edmund. 'Are they married, Mette?' he asked me in astonishment. 'But how? When?'

I shrugged. 'You heard the queen, my lord. She will explain.'

Owen carried Catherine into their bedchamber off the central hall and I followed them, leaving Edmund to kick his heels and wait. Earl of Mortain he may be but I could not consider his rank when I was so concerned about Catherine's condition.

'It will be all right, Owen,' Catherine was saying. 'Edmund will not betray our secret. I must tell him the truth and I am sure he will be sympathetic.'

Owen placed her tenderly on the bishop's great bed. 'Never mind about Lord Edmund. It is you that matters. Has it started? Is the babe coming?'

'Yes, but it will be hours yet. Leave me with Mette now and I will join you presently.'

As he backed away, looking a little crestfallen, I said, 'Perhaps you could send someone to the village to get the midwife. She will be needed come nightfall I expect. Childbirth is women's work.'

As soon as he had left, I laid my hand on Catherine's swollen belly and felt it hard and tight. 'There is something happening, Mademoiselle. Have you had any sharp pains?'

She shook her head and to my surprise started to heave her legs over the side of the bed. 'No, Mette. There is time yet. I just wanted a chance to think about what I am going to say to Edmund. And I would like to make myself more presentable and visit the guarderobe.' She gave me a mischievous grin. 'I will need all my faculties and guile to sweeten the gall he must feel that I rejected him in favour of a Welsh squire!'

I had to smile, reflecting that you might remove a queen from the court, but you could not entirely remove the courtier from the queen. There were times when I recognised that Catherine was very much Queen Isabeau's daughter, with many of her mother's wiles and stratagems.

A few minutes later we had swapped her loose country smock for one of the elegant tailor-made houppelande gowns acquired for her first pregnancy and I had dressed her hair into a gold circlet so that she more closely resembled the royal lady with whom Edmund was familiar. When we re-entered the hall we found him at the hearth, both hands braced on the chimneypiece and staring disconsolately into the fire. There was no sign of Owen but someone had placed a jug of wine and some cups on a buffet board. Catherine seated herself in one of the chairs by the fire and indicated that Edmund should take another.

'Mette will pour us each a cup of wine, my lord, and then I will tell you all that you want to know,' she said with a smile.

Edmund did not wait for the wine. 'But Owen Tudor has told me already.' His expression was mutinous. 'You married him only weeks after refusing me! Is he the real reason you turned me down?'

'No! You must not think that.' Catherine looked genuinely shocked. 'Marriage between us would have ruined you, Edmund. That is why I refused your offer. I did not even know then that Owen loved me.'

'Practically every red-blooded male in the royal household loved you, Catherine! Did you have to marry the first one who told you so?'

Edmund flung this reproach at her like a Greek fire cracker and Catherine flung one straight back. 'I said Owen loved me, my lord, not lusted after me! There is a difference, if you have not yet discovered it.'

I did not like the way this was going. Surely Catherine could not gain Edmund's cooperation by shouting at him?

'And you think that I would have married you for lust? How little you think of me!' Indignantly Lord Edmund took the cup of wine I offered and quaffed a huge gulp.

Catherine took a small sip of hers before replying. 'No, we would have married for the reason that all noble families inter-marry – for affinity and dynasty. And I would have done so gladly and honestly, but the council of regency – well, the Duke of Gloucester in particular – ensured that marriage to me would bring you only dishonour and disgrace.'

Edmund stared pointedly at her protruding belly. 'And what else has marriage to Owen Tudor brought you, Catherine?'

I braced myself for an indignant outburst, but all she did was smile benignly at him. 'It has brought me love and happiness, Edmund.'

Out of the corner of my eye I caught a shadowy movement at the door and saw that Owen himself was there, half hidden by a tapestry hung to exclude winter draughts. Catherine could not see him, but I knew he had heard her words.

Edmund dropped his head into his free hand and meditatively rubbed his brow. When he raised his eyes he looked calmer, even resigned. 'Well, long may it last, Madame Tudor. Far be it from me to deprive you of it.'

Catherine gasped and laid her hand on her heart. 'You mean you will not betray us? You will keep our secret, Edmund?'

He nodded. 'For as long as you wish me to. When I left you last time I swore I was your knight to command and I will not renege on that oath. Very soon I will be going back to France anyway. I am taking an army of reinforcement to the siege of Orleans. Our cause has been proceeding well up to now under the Duke of Bedford and when we take Orleans the whole Loire valley will be ours. But I suppose you have heard that some farm girl from Lorraine called Jeanne d'Arc has bewitched your brother Charles and promised to regain his crown for him? She is a fraud, of course, but incredibly for some reason people believe her. Suddenly the Pretender's forces show a new vigour. We need to nip it in the bud.'

I saw Catherine catch her breath and squirm slightly in her chair. It might have been solely due to the mention of her brother, but I suspected that her pains were growing stronger.

'It is surprising what a Frenchwoman can do when provoked,' she managed to say, taking another sip of wine and fielding a sharp look from Edmund. 'We do not lie down easily under the heel of tyranny.' With an effort she pushed herself to her feet, using the arms of her chair. 'I am afraid I must leave you now, Edmund, but I hope you will stay until tomorrow. I should like to hear more of the girl from Lorraine.'

She did not seem surprised to find Owen suddenly at her side, taking her arm and supporting her. Edmund also rose and Owen addressed him deferentially. 'No hunting during Lent, my lord, but we could course some hare later if you had a mind.'

The Earl of Mortain gave a small bow of acquiescence. 'Thank you, Master Tudor, I would relish that.'

Owen turned to lead Catherine away. 'Come, cariad, the midwife is here and you have work to do.'

30

Catherine gave birth to her second son soon after midnight. The two men had enjoyed an afternoon's distraction by bringing down a few hares for Sunday's permitted respite from the meatless Lenten diet and an evening swapping stories from the French wars beside the hall fire before Owen had been summoned to Catherine's bedside to view his firstborn son. Despite my protests that she should let a wet nurse suckle her baby, Catherine had laughed and declared that she would do it herself and begged me to show her how. After that Owen watched in fascination as his tiny son struggled to latch on to his mother's breast and whooped with delight when the newborn finally succeeded. I am not sure what the midwife made of it all but she was a taciturn widow who lived alone on the edge of the manor lands and was not much given to idle gossip, a quality which had greatly recommended her to us.

Compared to her first confinement, it was remarkable how swiftly Catherine recovered from the birth. By dusk the following day she was seated by the fire in her bedchamber eating supper with Owen and Edmund Beaufort. Geoffrey was absent in London so Catherine had invited Agnes and me to share the supper of roasted eel and fish stew, leaving the rest of the household to their own devices around the long trestle in the hall. They had been sent wine to toast the new arrival and we, too, drank the health of the tiny infant who lay sleeping within our reach in his carved wooden crib. Catherine toasted his health with the wine but otherwise, on the advice of the midwife, drank only freshly brewed ale to boost her milk supply. Although she was well cushioned in her arm chair, more than once I noticed a spasm of pain register on her face and made a mental note not to let her sit up too long.

Over the preceding twenty-four hours and despite their initial animosity towards each other, Owen and Edmund had clearly become, if not equals, at least friends. At the start of the meal they fell to discussing the relative merits of various forms of hunting but Catherine soon changed the subject.

'Enough of hawks and hares!' she said. 'You are only here for a short time, Edmund, and now that I am the happy mother of another son please tell me something of Henry. I miss him so and only get letters from him once a month, which I know are censored by his tutors. Have you seen him lately?'

'I was invited to spend Christmas with the court at Windsor but, to be honest, it was a paltry celebration – too much church and not enough cheer for my liking.' Edmund smiled apologetic-ally and shrugged. 'But the king loved it. He is very keen on the choir at St George's chapel. I do believe he would like to be a chorister himself, but of course with Warwick as his governor he is obliged to spend half his time at arms-training.'

Catherine frowned. 'But he is only seven. Surely he is not strong enough yet to lift a sword!'

'Clearly you are not acquainted with the long process of becoming a knight.' Edmund proudly felt the muscles of his own right arm. 'A boy has to start at seven to develop his strength. Warwick has provided the king with miniature versions of every type of weapon and even his own small suit of armour.'

Catherine looked unimpressed. 'And what about the development of his mind?' she asked. 'A king has to rule with wisdom. You do not get that with swords and maces.'

'I do not think you need to worry about his intellectual education. I am told that your son is prodigiously bright for his age when it comes to scholarship. I suppose that is why the Earl of Warwick feels he must balance his education with physical exercise, because if Henry was left to his own devices he would be constantly at book or prayer.'

'And music?' put in Owen. 'You say he likes singing. Does he have lessons in music?'

Edmund looked uncertain. 'That I cannot tell you. I only know that at the Christmas feasts he showed little interest in the dancing or minstrelsy. In fact he looked bored sitting through all the fun and games.'

'He takes after his father,' Catherine said. 'He was always impatient with too much drinking and merriment.' Her voice took on a yearning tone. 'Did you speak with Henry much? Did he mention me?'

Edmund gave an awkward shrug. 'It is hard to speak with him alone because his tutors guard him assiduously. However he did tell me that he was sorry you had been unable to come for Christmas at court.'

'Actually, I did not receive an invitation.' Catherine gave a forced little laugh. 'Which I suppose in the circumstances is just as well, for I would have been obliged to refuse.'

Edmund glanced across at the cradle where the new baby was making small snuffling sounds in his sleep. 'Will you tell him about his little brother? Surely it cannot remain a secret for ever.'

Catherine followed the direction of his gaze with maternal

pride. 'Of course I will tell Henry, but not while he is surrounded by people who wish me ill. When he is old enough to know his own mind I am sure he will understand my situation and even come to love his younger brother. After all, hard though they try to make him forget me I do not believe they will succeed.' When she turned back there were tears in her eyes, but she blinked them away. 'That is why I have a huge favour to ask you, Edmund. I should say we have, because Owen joins me in this. We wondered if you would do our son the honour of becoming his godfather and if you accept we would like to name the child after you. With the Earl of Mortain as his sponsor we feel confident that he would have at least one man in his life who would steer its course, should we ever be unable to do so. I know this would be an imposition, but the fact that you stand by your oath to me gives me hope that you will be generous enough to extend that affinity to our son.'

A silence descended on the room, punctuated by the sound of a log shifting on the fire. A fountain of sparks climbed into the chimney and Edmund followed their ascent, his brow creased in a frown, then his lips spread in a slow smile and he nodded. 'I would be honoured to know that your child was named after me and delighted to stand as his champion at the font. I shall take great pride in following the progress of a boy who, with such parents as you, is certain to make his mark in life.'

It was Owen who responded, dropping to his knee beside Edmund's chair and bending to kiss his hand. 'Thank you, my lord. I cannot tell you how much reassurance I feel as a father that my son will have such a powerful and noble friend. For what it is worth, in return you have my lifelong loyalty and fealty.'

'It is worth a great deal, Master Tudor,' said Edmund. 'For

you should know that I find you one of the finest fellows that was never knighted and I know you would defend your own family with the last breath in your body.'

Owen rose to his feet and Catherine raised her cup to the earl. 'Thank you, Edmund, with all my heart. And now, before I retire which I feel must be soon, please tell me more of the situation in France. You say there is a girl from Lorraine?'

'Yes. Her name is Jeanne and she is just some crazed country wench who seems to have convinced the Pretender that she is sent by God to lead his forces to victory. They call her La Pucelle – the Maid.' Edmund's voice acquired a brittle note. 'In reality she is a gold-digging putane who has the temerity to wear armour and wield a sword and has been given a banner showing Christ in a field of fleurs-de-lys. It would be laughable if it were not having such an extraordinary effect on the French fighting forces.' The earl fingered the hilt of his dagger as if he itched to sink it into the soft flesh of the French maid. 'Orleans had all but fallen to our siege, but now its defenders seem filled with new zeal, which is why I am taking reinforcements there.'

'And you say that Charles believes her?' I glanced sharply at Catherine. It was some years since she had spoken the name of her younger brother, whom the English called the Pretender.

'So it would seem, else why would he have given her armour and horses and a position in his high command? A woman in the high command! It is ridiculous.'

'Has he taken her as a mistress?' suggested Owen. 'Could that be the reason?'

Edmund grinned at him as man-to-man and nodded. 'It seems most likely, although she claims virginity, and that visions of St Catherine and St Margaret tell her what to do . . . and St Michael too, I believe. She is not short of saints to call on.'

'Ah – St Michael . . .' Catherine bit her lip pensively. 'Charles always had great faith in the Archangel Michael. Does this Jeanne also tell him that the saints confirm him as the rightful King of France?'

Edmund gave her a startled look. 'How did you know? Not only that, she says that God has sent her to crown him in the cathedral at Rheims.'

'She is clever,' Catherine said. 'She knows his weak spot. Do you not see? If she tells him God wants him crowned, she confirms his divine right to rule as the true-born son of our father. She lifts the stain of the Treaty of Troyes which declared him illegitimate, and restores his Determination to fight. Bastardy has long been the monster at Charles's shoulder. But how is it that a young peasant girl has acquired the knowledge and skill to manipulate him in such a way?'

Edmund threw up his hands. 'Jesu knows! The whole situation is incredible. A woman in armour, placed at the head of the army! No wonder our men are thrown into confusion. They are not used to waging war against women.'

'Not with blades and arrows anyway.' Catherine murmured this under her breath in French and I think only I heard it.

'When do you go to France, my lord?' asked Owen.

'The troops are mustering in Southampton now, ready to embark, so I hope the babe's baptism can be arranged for early morning for I must ride at Tierce.'

Edmund got to his feet as Catherine rose stiffly from her chair.

'Please stay and finish your meal,' she said, accepting my steadying arm. 'I will go back to bed and listen to your conversation from there, but while my baby sleeps I must try to rest. He will be ready to be taken to the church before the Hour of

Tierce and afterwards, every time we call him Edmund we shall think of you.'

Edmund of Hadham was baptised the following morning by Father Godric, with Agnes standing godmother beside Lord Edmund. Less than two months later, Catherine carried my own baby boy to the same font in the Church of St Andrew to stand as his godmother. They called him William after me, at Geoffrey's insistence, because he was so frightened that he might lose me.

I am left with little memory of that birth and so I must rely on what others told me afterwards. Childbirth is always hazardous. I already knew it to my cost, for at the age of fifteen I had suffered the stillbirth of my firstborn son, when I thought my world had ended. In fact it had just begun, because as a result I was recruited into the royal nursery to suckle Catherine. My next two children had arrived without trouble and although this time too the birth itself was relatively easy, something went badly wrong in the aftermath. I was vaguely aware that Agnes and the midwife fought desperately to staunch the bleeding while I drifted slowly into unconsciousness. As my senses faded, the last words that I heard were from Catherine, who was kneeling beside my bed, her voice desperate and pleading, 'Blessed Saint Margaret save her! Do not leave me, Mette.'

Later I dimly remember regaining consciousness and being told all was well, the bleeding had stopped. However, within hours a fever started and I grew hotter than a blacksmith's forge and apparently I began raving about black crows and blood-spouting gargoyles while Geoffrey sat by my side constantly sponging me down with cool spring water, praying to every saint he could think of who might intercede on my behalf. For two more days I hovered between life and death. It could have been his loving care, it could have been the beneficence of one or all of the saints or it could have been that I was, and happily still am, a hardy child of the Paris back-streets – but I survived.

It was only a fortnight later that I regained enough strength even to sit up and it was then that I learned how much I owed to Catherine, who suckled my little William along with her own son until I could do so myself.

'What could be more appropriate, Mette?' she declared in response to my weak bleats of gratitude. 'You suckled me as a baby and now I can repay you by feeding your child. The wheel of fortune turns full circle.'

Nor were these births the only legacy of that year of love at Hadham Manor. At the end of June, Anne and Thomas Roke were at last able to announce that she was with child and at the end of August there was much rejoicing when Agnes and Hywell were betrothed. He was to carry her off to Anglesey so that they could be married in the heart of his family and a lively farewell feast was given with much music and merriment, followed by a tearful leave-taking when Catherine begged Agnes to come back to her after the wedding.

'By then we will not only be friends but also relatives,' she pointed out. 'Owen has told me that his mother and Hywell's father were sister and brother and so you will have family here as well as in Wales.'

Agnes laughed and returned Catherine's hug. 'How wonderful that sounds to one whose own people cut her off without a penny! If Hywell agrees, of course we will return.'

'You must persuade him, Agnes.' Catherine clasped her friend's hands tightly. 'We have been together since we were five years old. I cannot bear to lose you for ever.'

I thought I had never seen Agnes looking prettier. She had

abandoned her nun-like coifs and wimples and taken to wearing pretty gowns, mostly Catherine's hand-me-downs, and dressing her hair like the young woman she was. Happiness seemed to radiate from her and I had an intuition that when the vows had been taken and the honeymead drunk there might well be an instant pregnancy to prevent her riding back immediately to Catherine. When I embraced her before she mounted her horse I dearly hoped it was not for the last time.

For my own part, until I regained my full strength, I was happy to tend my little son and hand most of the domestic duties previously supervised by Agnes and me over to a competent widow from London whom Geoffrey had engaged on a temporary basis. The only drawback was that we had to be careful she did not guess the real identity of the mistress of the manor, which meant watching our tongues in her presence. However, since she had her own quarters and chose to take her meals separately, it was not too onerous a task and by the time September came and John Meredith had returned from Anglesey I was fit enough to take up the reins again. As I predicted, Agnes had already fallen pregnant and she and Hywell were to remain in Wales until the baby was born. Happy in her marriage and motherhood, Catherine made no comment other than to express joy for her friend. But I knew how badly she would be missing Agnes since often they would pray together and Catherine had found a lot of strength in her old friend from the convent who loved her like a sister.

Autumn came and we began the seasonal tasks of stocking up for winter. Wood was gathered and cut, meat was salted in barrels, fruits were dried and preserved and grain stored. Much of the hard labour was done by cottars from the village, overseen by Owen who was accepted by them as the Bishop of London's appointed seneschal. One sad note to temper this period of happy productivity was that Anne lost the baby she was carrying. It was not a dramatic occurrence and she kept the loss to herself until Mildy noticed her sister's listless pallor and pestered her for the reason. We all felt Anne's despair and tried to comfort her, but work seemed to be the best healer and she busied herself supervising the women in the dairy, laundry and brewery and keeping as far away from the nursery as possible. Catherine and I of course spent much of our time there and in the gardens. I also picked and processed herbs to re-stock the medicine chest. Mildy looked after the cooks and kitchens and kept the keys to the spice cupboards and store rooms and sometimes accompanied Geoffrey on his frequent trips to London. He and I had to content ourselves with a hap-hazard sort of married life, but with little William in the cradle as compensation, we were happy enough.

Geoffrey always came back from these trips with news, especially of the war in France, and from the English point of view none of it was good. Despite Lord Edmund's reinforcements, they had been forced to abandon the siege of Orleans and Charles's forces had chased them out of the Loire valley, apparently inspired by the presence in their midst of Jeanne d'Arc, the strange soldier-girl from Lorraine. She had then escorted him to Rheims where, as she had promised, he had been crowned King Charles the Seventh of France. As Geoffrey imparted this news at the dinner table Catherine had remained impassive and made no comment, but when she raised her napkin to wipe her mouth I was sure I detected the hint of a smile behind it.

Before the autumn gales set in, Geoffrey was obliged to make another of his diplomatic journeys to Paris and, in view of the tense situation across the Sleeve, I fretted with Anne and Mildy until he sent word that he was safely back in London. His letter was short but it did contain the news that he would be coming straight to Hadham and bringing some unexpected visitors. 'They are refugees – a woman and two children. From charity I urge you to prepare a chamber in the house for them,' the terse message concluded. We were all agog.

The little cavalcade arrived on a cold, damp afternoon in early October, first Geoffrey on his big cob with a young girl riding pillion behind him. I watched from the entrance steps with William in my arms ready to greet his father and my heart began to flutter as they passed under the gatehouse and I saw the girl.

'Catrine!' I could not believe my eyes.

A laden cart came next into view with a hooded woman and a small child perched up beside the driver, followed by two hired men at arms.

'My Alys!' It was my daughter with her children, come all the way from Paris. I flew down the stair as swiftly as I dared while carrying my precious burden. Pleased though I was to see my husband, it was to the little girl on the pillion seat that I was rushing. Instead of the dimpled smile that I loved so much, her eyes were deep and sad and she did not speak or move, even in response to my greeting.

Geoffrey dismounted, passed the reins of his horse to a stable boy and came to greet me. 'Jacques died two months ago and the baby Guillaume a week later,' he told me in a low voice. 'I found the rest of the family in a sorry state and persuaded Alys to let me bring them all here.'

He turned to lift Catrine from the pillion while Alys climbed down from the cart and helped Louise after her. I went to her, still holding William, and I wrapped my spare arm around Alys's shoulders, tears spilling down my cheeks. 'Oh my poor little daughter, you have lost your love and your baby too. May God give you strength to bear it.'

She clung to me, wailing. 'It was the sweating sickness, Ma. Jacques caught it first and then the baby. They just burned up with fever. I thought we would all die.'

Alys's sudden wails pierced nine-year-old Catrine's grief-dulled mind and brought her to her mother's side. 'Do not cry, Mama. It will be all right now.'

I hurriedly passed William to Geoffrey and enclosed my daughter and granddaughters in my arms as best I could. 'My brave girls! You have suffered a terrible loss, but now you are here with your family. God has brought you to us and He will bring you solace.'

Gradually over the next few days we heard the whole story. Through the crowded and airless streets of Paris in summer, the sweating sickness had spread like wildfire, claiming victims in every house and workshop. Crucially it seemed to favour men and boys over women and girls and the result left many families fatherless, struggling to support themselves without a bread-winner, Alys and her children among them. Even those robes and gowns that Jacques had completed were not collected or paid for because customers were too frightened of the sickness. The little money Alys had put by was soon spent and when Geoffrey arrived at the workshop he found them penniless and desperate. Even so it had taken a lot of persuasion to get Alys to abandon the house and business that she and Jacques had so successfully established. Eventually Geoffrey convinced her and found a reliable notary to undertake the sale of the Paris business and the house in Troyes which Jacques had inherited from his parents. With a little luck, on his next trip to Paris, Geoffrey would be able to collect the revenue from both and Alys would not lose everything by coming to England.

It had not been easy to get permits for the family to leave Paris or to enter England, but by pulling strings with the clerks of the Paris council, Geoffrey had been able to prove that Alys was his step-daughter and begin legal proceedings for her and her children to become his wards, giving them licence to accompany him to England. After all the emotion and upheaval of Alys's arrival, it was only the following day that Geoffrey showed me a letter he had found lying in the Paris workshop, which had come to Alys through the council couriers at the Louvre. Luc had written again to tell her that she was now aunt to a little boy called Jean-Michel. He asked her to get word to me of this new addition to the family if she could.

I looked up from the letter with misty eyes. 'Oh, Geoffrey, he is called after his grandfather!'

'I knew that would please you. And now you have Jean-Michel's daughter here as well. Your family is not entirely scattered or divided.'

As usual Geoffrey showed an intuitive sense of my inner thoughts and as the days and weeks went by and Alys and her two girls began to settle into life at Hadham, I realised how much I had to be grateful to him for.

Catherine expressed deep sympathy when I confided this feeling to her. 'I know now how much it hurts to be apart from your children, Mette. I feel the lack of my Henry every day. So I am happy for you, but devastated for Alys of course. Can we persuade her to stay with us, do you think? Owen can find work for her in the household. Surely she cannot want to set up on her own in a strange country.'

'She says she does not like to trespass on your generosity, Mademoiselle. She feels she should be able to provide for her children.'

'And so she can, if she stays with me; but a widow alone with children faces a tough future, especially a Frenchwoman in England. When she is ready, Mette, you send her to me and I will explain how she can be of great help in my household, especially while we are without Agnes. Besides, Catrine is my god-daughter and I am only too happy to welcome her and her little sister into our growing brood – the more the merrier, is that not what they say?'

I felt a lump come to my throat as I fielded her beaming smile and reflected on how relaxed and comfortable Catherine had become since settling with Owen at Hadham. There was no doubt that the sophisticated French queen still lurked some-where beneath the surface but, already swelling with her next babe, her present aura was of a calm and fulfilled mother hen gathering her chicks under her wings. I prayed daily that nothing would happen to ruffle her smooth feathers.

31

I had feared disruption from officialdom in some way, but it came from a completely different source. When a chapman brought his pack to the village the following week, we in the house were unaware of his presence. He opened it in the church-yard and the village women soon flocked to inspect the contents spread out on the gravestones. I imagine it must have proved a box of temptations. Chapmen carried ribbons and braids, kerchiefs, buckles, belts, girdles, beads, needles and sewing threads, thimbles, charms, amulets, rosaries and reliquaries; anything small enough for the pack and pretty enough to attract the female eye. Every item would have been fingered and felt, unfolded and shaken and numerous purchases made and while he pocketed his coin and packed up his unsold produce, the pedlar also imparted some important news, which soon spread to the manor house.

'There is to be a coronation, Mademoiselle,' I told Catherine excitedly, having located her putting clean baby clothes away in one of the nursery chests. 'King Henry is to be crowned in Westminster Abbey. Anne heard it from the dairy maids.'

'When, Mette?' she asked, heaving herself to her feet encumbered by her growing belly. 'When is it to be?'

'Next month, on the sixth of November I believe. There was a pedlar in the village and he told everyone.'

'And I have received no invitation. Hah!' Her harsh laugh was more like a bark, sharp with disappointment. 'Evidence that the Duke of Gloucester is still conspiring against me, no doubt, but then I suppose I could not go anyway.'

My heart went out to her. 'You should not need an invitation to your own son's greatest moment – but you are right. It would be impossible for you to attend, invited or not.'

'When did the pedlar come?'

'This morning. He did not come to the house. I heard the news from a milk-maid.'

As it turned out we were lucky he had not come to the manor house, for pretty trinkets may not have been the only thing he carried.

The first villagers to fall ill were children. It was a form of pox. First they sickened and complained of headache and then spots began to appear all over their bodies; red blotches that produced little blisters like bubbles. Some children had only a few and soon recovered when these began to itch, but others were horribly afflicted and became insensible and delirious. Of these some, especially the babies, were quickly overwhelmed and died. Then the adults began to succumb as well and although few of them died, many were prostrated for days and left badly scarred from the blisters, which crusted into itchy scabs. Men crawled from their beds to try and bring in the harvest, but many of the late root crops and fruits were left to rot in the fields and on the trees.

Before anyone in the house fell ill, Owen urged Catherine to leave Hadham.

'It is not safe for you or the babes, born and unborn.' His usually carefree countenance was transformed by anxiety, deep lines creasing his brow. 'You must go somewhere else, cariad, to one of your other manors, away from the contagion. Hatfield Regis is only seven miles away. It will be less of a risk to travel there than to stay here.'

'But Hatfield is all tenanted, is it not? Would there be any supplies of food and is there anywhere for us to live?' Catherine asked. 'I have not heard that it even has a manor house?'

Owen shrugged. 'There is a hunting lodge by the forest, although it is small – smaller than Hadham – but adequate, I think, for all the mothers and children – you and Mette and the babies, and Alys and her two and Anne and Mildy should probably go too. It need not be for long. You can return here as soon as the disease stops spreading. Hatfield town has a market where supplies could be bought. Besides it would ease the strain on the Hadham stores. They are much depleted due to the poor harvest.'

As usual Owen was attempting to put a gloss on an awkward situation and Catherine was not fooled, but she smiled. 'I know you are telling me I must make the best of it and so I will. But how shall we explain ourselves to the local tenants? There is bound to be some curiosity about strangers who suddenly take up residence at a royal hunting lodge.'

Owen shrugged. 'Hatfield is a large manor and the farms are scattered, but the tenants are used to me by now. I have visited them all, collecting rents and checking boon work. The lodge is on the edge of the forest where few people go and the penalties for poaching are fierce. Most will not even realise you are there and when they do I can tell them you are retainers of the king's household who have been granted a royal favour. Thomas could even put your seal on a document that makes it look official.'

'You will stay with us though, Owen, will you not?' Catherine laid a hand cajolingly on his sleeve. 'I do not like the thought of living on the edge of a wild forest without your protection.'

He bent and kissed her rather sweetly on the brow. 'I will stay as long as you like, cariad. But I predict that you will find the Hatfield forest a serene and beautiful place. Some people call it Hatfield Broadoak because of its majestic trees. Perhaps you will not want to leave.'

Before he could raise his head, she reached her hand behind his neck and pulled it down to press her lips eagerly to his. 'That may be so, but only if you are there with me,' she said softly.

Carts were therefore loaded and the cavalcade of mothers and children departed the next morning for the seven-mile journey to Hatfield, escorted by several men at arms led by Owen and Thomas Roke. John Meredith remained behind to keep order at Hadham. For the sake of Catherine's unborn child, we travelled at a plodding walk, crossing the River Stort by ford after about an hour. Although the meadows around the river looked marshy, the autumn rains had largely held off and the sluggish stream barely reached the wheel-hubs as the carts rumbled through the water. Catherine travelled in one of them with Catrine, Louise and the babies while Alys, Anne, Mildy and I all tucked our skirts up under our saddles as a precaution, although the water on our horses' legs was less than hock-high. A group of about ten Hadham servants, stable hands, cooks and laundry maids, waded through beside us, excited at the rare prospect of visiting a new place. I counted heads and hoped Owen was right when he said there would be enough room for all of us at the hunting lodge.

Over the next hour the countryside gradually altered from fields and meadows to common scrub and then to forest, the narrow track winding through groves of magnificent ancient oaks whose leaves had already changed to russet and deep crimson. The ground beneath them was thick with withered leaf-fall and full of the rustling sounds of small woodland creatures scuttling away from the noisy rattle of the carts. Little birds with jewel-coloured wings flitted around in the canopy and the occasional deer was glimpsed fleeing our presence, its white tail flashing through the sparse undergrowth, or squirrels could be spotted darting among the overhead branches. Otherwise it was shady and peaceful in the forest and we encountered no other travellers.

Owen seemed to know the way, although the tracks all looked the same to me and it was something of a surprise when we eventually emerged from the peaceful shadows into bright sunshine and found ourselves joining a wide thoroughfare which, judging by the number of hoof-prints and cart-tracks in the dusty surface, connected well-populated habitations. Like all roadways it would be deep with mud once the autumn rains arrived, but for the present it was firm and springy. On this side of the forest much of the land was given over to pastures. We had reached the edge of the wealthy East Anglian sheep-country which, according to the London tailors I had dealt with, supplied the best weaving wool in the world. The presence of so many sheep in the fields delighted me because I had been supplementing William's suckling with ewe's milk and I knew that Catherine would soon be weaning Edmund in favour of her new babe. We should be able to obtain a good supply.

None of us were cheered by our accommodation however, when we finally reached it. While income from the manor of Hatfield Regis formed part of Catherine's dower, it all came from rents. There was no manor hall as at Hadham, only scattered farmhouses, all of which were inhabited by the families of their tenants, so the lodge, built as a base for hunting parties, was the only accommodation available to us. Although the forest had been a royal park for hundreds of years, the privilege of hunting there had gradually been offered to courtiers of lower rank. Owen said that the post of Forest Warden had now been granted to one of the manor tenants, a minor esquire who was permitted restricted hunting rights in payment. As a consequence, while the forest itself was well managed, recently the lodge had been more or less abandoned.

Viewed from a distance it was a charming sight. Under roofs of thick grey thatch was a large central hall flanked by two cross wings, set on bailey ground within a well-filled moat and surrounded by an orchard of fruit trees, their autumn livery flaming orange and red in the midday sun. It was built in the local fashion, using a frame of heavy oak beams from the forest, which had seasoned to a mellow grey-brown and were filled between with a willow lattice plastered with ochre-coloured clay but on closer inspection several patches revealed where the clay had crumbled away and the lattice showed through, leaving scope for wind and rain to penetrate. The shutters looked weather-proof and diamond-shaped leaded glass in the windows indicated that at one time there had been a certain investment in the comfort of noble guests, but now several panes were missing and those that remained were obscured by a thick deposit of the dust of ages.

As at Hadham, the moat was there to keep animals out of the domestic area rather than as a defence against attack, but there was no gatehouse and the drawbridge had clearly not been raised into its timber cradle for some time. We crossed it with bated breath because the ropes looked frayed and some of the planks were half-rotten. It was a subdued party that dismounted onto the cracked and weed-filled paving of the courtyard.

'I will hire some labour in Hatfield market and get the place spruced up,' said Owen apologetically, dismounting and leading his horse to a hitching post. 'A few days' work by a few men will make a world of difference.'

For the first time since leaving Hertford Castle I saw an expression of despondency on Catherine's face. 'I hope it looks better inside than out,' was all she said when Owen came to lift her down from the cart.

It did not. Every surface in the hall was covered in dust and an army of spiders had been busy spinning webs in the exposed rafters. There were also ominous beams of light descending through the sarking boards which supported the thatch and puddles on the floor below confirmed that neither roof nor walls were weather-tight. The light was welcome though, because the filth on the windows rendered the place as gloomy as our mood.

'Perhaps we should have recruited a team of people to clean the place before we arrived,' squeaked Anne, flapping frantically at something with long legs which had fallen on her from the beams above.

'There was no time,' I reminded her. 'Dust and a few insects are infinitely preferable to the pox.'

'You are right, Mette,' said Catherine. 'Let us look over the rest of the house while the babies are quiet and then we can make a plan of attack.'

I loved her for her down-to-earth practicality that day. As a queen she could have sat down and let the rest of us toil to make the place habitable, but the thought obviously never occurred to her. During a quick tour of the wings that led off each side of the hall, we discovered enough bed-chambers on the upper floors to allow each family one of their own and one to set up as a nursery for the babies. At the back were a pantry and a servery, lean-to store-rooms and still-rooms and, located separately, a brick-built bake-house and kitchen with a hearth wide enough to hold a roasting spit. Later we found a tumble-down brewery and some rickety latrines built out over the moat. Catherine held her nose at these and Thomas assured her that there were close-stools packed on the carts which would serve the same purpose.

'We will establish stool-rooms in the house,' he suggested.

'Yes, Thomas,' observed Catherine darkly. 'But who is going to empty them?'

'The usual people, Madame,' he replied with a broad smile. 'Servants and gongfermours. Such things should not concern the king's mother.'

'The king's mother is concerned, Thomas.' Catherine sounded rather cross. 'It is important.'

The stocky receiver-general blushed. 'I apologise, Madame. I did not mean to imply otherwise.'

'Well, we must make plans and that is one of the first things to consider. We have few servants with us, let alone – what did you call them, gongfermours? – and jobs must be allocated among us all.'

Funnily enough, scrubbing the filthy flagstones on the kitchen floor seemed to bring the sparkle back to Alys's eyes in a way that no coaxing or sympathy had achieved. The physical effort of bringing a neglected room back to useful service seemed to be of more therapeutic value in restoring her love of life and sense of purpose than any amount of heart to heart persuasion on Catherine's part or mine. When I actually heard her humming a little tune to herself as she showed Catrine how to clean out a rusty cauldron with river sand and a hank of old sacking, I began to believe that we might succeed in getting her to stay on with us.

It took three days to get the house into a reasonably habitable condition and at the end of it Catherine decreed there should be a feast to celebrate. In view of the ride there and back, she even suggested that, being pregnant, she should stay behind with the servants and look after the babies while the rest of us went off to Hatfield to buy food and other necessities.

On a busy market day our presence in the town sparked no special interest apart from a few admiring male glances cast at Mildy and Alys, pretty in their colourful shawls and coifs as they filled their baskets with vegetables and fresh ewe's milk cheese. Out of nostalgia for my childhood, I was drawn by the smell of fresh bread to the baker's stall where I discovered that Hatfield boasted only one bakery but as many as eight breweries and two wine shops. What that said about the priorities of the populace I hesitate to suggest, but it certainly meant that we need not run short of ale, should we fail to brew enough of our own. The bakery was run by laymen at the nearby priory and, in my humble opinion, produced an inferior loaf, but then I often complained that I had not tasted decent bread since leaving France. However, the wafers and fruit pies looked delicious and I loaded my basket with these as a sweet treat for the feast.

On the way back to the lodge we made a detour to collect a fresh supply of ewe's milk from the nearest farm, which nestled at the edge of the forest. I watched fascinated while in a matter of minutes two sturdy milk-maids filled the new wooden buckets we had bought at the market. The small sheep stood quiet and patient, staring at us with their limpid yellow eyes, little knowing that their curly pelts of fleece, almost fully re-grown after their summer shearing, were the primary source of England's wealth. Geoffrey had told me that when the barons held their parliaments at Westminster Hall, the lord chancellor, who held the nation's purse-strings, sat on a sack stuffed with wool to demonstrate its value to the English crown. However, for little Edmund Tudor and my own sweet William, the ewe's milk was of far more worth.

At the feast, queen, courtiers and servants all sat around a big trestle in the hall and Owen opened a cask of wine, brought by Geoffrey from his brother's vintry. He had loaded it on a pack-horse, which he led from London to Hadham then, after discovering our absence, on to Hatfield, arriving just as the cloth was spread. He surprised me at the kitchen hearth, putting pies into the warming oven and our kiss was hot and hungry – hot on my part, hungry on his.

'I could swallow one of those in a mouthful,' he said as I closed the oven door. 'I have not eaten since dawn. My belly thinks my throat has been cut.'

I tapped the front of his padded doublet. 'It does not look like it,' I said. My cheeks were fiery from the heat of the fire, where only minutes ago a spitted stag had been roasting, brought down in the forest by Owen and now being carved in the servery. 'How did you know where we were?'

'John Meredith told me. I rode through Hadham village but I did not speak with anyone. I noticed there was a row of fresh graves in the churchyard though. John said it was the pox.'

'We did not like to leave but we have the children to think of and you will see now that Catherine is pregnant again.'

'You did the right thing.' He looked about him; the sooty ceiling of the kitchen still bore remnants of its festoon of cobwebs. 'Not exactly a palace, is it?'

'You should have seen it before we cleaned it up. I do have a chamber though and it has a bed in it with a mattress and I might even share it with you.'

He laughed and tweaked my bright-red cheek. 'I'll be warm tonight then. But bed can wait. Show me the board first, please!'

When we had all eaten our fill, while the cloth was being cleared and Owen was tuning his harp, Catherine brought her cup to sit beside Geoffrey and me on a bench. 'I have a favour to ask of you both,' she said.

She was at a glowing stage of her pregnancy and, in honour of the feast, wore one of her court gowns. Its blue brocade skirt and sweeping fur-lined sleeves gleamed in the light of the fire, looking royally out of place in the yeoman surroundings of the hall's open rafters and mud-plastered walls. But the torn nails and grazed skin on the hands that rested on the small mound of her baby-belly bore mute witness to her thorough share of the clean-up process.

'I want you both to go to London for the king's coronation.' One hand moved indicatively over the brocaded bump. 'Because of this I cannot support my son on his day of days, but I know Henry will regret my absence. I am the only one who knows the powerful force of the anointing, the only one who could offer him the strength of experience; how to pray for divine guidance in the God-given task he has been born to.' Tears welled in her eyes as she contemplated her son's future and the void her absence formed in it. 'I ask you to witness anything you can of the event and bring me back your impressions. Go to Westminster. The king may be hearing petitions and if Henry should chance to hear your name or see your face he might insist on you being admitted. I will give you a letter for him just in case. It would be so good to know if it is actually placed into his hand, for I fear that those I send each month do not always reach him and those that do are always read first by another.'

'Of course we will go to London, Mademoiselle,' I said, moved by her earnest pleading. 'But I do not know how much we will be able to achieve.'

Catherine reached out her hand, lacing her rag-nailed fingers with mine. 'We have shared so much, Mette, and we will share much more. You are the only one I can send. I know you will do your best.'

32

Londoners watching King Henry the Sixth's coronation procession began murmuring about bad omens when the rain started falling. Three days previously, Geoffrey and I had made good speed from Hatfield because the roads had still been dry and the streams and rivers low, but on the sixth day of November we peered out of our bedchamber window at dawn to find that autumn had suddenly taken a firm grip. Heavy dark clouds reached grey fingers down to the rooftops and icy winds were making whirligigs with the dead leaves that had dropped from the fruit trees in the garden.

'We had best make haste to the Strand if we want to arrive dry,' said Geoffrey, pulling on his hose. 'Let us hope we have a good viewpoint.'

As a member of the Middle Temple, Geoffrey had reserved places for us to watch the procession in one of the stands erected outside the Inns of Court. I dressed hurriedly in the warmest clothes I could find, extremely grateful that Catherine had made me borrow her sable-lined hooded mantle especially for the occasion. It was a sleek and beautiful garment of the inheritable quality worn only by the highest in the land and I had protested my eligibility to wear it, but she had dismissed my doubts.

'You are going on my behalf, Mette,' she had insisted. 'I would not like you to catch a chill as a result.'

As we waited for the procession to begin, I recalled the preparations Catherine had made the night before her own coronation and wondered if her son had undergone the same long prayer vigil and ritual of bathing and robing in the Tower. There could surely be no doubt that childish Henry would be even more nervous and fearful than she had been as a grown woman, contemplating the prospect of a grand ceremonial ride from the Tower of London to Westminster, the solemn anointing and crowning at the abbey and the protracted feasting afterwards. How sad it was, I thought, that he should be denied the reassuring presence of his mother, the only one with the experience to guide him through the ordeal.

Our seats in the flag-draped wooden stand were good ones, commanding a panoramic view down Fleet Street to the Strand, a thoroughfare which ran down to Westminster from Ludgate, passing a fringe of monasteries and noble mansions fronting the Thames. The rain held off while we settled down to wait, grateful for the arrival of a pie-man and a wine vendor who threaded their way between the benches to sell us some much-needed breakfast. We had napkins tucked in our purses and horn cups tied to our belts and the warm pies and spiced wine soon stilled our shivers and loosened the tongues of our fellow spectators.

The wimpled woman in front of me turned to address the man in a coney-trimmed hood, evidently her husband, who sat beside her. By the loudness of her voice she intended everyone around to hear. 'I fear the king is over young for such a momentous occasion. What if he drinks too much ale at breakfast and gets caught short during the procession? I mean, he is just a child – still not eight years old.'

'But kings are different, are they not? They are taught discipline from the cradle – have to be, I suppose.' It was another goodwife who spoke, twisting round from the row in front and obliged to look up at the first speaker due to of the rake of the stand. Their male companions exchanged frowns, uneasy about the nature of the conversation.

The first woman shrugged and sniffed, unconvinced. 'I would say my son was well brought up, but at seven when he needed a pee he had to go, there and then.'

'Shush, madam!' interrupted her husband. 'It is the king you are talking about. We owe him the respect of his rank, especially on his coronation day.'

'And for the sake of his great father, the hero of Agincourt,' added the other woman's companion, a florid man wearing a tarnished black chaperon. 'It seems no time since we cheered him through here with his French bride. The noise was deafening then, but there are no triumphs for today's warlords. The vanishing earls, I call them. Somerset has still to be ransomed, Salisbury got himself killed and now Suffolk has been captured.' He ticked them off scornfully on his fingers. 'Meanwhile, a French tart marches the Pretender to Rheims to be crowned king of France. Half a dozen cities opened their gates to him en route, even Troyes where good King Hal was married!'

This was news to me. Troyes had welcomed Catherine's brother? I could not believe it. When I was last there, the people had been solidly against Prince Charles, whom they blamed for the murder of the Duke of Burgundy's father.

The man in the fur-hood nodded vigorous agreement. 'How does the French whore get away with it? She claims she is sent by God to save France – hah! In England we call bitches who rant like that witches.' He made the sign of the cross to reinforce his point. 'And put them to the flames.'

'But the regency council is rattled enough to rush the young king into this coronation,' grubby coif pointed out. 'And next year he will travel to Paris to receive his French crown.'

'If John of Bedford can hold Paris long enough.' Fur hood was becoming more agitated. 'The whore has already tried to storm the gates, but at least this time she was sent packing.'

'Someone should put a stop to her before she bewitches the whole of France. She is costing us a fortune! Ugh, here comes the rain.' The second man pulled his hood over his coif.

There was the nub of it, I thought, retreating under my own hood. London merchants were sick of financing wars in France that did not result in rich pickings and the success of this girl Jeanne, who these men called a whore and the French knew as the Maid, was seriously affecting trade. For her own sake I prayed that she would go back home before it was too late, because I knew exactly what kind of man her 'king' Charles was and I would have wagered my best silver belt buckle that he would do nothing to help her if she fell into English hands.

Geoffrey slipped his hand into mine under the folds of my cloak and squeezed it in warning. He could see I was fulminating and feared that if I opened my mouth I would spark an argument. Luckily at that moment we heard the sound of trumpets and everyone's attention switched to the Ludgate where heralds on the battlements were signalling that the king's procession was about to leave the city walls. On a platform beside us at the Temple Bar a group of costumed boys hastily assembled themselves into a choir of angels, each of them harnessed with feathered wings and crowned with a gilded halo, while a beautiful girl in a blue robe mounted a raised throne in their midst and someone passed up a small child with golden hair, perhaps her own offspring or it might not have sat so calm and still on her lap. The Blessed Virgin Mary and the Christ Child

382

were waiting to honour the king as he passed by – an appropriate image in view of the tender age of the monarch, but ironic too, I thought, in the absence of his own mother.

Out of every window and from the city battlements people waved banners and shouted greetings. The Lord Mayor and Aldermen in robes of scarlet and gold led a column of guild masters through the Ludgate, resplendent in their tasselled hats and chains of office, dispersing to either side of the roadway, ready to bow the king from the city precincts. They were followed first by a detachment of the royal guard, marching in gleaming breastplates and sallet helmets under a forest of long pikes and then by the king's retinue of knights, wearing highly polished plate armour and crested surcôtes, their horses in full trappings, embroidered with colourful heraldic devices. Behind them and surrounding the king came his most noble vassals led by the Duke of Gloucester and the Earl of Warwick, who, as the king's governor, held the lead rein of Henry's prancing white pony.

A lump came to my throat when I saw the little king, for he sat ramrod straight in his saddle like a true chevalier, a gold coronet on his head and an expression of intense pride on his face. Riding beside the warlike Earl of Warwick, he could not help appearing small and vulnerable and I was too far away to glean any sense of his true feelings from his expression, but there was no doubting his self-belief. Henry was playing his role to the manner born. Catherine would have been immensely proud of him. Then we were all given a clue to his character, for as soon as the angel choir began to sing he turned his head to listen, ignoring the deep farewell bows of the London guildsmen. When Warwick drew them to the king's attention, he shook his head impatiently and drew rein, raising his hand to indicate that he wished the procession to halt.

'I want to hear the angels sing,' he declared in a voice high enough and loud enough to carry up to the stands.

Faced with this very public display of the royal will, the Earl of Warwick had no choice but to acquiesce and the whole procession ground to a halt behind them, waiting while Henry sat on his fidgety pony and enjoyed the whole anthem, ignoring the steady curtain of rain which soaked his ermine-trimmed mantle and dripped off the helmets of the stern-faced pike-men. Just as Edmund Beaufort had told us at Hadham, the king obviously preferred a choir above everything.

Meanwhile the rain increased in intensity and once the procession had passed, no one was sorry to quit the stands. As fast as they could, the lawyers, their wives and families hurried to their respective Inns to indulge in the celebratory feasts provided. When the bells of London began to peal from every direction we knew that in St Peter's Church at Westminster Abbey the probably still damp boy-king had been crowned.

We heard that King Henry would be meeting petitioners at Westminster Hall the following day, and I had announced my intention of being among them. Sensibly, Geoffrey would not let me walk to the Palace of Westminster. 'You will want to wear your finest clothes to meet the king,' he said, 'and the hem of your skirt will get filthy. We will ride there and take Jem to hold the horses.'

He was more confident than I was of getting anywhere near the king but, early the following day, the rain mercifully having stopped, we rode down the Strand, open to traffic once more and bustling with people, carts and flocks of farm animals being herded to market. Although the muckrakers had cleared the thoroughfares for the king's procession, the previous day's downpour had turned them to mud, which was already foul with refuse and droppings and I patted Genevieve's neck, grateful that it was her feet and not mine that squelched through the mire. Under Catherine's magnificent mantle I felt suitably clad for court in the gown I had worn to my own wedding and, safely tucked into my best red leather purse, I carried her sealed letter to her son.

As a meeting-place for parliament, both lords and commons, and many sessions of the various courts of law, Westminster Hall was used to crowds and many hundreds of people could cram in under its wondrous network of rafters and beams. Being among the first to arrive, we waited for hours while more and more petitioners jostled in behind us, pushing us to the foot of the steps which led up to the royal dais and the guarded entrance to the palace and council chambers. There had been some coming and going through this privy entrance, but no one had emerged that I recognised or who we felt bold enough to approach to ask whether the king would be coming or not. We ate the bread and cheese I had stuffed into Geoffrey's purse and bought some ale from an opportunistic man with a barrel strapped to his back, but when the None peal began to ring from the abbey bell tower for the monks' mid-afternoon Office, we became tired and despondent. Even the patient Geoffrey decided that we had waited long enough.

'You have tried, Mette, and that is all you can do. Queen Catherine will understand.' He put his hand under my elbow to steer me through the milling crowd of petitioners back to the main door, but just as we were turning away we heard a commotion and the elaborately carved palace doors were flung back to admit a procession of stylishly clad courtiers and richly apparelled clergy with the young king in their midst. The royal party moved to the centre of the stone dais and gazed down at the mass of onlookers who dropped to their knees and broke into a ragged burst of cheers and greetings.

'God save the king!' 'God bless your grace!' 'Heaven protect our little king!'

I made no shout myself but gazed up intently at Henry, letting his image etch itself on my mind so that I would be able to describe it to Catherine. From close to he did not look as proud and confident as he had the previous day. His shoulders drooped and his head sagged forward as if he was very tired. I even wondered if, the day before, he could have been wearing some kind of brace under his furred gown when he rode his pony so erectly in the coronation procession. His brow, which yesterday had felt the touch of the holy chrism, was today deeply furrowed in a way I did not like to see in one so young and the expression in his eyes was wary rather than keen. His face was pale and possessed of a large jaw for a boy, his nose long and straight as I remembered his uncle Charles's had been and he looked tall for his age, despite being dwarfed by the imposing stature of Warwick who stood beside him. My abiding impression was that he would prefer to be somewhere else.

Briefly I dragged my eyes from the king to scan the people gathered around him, dreading to see the Duke of Gloucester, but to my intense relief he was not there. When I returned my gaze to the king, it was to find that he was staring straight at me. The cheers and blessings in the hall had dwindled into murmurs and subsided into complete silence as King Henry raised his hand and pointed at me.

'I know that woman,' he said, turning to the Earl of Warwick. 'I would like to speak to her.'

Warwick looked down at me, frowning, clearly unable to identify me, but he jerked his head at a squire who took note of me and returned the nod. Meanwhile the earl bent down to address the king. 'Very well, your grace, but first, have you remembered what you would like to say to the people here?'

'Of course I have remembered,' declared Henry indignantly and cleared his throat to deliver his well-rehearsed speech to the assembled company. 'Beloved subjects, I thank you for coming here today. Now that I am your crowned king I will be attending to as many of your petitions and grievances as I can, as soon as I can, but you must be patient. Please hand them to my squires if they are written and tell them to my clerks if they need taking down. May God bless you all.'

He looked rather pleased with himself when he had completed this speech and a ripple of polite but not very enthusiastic applause broke out behind me while the royal party immediately turned and headed once more for the carved double doors. I got to my feet, my knees complaining bitterly at the minutes spent in contact with the cold stone floor and saw the squire who had been detailed to fetch me move down the steps in my direction. When he asked my name I thought it wise to tell him it was Madame Lanière. Even so I doubted King Henry would remember it. It was nearly three years since I had been a regular visitor to his nursery.

'Please follow me.' When Geoffrey made to come with me the squire shook his head, saying, 'The king only asked for the dame.' Then he set off at such a pace that I only half-heard Geoffrey's promise to wait as I hurried to keep up.

King Henry had retired to his presence chamber in Westminster Palace and was perched on an over-sized plush-cushioned throne set on a dais several steps above the floor and under an imposing canopy of gold-embroidered and tasselled crimson velvet. His small frame occupied less than half the seat and his thin black-hosed legs stuck straight out from under the furred hem of his scarlet gown, too short to allow his knees to bend over the edge. The Earl of Warwick stood protectively at his side.

'What is your name?' young Henry asked rather petulantly, as if he blamed me for his own inability to remember it. 'When I was in the nursery you used to sing me lullabies at bed time if my mother was called away. I liked hers best but yours were better than nothing.'

I had sunk to my knees before the throne that swamped him. 'My name then was Madame Lanière, your grace, but the queen mother called me Mette. You may recall that name perhaps.'

Hearing this he pulled himself forward enough to allow his knees to bend and his feet to swing down. 'Mette! Yes, I remember you now. You used to tell me stories – fairy tales and stories of the saints' lives. You knew so many.'

I smiled, relieved by his sudden enthusiasm. He seemed more human somehow, more like the little boy he was. 'Well I used to tell them to your mother when she was a child.'

'Did you? I know nothing about my mother's life when she was my age. Was she good? I mean did she say her prayers and learn to read and write like I do?'

'Yes your grace, she did, although I think she may not have been as good at her letters as you are.'

He looked pleased to hear this. 'I can read the Gospels in Greek,' he said proudly. 'My lord of Warwick says that is unusual for someone of my age.'

He looked up at his governor for confirmation of this and the earl nodded. He also noticed me shifting painfully on my already-sore knees. 'Perhaps you would like me to have a stool brought for Madame Lanière, your grace? Then you could talk together more comfortably.'

King Henry scrambled down off his throne and sat on the

top step of the dais. 'Or she could sit on the next step down,' he suggested accommodatingly, adding solemnly, 'you see your head must not be higher than mine, Mette.'

I crawled forward and sank gratefully onto the second step, taking care to crouch low enough to ensure my head stayed below his. 'Thank you, your grace. That is very kind of you.'

'I should like to hear one of your stories again. I remember one about St Margaret, I think. But first, tell me about my mother. Are you still in her household? When did you last see her?'

From the corner of my eye I saw the Earl of Warwick tap his nose at me, as if to signify that I should be discreet and I felt my heart begin to beat faster. What did he mean? Should I say nothing about Catherine, or just as little as possible? What was he worried that her son might hear?

I decided on half truths. 'My home is in London now but I did see her grace your mother quite recently and she was delighted to hear about your coronation. Had she known I was going to speak with you, I am sure she would have asked me to give you her blessing.'

Henry's face clouded. 'I would have liked her to come and see me crowned, but my lord of Warwick explained that it would be only men in the Abbey.'

With Warwick glaring down at me, I was wondering how I was going to give Catherine's letter to her son without being seen.

The king was chattering away, asking questions like his mother always had. 'Was she well when you saw her? Where is she living? I wish I could visit her, but after Christmas I am going to France. I am to be crowned there as well. Then I shall have two kingdoms. Even my father did not have that.'

I found this proud boast quite endearing, but Warwick obviously did not.

'Your father was taken from us before he could claim the greatest fruit of his victories, your grace.' The earl's voice was stern with admonishment and his royal charge flushed scarlet. 'Your councillors strive to preserve his achievements so that you may continue his noble enterprise, Henry. Remember that.'

I saw a mulish look steal over the boy's face, but before he could speak the earl's attention was caught by one of his squires. He bowed to the king, murmured, 'Stay here,' to me and strode away to speak to him.

Swift as a hawk I pulled the letter from my purse and pressed it into the boy king's surprised grasp. 'It is from your mother,' I whispered. 'Tuck it away and do not tell anyone. It is for your eyes only.'

King Henry's eyes flitted nervously to Warwick's retreating figure as he slipped the letter inside the doublet he wore buttoned up under his gown. I leaned forward to help him refasten the buttons and he smiled at me, excited by the subterfuge. 'She loves you very much. Never forget that,' I said softly before sitting back again.

'Now, you wanted the story of St Margaret and the dragon, your grace.' I made sure to say this loudly enough to carry across the room. 'A very good choice. It was one of your mother's favourites.'

33

To Mistress Guillaumette Vintner from Mistress Catherine Tudor.

Greetings to my beloved Mette,

That is the first time I have actually penned our new names and I must tell you that I am very much taken with the look of mine, but then as you know I am very much taken with the look of my husband. How wonderful it is that O and I can be together as we are, honourably married, blessed with our beautiful Edmund and looking forward to a sister or brother for him in a few months time. Truly I never knew happiness like this before. I admired and respected H and loved him as a wife should love her husband, but he did not really love me, not wholly and unconditionally as O does. He is a man like no other I have ever known – warm and honest and beautiful and I thank God for allowing us to be together.

I am writing this on the day of little H's coronation, knowing that you are witnessing his great day whilst I cannot. I should be desolate about that, yet strangely I am not. My deepest regret is that he cannot share in my happiness or become acquainted with his brother or stepfather. I pray that one day this will come to pass and that he will learn what *a strong and wise father O could be to him, in the absence of his own. I wait impatiently to hear your account of the coronation procession and I hope against expectation that you may have been able to speak to H and to give him my letter.*

I must mention how all the little children give me enormous joy, not just my own Edmund, who by the way now has four teeth and is your granddaughter Louise's greatest love. I think if she had the strength she would carry him around all day, but I fear she may drop him and so she is only allowed to cuddle him sitting down. And my godchild Catrine is enchanting, always ready to run an errand or perform little tasks for me. We have started to call her Cat because there is sometimes confusion but she does not seem to mind and I think Cat suits her for she is clever and independent – and so pretty, with her curly brown hair and merry eyes like yours. Alys had started to teach her letters but she has little time and so I have taken over. It makes me sit down in the afternoons, which is good because the babe tires me. Alys asked me if I still had the ring I lent you when little Cat was born. She said the gemstone was jasper and has a God-given power, a precious gift of healing and vigour, which it shares with women who are nearing their time. I believe she is right; now I will not let it leave my finger.

Then last but by no means least, there is your William. Young though he is, he must be the most cheerful, good-natured child in the world. When I put the two babies together on a blanket and let them play, William tries to copy everything Edmund does and for the most part he succeeds. He is so determined. By the time they are both running about they will be like a pair of young pups and

into all kinds of mischief. We will have to watch them like
hawks.

You can tell that I am missing your company, Mette, for
if you were here I would be able to share these thoughts with
you directly and not have to commit them to paper.

I must now be patient and wait for you to come back and
regale me with a vivid description of London en fête for the
coronation. You are my eyes and ears, Mette, and you are in
my heart.

Your fondest friend,
Catherine

Written on this Coronation Day of Henry I, King of
England, the sixth of November 1429.

—ξξ—

I smiled at Catherine's attempt to disguise her identity and
location; not a very subtle disguise, I concluded, but then the
letter was unlikely to fall into the wrong hands since it was
brought to London by Walter the day after I had managed to
deliver hers to her son. I was surprised that he managed to
complete the journey from Hatfield in one day because the
roads were starting to dissolve into quagmires owing to the rain.
Geoffrey and I were unable to return to Hatfield for two weeks
as the rivers became torrents, the fields disappeared under lakes
and the highways turned into streams of liquid mud. Desperate
though I was to get back to little William, it was not until the
floods had subsided and a sharp frost had hardened the ground
that we felt we could risk the country tracks. Even then our
journey took the best part of three frustrating days because of

the many times we had to make diversions where floods had washed away bridges or rendered fords too deep to cross. I saw parts of Essex I had never expected to visit, because we took the high ground between valleys to try and avoid river crossings.

For the first time since I had married Geoffrey, I seriously began to question whether we needed to continue splitting ourselves between London and Catherine's rural hideaway. As faithful Genevieve fought her way through yet another fast-flowing ford, belly deep in freezing water, I asked myself whether, happy as she was with Owen, Catherine really needed me constantly at her side? When we finally struggled over the rickety drawbridge at Hatfield Lodge, I rushed straight up to the nursery to cradle William in my arms, listening to his gurgles and nuzzling his gorgeous baby skin and decided that once Catherine's latest child was safely delivered, I would make some major changes in my life.

I said nothing of this inner turmoil however because I quickly discovered that the household was alive with preparations for Christmas and Alys and Mildy immediately roped me in to help with a costumed masque they were planning as part of the entertainments. Any time left spare for quiet conversation was spent giving Catherine detailed accounts of King Henry's coronation procession and my conversation with him the following day.

Predictably she was thrilled. 'Imagine, you talked to him face to face, Mette, and actually gave him my letter – and he picked you out of the crowd, you say? He remembered your face?'

'He did, Mademoiselle, although he did not remember my name. In fact he still does not know it because I did not tell him I had married again. He understood about keeping the letter secret but I feared he might mention me in conversation at court and I do not want to be traced. I was greatly relieved that the Duke of Gloucester was not present at the audience, but I believe the king will be spending Christmas with him and his duchess at Greenwich. The last thing we need as you are nearing your time is a visit from the duke.'

The mention of Christmas with the Gloucesters fired Catherine's anger. 'It is not right that Eleanor Cobham should see more of the king than I do,' she complained. 'She is not a fit person to have influence on my son.'

'At least she did not attend the coronation,' I consoled her. 'And now that the king has been crowned, parliament has declared that Gloucester is no longer to be called Protector of the Realm. As the king grows older, perhaps Gloucester grows weaker. As I remember, your brother was made Governor of Paris at only fourteen.'

Catherine made a scornful noise. 'Pah! That was just a title. Others did all the governing. And speaking of my brother, what was the talk of him in London?'

I told her what I had heard in the crowd during the coronation procession. 'People deride him for his attachment to Jeanne d'Arc, but she seems to have gained much support for him in France. Did you know that even Troyes opened its gates to the dauphin as he travelled towards Rheims?'

Her eyes grew round on hearing this. 'But Troyes was always staunchly for Burgundy! Surely Philippe has not forgiven Charles for the death of his father? That was the main reason Burgundy made an alliance with England – the main reason I married King Henry.'

I shook my head. 'No, the English alliance with Burgundy

holds. I have had time to consider this. The coronation in Rheims was in July. Your brother would have been passing Troyes with his army just before the Hot Fair, when the merchants make all their money. They would not want trouble at that time. The flags were probably flying again for Burgundy the day after the dauphin left.'

Catherine eyed me with interest. 'You are becoming quite a strategist, Mette. Geoffrey's diplomatic skills are obviously rubbing off on you. But tell me more of this mysterious girl, Jeanne d'Arc. Does she actually fight with the army? Is she still with Charles?'

I shook my head. 'Apparently not, he has gone back to Chateau Chinon; but she does fight, yes. She and the Duke of Alençon recently led an abortive assault on one of the Paris gates and then had to flee into Picardy. They say her star may be waning.'

Catherine shrugged. 'Perhaps now that Charles has been crowned, she has served her purpose as far as he is concerned. And if she pits herself against Paris and Bedford I would not give her much chance. He will go to any lengths to preserve his brother's conquests.'

'Let us hope so, Mademoiselle, because the king is leaving for Paris in the New Year. To counteract your brother's ceremony in Rheims, the council wants your son to be crowned King of France at the cathedral of Notre Dame.'

Her eyes widened. 'Really? God keep him safe! So effectively France will then have two crowned kings – my son and my brother.' She crossed herself and her expression grew melancholy. 'That is a sorry situation. It cannot end well.'

She did not say for whom.

*

Edmund's little brother was born almost exactly a year after him at Hatfield, in the middle of a March snowstorm. There was no chance of the midwife getting to us because the wind had whirled the snow into deep and treacherous drifts, so Alys and I tended Catherine through her labour, while Owen refused to obey the traditional rule that fathers had no role to play in childbirth. He remained with her all the way, as if he believed only his presence could guarantee a successful delivery. At first he made music on his harp and sang the epic lays he had learned in France, endeavouring to distract Catherine with romantic tales of knights coming to the rescue of ladies in distress, until her pains grew intense and he abandoned the harp to rub her back and stroke her brow. Alys and I shrugged our shoulders and left them to it, restricting ourselves to regular checks on the baby's progress and supplying spiced wine and nourishing possets.

All went well until the final stage when Catherine suddenly screamed that the pain was unbearable and started thrashing about, trying to escape its onslaught, much as she had at King Henry's birth. Understandably, Owen grew fearful and began to panic and I firmly pulled him away and told him to play his harp again and close his ears to his wife's cries. It was Alys who found the magic formula for calming Catherine's distress.

'All will be well, Madame,' she crooned, taking Catherine's hands and putting them together. 'Here, feel the jasper ring on your finger. Take its energy and use it. It will help you to bear the pain and push the baby out. It will not be long now and my Ma will help you. You must not worry. The jasper will bring you a healthy babe.'

I remembered the previous births I had witnessed and copied what the midwives had done, turning the emerging baby's body to allow the shoulder to pass through more easily. There was no drama of the caul as there had been with Henry. This little baby boy catapulted into the world like a knight at full charge and was soon cleaned and wrapped and placed in his tired but exultant mother's arms.

'He is so full of life!' Catherine exclaimed gazing at the baby's wide open eyes and watching his hands wriggle free of the restricting shawl. 'I swear he is about to jump up and speak. Look, Owen, he is grasping the ring! It has given him its energy. Let us call him Jasper.'

Owen protested. 'But we should give him a family name, cariad; Charles perhaps, after your father, or Meredith after mine, or even Owen. We have heritage to preserve.'

Catherine reached out to take her husband's hand. Her other arm cradled the baby whose tiny fingers remained clasped over the large red gemstone in her ring. 'I know we should call him Owen after you, my dearest love, but I am sure this one is different. He does not need to be saddled with the weight of heritage. He needs to be free to make his own mark.' She pushed the edge of the shawl off his head to reveal a fast-drying mop of curly hair. 'Look, his hair is not fair like mine or dark like yours, it is red – red as the bloodstone. If we do not call him Jasper, others will.'

34

Almost two years after Jasper's birth, a letter from the king arrived at Hadham that threw us all into panic. Since the king and court had left England for France, letters from King Henry had become rare and irregular and each one was a cause for celebration. They always came via Hertford Castle, which as far as the court was concerned was the queen dowager's official residence, and this one had waited nearly a week to be carried to Hadham by Thomas Roke returning from one of his auditing tours.

At dusk in the fire-lit hall, as the household gathered for the main meal of the day, Catherine revealed its contents to us, her manner unusually flustered. 'The king is to honour us with a visit. He is back from France and will be making a pilgrimage to the shrine of St Edmund in time for Lent. On his way he will stop at Hertford.'

I immediately understood the reason for her extreme agitation. 'But, Mademoiselle, Lent begins next week.'

'Yes, Mette, the letter has been waiting at Hertford for several days. Henry will arrive there on Saturday. We have only three days to get to Hertford and prepare to entertain the king.'

Owen and Catherine had been standing at the hearth while the rest of us waited to seat ourselves around the trestles, laid out as usual on three sides of a square. The warmest places, nearest the fire, were for Catherine, Owen and other officials of her small Hadham household who were present, which on this occasion were myself, Thomas Roke and the priest, Jean Boyers, who was on one of his regular confessional visits. The previous year, learning that he had taken a teaching position at one of the Oxford Colleges, Catherine had invited him to attend her Easter celebrations, which she had held at Hertford Castle in order to keep up appearances and entertain some local dignitaries, including the kindly Bishop Grey of London. During that year she had felt safe from any intrusion by Gloucester because the duke had been in France with the king. The result was that under protection of the confessional, she had revealed her family situation to Maître Jean and he had agreed to make regular visits to Hadham during university holidays, in order to revive his role as her confessor.

Owen sought to calm Catherine's nerves about the king's imminent arrival. 'There is plenty of time, cariad. We can be at Hertford by noon tomorrow. The weather is good – cold but dry – and we should not need to take much baggage; just a couple of pack horses I think. It might be best if I supervise the preparations and return here before the king arrives.'

Catherine frowned at this but said nothing, choosing instead to take her seat at table, allowing the rest of us to do the same. Under the buzz of conversation, from my place beside Owen I heard her murmured words to him. 'I wish you would stay on with me at Hertford, *mon cher*. Henry will expect to see you there. You know how much he likes you. You can play my master of the wardrobe for a day or two, can you not?'

Owen shrugged and there was doubt in the tone of his reply. 'Of course I will stay if you wish, but I fear he may suspect something if he sees us much together.'

'It may be the right time to tell him,' she replied, still speaking under the sound of chatter in the room. 'He is ten now and I would prefer him to hear of our marriage from my lips and not through those of some spy from the court.'

I saw alarm flare in Owen's eyes, but he said nothing because at that moment Maître Jean stood and raised his hand to deliver the grace.

As Owen had said, no carts were needed to slow our journey back to Hertford. Most of Catherine's more elaborate gowns were stored there and her court jewels were kept in a strongbox in the castle treasury. All she took in the way of furniture was her portable altar with its secret compartment, which conveniently fitted into a pack-horse pannier.

Earlier in the year, soon after Epiphany, Geoffrey had taken Mildy back to London where a marriage was being arranged with one of her cousins from the wine side of the Vintner family. William and I were to join them shortly before Easter when the wedding would take place. Meanwhile, Agnes and Hywell had returned from Wales with their toddler, a shy little girl called Gywneth, who with all the other children was left temporarily at Hadham under the care of Alys and Anne, who was nervously pregnant again and taking every precaution in the hope of carrying this child to full term. We travelled discreetly, displaying nothing to reveal Catherine's identity and, being a small group, were able to ride fast, reaching the castle by midday.

Prudently King Henry's party adopted a similar policy. There were no royal banners flying when he rode in three days later on a pony in plain harness, with only twenty guards, his confessor, a tutor and a couple of body squires. The regency council was represented by Owen's former troop-captain Sir Walter Hungerford, now a baron and lord treasurer of England, with his entourage of clerks and squires.

To do honour to her twice-crowned son, Catherine had arrayed herself in full court finery; or rather Agnes and I had arrayed her, forcing our fingers to perform grooming tasks which had lately become unfamiliar. We were proud of our handiwork as we watched her perform her role as the stately queen dowager in an ermine-trimmed mantle and gem-studded headdress. On a carpet spread over the courtyard paving she knelt to greet the boy-king.

'You are greatly welcome, my liege; joyful and humble greetings from your grace's most loyal subject.'

King Henry seemed impressed by her words and her appearance. He dismounted from his pony and bent solemnly to take her hand and raise her. 'It is good to be with you, my lady mother. We have been too long apart.'

I felt a lump come to my throat because his words echoed Catherine's own thoughts, fervently expressed to me the previous evening as she anticipated Henry's arrival. 'It is nearly four years since we laid eyes on each other, Mette. How terrible it will be if we meet as total strangers!' she had said.

I thought as they exchanged formal kisses how much had happened in those four years, and how little this young mother and son knew of each other's lives and activities during that time.

Having been closed up for a year, the Presence Chamber at Hertford had looked cold and uninviting when we first returned, but once the furniture had been polished and made comfortable with embroidered cushions, bright-coloured tapestries had been hung and a blazing fire lit in the hearth, it had become a warm and pleasant place for mother and son to sit and become re-acquainted. A meal had been served in the great hall, also warmed and polished and hung with banners, after which Owen had taken Lord Hungerford off to the castle butts while there was still enough light to prove that his skill with the bow was as keen as ever and Catherine and Henry had settled themselves cosily by the fire. Agnes and I served drinks and sweetmeats and the young king commented on the preserved pears from last year's crop which I had brought specially from Hadham.

'I had some very similar to this in Paris,' he remarked, taking a bite and reminding me uncannily of Catherine's brother Charles doing the same while breakfasting with her at a similar age. He had discarded his fur-lined riding heuque to disclose a short gown of murrey wool over royal-blue hose and sported a plain bucket hat with a feather in it, of the sort that any well-to-do schoolboy might wear.

Catherine smiled at me as I poured wine and spring water for her and weak ale for Henry. 'Madame Lanière learned the recipe at the Hôtel de St Pol, did you not, Mette?'

'Yes, your grace, although I have changed the spices to suit the English pears.'

'I went to the Hôtel de St Pol to visit my grandmother, Queen Isabeau,' Henry said, glancing at his mother a little uneasily. 'I hope you will not be offended, my lady, if I say that I did not enjoy the visit very much. My uncle of Bedford did not want me to go but I insisted. He thought I would be shocked at her appearance.'

'And were you?' Catherine asked gently.

'She does look quite . . .' Henry sought for a suitable word, '. . . messy. Her face is a mask of flaky white paint and her hands are gnarled and swollen, with rings embedded in the flesh. I could not believe she was your mother.'

Catherine shrugged sadly. 'She is old now – over sixty – but she was once a beautiful and formidable queen; not a good one perhaps, but forceful and determined.'

'I think she was a little drunk,' Henry murmured, leaning closer to confide in Catherine. 'She kept forgetting what she was saying and her servants sniggered behind her back. Her clothes were dirty too and . . .' After a pause he continued almost in a whisper, '. . . she smelled rather unpleasant. I did not go again.'

I watched Catherine absorb this description of her mother and wondered how she would react. Queen Isabeau had shockingly ignored and neglected her children and was now apparently being neglected in her turn, but it would be typical of Catherine to regret this situation rather than see it as her mother's just deserts.

Eventually her response was neutral. 'It was kind of you to visit her, Henry. I have not seen or heard of her since your father died. I am sure Queen Isabeau was pleased to see you. But let us talk of your coronation in Paris. Did the people greet you well?'

Henry immediately became animated. 'Oh yes! On the streets they all wore red and blue in my honour. There were tableaux in the squares, even mermaids swimming in the fountains. They were not real mermaids, of course, but young girls in costume. Imagine that though, in December!'

Catherine laughed. 'Perhaps the water had been warmed. And the ceremony – was it very solemn?'

The little king nodded. 'Yes, very. I walked beneath a blue silken canopy sprinkled with gold fleurs-de-lys and carried by the greatest of my nobles and the Bishop of Paris anointed me with the holy chrism, but it was Cardinal Beaufort who set the crown upon my head. I believe there was an argument over this. The bishop said that he should do it in his own cathedral, but you know how forceful the cardinal can be and I suppose he pulled rank. There were several anthems but they were not as fine as the one I heard last night when we stayed at Waltham Abbey. The Windsor choir is great, but I think Waltham is better.'

His mother smiled. 'Well, you are the expert on choirs I am told. Where did you live while you were in France?'

'I went to Rouen first and we stayed a long time because there was all that business with the girl, Jeanne d'Arc. She had been taken prisoner by the Burgundians, but they handed her over to the English and my uncle of Bedford organised her trial. It was very thorough. The Bishop of Beauvais was the judge and the woman was questioned over many weeks.'

'Did you see her? What did she look like?'

The king shrugged. 'I saw her only once. She was ordinary, a peasant girl. You would not have noticed her in a street crowd but she was a sorceress, of that there is no doubt.'

'Oh?' Catherine's eyebrows arched in surprise. 'Did she cast spells and fling curses?'

'Not that I heard, but she claimed to hear voices. She said they were saints telling her what God wanted her to do.' Henry shifted uneasily in his chair. 'Everything she did was against the teaching of Holy Mother Church. She wore men's clothes and carried a sword, she said because Saint Margaret and Saint Catherine told her to do so. Also she claimed to have been sent by God to save France. From what, I would like to know? I am God's chosen King of France. She was blasphemous.'

'And what happened to her? We heard she was burned.'

'Yes. At first she repented and was sentenced to prison for

life but then she recanted and somehow she acquired male dress in her prison cell and dressed as a man again.'

'As protection perhaps,' murmured Catherine, 'from the guards.' I could tell that she felt certain sympathy for this girl whom her brother, Charles, seemed callously to have used and then abandoned.

Henry shook his head and took a sip of his ale. 'No I do not think so. She was ugly. Warwick said that if she was a virgin it was only because she was unattractive to men.'

His mother's eyes rounded in shock at this flagrant masculine bigotry and her tone became indignant. 'So they burned her?'

Henry did not appear to notice the reproach in her question. He nodded. 'Two days later, in the main square at Rouen.'

Catherine shivered visibly. 'You did not watch?'

'They would not let me,' Henry said almost bitterly. 'She deserved to burn though. She was a schismatic, a witch, a heretic!'

I saw Catherine wince at the strident tone in which her son made these terrible accusations. Nevertheless she managed to sound matter-of-fact.

'So the maid is dead?'

'Yes.' At this point Henry suddenly began to sound uncertain, more like the ten-year-old boy he was. 'Some of the French now call her a saint. They say her soul took the form of a white dove and flew out of the flames and up to heaven.' He stared into the fire for a few moments, then turned haunted eyes to Catherine. 'Would that not be terrible if it were true?'

A mother's urge to console overcame Catherine's misgivings. 'Perhaps, Henry, but it would be her followers who want you to believe that. To me she seemed a poor young girl who was given to wild fantasies, which misled her into believing she was God's chosen vessel. Such things happen in convents when young nuns pray too much and eat too little. I saw it at Poissy when I was young.'

The alarm in Henry's eyes faded and he smiled. 'They say she hardly ate at all,' he said, 'so perhaps you may be right.'

His mother abruptly changed the subject and became brisk and businesslike. 'Have you seen the Duke of Gloucester since your return?'

'Yes, of course. Did you not hear? He organised a big parade through London to welcome me back and we are to spend Easter together at St Edmund's Bury. I would ask you to join us but it will be men only.'

She smiled. 'It is much better to see you now, alone. Will you stay with the monks all through Lent then?'

He nodded enthusiastically. 'I am to have lessons from a famous scholar who is very old and cannot leave the abbey. He will teach me how to translate Aristotle.'

'And will you like that, Henry?'

I could not blame Catherine for sounding a little incredulous, but her son looked remarkably keen. 'Oh yes, and it means I will escape the Earl of Warwick's daily arms practices for a while.' Henry leaned forward confidingly again. 'But do not tell anyone I said that, will you, Mother?'

She leaned forward and patted his arm. 'No, Henry, I promise I will not – especially if you promise to visit me again on your way back from Bury. Will you do that?'

He gave her a gratifyingly determined nod. 'I will, my lady mother, whatever anyone says!'

A bright laugh greeted this response. 'Well said, my son. You are the king; do not let anyone bully you, whoever "anyone" is. Now, what would you like to do while you are here at Hertford?

Would you like to hunt with Master Tudor tomorrow? The park is full of game.'

Henry looked shocked. 'Tomorrow is Sunday. I cannot hunt on a Sunday. Will your chaplain not celebrate a high Mass?'

Catherine blushed. 'Do you know, in the excitement of seeing you again I had quite forgotten what day of the week it was. Of course Maître Boyers will be honoured to say high Mass tomorrow with the king.'

That night, because of her elaborate apparel, both Agnes and I were needed to help Catherine prepare for bed and as the three of us discussed the events of the day, it felt quite like old times, before her marriage to King Henry's father. As part of their pretence during the king's visit, she and Owen were keeping separate chambers but it quickly became apparent that Catherine was seriously considering telling her son about her second marriage and the existence of his stepbrothers.

'I so dislike the need for this deception,' she fretted, pulling one glittering ring after another from her fingers in a series of vexed jerks. 'I feel as if I am performing in a masque. It is like these jewels – all sham and show. I have not actually had to deny that I am married to Owen, but the longer I continue to keep it from Henry the less he will be able to trust me afterwards. He seems so mature for his age. Two coronations would be enough to make anyone grow up fast. I believe I can trust him to keep our secret.'

Agnes ventured a mild protest as she hastily gathered up the rings Catherine had discarded. 'But, Madame, if you tell King Henry might he not have to lie to protect you? That would be hard for one as young as he – and so obviously devout? He will be torn between God's commandment to honour his mother, and obedience to the Church's teaching on truth.'

Catherine pondered this briefly, then shook her head. 'No, he will not have to lie because I am scarcely a part of his life. I am willing to wager that my name is only mentioned when he writes his censored letters to me. Lord Hungerford is the only member of the government he could ask to escort him to Hertford. I suspect the Duke of Gloucester and the Earl of Warwick would have refused to bring him to visit his mother because they want him to forget me and learn to pursue the war with France. Henry will not have to lie; he will be able to keep the secret by saying nothing.'

'And will Owen be happy for you to tell the king?' I asked, lifting the heavy gold templette from her head.

'I do not know and I cannot ask him because he is not here, where he should be!' She put her hands to her forehead to scratch irritably at the red marks left by the headdress. 'I know, I know, Mette, you are going to tell me that he is the one who will suffer if it gets out that he has defied the heinous Marriage Act. And you are right. They may throw him in jail – or worse. Aaah!' She sank her head into her hands and her next words were muffled. 'It is not a decision I want to make.'

In the event it was not a decision she had time to make, because the next morning a warning trumpet blast was heard and a troop of horsemen cantered over the drawbridge under the banner of the Duke of Gloucester. Catherine had just finished dressing for Mass, donning once more the sober widow's barbe and wimple she had abandoned on moving to Hadham, and immediately sent Agnes to find out who had arrived. The news did not please her.

'No visit from Gloucester augers well,' she observed grimly as I handed her her breviary. 'He would never come here except to bring bad news or else to gloat.'

'Then you must be careful, Mademoiselle,' I said. 'Do not allow him to rile you.'

She took a final look in the Venetian glass; an unusual event these days because it never went to Hadham for fear of breakage. A prim figure in a plain dark-blue gown stared back at her. Framed by her linen coif, her face was pale, the eyes steely blue and the answering smile resolute. 'I would not give him the satisfaction, Mette. Please accompany me.'

The great hall was crowded with men in Gloucester livery and half-armour, whose arrival had sent the servants scurrying as they struggled to answer strident calls for ale and meat. Catherine checked her pace at the entrance and advanced with slow, regal tread towards the hearth where the Duke of Gloucester stood impatiently tapping his booted foot. His meagre bow of greeting was made grudgingly.

Catherine made no effort to greet him in return, but stared pointedly down at the duke's sword, hanging in its jewelled scabbard from his gilded leather belt. 'You must know as well as anyone, my lord duke, that where the king is in residence all arms must be left at the gatehouse – even yours.' Her tone was calm but not pleasant.

'Then the king is here. That is what I came to find out,' said Gloucester curtly. 'I have no time for niceties. I must speak with the king and my men need refreshment. We ride on for St Edmund's Bury afterwards.'

Catherine seated herself in a chair by the fire. 'I repeat. All arms must be taken to the guardhouse before anything further can be done.'

Across the hall I saw Owen enter from the screen door. He heard this request, strode swiftly up to the duke, made a bend of the knee and held out his hands. 'Allow me to take your sword, my lord, and I will show your men where to leave theirs.'

Gloucester's scowl deepened, but he unbuckled his weapon and handed it to Owen. 'It is of great value. Take care it is kept separate from the others,' he snapped and rounded on Catherine. 'Now, Madame – the king?'

From close behind Catherine's chair I watched her ignore the duke's rude demand for her son, gazing down at her hands, carefully folded around her leather-covered breviary. 'It is Sunday, my lord of Gloucester. You should be even more aware than I that the king always hears Mass before breaking his fast on a Sunday.' Her chin lifted as the bell began to ring from the castle chapel and she rose swiftly. 'You and your men may join us if you like, my lord. The meal will be served after Mass.'

I followed Catherine's rigid back through the main entrance and down the steps without looking back to see whether the duke came or stayed. We met with the king and Lord Hungerford as they emerged from the privy entrance where Gloucester had accosted Catherine so roughly four years previously.

Henry took her hand as she made her curtsy to him. 'God's Sabbath greeting to you, my lady mother.' She bent to let him plant a kiss on her cheek and gave him one in return. Henry gazed around at the bustle in the courtyard. 'Who has arrived so early on a Sunday?'

'Your uncle of Gloucester. He wishes to speak with your grace. I told him he was welcome to join us at breakfast after Mass.' Catherine managed to keep any hint of antipathy out of her voice.

'Did he not wish to join us in the chapel?'

'I invited him but it seems not.'

Lord Hungerford coughed and interjected. 'Perhaps I should go and see what he wants, your grace?'

Henry frowned but nodded. 'If you wish, my lord. I hope you will join us in the chapel later.'

But Lord Hungerford did not come to Mass at all, nor was he in the great hall for breakfast.

'Hungerford had to leave for London,' the duke explained baldly to the king. 'Regrettably he will not be continuing as treasurer here and his place will be taken by your new steward, Sir Robert Babthorpe.'

'What? But why?' The little king was far from happy at this news and immediately grew petulant. 'I do not know this Sir Robert Babthorpe. I wish Lord Huntingdon to accompany me to Bury.'

'That will not be possible, I fear, but you know Sir Robert's son Ralph. He is one of your squires of the body. He is here with me now and will come with us to St Edmund's Abbey.' Gloucester put an arm around the boy's shoulders and guided him to his place at table. 'Come, Henry, I expect you are hungry. Some breakfast will set you up.'

My place was further down the board and I was not able to hear what followed, but I could see that Catherine's questions to the duke were not answered to her satisfaction for she became morose and ate little, taking only a small portion of bread and a few sips of the breakfast ale. Meanwhile Gloucester's smiling overtures seemed to be working on the king, who grew more animated and amused by his uncle's conversation as the meal progressed. It was a cheerful boy who withdrew with his mother and the duke to the solar at the end of breakfast.

I slipped in after them, not wanting to risk any chance of Catherine finding herself alone with Humphrey of Gloucester.

Behind me Ralph Babthorpe, the squire whose father had suddenly and mysteriously been appointed King Henry's new steward, smugly brought the duke's sword and belt into the room and informed him that everything was prepared for departure.

'His grace's bags are packed and loaded as you instructed, my lord,' the young man added.

Henry looked at his mother in surprise. 'I thought I was to stay here with you until tomorrow,' he said. 'I was so busy telling you mine, that I have hardly heard any of your news.'

Catherine smiled and tucked her hand in the crook of his elbow, turning him pointedly away from the duke. 'You may stay as long as you like, my dear son. And you are right; we still have much to tell each other.'

'On another occasion perhaps, my liege,' Gloucester said, moving in on Henry's other side. 'The plans have changed. I am to escort you to Bury and must leave at once.' He took the king's other elbow, removing him firmly from Catherine's grasp and letting his gaze travel contemptuously over her plain attire and concealing coif. 'Besides, now that your mother lives in such nun-like seclusion, she can have nothing of much interest to tell you. Far better we should make a more leisurely journey and arrive in good time to enjoy the abbot's lavish Fat Tuesday feast before Lent turns our thoughts to our salvation, do you not agree?'

'Actually we have a sumptuous feast prepared here for you today, Henry,' countered Catherine, refusing to admit defeat. 'Master Tudor brought down a fine hind and it is already roasting at the kitchen fire. I believe we can smell its tantalising aroma.' She sniffed appreciatively.

'It is pointless to tempt the king with the smell of venison,

Madame,' said Gloucester on an unmistakable note of triumph. 'I happen to know it is the one meat that is not to his grace's taste, is that not so, nephew? Your mother has either forgotten, or else you have changed. Young boys do change their tastes as they grow, Madame, but of course you can have little experience of that. Now I think you should go and make yourself ready for the journey, Henry, and let Ralph clothe you in your warmest attire. Remember it is February and the wind is blowing cold from the east.'

The squire, a sturdy-looking young man approaching the age of knighthood, bowed low to the king and gestured him point-edly towards the door. Henry's gaze flickered uncertainly between Catherine and the duke and then he shrugged.

'It seems I must go, then,' he grumbled, 'but I do so unwill-ingly, uncle.'

'We will make our farewells in private before you go, my son,' Catherine called after his small, departing figure, waiting for the door to close before turning angrily on the duke. 'Shame on you, Gloucester! There is a boy who is baffled and bemused – and no wonder. We were fighting over him like the two women before Solomon. He was happy with Lord Hungerford. Now he does not know if he is coming or going. Boys of his age need security and a regular routine.'

Gloucester sneered down at her from his superior height. 'Neither of which you are in a position to give him, Madame. So do not lecture me on the upbringing of boys. At least I was one once.'

She was holding the breviary she had taken to Mass and suddenly raised it high under his nose. 'Using my son for revenge on me is the devil's work. Have a care for your soul, my lord!'

Gloucester adopted an incredulous expression. 'Revenge on

you? You are not of enough significance. Even less so now that the fool who sought to advance himself by marrying you has secured himself a bride of rather more worth. You probably are not aware that, lacking English estates, Edmund Beaufort has married Warwick's daughter Eleanor, Lady Roos; a widow with enough lands and wealth to satisfy any impecunious younger son.'

Humphrey took his sword from the table where the squire had left it and made a great show of buckling it on. 'However the upstart Beaufort pup has not learned his lesson. He married her without licence from the council, so when the formalities are finally concluded, which may take some time, he will be paying a sizeable sum into the Treasury by way of a fine. Still, the penalty for marrying you would have been penury and dishonour and no woman is worth that, however royal her blood.'

To show his disdain for her ban on weapons, he half drew his sword, slammed it fiercely back into the scabbard then, without bow or farewell, made his exit.

Catherine took a deep breath to shout after him in protest, then caught my eye and expelled air instead. 'Ugh! Abominable, self-satisfied, pompous man! And I have to let him ride away with my son. God give me the patience to bear it!' She paced furiously around the room. 'Power has corrupted Humphrey of Gloucester and I hope it will be his downfall and that Henry, when he is old enough, will be the one to bring it about!'

As we were alone, I risked the remark that it was fortunate she had not told Henry about her marriage and his brothers. 'For it appears that at present the king is too much in Gloucester's thrall to be trusted not to reveal your secret.'

'Yet I must tell him, Mette,' she declared with grim determination. 'He must hear it from my lips. If there is to be trust between any two people, surely it must be between mother and son.'

35

A week before Easter, Geoffrey came to Hadham to accompany me and William to London to prepare for Mildy's wedding, which was to take place immediately afterwards. It was an affecting sight to see our three-year-old son grinning from ear to ear as he rode in a pommel-seat on his father's saddle, but I have to admit that my heart was in my mouth all the way to Tun Lane. I knew from bitter experience that life was God's to give and take as He saw fit but, being what Catherine teasingly called 'autumn' parents, William had become of such supreme importance in our lives that to have him taken from us by some dreadful riding accident was not something I could bear to contemplate. However all went well and William attended his half-sister's wedding in a new blue doublet and a jaunty felt hat with a red feather in it. I may be biased, but the sight of our lively little boy with the curly brown hair and ready smile made me almost burst with pride.

The marriage was an interesting match between two people who had known each other since childhood and were friends rather than sweethearts. At twenty-three, Mildy had reached an age when she understood the obligations of matrimony and looked forward to keeping a house and raising a family. Hugh Vintner was her cousin, a few years older and just the right side of the Church's rules on consanguinity, who had recently returned from a lengthy period acting as the family's agent in Bordeaux, where he had learned all there was to know about the wine from that region and so was amply suited to take over his ailing father's London import business. I suppose it could have been called a marriage of convenience, but watching them talking and laughing together as they shared a cup at the wedding feast I thought the omens looked good for this particular union.

Our intention had been to stay in London for a few weeks before returning to Hadham. Shortly after the episode at Hertford, Catherine had revealed to Owen that she was pregnant again and I planned to return to her side well before the birth of their third child in the summer. However, less than a week after Mildy's wedding, a letter came from Hadham. In truth it was more of a cry of distress; a scrawled note penned in obvious haste and agitation, without any greeting or signature.

Oh, Mette!
As so often I am in sore need of your wise counsel for I am torn between my eldest son and my husband and cannot reconcile my loyalty to each. Henry has written to say that he is to stay an extra month at St Edmund's Bury, but will visit me in early May on his way back to Westminster for the opening of Parliament on the sixteenth. I have written to tell him that I will be at Hadham and not Hertford and Owen is furious with me, saying I have betrayed his trust by not consulting him first. He says he will not be at Hadham if the king comes because he cannot preserve the deception here in our sanctuary and forbids me to tell Henry of our marriage. I have declared that I must because by then it will be obvious that I am with

child. He wants me to tell Henry not to come. We have argued as never before and he has left Hadham – gone I think to Wales. Suppose he does not return? I cannot live without him. Dear God, what should I do?

I had procured refreshments for the courier while he waited for a reply, then taken the note straight to Geoffrey in his library where he was working. He had not looked pleased at being interrupted, but I had pushed the letter at him.

'I am sorry, Geoffrey, but you must read this. It is from Catherine. We have to go back to Hadham.'

He scanned the note and shook his head impatiently. 'It is time you let her fight her own battles, Mette,' he declared. 'She expects too much and you have other commitments now.'

'She sounds desperate, Geoffrey. Look at the writing. The ink is spattered. Her hand is shaking as she writes. This is a frantic note. She might do anything and there is the babe to think of.'

Geoffrey sighed. 'We have our own child to consider, Mette. Why should we take William on a rushed and hazardous journey to Hadham just because Catherine and Owen have had an argument? Owen will probably have returned by the time we get there and our haste will have been for nothing. Reply to the queen with your advice in a letter and let us not change our plans because of a slight marital disagreement.'

I demurred. 'This is not a trivial tiff. It has been brewing for weeks and the problem is of major significance. If she tells the king of her marriage and he decides he cannot keep it a secret, it could spell the end of everything.'

Geoffrey was perusing the letter again, more carefully. 'I cannot believe Owen will have gone far. He is too honourable a man to leave Catherine in such a predicament. She says she thinks he has gone to Wales, but she does not know that. It is my belief that he has galloped off in a fit of pique to the next dower manor and once he has calmed down he will turn around and go back to Hadham. He is probably there already.'

Stubbornly I stood my ground. 'Then he could do with your legal advice, Geoffrey. What is the likelihood of him being arrested if their marriage comes to the attention of the council, and what would be the position of the children? Contingency plans should be made.'

With another sigh he pushed away the scroll he had been consulting and stood up. 'Very well, I can see you will not be dissuaded. But we cannot leave until tomorrow. I have to make arrangements for another lawyer to take this case and besides there is not time to make it to Hadham in daylight if we leave today. I refuse to submit William to the dangers of a night journey.'

I walked round the table to give him a kiss and took back the letter. 'Thank you, husband,' I said with a conciliatory smile. 'I will send a note to that effect with the courier. Apart from anything else, William will be delighted to go back to Edmund. I fear the company of his parents is no substitute for that of his boon companion.'

As Geoffrey had predicted, Owen had returned to Hadham by the time we arrived, but the mood between him and Catherine remained tense. He greeted us cheerfully enough, but over the evening meal he exchanged hardly a word with her and instead of sharing a game of chess with Geoffrey afterwards, as he often did, or else playing his harp for us all, he disappeared with Hywell and John on some business concerning weapons or armour. Clearly he and Catherine had not resolved their differences and when I had a chance to talk to her, I soon learned that she remained adamant that she would not put off the king's visit, nor would she consent to keep her marriage a secret from him any longer. She appeared pleased with our return and listened to Geoffrey's advice on the legal ramifications if the marriage should become public; however, even the possibility that Owen might end up in Newgate Prison did not cause her to swerve from her intended purpose. Observing how pronounced her five-month baby belly was already, I confess I could appreciate her point of view, but I nevertheless tended to agree with Owen, that it was not too late to postpone the king's visit, being of the opinion that even for a king, ten was too young for a boy to be saddled with knowledge of his mother's clandestine marriage and secret children.

'I will not turn my own son away from my door,' she retorted when I expressed this thought. 'And Henry is not like your average page boy. He is highly intelligent and well educated. He may dislike the idea of my marriage at first, but I am sure he will appreciate my point of view eventually.'

I made no reaction except to purse my lips and she must have noticed because she tossed her head and called Agnes to bring the chessboard. Geoffrey and I were obviously dismissed.

The king came a few days later, in the first week of May, sending a messenger on ahead to warn us of his imminent arrival. This gave Catherine time to change her drab workaday clothes for something her royal son might recognise as queenly attire and, since she chose a tight-bodiced houppelande gown with a full skirt that flowed from a high waist, I suspect she was hoping that the king might not notice her gravid state.

However she did not risk welcoming him outside in front of

his steward and retainers. Owen performed this task, ushering King Henry into the house and straight to Catherine's solar, where a canopied chair awaited him across the hearth from his mother's. Catherine bent her knee in greeting and embraced him warmly before they both took their seats. I too made my obeisance to the king and waited in my usual place behind the queen's chair in the shadow of the chimney-piece, discreetly removed but ready to be of service. The door had barely closed behind Owen when we were startled by King Henry's frantic, stuttering inquiry.

'My lady mother, please tell me that my eyes deceive me and that you are not . . . are not . . . well, are not . . .' His treble voice seemed to fail him and vanished altogether in a gulp. For several seconds there was silence.

Catherine gave a nervous cough. 'That is why I wanted you to come here, my son, so that I could tell you myself. Yes, Henry, I am expecting a child.'

Henry's arm moved rapidly as he crossed himself repeatedly muttering, '*Ave Maria, gratia plena, Dominus tecum, benedicta tu in mulieribus . . . ora pro nobis peccatoribus . . .*'

Catherine interrupted his recital, speaking slowly and clearly. 'Why do you say the Ave, Henry? Why do you pray for "us sinners"? I do not believe you are a sinner and I am certainly not a sinner.'

The king's response emerged like a chicken's squawk. 'You must be a sinner! You are condemned by your condition. How can you deny that you are a fallen woman? A Mary Magdalene!' I detected a frightening build-up of hysteria and took a step forward, ready in case he threw himself at his mother in ferment, but Catherine raised her hand to stop me.

'Even Lord Jesus let Mary Magdalene wash his feet,' she

reminded him gently. 'But, believe me, Henry, I am not a fallen woman, as you put it.'

'What is this, then?' her son demanded, pointing his finger accusingly at her stomach. 'I may be only ten but I know full well that a child born out of wedlock is a bastard and its mother is a-a-a whore!' He tripped over the word but eventually spat it out with venom, his young face twisted in distaste. Falling from his chair onto his knees, he raised his clenched fists skywards in a dramatic appeal to the Almighty. 'Ah dear Lord be my aid! I am shamed and betrayed by my own mother!' Then he covered his face with his hands and broke into wild moans of anguish and denial, choking and sobbing by turns.

Catherine swung round to look at me, her eyes rounded in alarm. I knew what she was thinking. This kind of sudden and uncontrolled behaviour was reminiscent of her father's fits of madness, when he had screamed that he was made of glass and would not let anyone near him in case he shattered. Could this tragic feebleness of mind be re-appearing in King Charles's grandson?

'Listen to me, Henry!' Catherine grabbed her son's hands and hauled him to his feet. 'Stop screaming or you will not hear me.' She pushed him back into his chair. 'Stop it! Now!'

Henry lapsed into silence as if suddenly aware of how childish he had been sounding, like a toddler in a tantrum over a sweet-meat. He had the grace to look a little shamefaced and sat in his chair swinging his feet, eyes downcast, sighing, fiddling with his fingernails. The door opened and a rather portly grey-bearded man in a dark chaperon hat poked his head tentatively into the room, only to be waved regally away by Catherine, who carefully kept her back to him.

'Take no notice, Messire, the king has had a surprise but he is now recovered. Leave us please. We wish to be alone.'

When Catherine spoke in that regal ignore-me-at-your-peril tone of voice it was beyond the bravest of courtiers to disobey and the door hastily closed again. I had recognised the man as Sir Robert Babthorpe the royal steward who had been foisted on King Henry by the Duke of Gloucester at Hertford. My heart sank at the possibility of him having noticed Catherine's condition. If he had, the news would go straight to the duke himself.

'I think you might fetch Maître Boyers, Mette.' Catherine was keeping up a calm front and seated herself back in her chair. 'Henry obviously needs the reassurance of a priest. Meanwhile I will endeavour to tell him the truth without him jumping to any more false conclusions.'

As I crossed the room to the door, I saw Henry raise his head to look at his mother. His expression was still thunderous but his tantrum seemed to have subsided. I found Maître Boyers in the hall conversing with Owen, Geoffrey and Sir Robert while servants laid cloths and napkins on a trestle ready to serve the steward some refreshment. Two of King Henry's squires were playing dice beside a brazier in a far corner. I beckoned the priest aside in order to convey Catherine's message out of earshot of the visitors.

When we reached the solar, the little king was slumped, whey-faced, in his chair and Catherine was kneeling before him, his hands held tightly in hers. She was evidently trying to reassure him as best she could, but she looked relieved to see her confessor. 'Ah, Maître Boyers is here now. He will confirm what I have said, Henry, that I am married to Owen Tudor and that this child will be your legitimate half brother or sister.'

The priest did not appear surprised to be summoned for this purpose and I concluded that Catherine must have primed him beforehand to be ready to administer divine comfort to the bewildered young boy. She stood up, gestured to her confessor to approach the king and came over to join me.

'My poor son,' she murmured, shaking her head sorrowfully. 'He has taken it badly. I hope some prayer and priestly advice may calm his anxiety. What is Owen doing with the steward?'

'He is arranging some refreshment, Mademoiselle. Have you told his grace about his brothers yet?'

Catherine shook her head. 'No. One step at a time, I think. It took me quite by surprise when Henry made so much fuss before I was able to explain. He is still as temperamental as he was when a small child. I am surprised the Earl of Warwick has not managed to instil more self control. Do you think Sir Robert noticed my condition when he burst in?'

'No, Mademoiselle, you were very quick to turn your back. When I saw him in the hall, Sir Robert was eyeing the table hungrily as the cloth was being spread; I would say he was more concerned about filling his belly than measuring yours.'

As we spoke together quietly, the priest had drawn Henry out of his chair and over to the prie dieu. Soon there was the familiar sound of chanted prayer and King Henry bowed his head over his hands in reverence of the Virgin's image.

'He is so very devout,' his mother whispered. 'Prayers and psalms soothe him. I will tell him the whole story after they finish. Perhaps you would arrange for us to dine together in here, Mette; and Owen too I think. Ask Geoffrey to distract Sir Robert with an inspection of the dower accounts after his meal so that we can bring Edmund and Jasper down here to meet their brother without the steward noticing.'

I had to hand it to her; she had it all planned and, the Lord be praised, things proceeded just the way she intended. Sir Robert relished his meal and then dozed over the income and expenditure of Catherine's dower manors under the watchful eye of Geoffrey, while Owen and Catherine gently eased King Henry into acceptance of their marriage and life at Hadham. To my surprise, casting aside his doubts and fears, Owen assumed the lead role in this task. With a courtier's skill, he was careful to afford the young king all the deference due to his rank, but for once he asserted himself, gently but firmly impressing on Henry the love and respect he felt for Catherine and the desire they both had to live quietly removed from court, while remaining his loyal and faithful subjects.

At first the young king avoided their gaze as he picked at his roasted birds and jellied parsley and sipped his weak ale, his brow knitted in a fierce frown. I served their meal and at one point, as I was filling his cup, he fixed me with his flecked brown eyes, so like his father's they made me blink. 'You are the one who brought me the letter from the queen after my coronation,' he said accusingly. 'I was very pleased to get it. And you used to come to my nursery at Windsor. Have you stayed with my lady mother all this time?'

My hand shook with surprise at such a direct question and some ale spilled on the cloth, making me even more flustered. 'Er – yes, your grace. I live sometimes here in the queen's household and sometimes in London with my husband.' I was acutely conscious of the white lies I had told him at Westminster Palace, regarding my name and my domicile, but this did not seem to concern him.

'So you came with her from France and you have been with her ever since? You are very loyal.'

I did not know how to respond to this observation so I just said, 'Yes, your grace,' and moved round the table with my jug.

'Mette used to tell you stories when you were a little boy at Windsor,' Catherine interjected. 'Do you remember?'

At last the king responded to his mother directly. 'Yes, I liked her stories, but I liked Master Tudor's better,' he said, suddenly turning his attention to Owen, 'especially when you sang those wonderful songs about knights and their quests. I am very fond of singing.'

Owen smiled. 'So I understand, your grace. I would happily teach you some lays if you would like to learn them.'

The king's frown returned. 'I do not think I will have time today. Sir Robert says we must get to Waltham Abbey before sundown. He is anxious to reach Westminster early tomorrow. Perhaps I could learn the songs on my next visit?'

'Of course, my liege. We are delighted that you would like to come again.' Owen made an acquiescent bow and seized his opportunity. 'With that in mind, I hope you will not mention to Sir Robert anything we have told you of our marriage, or indeed to anyone at all. I am afraid that if you do, when you come again I may not be here to teach you anything, your grace.'

King Henry looked puzzled and was about to speak when Catherine broke in again. 'You see, Henry, our marriage is regarded as honourable by the Church and legal according to the laws of England. It is important that you remember that. However, we have fallen foul of a recent Act of Parliament that says I can only marry with your permission, which sadly you are still too young to give. I hope you understand that we must ask you to keep our secret until you come of age and can give that permission, otherwise Owen could be arrested and imprisoned and that would upset me enormously. Will you – can you – guard this secret for us?'

King Henry did not respond immediately, but gave himself some thinking time by fiddling distractedly with one of the pearl buttons on his blue velvet doublet. Owen made as if to speak, but Catherine shook her head at him and laid a finger on her lips. A log shifted on the fire and the noise it made was the only sound in a silence that seemed to last for long minutes. When at last the troubled boy lifted his head, there were tears in his eyes.

'I remember copying a letter to you concerning a proposed marriage to the Earl of Mortain,' he told Catherine. 'My lord of Warwick said the marriage would not be in England's interests. I was sorry because I like Edmund Beaufort.'

Catherine leaned forward to place her hand over his. 'I was sorry then too, Henry,' she said, 'but now I am glad because I found love with Owen and married him instead.'

King Henry blushed and removed his hand from under hers. 'Yes, but I would have preferred it if you had married Edmund Beaufort. Of course I like Owen and he is a very good archer and musician, but he is a commoner and your child will not be of true royal blood.'

Not for the first time I felt my common blood begin to boil at the way this trainee king was being educated for his vital role as ruler of his country. Of course he needed to be aware of his own birth and heritage, but it seemed to me that he also needed to acquire some of his father's appreciation of his subjects' worth. England needed a king with pride and charisma, but also with the common touch.

Catherine countered her son's received prejudice from a rather different angle, however. Noticing Owen's rueful expression, she flashed him a placatory smile and turned again to the king. 'You will be happy to hear then that Master Tudor is directly descended from a line of Welsh princes and, disinherited though they may be, their blood is as royal as yours, my son.' This appeared to give her son pause for thought, and while he was thinking she delivered her final thrust.

'And I must tell you now, Henry, that apart from the baby I am expecting, we have two sons already. They are called Edmund and Jasper. Would you like to meet them?'

Now the young king looked completely stunned. His jaw slackened and for several seconds he gaped at Catherine, his mouth and eyes open and staring, like a fish in a monger's basket. Before he could speak, Catherine beckoned to me. 'Would you fetch the boys please, Mette – and bring some toys and games.'

I have always considered it curious that children, no matter the difference in their age and size, invariably recognise each other as children and quickly form a bond that is a mystery to adults. Despite King Henry's evident shock at receiving the news that he had two half-brothers, after they had been introduced and had stared at each other for several minutes without speaking, when I suggested that they might like to play the game of indoor skittles I had brought from the nursery he was the first to agree. Obviously familiar with the game, he was quickly down on the floor placing the pins ready to start and proved to be a good shot, knocking down the king pin twice during his first turn. The two little boys took a few moments to lose their shyness, but it was not long before they were also throwing the wooden balls enthusiastically at the pins; sometimes a little too enthusiastically so that Owen had to restrain them and show them how to aim more accurately. Inevitably Henry won the match but he showed sensitivity towards the younger boys' disappointment by asking what other games they liked to play and letting them each win a game of Claim the Castle.

When the time came for the king to leave, he did not wait for Owen or Catherine to remind him of the secret he had to keep. He even realised that he must not mention what that secret was, nor refer to his relationship with the little boys in their earshot.

'I will remember all that you asked of me, my lady mother,' he murmured to Catherine when she hugged him before he quitted the room. 'I will think of you all and pray for you. And I will find a way to come back and visit again soon.'

Edmund and Jasper broke off sharing another game to say their farewells to Henry. 'Next time I will beat you at skittles,' declared Edmund, his chin jutting determinedly. 'I will be practising.'

'Me too,' said Jasper stolidly.

'Then I shall have to practise as well,' retorted Henry with a grin. 'Next time will be a fine battle.'

'Who was that, Mama?' Edmund asked when the king had left the room, escorted by Owen and Maître Boyers. 'I liked him.'

Catherine ruffled Edmund's gold head. 'I am glad,' she said. 'He is a good friend of ours.'

Such reticence was essential. Trusting a ten-year-old boy with her all-important secret was nerve-wracking enough, but to reveal the truth of their birth to these two, that were little more than toddlers, was a risk too far.

36

Catherine and Owen's third child was born on the Feast of St Margaret, the twentieth of July 1432, and duly baptised in honour of that saint, which surprised Catherine who had thought she was destined only to have sons and thrilled Owen because Margaret was the name of his mother who had died when he was six years old.

'Now I have a living reminder of the beautiful Margaret Vychan, whose voice I have inherited and who taught me my first notes on the harp!' he cried, cradling the tiny girl carefully in his brawny arms, 'As I shall teach you, cariad bach!'

There was no sign of the fear and anger that had caused his dispute with Catherine and driven him temporarily away three months before. After the king's visit they had spent several hours closeted alone together and then it was as if there had never been a rift. In the glorious sunshine of that balmy Hadham summer, their idyll was restored.

Nor, after Margaret's birth, could I bring myself to leave Catherine's household as I had considered doing. Geoffrey and I had discussed taking William to live with us permanently in London, but he and Edmund Tudor were so close it seemed a shame to separate them. For two months of their earliest infancy they had shared milk from the same breast and it may have been this that had forged the tight bond between them so that

431

they were seldom to be seen apart, even sharing a cot bed at night. Little Jasper tried to shadow their every move and most of the time they tolerated the younger boy, but now and then they managed to give him the slip to go off on 'big boy' expeditions into the woods. So adventurous did they become that a student from Hatfield Priory was hired to keep them from danger and also to teach them the rudiments of writing and reading.

For the sake of this harmonious attachment Geoffrey continued to journey patiently through fair weather and foul between his law practice in London and his work at Hadham as Catherine's treasurer, when we managed to live like married people for spells of time. He was our main source of news from the outside world and so it was from him that we learned the following year of a new and more serious outbreak of hostility between Cardinal Beaufort and the Duke of Gloucester. Once again it was over the war in France and the cardinal's calls for peace negotiations. Gloucester accused him of treachery and urged the Commons to raise taxes to underwrite further armies in order to defend England's threatened territories, a move the cardinal deplored. These disputes became violent within the council and among their supporters on the streets of London, which eventually led to the return of the Duke of Bedford from France to try and restore calm and avert a very real threat of civil war.

However John of Bedford had done more than broker a much-needed peace between warring magnates. Having lost his first wife, Anne of Burgundy, to a sudden outbreak of plague in Paris, he had re-married and brought his new wife to England, seventeen-year-old Jacquetta of Luxembourg, the niece of Holy Roman Emperor Sigismund. The whole country began to speculate whether this union might not only strengthen England's position in Europe, but also produce a potential second-generation heir for the English throne. In June, to Catherine's delight, John of Bedford sent her a letter proposing that he bring his new wife to Hertford to meet her. On this occasion we had plenty of time to prepare, which was fortunate because Catherine wanted to put on a grand show for her favourite brother-in-law and his young and well-connected bride. She had new accessories and trimmings sent from London to spruce up her court attire and Alys was urged to recall all she could remember of the fashions seen around the hotels of Paris before she left.

'I imagine a girl of seventeen will display the very latest styles, and I shall be made to look frumpish and dowdy unless something is done,' Catherine fretted. 'We are so out of touch here in the country.'

Alys sought to reassure her. 'The first gown that Jacques ever made for you was so ahead of its time that I think you may find it is now the height of fashion, Madame. If it would please you, I could re-line the sleeves in some of that beautiful, patterned Milanese silk I brought over from Paris. The court ladies will believe you had it specially made for their visit.'

Certainly, the striking turquoise-coloured gown with its underskirt of gold-embroidered cream satin was brilliantly lifted by the addition of Alys's pale sea-green Italian silk, turned back on the long trailing sleeves to form a deep cuff with a trimming of costly Flemish lace. A padded V-shaped roll of the same fabric set off Catherine's lofty headdress of gold netting with its ropes of pearls and shimmering veil of finest gauze. There was nothing dowdy or frumpish about the dowager queen of England as she stood in the June sunshine at the entrance to Hertford Castle to greet her distinguished guests. The great hall was decked with flowers and festooned with heraldic banners and an aromatic feast of six or seven courses was being prepared in the kitchens; there was nothing to suggest that this was not the well-established residence of England's highest-ranked lady. Even her ladies-in-waiting were arrayed in elegant court attire and decked out in items from the royal jewellery boxes. Of course we no longer numbered the Joannas in our ranks, but Geoffrey had brought Mildy to join Agnes and Alys and Anne. The five of us stood proudly at Catherine's back as the Duke of Bedford's cavalcade trotted under the gatehouse tunnel.

In a gold-tasselled blue velvet side-saddle, Jacquetta of Luxembourg rode a high-stepping chestnut palfrey trapped out in azure silk, embroidered with the Bedford badge of a golden stump and harnessed in gold-embossed white leather, making it clear to the world that John of Bedford had showered his new bride with gifts. As gossip had proclaimed, Jacquetta was indeed a beautiful young woman; clad in butter-yellow under a nutmeg-coloured riding heuque, slender and fair with porcelain skin and a wide smile displaying perfect white teeth framed by soft, cushioned ruby lips. No wonder her new husband now appeared handsome and rejuvenated compared to the grey-faced and weary man Catherine and I had last seen in his brother's funeral procession.

However, it was not the arrival of the lissom young bride or the statesmanlike bridegroom that widened my eyes, but the sight of the woman who rode beside them resplendent in a forest-green gown, her fine, dark features a striking contrast to Jacquetta's apple-blossom delicacy. Those slanting violet eyes appraised us and I could tell from the sudden stiffening of her neck and shoulders that Catherine saw their enmity too. It was Eleanor Cobham, Duchess of Gloucester.

Through the formal greetings and protracted banquet that

followed, there was no opportunity for any private conversation with Catherine but from my position beside Owen at the reward table I watched her conversing animatedly with the Duke of Bedford and, across him, to his luminous bride, effectively cutting out the Duchess of Gloucester, whose place was at the end of the table on Jacquetta's other side. This was the correct order of placement, according to rank, but I could see that it riled Eleanor of Gloucester, who was left for extended periods without anyone to talk to.

'Why did no one inform us that the Duchess of Gloucester was coming?' I asked Owen early on in the proceedings. 'Would that not have been the correct etiquette?'

Owen was stressed by having to reallocate accommodation in order to find suitable chambers for the Gloucester entourage and finding it hard to school his expression into that expected of the calm and capable master of Catherine's household. A mutinous look crept over his countenance. 'It is my guess she invited herself along at the last minute, possibly under orders from her husband,' he muttered. 'The Gloucesters will not want Catherine to become too cosy with Bedford. And do not forget that Eleanor has been spurned more than once by the queen. Petty though we may consider it, she might be looking for ways to get back at her. If you are going to pry into someone's affairs, you need to take them by surprise.'

'What do you mean, pry?' I looked down the main trestle where Eleanor's two lady companions were engaging gaily with Agnes and Mildy, laughing at one of Mildy's witticisms no doubt. 'Should we warn Catherine's ladies?'

Owen made a rueful face. 'It is a little late for that. We must pray they are all discreet. You can be sure that every word they say will be reported back to Eleanor.'

'And through her to the Duke of Gloucester,' I commented sourly. 'No wonder Catherine wanted to retire from court life.'

Suddenly Owen's infectious smile crinkled the corners of his eyes and mouth and reminded me why women, and Catherine in particular, found him so attractive. His voice sank to a throaty whisper and he leaned closer. 'Do you not think I might have had something to do with that?'

Returning his smile, I wagged a finger at him and whispered back, 'Do not flirt with me, Master Tudor, just because you are obliged to avoid your lady's eye!'

His head was turned away from the high table, but he must have had eyes in the back of it. 'It is called diversion tactics, Mette. While her grace of Gloucester stares at us, she is not thinking about the queen.'

I glanced up at the high table. Lacking any conversational distraction, Eleanor was watching us curiously. Despite my best intentions, I found myself blushing.

After the feast we watched an entertainment in the castle garden. A stage had been erected, complete with a painted castle where a troop of mummers put on a pageant celebrating King Henry the Fifth's famous run of siege victories in France. With glorious disregard for historical order, it culminated in a staged Battle of Agincourt, complete with volleys of blunted arrows and knights in armour galloping on hobby horses. Music was provided by a band of minstrels and some flowery and grandiose speeches were proclaimed by a master of ceremonies dressed as a herald. In a theatrical gesture to the Duke and Duchess of Bedford, a final tableau depicted the wedding of a beautiful golden-haired bride to a knight in shining armour at which Peace was the guest of honour.

'Of course that final scene could equally have been referring to your own marriage to the king's father, could it not, Madame? Was it not also meant to bring peace?'

Eleanor of Gloucester made this observation to her hostess as the three royal sisters-in-law, surrounded by their ladies, walked back through the garden to the great hall. The evening sun cast slanting shadows across the formal pattern of small hedges, flower beds and gravel paths as it slipped below the crenellations of the curtain wall. A perfect evening for schemes and subterfuges, I thought.

Catherine cast a swift glance at Eleanor. 'You are right, my marriage did seal a treaty, but we should not detract from the compliment to Duchess Jacquetta. Many hopes of peace are invested in her marriage to his grace of Bedford.'

She made a small bow in Jacquetta's direction and was rewarded with a dazzling smile. Not for the first time the new duchess put me in mind of Catherine at the same age. Although both were fair, they did not look much alike and the duchess was taller, but each moved with the grace and carriage of a dancer. Eleanor's gait, on the other hand, reminded me of a cat's, stealthy and sinuous, like one of the wild pumas I had seen in the royal menagerie at the Tower of London.

When she spoke again her voice was a deceptive purr. 'Of course the peace treaty is usually secured before the marriage is made. However, when the bride is as beautiful as her grace of Bedford, it is no wonder the bridegroom was anxious to hasten the nuptials and seek peace to enjoy them. Meanwhile, my own lord endeavours to defend the territories so fiercely won by their conquering brother, rather than surrender them at the negotiating table.'

'There has to be a time for everything, does there not?' Jacquetta did not say much but whenever she did, she went higher in my estimation. 'We should remember those words in the bible; "a time to love and a time to hate, a time of war and a time of peace". My lord of Bedford believes that France – all of Europe – needs peace.'

There was silence between the royal ladies for several paces. I could not see Eleanor's face, but I detected a definite edge to her voice as she made a sweeping gesture towards her two companions. 'It is remarkable that we are sisters, is it not? How much pressure could we exert on the policies of our lords if we combined our efforts?'

'Are you suggesting an alliance, Eleanor?' Catherine sounded astounded. 'Because I fear your own lord would be the first to cry witchcraft if he caught a whiff of such female conspiracy. Besides, I suspect our aims and objectives are very different. Jacquetta here may have motherhood more in mind than meddling in government.'

Jacquetta turned to face the other two ladies. 'Are children not the hope of every marriage?' she said, her cheeks the colour of a linnet's breast. 'I know my lord prays for an heir and surely it is every woman's wish to fulfil God's holy ordinance.'

'I do not believe motherhood is God's only intention for women,' Eleanor said. 'So many female saints are virgins, are they not? I believe we can aspire to more than simple motherhood.'

'Do you have children, my lady of Gloucester?' It occurred to me from the way Jacquetta posed the question that she may already have known that Eleanor did not.

'No,' Eleanor snapped. 'But nor is a child the only thing for which I pray. I believe we are on this earth to fulfil ourselves in many ways. It is not enough to let things happen. We owe it to ourselves to make them happen.'

'But not at the expense of others, I hope,' suggested the young bride, showing signs of alarm at Eleanor's fervour.

The Duchess of Gloucester glanced briefly at Catherine, then away. 'Not unless it is necessary,' she said.

When the Lords and Commons met in the second week of July, John of Bedford claimed precedence and took over the presidency of the Parliament from his brother. His first action was to reverse the changes in the king's household made by the Duke of Gloucester eighteen months before, with the result that when King Henry made a surprise visit to Hadham on his way to spend Christmas at St Edmund's Abbey, he brought with him his new steward, William de la Pole, Earl of Suffolk, a replacement for the incompetent Sir Robert Babthorp.

'I like my household much better now that my lord of Suffolk has made changes to the staff,' King Henry told Catherine when they were seated together in the hall after dinner, set slightly apart from the rest of us but not entirely private. 'He has recently been ransomed from two years captivity in France, you know.'

Catherine cast a glance at the earl, a rather aloof figure who was leaning against the chimney hood, staring into the fire. A handsome and well-built man in his mid-thirties, he was a protégée of the cardinal and married to his great-niece, Alice Chaucer, a strong indication that his new appointment was another Beaufort move against Gloucester. We were told this by Geoffrey, who was professionally involved with Alice's father, Sir Thomas Chaucer, son of the famous poet whose wife's sister had been the cardinal's mother. Alice was a famous beauty still in her twenties and a widow since the Earl of Salisbury was killed at the siege of Orleans; no doubt she had brought her new husband a sizeable dower. The Earl of Suffolk seemed to be on the way up, despite the fact that under his military command England had lost much ground in France. Catherine alluded to this fact in a voice loud enough for the new steward to hear.

'We hear that a lot of ransom money has gone to France in recent, years Henry, and a lot of territory. Your present commanders seem intent on losing all that your father fought so hard to win.'

Suffolk swivelled his gaze from the fire to fix it on Catherine and bowed before speaking. 'I am one of many councillors who argue that we should seek a peace settlement with your brother in France, Madame. But I understand you no longer take an interest in affairs of state.' He delivered this last statement with such a charming smile that it was not clear if he was criticising Catherine or congratulating her.

'I have told my lord of Suffolk about your marriage, my lady mother, and the existence of your new family,' Henry put in quietly. 'So Master Tudor may come out of hiding, wherever he is.'

After seeing the king in Suffolk's company, Owen had judged it sensible to make himself scarce and had not appeared for dinner. Alarmed by her son's dramatic and disturbing revelation, Catherine paused to collect her thoughts, taking a few deep breaths while never taking her eyes off the earl.

'As far as I am concerned, the state has always taken far too much interest in my affairs, my lord,' she said at length, meeting his smile with a cool sapphire stare, 'especially over the matter of my marriage. I am deeply grateful to the Bishop of London for allowing me to stay here at Hadham, where the long nose of the state rarely sniffs. I dearly hope it will remain that way. If you wish to consult me on the chances of the council achieving a peace settlement with my brother, then I suggest you make an appointment to meet me at Hertford Castle, where I conduct the small amount of official business that comes my way.'

The earl looked quite startled at this pronouncement, as well he might I thought. Catherine went on remorselessly, 'And since the king has apprised you of my marriage to Master Tudor and of our quiet, secluded family life, I must beg you to recognise that his grace is still very young and probably unaware of the consequences there could be for his stepfather and siblings if these facts were to become known to certain members of the regency council. Here at Hadham we live as the Tudor family. People are not aware of my connection to the king and I hope and pray that our existence can remain a secret from your world of high schemes and state policies. I must ask you to keep that secret, my lord. Indeed, I require your oath on it.'

Suffolk's reaction was abrupt and solemn. He took three long strides to her chair and bent his knee to the floor, holding out both his hands and gazing up, his pale-blue eyes locked with hers.

'You took my oath of fealty at your coronation, your grace, and I have no intention of changing my allegiance now. I am your liegeman in life and limb. I will do anything that you require of me as long as it is good in the sight of God and my king, which in this case it clearly is.' A pulse could be seen throbbing in his temple as he waited for her reaction and it seemed an age before she stretched out her own hands and briefly touched them to either side of his in token of the oath of fealty made between lord and vassal. At this he bowed his head and rose, backing away to his former position by the fire.

'You may rest assured that I will keep your secret,' he said, 'as I was required to do by the king also, until such time as either he or you release me from this oath. This I swear on my life.'

Then he crossed himself and made a bow in King Henry's direction. The Earl of Suffolk might be an English nobleman, but with his thick blond hair and fresh complexion he looked more like a wandering Teutonic knight as depicted in the *Romances d'Arthur*, which I had heard read in Catherine's salon in the days before we left Paris.

King Henry smiled back at the earl. I could see that he greatly admired his new steward and his mother did not look entirely immune to his physical charms either. They both listened attentively as he held forth freely from the kind of dominant position that would not have been tolerated at court.

'As for the two of us discussing a French peace, I believe the Duke of Bedford is returning to Paris very soon in order to try and mend the relationship with Burgundy which Gloucester has done so much to damage. It would be foolish of me to undermine his efforts by holding clandestine discussions at Hertford with the sister of the Pretender, would it not?'

She shrugged and signalled me to pour wine from the flagon on the nearby buffet. 'As you wish, my lord. Shall we drink to the possibility of peace at least? Although I must say that I do not envy the negotiators of such an agreement. My brother was never very good at making up his mind, except about our mother, of course, whom he never could bear.'

'It must be owned that she never gave him much to thank her for,' remarked Suffolk dryly. 'The Treaty of Troyes declared him a bastard and it carries her signature.'

Catherine frowned. 'She is an old lady now. I doubt if she remembers what she signed or even that she has a son still alive.'

I offered her wine and she took it. 'Let us look to the future, not the past.' She raised her cup and Suffolk took one and did the same. 'To peace between France and England!'

They both drank, but the king shook his head at the cup I offered him. 'I do not care for wine,' he said.

'The queen drinks her wine watered, your grace,' I told him. 'Shall I water some for you?'

He shook his head. 'No. The ale we had at dinner was enough.'

The earl then shot a question at me, which I decided was really aimed at Catherine. 'I wonder, is your mistress still a queen now that she is the wife of a commoner?'

Catherine and I exchanged glances, neither of us sure how to respond, but King Henry had no hesitation. 'She has been crowned, so she will always be a queen,' he declared indignantly.

'And my husband is not exactly the commoner you think him, Lord Suffolk,' added Catherine with pride. 'Owen Tudor is directly descended from Llewellyn the Great, Ruler of all Wales, as was the king's grandmother, Mary de Bohun.'

The earl's eyebrow rose in surprise. 'Indeed? Then I see why your secret must be preserved, Madame. If this can be proved, then your Tudor sons have as much royal blood as Humphrey of Gloucester.'

'Who says it cannot be proved?'

It was Owen who spoke from the shadows. He had entered the hall quietly and had obviously heard the exchange between Catherine and Suffolk. Now he moved into the room, approaching the group around the fire with a deep frown on his face. 'My family ancestry, as sung by bards, goes way back before Llewellyn. I can sing it myself, only not in a language you would understand, Lord Suffolk.' He bent his knee to the earl, but it was hardly a subservient salute. 'But you are right about one thing, my lord. It would not be music to the ears of Humphrey of Gloucester.'

He stooped to kiss Catherine's hand and cheek and then knelt before King Henry's canopied chair, bowing his head respectfully. 'God give you good day, my liege. I beg your grace's pardon for not greeting you on your arrival, but I was not aware that Lord Suffolk was apprised of the situation here.'

The king stood up and signalled Owen to rise. 'It is good to see you, Master Tudor,' he said and I was surprised to see that he was not dwarfed by his stepfather. The little king was not so little any more, promising to follow his father in height. 'You need not be worried that my lord Steward is aware of your marriage to my mother. The Earl of Suffolk is a loyal vassal of the crown and a good friend to the House of Lancaster.'

'Of which the Duke of Gloucester is a leading light, my liege,' Owen pointed out. 'And he is not well-disposed towards us Tudors.'

'And he and I are not well-disposed towards each other,' the earl broke in. 'You need have no fear that I will be making a confidant of his grace of Gloucester.'

Owen shrugged and went to stand behind Catherine's chair, touching her shoulder reassuringly. 'My wife and I are in your hands, my lord. The king has put us there and we must trust in his judgement.'

'It seems that you must, Master Tudor.' King Henry favoured his stepfather with a grim smile, which looked out of place on the face of a twelve-year-old boy. Then he gestured to his clerk, who had been waiting in a corner, obviously expecting to be summoned. He brought the king a parchment scroll from which hung a heavy wax seal on a red ribbon.

Henry held it out to Owen. 'This is for you. It is a deed of denizenation. I had my lawyers seek it in your name in Parliament in recognition of your loyal service to my father and my mother. It makes you exempt from the restrictions imposed on Welshmen under English law. More importantly, your children will be classed as English.'

It was not until later, when Geoffrey explained it to me, that I realised the significance of this gift. The king could still not bestow land or a knighthood on Owen as a Welshman, but this move would lay the foundation of a future for his children in the land of their birth. Owen was immediately aware of this and dropped to his knees once more before the king. His voice was hoarse with emotion as he took the document.

'I thank your grace for honouring me in this way,' he said, clearing his throat. 'I was a loyal servant, but now I will be a loyal subject, which is a fine and precious gift. And your brothers will be Englishmen of whom I hope you will one day be proud.'

I wondered then why no mention had been made of little Margaret, who was now a bright and bonny toddler in the nursery, a playmate for Anne and Thomas's precious daughter Hester born two months before her and Agnes's two-year-old Gladys. It was not until much later that I learned the reason for this.

PART THREE

Journey into Jeopardy
(1435–1437)

37

O n a cold, wet day in early 1435, I saw two women in hooded mantles talking together under an arched side door to Westminster Palace. At first they were of no particular interest, but as I passed closer I could see under their hoods and I realised that one of them was the Duchess of Gloucester and the other was Margery Jourdemayne, the girl who had assisted the midwife at the birth of King Henry.

Pulling my own hood lower over my face, I calculated how long it was since I had encountered the same two women consulting together in the herb garden at Windsor Castle. It was at least seven years. From what I knew of the proud and image-conscious Eleanor Cobham, such an enduring friendship with someone of yeoman stock like Mistress Jourdemayne was unlikely and yet the relationship had clearly persisted and, judging by the way they were conversing, cheek by jowl, some well-established intimacy was indicated. Then, as I watched, a package was passed furtively from Margery to Eleanor, and the two immediately parted. Perhaps it was not a friendship but a business relationship. The duchess disappeared inside the building and Mistress Jourdemayne made for the palace gate. On the spur of the moment, I decided to follow her.

I had come to Westminster to deliver a gift from Catherine to the king, a baldric she had embroidered for him in bright silks and glittering gold thread, 'To wear around your hips or across your shoulder as you choose,' she had written in the accompanying letter. 'It was all the fashion among the young courtiers in Paris when I was your age and you could make it so in England. They had bells sewn on theirs, but I have not done that because I think it rather undignified and a king must never be that.' The relationship between the royal mother and son had improved quite markedly now that King Henry had reached his fourteenth year and taken an observer's seat on the council of regency. He had not yet been declared of age, but at least his letters were no longer vetted so that he and Catherine could exchange news and ideas. The young king was beginning to make his preferences felt and to choose the people whose counsel he preferred. Cardinal Beaufort, the Earl of Suffolk and, secretly, his mother were among those favoured; unfortunately in Catherine's eyes, so was the Duke of Gloucester.

I had come to London to visit Mildy, who had given birth to her first child, a boy named Gilbert. Geoffrey had been unable to accompany me to Westminster due to an out-of-town case, and so my stepson Walter, who had escorted me from Hadham, was once again my companion.

'Quick, Walter, I must speak to that woman,' I urged him, indicating the hooded figure heading for the gate. 'Did you see who she was talking to? It was the Duchess of Gloucester.'

No longer a callow youth but a vigorous man in his prime, though unmarried still, Walter did not hesitate but obligingly loped off in pursuit of Margery Jourdemayne. She was setting a fast pace across the wide palace courtyard, her dark cloak pulled protectively about her against the steadily falling rain, and it was not until she had passed through the main gate and out into the thoroughfare beyond that he managed to reach her.

I hurried after him and found them sheltering together in the lee of the gatehouse bastion. Walter was in the process of calming Margery's understandable alarm at being accosted by a strange man.

'I am sorry to send my stepson after you, Mistress Jourdemayne,' I hastened to reassure her, panting a little. 'I am not as quick on my feet as he is and I saw you crossing the courtyard. Perhaps you remember me. I attended Queen Catherine at the birth of King Henry. I was called Madame Lanière then, but I am now Mistress Vintner and this is my stepson, Walter.'

Margery's frown gradually faded. 'I do remember you, mistress, but your English is greatly improved since then.' She smiled to offset any potential insult and nodded a greeting to Walter. 'Master Vintner, God be thanked that you are not the cut-purse I first thought you to be. Let us by all means talk together, but shall we go to the chapel porch? This rain is penetrating, is it not?'

Dark clouds hung low overhead and the porch of St Stephen's chapel was full of shadows as we shook the moisture off our outer clothes. With her hood pushed back, Margery could be clearly seen as the shrewd countrywoman she was; deep, intelligent eyes, cheeks laced with broken veins and skin weathered and lined. Although I knew her to be younger than Catherine, she looked ten years older. Not wishing Walter to hear our conversation, I drew her aside to sit on the stone bench along the wall. Prudently he kept us in view, though out of earshot, hovering in the doorway that led into the chapel.

I began cautiously. 'I could not help noticing that you were speaking with the Duchess of Gloucester. I remember encountering you together in the herb garden at Windsor after the last king's death. Are you still helping her with herbal cures?'

Margery's expression grew wary. 'Ye-es,' she said hesitantly. 'But I am well known to many court ladies who come to me for cures and potions. My home is not far from Westminster.'

'Are you no longer a midwife?'

Her harsh laugh, more like a bark, startled me. 'I am a little of everything, Mistress Vintner,' she answered. 'Midwife, herbalist, healer – some people call me a wise woman or even a sorceress, but they all come to me when in need. Some want to get a baby, others to get rid of one. Some want love potions, others beauty lotions, and some want their fortunes told. I can do it all.' She leaned forward until her shadowed face was close to mine, eyes glittering. 'What do you want, Mistress?'

Her breath was sour, but if she sought to frighten me she did not succeed. I remembered her as a girl and I knew that although she was trying to disguise it, at heart she was kind. I smiled benignly at her and shook my head. 'Nothing like that, Mistress Jourdemayne. I want some information, if you will be so kind.'

That appeared to shock her. Even in the gloom I could see that her cheeks had paled under their sun-browned surface. 'About what?' she demanded sharply. 'I never discuss my customers. Everything I do is confidential, otherwise no one would consult me.'

I held up my hands to placate her. 'This does not concern your customers – at least not present ones. It is merely for my own interest. I want to know what became of the king's caul? Do you know?'

She pretended not to understand me. 'The king's caul? I have no idea what you mean.'

I held her gaze, my expression, I hoped, firm. Despite the intervening years I had not forgotten the midwife's warning that we should never mention the king's birth 'in the Veil' or its mysterious disappearance afterwards. 'I am sure you remember, Margery. Mistress Scorier slit the caul and the veil slipped away from the baby's face. The king breathed and we all sighed with relief. It was a tense moment. I have since learned that such cauls are believed to hold magic powers and can be very valuable, so did you keep it or did Mistress Scorier?'

I could see fear flicker in her eyes just before she dropped her gaze and whispered. 'I was the apprentice. It is the midwife's responsibility to take the afterbirth and burn it.'

'But did she?' I persisted. 'Or did it travel from Windsor to your village? It is called Eye, as I remember – well-named, I think, for a woman with the sight. A caul must be useful in some magic spells.'

Abruptly she stood up, having gathered her forces. 'I told you, I do not know what you mean and I advise you not to ask any further questions on this subject, Mistress Vintner – of anyone.'

I rose to confront her. 'Of the Duchess of Gloucester for instance?'

Her eyes flashed and she glanced about to check for listeners. 'This has nothing to do with the Duchess of Gloucester, do you understand. Nothing!'

'Are you sure? Does the caul have power to aid conception, perhaps? And does the duchess not long to give her lord an heir?'

With an angry hiss Margery Jourdemayne turned her back. 'Shh! No – more – questions. Good morrow, Mistress!' She flicked her hood over her head and strode towards the exit, flinging one parting shot over her shoulder. 'Be careful. I warn you, be very careful!' The church door slammed.

Walter wandered over from his watchful stance at the inner

door. 'She left rather suddenly,' he remarked. 'Is everything all right, Mette?'

'I am not sure,' I rubbed my nose thoughtfully. I had wondered if pieces of the caul might have been sold as fertility aids, but now I suspected there was more to it than that. 'Walter, please run out and see which way she goes – towards the palace or away?'

He was back in seconds. 'She went back to the palace and she was in a great hurry. What did you say to her?'

'It is not so much what I said, as how she took it,' I replied enigmatically. 'I think I have rattled a cage.'

That evening, as we sat beside the hall fire after our meal, I described the meeting to Geoffrey. Usually I took the opportunity of mending my husband's chemises and the household linen as we talked over the day's events, but on this occasion my mind was otherwise occupied.

'I must admit I had not expected her to be so agitated by my enquiries,' I added, when I had concluded my tale. 'I am beginning to suspect Margery Jourdemayne of dabbling too deeply in spells and I have a bad feeling about Eleanor of Gloucester's use of her services. The caul has a direct connection to Catherine as well as the king and Eleanor has no love for her.'

Geoffrey stroked his beard thoughtfully. 'Margery Jourdemayne,' he murmured. 'For some reason that name rings a bell. I can check tomorrow, but I think there was a case before the council of regency a few years ago concerning charges of witchcraft and a plot against the king. It was a serious case and some of those found guilty were hanged, but some were given prison sentences and I think Mistress Jourdemayne may have been one of them.'

'A plot against the king,' I echoed, my stomach lurching unpleasantly. 'What kind of plot?'

'Something about foretelling the king's death, as far as I remember. One of the men accused was an astrologer and one woman – Mistress Jourdemayne if it was her – was charged with something called "image magic". That is when a wax figure is made of a person, either to do them harm or to read their future.' Geoffrey frowned deeply and scratched his head. 'But I may not remember it right. I will take a look at the Council Rolls tomorrow if I can.'

'Well I hope you can, *mon amour*, because if it was indeed Mistress Jourdemayne, I do not like the way my thoughts are turning. Why would she have suddenly decided to return to the palace after speaking to me, when prior to that she had clearly completed her business there and was heading home – unless it was to warn someone that I was asking awkward questions about the king's caul?' I leaned forward to engage his full attention and continued earnestly, 'Tell me exactly what this "image magic" involves. Does this wax figure need to contain something from the person it is supposed to represent? Some hair, for instance, or some nail parings? Or a piece of the person's birth sac – the caul?' I gave this last example added significance by lowering my voice and more or less whispering it.

Geoffrey stared at me, his mouth half open. 'Exactly what are you implying, Mette?' he asked.

I shook my head. 'No, I do not want to voice my suspicions until you can confirm the identity of the woman accused of plotting against the king. Until then let us talk of something else. What fraud or felony did you defend in court today?'

*

The following morning I walked down to Mildy's riverside house and spent a few delightful hours talking of births and babies and holding little two-month-old Gilbert in my arms. Our conversation would have bored any man to death, but it kept two mothers chattering away busily, swapping cures and theories on everything from the merits and demerits of swaddling to the significance of cradle cap. The house Hugh Vintner had bought for Mildy overlooked the Vintry Quay where barges laden with the huge barrels called tuns manoeuvred in and out of the docks, and were loaded and unloaded at what seemed to me an extraordinary rate. From every window in the house there was a view of masts and cranes and heavy tuns swinging alarmingly at the end of ropes and our constant companions were the shouts of dockers and the heady smell of wine. On the dock itself carts lined up at the warehouse doors to carry away loads of the smaller casks and hogsheads into which the contents of the giant tuns had been transferred.

When I arrived home Geoffrey was waiting for me and he wore an expression I did not like. 'We must talk now, Mette,' he said. 'I have had Jem light the fire in my library.'

I shed my pattens and fur-lined mantle and made my way to the private chamber at the back of the hall where Geoffrey kept his precious collection of books. They were stored flat on strong, purpose-built shelves; law books, almanacs and some treasured volumes of poetry and scholarship, bound in cloth-covered wooden board and clasped with pewter or silver – about two dozen in all. When I was at Hadham I knew that his books were his chosen companions when he was not working. There was an impressive lock on the library door, to which he held the only key and he used it now to lock us in.

Two chairs had been placed by the fire and as soon as I sat

down he passed me a sheet of paper covered in writing in his own neat hand. 'This is a copy I made of the judgement. I found the account of the council hearing; it was in 1430 and the accused was Margery Jourdemayne. You will see she was sentenced to imprisonment at the king's pleasure – or in this case the regency council's. She could have been sentenced to burn but instead she spent only a year and a half incarcerated at Windsor Castle. It seems a light sentence. She was either lucky or well connected.'

I ran my eyes over the carefully copied tract looking for the words 'plotting the king's death', but I could find nothing. 'I do not see any charge tantamount to treason here,' I said. 'What was her offence?'

Geoffrey shook his head. 'It is not specified, but in the same roll there is the account of a trial of seven women accused of plotting the king's death by witchcraft and they were sent to the Fleet prison. Their names are not given, but it seems likely that she was implicated with them in some way. I do not know why she was sent to Windsor, which is certainly preferable to the Fleet. The important fact is that when she was released her husband paid a surety of twenty pounds that she would abstain from all sorcery in the future. If she is still performing spells and magic for the likes of the Duchess of Gloucester, your questions would have put the fear of God into her. If she were to be charged with sorcery a second time she would be unlikely to escape the flames.'

I shook my head in bewilderment. 'I am not surprised that Margery is involved in magic cures for she clearly has acquired skills that are much in demand, but I would be amazed if she was plotting against the king. After all she was one of the people who helped him into the world.'

Geoffrey considered my argument. 'But Eleanor Cobham, our duchess of Gloucester, may have discovered more sinister uses for Mistress Jourdayne's skills. Her star is rising at court and she is now regularly to be seen in the company of the king. If she believes that magic is helping her to achieve her goals then she will not want nosy members of Queen Catherine's household asking impertinent questions. I fear that you may have stirred a hornet's nest, sweetheart.' Geoffrey leaned over and took back the paper. 'I will keep this safe,' he said with a grim smile. 'If you are found with it you could also be suspected of being involved in sorcery.'

'What do you think I should do?' I asked my husband.

'I think you should go back to Hadham and lie low. If there is sorcery afoot, you certainly do not want to be implicated and nor do you want Eleanor to turn the Gloucester lantern beam onto you and thus discover the Tudor family. Loath though I am to see you go, I think you should leave tomorrow.'

38

Six months later, Alys, Cat and I were taking advantage of some early October sunshine to gather herbs for simples in the riverside garden at Hadham. On a spread blanket, little Margaret was contentedly burbling nonsense to her wooden doll as she rocked the miniature cradle which Owen had fashioned as a present for her third birthday. The three boys, now six and five respectively, were loudly playing a game of sheriffs and outlaws on the island with Jasper as the undaunted sheriff upon whom blunt arrows and cat-calls were raining down from the two older boys hiding in the bushes.

The clang of the bell from the watch-tower silenced the boys and in seconds they had broken cover and were racing over the bridge to go and see who was approaching the gate-house. Alys and I and the girls followed more sedately, gathering up the baskets, toys and blanket and letting Margaret toddle industriously along, holding my hand, as we made our way to the sally gate in the curtain wall. By the time we had crossed the bailey and entered the courtyard, the visitor had dismounted. By the bollard badge on his livery I knew him to be the Earl of Suffolk's herald, presumably with a message for Catherine.

She had not emerged from the house, but Owen had arrived from somewhere and now introduced himself and offered to take the visitor in to see her. I told the children to stay with Alys, handed over my basket and followed Owen and the herald inside. In Catherine's chamber Agnes was helping her to change into a formal gown and I took a veil from a chest to fix over her hair.

'Where are the children, Mette?' she asked anxiously. 'I trust Suffolk has not told his herald about them!'

'They are all with Alys, Mademoiselle. He will have seen them, but he will not know whose they are.' I began pinning the veil in place.

'I wonder what news he brings,' she fretted. 'It must be something important for Suffolk to send his king of arms. I do not have a good feeling about this.'

By the time we three reached the hall, Owen had acquired refreshments and a servant was pouring wine into cups. Both men bowed low as Catherine entered and walked to her canopied chair, which always stood opposite the fireplace against just such an occasion. Owen stood back as the herald bent his knee before her. Appearances were being scrupulously preserved.

'My lord of Suffolk humbly greets your grace and sends me with grave news.' The visitor had left his sword and mail coif at the gatehouse and he knelt bare-headed, the sweat from his hectic ride still damp in his reddish-brown hair. He withdrew a folded and sealed letter from the purse belted around his padded gambeson. 'This comes from the Earl of Mortain, my lady.'

Catherine took the letter and examined the seal briefly. 'Thank you. But you can tell me the news, can you not, Sir Herald?'

The messenger nodded. 'Mortain Herald came from Normandy yesterday to inform the council that his grace the Duke of Bedford died suddenly in Rouen two weeks ago. My lord of Suffolk has instructed me to convey his condolences on the loss of your royal brother-in-law, a great general and a noble statesman.'

There was a long silence as Catherine absorbed these sad tidings. 'This is sad news indeed,' she told the herald. 'But why was Bedford in Rouen? I had heard he was attending the peace conference which the pope called at Arras.'

'He did go to Arras, Madame, but there was a stalemate. My lord of Bedford left the conference and travelled back to Rouen in early September.'

'He walked out, you mean. Was there a result of the conference?'

'There was, eventually. The Duke of Burgundy and Charles of Valois have agreed a truce. It has taken the English commanders in France by surprise and at Westminster his grace of Gloucester has called an urgent session of the council.'

'As well he might!' Catherine was more aware than anyone of the significance of such a truce. 'That Burgundy and my brother should exchange the kiss of peace is nothing short of miraculous. The Duke of Bedford's death may be a dreadful consequence of it, for it places my son's French crown in grave jeopardy and Bedford of all people would feel it as a mortal blow. He was the backbone of England's rule in France. You say he died suddenly – was there any reason given?'

The herald shook his head sadly. 'No, your grace. That is all I know.'

Catherine stood up, crossing herself. 'I will pray for him and his poor widow. Jacquetta is so young to be left without a husband. Thank you for performing your duty, Sir Herald. Master Tudor will see that you are well rewarded and that you are rested and refreshed before leaving. Good day.'

As good as her word, Catherine went immediately to the church and settled herself before the altar of the Lady Chapel for a long period of personal prayer and reflection. I followed, worried by her pallor. Of all the late king's brothers, John of Bedford had been her staunchest friend and champion. Had it been he who had led the regency council in England she might not have suffered the humiliations meted out to her by Humphrey of Gloucester. Catherine may have been praying for the soul of her brother-in-law but, kneeling discreetly behind her, I was praying that the collapse of the Burgundian alliance would ensure that Gloucester's attention remained focussed well away from Hadham.

Catherine's thoughts in the church cannot have been entirely for the soul of John of Bedford however, because that evening, when the trestles had been cleared, she stopped Owen from fetching his harp.

'Do not play yet, Owen,' she said. 'I would like to read you and Mette the letter Suffolk's herald brought from Edmund Beaufort. I think we need to discuss its contents. We will not be overheard here.'

Owen glanced across the room to where his two boys and my William were playing some game of their own devising, crawling over and under a makeshift obstacle course of trestles laid over benches. Pools of candlelight lit the occupied areas of the hall, while the abandoned corners were draped in shadow, rendering them dark and mysterious as the light died through the windows. Anne and Agnes had taken little Margaret up to bed with Gladys and Hester and Thomas, John, Walter and Hywell had gone off on some business of their own. Near the hearth Cat and Louise were playing a board game with Alys, occasionally protesting as the boisterous boys bumped or jostled their stools. I sat in the hearth-light with Catherine and Owen. As happened all too often for my liking, Geoffrey was absent in London.

Catherine unfolded the letter on which the seal had already been broken.

'I will dispense with the greetings,' she said, 'and just read the content.'

I am sorry that I cannot tell you myself of the death of my lord of Bedford, but must rely on my cousin of Suffolk to convey the news to you. Everything here in Rouen is thrown into disorder as you may imagine and it is impossible for me to leave, especially with the funeral to organise and his widow to assist. According to his declared wish, the Duke of Bedford is to be buried in Rouen Cathedral. I would like to be able to tell you more about his death but alas his illness was short and I was not there in time. It seems to have been a sudden collapse and he died within hours. May his soul rest with God.

Now to my concerns about you and your children, which have been much on my mind, especially now that I am a father myself. My own two girls are strong and healthy, but I am aware how fast they grow and realise that my godson and his brother must now be quite big boys and old enough to start their education. I am sure that you and Master Tudor will have made more than adequate provision for this, but it occurred to me that if anything were to happen to either or both of you there should be someone who would be in a position to take care of them and raise them as befits their birth, until such a time as their brother the king shall reach his majority.

As you will know, my marriage to the Lady Eleanor has yet to be licensed by the council so I prefer to stay out of England until that situation is rectified. I expect to remain as a commander of our armed forces in Normandy, where I hold the Western border against the Duke of Alençon. It will not be the same here without the strength and wisdom of my lord of Bedford, but we will struggle on and it does mean that I am not at present in a position to offer your sons a position in my household.

Catherine paused here to make an observation. 'I read between these lines that it is the Duke of Gloucester who makes difficulties over their marriage licence, perhaps in retribution for Edmund's attempt to marry me. Gloucester can be vengeful, as we know to my cost. However, here is where we get to the proposal I wish to discuss.' She cleared her throat and continued reading.

Another possibility is open to us however. My noble friend the Earl of Suffolk has a sister, Lady Katherine de la Pole, who has been a nun at Barking Abbey for many years and is now abbess there. As you may know, it is an ancient and well-endowed community which takes in numerous students; most of them are wards of the crown, and are provided with care, religious guidance and education of a high standard. If you are agreeable, I will make arrangements with Suffolk that, in my stead, the abbey would shelter your sons in the event of any misfortune to you. You can be sure that, no matter the opposition, the protection of the name de la Pole would guarantee security and safety for your precious sons.

Catherine dropped the letter to her lap and glanced question-ingly from Owen to me.

Owen leaned back in his chair and made a face. 'Lord Edmund is right. We should make provision of that kind, but I am not sure that Suffolk is the one to trust. We hardly know him.'

'The letter would suggest that Lord Edmund is not aware that the Earl of Suffolk already knows your situation, Mademoiselle,' I said. 'Even so, he seems happy that Lord Suffolk should be told.'

'Mette, is right, Owen.' Catherine looked at him earnestly. 'In fact it would not alter the position very much, except to bring the Abbess of Barking into our confidence.'

He was not mollified. 'But what do we know about her? She may be a Mother Superior of the worst kind. I do not want my sons submitted to a regime of prayer and mortification under the rule of a bunch of pious virgins.'

'Not all nuns are pious virgins. And if Burgundy invades England, as he now very well might, at least they would be safe in a convent, would they not?'

Owen stared at Catherine as if he thought she had gone mad. 'Who says Burgundy will invade England?'

I must admit that I grew wide-eyed myself at the thought of such a thing, but Catherine was adamant. 'It is not unlikely,' she insisted. 'Now that he has made peace with my brother, the duke may well turn his ambitions towards England. Philippe of Burgundy admired my valiant Henry and the good John of Bedford, but he has scores to settle with the Duke of Gloucester, not least over the matter of Humphrey's outrageous attempt to annexe Hainault by marriage to Jacqueline. I only make the point that a convent would be a place of refuge in a time of war.'

'Perhaps our first act should be to find out more about Barking Abbey and its abbess,' I suggested. 'Geoffrey could make some enquiries. Barking is in the diocese of London and he has made friends with the new bishop.' William Grey had been translated to the bishopric of Lincoln and Geoffrey had made a point of establishing good relations with his successor, Bishop Robert Fitzhugh, in order to extend Catherine's arrangement at Hadham.

'That is a good idea, Mette.' I detected a note of relief in Owen's voice. 'If we learn more we can make an informed decision. Meanwhile I suggest we let the matter drop.' He downed what was left in his cup and stood up. 'I am going to make my final check on the guard.'

Catherine watched him cross the hall to the main door, then caught my eye and shrugged. 'He becomes more nervous every time someone else is told about the children,' she sighed. 'When is Geoffrey due back at Hadham, Mette?'

'Not for some time,' I told her ruefully. 'The Michaelmas term has only just begun in the courts and he has quite a few cases to deal with. But if you can do without Walter for a few days he could take me to London. I might even make some discreet enquiries myself before I return.'

Catherine looked grateful and reached over to take my hand. 'Would you, Mette? It is getting a little late in the year for comfortable travelling but I would be grateful. Will you mind leaving William again?'

'As long as he is with Edmund, William is happy.'

Catherine laughed. 'Well that is true. If they did not have such different colouring, one would almost think they were twins.'

I shuddered. 'I am glad they are not. I would not wish the birth of twins on any woman!'

Catherine shook her head solemnly. 'Nor I. Look what happened to poor little Joan Beaufort.'

It was five years since we had heard that the Queen of Scotland, Catherine's former lady-in-waiting, had produced not one but two male heirs, but sadly the younger one had died during the first fragile month of life.

'At least one of them survives and so there is another James to inherit his father's throne,' I said. 'I do not suppose Scotland is any more willing to accept a female ruler than England or France.'

Catherine's face clouded. 'Princes and barons will always squabble when there is no strong leader to bring them to heel. I am serious about Burgundy being dangerous now that he has made peace with Charles. All Henry's territories are vulnerable without John of Bedford's wily rule. Gloucester does not have the moral strength needed to get a grip on the government of one kingdom, let alone two.'

39

I nstead of heading straight for London, Walter and I took a detour and spent a night at an inn in Highgate recommended to us by Thomas Roke. When we left next morning we found ourselves transfixed by the view from the top of Highgate Hill. In the distance to the west the River Thames wound its way in a series of loops through the Chelsea marshlands, north past the palace of Westminster and the mansions of the Strand, then east to the City of London itself, tucked snugly behind its high walls and spewing clouds of smoke into the sky. Directly below us lay our destination, the village of Eye, one of several incorporated into the manor lands of Westminster Abbey.

A hilltop wind had whipped the blood into our cheeks and we soon headed for the shelter of some woodland on the lower slopes. It was a cold autumn day and fallen leaves swirled under our horses' bellies making them dance excitedly and heavy grey clouds rolled off the horizon across a chalk-white sky. The main purpose of our journey was to make enquiries in Barking about a lady who I was sure would be a perfectly respectable abbess of a long-established abbey, but first I intended to learn more about a woman whose activities concerned me much more; Margery Jourdemayne. At the end of our last meeting, the Wise Woman of Eye had warned me, somewhat menacingly, to be careful. Since then I had learned of her previous trial and imprisonment for practising sorcery. Now I wanted to find out more about her connection with Eleanor of Gloucester. Where I came from, sorcery was a weapon much to be feared, and while the duke had shown Catherine a very male antagonism in his quest to dominate the king, I knew his duchess to be a devious character who would use more dangerous and subtle means to further the cause of Gloucester.

As we turned off the road onto the field paths of Eye, it began to rain and I pulled the hood of my mantle over my head. Walter led the way and hailed the first person we saw, a man who was mending a gate leading into a neatly hedged pasture containing a herd of shaggy brown cattle.

'God keep you, goodman, I seek the house of Jourdemayne,' Walter called. 'Can you direct me?'

The fellow dragged off his grubby hood and scratched his stubbled chin. 'Is it the Master or Mistress Jourdemayne you seek, sir?'

'Do they not both dwell in the same house?' Walter flashed the man a mischievous smile.

The returning grin revealed only a scattering of teeth. 'Aye, that they do but the Master is away at this time finding a market for these beasts.' He indicated the cattle grazing peaceably on the still-plentiful grass of the meadow, their backs turned against the wind and rain. 'But if you seek Mistress Jourdemayne, she is up in the woods collecting herbs for her cures.'

He jerked his head towards the belt of trees that ran along the field's edge and up the side of the hill beyond. Walter glanced at me with one eyebrow raised and I nodded agreement that we should go there.

'There is a path between this field and the next,' said the gate-mender, interpreting my nods. 'It takes you up to the woods.

You will have to find her though. She wanders hither and yonder up there.'

'Does she make many cures?' I asked on impulse.

He gave a throaty chuckle. 'That is like asking if the king wears a crown. Ladies like you come to her from far and wide.'

'Do you know who they are?'

'If I knew that they would kill me. No, lady, I do not know them, just as I do not know you. Some of them wear more jewels than you though.' His chuckle increased to a guffaw and he turned back to his task, the sound of his hammer indicating that, as far as he was concerned, the interview was over.

As we set our horses' heads for the woods, I pondered his words, fascinated by the tolerance he obviously felt towards Margery and her 'cures'. I wondered if his attitude was typical of the local people and whether they were all as tight-lipped about her customers. If they were, it meant she had won their respect – no easy task when the Church preached hellfire and damnation against anything resembling sorcery. Perhaps they did not see Margery's activities as sinister in that way.

Like all woods close to habitation, the undergrowth had been well cleared for use as fuel and it was possible to ride easily between the trees but I kept a sharp eye for low branches and foxholes. I did not want a cracked skull and I did not want Genevieve to break a leg, either injury being almost certainly fatal to its recipient. My Genevieve was getting old now, but she still carried me stoutly and proudly. At least under the trees the rain was less penetrating and after a short search we found Margery Jourdemayne sitting on a log under a sheltering oak at the edge of a clearing, inspecting the contents of her basket.

'I heard you as soon as you entered the wood,' she called across the open space. 'You would not make very good assailants.' She had not looked up but continued to sort the results of her foraging.

'That is because we mean you no harm, Mistress Jourdemayne,' I replied, kicking my horse closer to her mossy seat.

This made her glance at us and by her frown she did not like what she saw. 'Oh, it is you again. Did you heed my warning, Mistress Vintner? Were you careful? Well, you must have been or you would not be here.' She put down her basket but otherwise did not move. 'Did anyone see you come?'

'Only an old man mending a gate.'

She made a deprecatory gesture. 'Old Matt. He is my husband's man. He will not tell anyone.'

I got down off Genevieve and handed the reins to my companion who remained in the saddle. 'Would you mind taking the horses off somewhere, Walter?' I requested apologetically. 'I would like to speak with Mistress Jourdemayne alone.'

Walter obliged and the hem of my skirt soon became soaked as I trudged across the damp grass, grateful to be wearing long leather riding bottins. The log was big enough for two and I sat down. 'Why do I need to be careful, Mistress Jourdemayne?' I asked. 'Me in particular?'

She turned her penetrating brown eyes to mine. 'There are dark forces building against you,' she said. 'I have the sight.'

I laughed and shook my head. 'That kind of jargon will not work on me. I am not a naive young girl who wants her fortune read.'

'What do you want then, Mistress?'

'I want to help you escape the clutches of Eleanor Cobham, who calls herself the Duchess of Gloucester.'

It was Margery Jourdemayne's turn to laugh. 'Who says I am in her clutches? She is my customer, not I hers.'

471

'That is not how I read it.'

'Indeed? And how is that?'

'She was your customer at first and you were flattered that she made you her friend but then the situation turned, did it not? First she sought love potions to snare Humphrey of Gloucester and then she asked you to help her become pregnant by him.'

Margery shrugged, but her eyes shifted about uncertainly. 'There is nothing unusual in that. Many women ask me for help on that count. She was desperate – said it must be her fault because the duke already had two bastard children.'

'Only two? You surprise me.' I said it sarcastically but actually she did surprise me. I had never heard of any Gloucester by-blows. 'He is lecherous enough to have fathered a dozen or more. Eleanor was desperate you say – but how desperate? Is it perhaps she who has begun to harness those dark forces you mentioned? I believe it was her you warned me against. Does she force you to conjure dark spirits? She knows that you have been bound over not to practice sorcery. One word from her to the council and you would be facing the flames.'

Margery's face had gone the colour of the fungi in her basket, a pallid grey. 'How do you know this?'

'My husband is a lawyer with access to the council rolls. It is all down there in black and white. We could have reported you to the council at any time in the last six months, but we have not because I do not believe you practice the black arts. You use your skills to do good and many people have to thank you for your cures and potions. Not one of them would speak against you.'

I paused, watching her, waiting for her to realise that I was her friend. When she said nothing, I risked another question.

'So what is Eleanor using you for, Margery? And, more importantly, what is she using the king's caul for?'

She seemed to shrivel into herself. All her strength and bravado vanished and she looked at me like a cornered hind. Her voice became small and hesitant. 'That is the thing. I do not know. At first her need was straightforward. She wanted a potion that would make her fertile. When that did not work, she demanded something more potent. I told her about image magic and I made her a wax doll. I explained how she could use it in various ways as a fertility symbol, employing certain items as catalysts for the spell. One of them was waste-matter from a birth. That was when she revealed that she knew King Henry had been born in the caul. She was there at the birth with the Duchess of Hainault and I do not know if she saw it or if she heard one of us talking about it, but she knew that the caul had magical powers and she wanted to use them, I thought for the fertility cure. I did not have the caul but I said I would get it for her if she paid well. I bought it off Bet Scorier and I sold it to the duchess.'

This much I had more or less guessed and I smiled at her encouragingly. 'I hope you made a healthy profit on the transaction,' I said.

The side of Margery's mouth tilted slightly. 'A few crowns. Bet was happy and so was I – at the time.'

'And now? What has changed?'

My question hung in the air and it was many seconds before she answered it.

'The duchess has now asked me to make a larger wax doll and bring it to Greenwich. She wants me to take part in a ceremony there with others who she says are "of a like mind".' There was panic in Margery Jourdemayne's eyes when she looked at me then. 'What does that mean – "of a like mind"? Are they going to hold a Black Sabbath? Is she desperate enough to summon Beelzebub?' A shudder ran through her. 'I do not like it and I do not want to be part of such a ritual.'

I was equally appalled, unable to believe that Eleanor might have sunk to such depths. Surely she did not believe it was worth sacrificing her soul to the devil merely in order to conceive a child?

Then my thoughts took a sudden and more sinister turn. 'Tell me, when did the duchess make her request?'

Margery's brow creased in concentration. 'It was not long ago; two, maybe three weeks.'

I counted back in my head. John of Bedford had died on the fourteenth of September. Eleanor must surely have heard about his death when she asked Margery for the new doll – after she knew that Humphrey of Gloucester was now heir to the throne. Was it just a child she wanted – or was it also a crown?

I stood up and brushed bark and moss from my skirt. 'Well, there is no longer any point in my pursuing the king's caul,' I said. 'Not if Eleanor of Gloucester has it. Why do you not send someone else to Greenwich with the doll, Mistress Jourdemayne? If you do not take it yourself, you cannot become involved in any sinister ritual.'

Margery rose to face me, shaking her head. 'No, I must take it myself because I need to remain friends with my lady Eleanor. Otherwise she will become my enemy and that would be fatal.'

I inclined my head and sighed. 'I understand your dilemma and you have my sympathy. I am glad we have had this conversation. Please let me know if I can ever be of help to you. I live in the city, at the House of the Vines in Tun Lane, down near the Vintry. Will you remember that?'

A smile briefly lit her weather-worn face. 'I will remember. But it is not wise to befriend a wise woman, Madame. I am afraid that if I was ever to need your help, it would not be wise to give it to me. But thank you for the offer. I will remember that too.'

When, later that day, I described this encounter to Geoffrey, it brought a worried frown to his brow.

'She is right, Mette,' he said. 'Anyone known to be a friend of hers risks the taint of witchcraft, however innocent they may be. That is the price she pays for the way she makes a living.'

'Then why does she do it? Why does her husband allow her to continue doing it?'

He laughed then. 'Whatever the law may say about husbands having rule over their wives, you may have noticed that often this is not the case.'

I bridled. 'Whoever can you mean, Geoffrey?'

'Well, I'll name no names. But has it occurred to you that Mistress Jourdemayne's line of work probably pays quite hand-somely? Perhaps her husband likes the money it brings in. He certainly seems to have been able to raise the twenty pound surety that was paid for her freedom after that previous misde-meanour and that is no mean sum for a yeoman cattle-trader.'

'I take your point, but how would he feel if his wife went to the stake for being involved in real sorcery, however unwillingly?'

Geoffrey shrugged and he raised a sly eyebrow. 'Not all husbands are as honourable as yours, Mistress Vintner. He would probably take another wife within half a year.'

'Whereas you would wait all of eighteen months I suppose?' I retorted.

'Oh, I think a twelvemonth would be quite enough.' He dodged the cushion I threw at him and assumed a more serious demeanour. 'On the subject of marriage, you know that Eleanor's has yet to be licensed by the council and unless it is she would not be recognised as his queen should Humphrey ever take the throne, whether by fair means or foul.'

'No, I did not know that. But I imagine Eleanor thinks that now Humphrey is heir to the throne he will be able to force the licence through the council, especially if she becomes pregnant.'

'Until such a time though, would it be worth selling her soul to the devil as you suggest she might?'

I felt my heavy heart lighten a little. 'Probably not,' I conceded. 'And there is little to be done about it anyway, so let us turn our attention to the Abbess of Barking. Please tell me that you have found nothing sinister about her.'

40

In his capacity as Catherine's treasurer, Geoffrey had requested a meeting with Bishop Fitzhugh of London, on the pretext of discussing Catherine's continued residence at Hadham and paying another year's dues for use of the manor hall, produce and bondsmen. In the course of this meeting the subject of Barking Abbey was raised as a possible place of religious retreat for Catherine in the future and the bishop spoke with great enthusiasm about Abbess de la Pole and her firm but compassionate rule over the community of nuns and tertiaries and the various royal wards and hostages who were sent there for safe-keeping.

'To be honest, Mette,' Geoffrey told me, 'it sounds like the abbess has a demanding job which she performs with notable skill and sensitivity. The Tudor boys would not be alone there because the abbey houses and educates several heirs who are too young to administer their estates and whom the crown has not placed in ward with other noble families. The bishop says they even employ a Master at Arms to provide military training for these young nobles. The abbess understands the importance of preparing them for their future roles, as well as bringing them up in the fear of God. If Queen Catherine should need to go there herself, as a tertiary she would have her own apartment and would follow the rule of St Benedict.'

'I do not suppose she will ever go back there now, but Catherine was made a tertiary of the abbey of Poissy,' I informed him. 'She was sent there as a punishment by her mother for daring to contest the way the government of France was being handled by Duke Jean the Fearless of Burgundy.'

'Is that so?' Geoffrey cocked his eyebrow in surprise. 'She has a record of rocking the boat then, your Queen Catherine?'

'I will tell her you said that.'

He raised his hand in a placatory gesture. 'Please do not. I am sure she had every reason to criticise Burgundy,' he said. 'Jean the Fearless was a man on the make, particularly where the French exchequer was concerned.'

'A monster on the make, I would say.' I had never told Geoffrey anything of what Catherine had suffered at the hands of the present Duke of Burgundy's father. In fact I had never told anyone, and I do not believe Catherine had either, not even Owen. Those sufferings were in another time and another country; our lives were very different now. 'Barking Abbey sounds very like Poissy and its abbess sounds very like Catherine's sister Marie, who is in charge there.'

'So on that basis you think we can recommend it to her? Given that it will only be a refuge should the need arise.'

'Well, it will be a refuge for Edmund and Jasper, and possibly for Catherine herself. Nothing was said about little girls being accepted as wards there.'

'A girl does not have the same political significance as her brothers,' said Geoffrey. 'The queen may hope to keep Margaret with her.'

I silently prayed that this may come to pass, but in the long term I could see many hazards threatening such a happy outcome.

*

On his saint's day, November the twentieth, Catherine took Edmund to the church in order to light a candle to the martyred Anglo-Saxon king. Although its patron was St Andrew, Hadham's beautiful church contained a small chapel dedicated to St Edmund and often visited by pilgrims travelling to his shrine only fifty miles further north. The chapel boasted a relic which fascinated the boy – one of the arrows which had pierced the saint's flesh when he had been martyred by the Viking heathens who had invaded East Anglia five hundred years before. It was kept in a carved and gilded glass-topped box and exhibited on the saint's holy day, always an attraction to the villagers who saw St Edmund as a stalwart defender of England's shores. I had accompanied Catherine and her son on this minor pilgrimage and taken William with me, as he seldom liked to be separated from his friend.

The church was crowded and we took our place in the line of villagers which had formed in the side-aisle leading to the chapel. Disconcertingly, as soon as we joined it, the hitherto orderly queue began to rumble with an undercurrent of discontent. We had been talking among ourselves in low voices and at first were merely puzzled by the mood of growing hostility around us, but then the father of the family standing immediately ahead turned with an ugly glare and began hurling angry invective in a low growl.

'Filthy foreigners! You have no business with St Edmund. He is England's saint. You with your ungodly French talk. You defile our church and poison our village.'

Instinctively both Catherine and I clutched our boys to us and I saw her face drain of colour, as I am sure mine did too. Such bitter hatred was alarming, coming completely unexpectedly from a source which up to now had always been civil, if not consistently friendly. Since settling in Hadham we had believed ourselves accepted by the locals. Certainly many of them were happy to earn extra pennies working in and around the hall and we had never heard of any complaints about our residence there. I frequently ventured into the village to distribute alms and visit the sick and the men in the household willingly offered their labour at busy times on the manor, such as stock musters and harvests. There had never been any animosity between hall and village – until now.

I recognised the angry man as one of the older churls seen frequenting the village alehouse and wondered if perhaps he had been there already. Whether he had or not, he was not alone in his resentment, for others in the queue were quick to register their disapproval of our presence, moving to surround us in a threatening manner and to echo the gist of his tirade. Even some of the children took to verbal intimidation.

'Foreigners! Filth! Poison!'

Catherine cleared her throat and nervously protested, 'St Edmund is my son's patron saint. He is named after Him and born in the village. He has as much right as anyone to visit His shrine.'

'You have no rights here, Madame Stranger!' The man spat the last words like a curse, his face so close that his spittle showered Catherine's face, making her jump back and canon into the folk behind who began to stamp their feet while the chants continued, louder and fiercer. 'Strangers out! No Frenchies! No Welshies! English soil for Englishmen!'

'Strangers out! Out! Out!'

Gradually the whole queue took up the chant, their faces twisted in hatred. Probably because we were in a church, no one actually assaulted us but we were closely beset, herded into a small protective huddle and the little boys were understandably terrified, clutching our skirts, eyes wide with fear.

Catherine gave up trying to reason with the villagers and spoke instead to Edmund, whom she kept tightly encircled in her arm. 'Have no fear, my son,' she said clearly and slowly in English. 'These people are mistaken. They think us enemies because we sometimes speak French to each other. But they will not harm us because violence would desecrate God's house. They want us to go and so we shall go – if they will just let us through.' But the circle of antagonism held fast and I found myself back to back with Catherine, clutching William tight and growing more fearful by the minute. Weapons were banned in God's house, but I was suddenly terrified that the ringleader might have a knife concealed under his tunic, so ugly was his expression.

Then, as I looked around for any source of help, I saw Father Godric emerge from his vestry. For once he wore a look of authoritative anger rather than his usual benign air and he paused, frowning deeply, before striding down the nave towards us, his deep bass voice booming loudly through his tangled beard, above the villagers' hateful chanting.

'Silence! Silence in the church! You offend God with your raised voices. Quiet I say! If I am forced to inform the bishop of this uproar there will be punishments – women on the cucking-stool, men in the stocks. Give way now, churls, and let me through!'

Taunts and curses subsided into sporadic mutterings and expressions altered from open aggression to mulish resentment. The men, women and children ceased to jostle us and began to shuffle back into their family groups, allowing the priest to push his way to our side.

'Mistress Tudor, Mistress Vintner, boys, I think it would be advisable for you to leave the church,' he said, casually cuffing an obstinate urchin back into line. 'Follow me.'

He turned towards the door and we all hastened to obey his order, avoiding eye-contact with the scowling villagers and grateful for the protection of his wake. With his hand tight in mine, I could feel William's fearful shivering and as soon as the church door banged shut behind us I cast him a consoling smile. Outside, the churchyard seemed reassuringly peaceful; one or two groups of villagers stood gossiping together, apparently unaware of the drama which had unfolded inside. We followed Father Godric to the gate where he stopped and spoke to us, keeping his voice low so as not be overheard.

'I must apologise for any alarm you may have suffered, especially the children. They of all people should be safe in a church. But there has been much unrest in the village lately, of which you may be unaware. It has been fermenting since we heard news of the alliance between the French and the Burgundians. People now fear an invasion. It may be unwarranted, but there is growing suspicion of you and your household, Mistress Tudor.'

Catherine looked up from giving Edmund a reassuring hug. 'Well some of us are French, it is true, but Mistress Vintner here is married to an Englishman and I am married to a Welshman.' Her protest was made calmly, but there was no mistaking the note of indignation in her voice. 'I do not think we deserve to be treated as spies and interlopers. We have lived among you for six years now without incident.'

Father Godric wrung his hands apologetically. 'Yes and I have promoted tolerance among the villagers, but you must know that the Welsh have not been liked in England either since they rampaged over the border twenty years ago. I am afraid being married to a Welshman does not improve your popularity in English eyes.'

'Are you telling me that we are in danger from your flock, Father Godric?'

'N-no, not in danger of your lives, but you should be aware of the ill-feeling. I did not mean to imply that everyone in the village is against you; it is just that some of the elders stir things up, particularly those who fought in France. Unfortunately they tend to be the men the younger ones listen to.'

'I will tell Master Tudor what you say. Perhaps we should double the guard,' said Catherine, her frown deepening.

Father Godric tugged at his beard in agitation. 'No, I would not do that – not obviously anyway. It might aggravate the situation. But may I suggest that the boys stay away from the village? Sometimes their antics can irritate the cottars.'

William and Edmund exchanged glances and went bright red at this and I made a mental note to question my son on what these 'antics' might be. When the two of them put their heads together they could come up with some mischievous pranks which were not universally appreciated, even within the household.

Catherine glanced at Edmund, apparently thinking on similar lines. 'We will take your advice, Father Godric, and thank you for coming to our rescue. It was an alarming experience and there was no way of telling what the outcome might have been had you not intervened.'

The priest bowed in appreciation of her gratitude. 'I hope it will not put you off coming to worship at St Andrews. I will make every effort to ensure that there is always a welcome in God's house for the bishop's guests.'

Despite what the priest said about a welcome, none of us felt brave enough to attend Mass in the church the following Sunday or for several weeks afterwards. Maître Boyers came from Oxford and said Mass for us in the house and, for a time, we kept a wary eye on those villagers who worked as domestic servants but they did not seem restive. Catherine, Owen and I summoned Edmund, Jasper and William to the main hall for a serious enquiry into their behaviour towards the locals. They often played outside the bailey wall and we had never thought twice about them going to the village, but it turned out they had been chasing the cottagers' chickens and throwing stones into the duck-pond and some of the women had complained to the reeve about it.

Jasper and William were contrite, but Edmund took a different view. 'We were only skipping stones on the pond,' he complained. 'Those women are as stupid as their ducks.'

Owen strode forward and took his son by the ear, turning his face up so that their gazes met. Edmund tried to turn away, but his father grasped the other ear and compelled the boy to look him in the eye. 'Those women are not stupid, son. The ducks and chickens are their livelihood. If they do not lay eggs they do not make any money and they do not lay eggs if stupid boys throw stones at them. Do you understand, Edmund?'

'No!' squealed the boy, trying to wiggle out of his father's painful grip. 'She was an ugly hag. She cannot tell me what to do. My mother is a queen! I can do what I like.'

'Edmund!' Catherine almost shouted in her anger. 'You are so wrong. No one can do as they like and particularly not queens, or their sons. You will be punished for even thinking so.'

'I hope you did not say that to the woman, Edmund,' Owen snapped. 'You know we do not refer to your mother's rank.'

'Yes I did!' declared Edmund defiantly. 'But the stupid hag

484

just cackled at me like one of her hens. I never want to go there again anyway.'

'Good, because it is forbidden territory from now on and you are not to leave the house for a week. You will not ride your pony or play outside and you will remain in your chamber until one of us comes to get you. Starting now – go!' Owen pushed his son towards the stair which led to the upper floor. 'And if I see your face outside your door, I will fetch my horse whip.' Edmund stumbled past me, his bottom lip trembling. William and Jasper watched him go and began to sniffle.

I did not feel sorry for Edmund. Owen was right and he had important lessons to learn, but so did my own son. 'William you will not go to the village again either. Nor will you sleep in the same room as Edmund until you have learned not to follow blindly when you know something is wrong.'

'And, Jasper,' Catherine broke in. 'Do not think you have escaped. No riding for you either and you will sleep with Margaret for a week, until you and Edmund have both learned your lesson.'

The house was unusually quiet during the boys' punishment week but gradually, as Christmas drew nearer, plans for celebrations lightened the mood and tension over the incidents in the village abated. No one went there unescorted any more, but in the cold winter months we kept close to the hall anyway. However, reports reached us of riots and demonstrations against foreigners in other parts of the country. Thomas returned from his Michaelmas tour of Catherine's dower lands having received protests from a number of tenants about paying their manor dues to a Frenchwoman. Then, in spring, a message came from Anglesey saying that the tenants and villeins on two adjoining dower manors had rioted, chasing out the reeves and burning down the granaries and mills. This was very serious because, apart from the need to prosecute those responsible for terrorising manor officials, much of Catherine's income was derived from the sale of grain to the crown and the fees paid by tenants for having their own corn ground.

'What worries me most is how will they get flour for their own bread?' she said when Owen told her of the sabotage. 'Did these men not think of that when they fired the mills and granaries? Their families will starve. We must do something quickly.'

Owen's anger was from another cause. 'I do not know what came over them,' he growled. 'These people know me and my family. They are not dealing with foreigners. I do not want to leave you now that you are with child again, cariad, but I will have to go to Anglesey. Only I can deal with this vexing situation.'

Catherine had not yet let it be known generally that she was pregnant again because she was not best pleased herself. Happy with her three healthy children, she had been wearing a jet-stone pendant, a way of preventing pregnancy popular among noblewomen at court, but one which manifestly did not work.

'Yes, of course you must go. There is plenty of time; the babe is not due until September. But, Owen, what is the penalty for sabotage? I do not want hangings among my tenants.'

Owen shrugged. 'Yours are crown lands, Catherine. These offences will go before the king's justices. It is up to them what penalties are imposed.'

She looked seriously concerned. 'Then for my sake you must make sure you are away from there when sentences are passed, because I expect the justices are as anti-Welsh as the rest of England. Those fools have rioted against paying dues to a French overlord, but they will be tried by an English judge. They are dead men.'

'I fear you are right, but I will only arrest the miscreants, organise the building of new mills in time for harvest and bring in supplies to avoid starvation in the meantime. By the time the King's Bench judge comes out to North Wales and sentences are passed, I will be safely back here with you.'

Catherine smiled doubtfully at him. 'You make it sound easy, Owen, but I know it will not be. These are your countrymen and you will know them personally. Are you sure it would not be better to send Thomas?'

Owen shook his head emphatically. 'I could not put him in such a position. There will be protests and maybe even more riots, but I will have local support as well. He would have none. I will take Hywell and John and plenty of men. The law must be upheld and it is my job to do it.'

Catherine crossed herself. 'I will pray for you daily while you are away,' she said and kissed him on the lips.

Two days later, Owen, Hywell and John set off for Wales intending to hire men at arms on the way north and leaving three women at Hadham praying for their safety – Catherine, Agnes and Alys. To my surprise, Alys seemed to have succumbed to Welsh charm as well and had been mending John's shirts for him ever since Christmas. Having chosen an Englishman, I could not begin to understand what it was about the Welsh character that appealed to my fellow countrywomen and I sometimes teased Alys about her new amour, but she was as tight-lipped about this relationship as she had been when she fell for Jacques, the father of her children. There had been no suggestion of a marriage to John and I supposed I would not know if they were actually lovers unless another child came along.

It was different with Catherine, who had neither hidden her use of the jet-stone from me, nor her disappointment in its failure.

'I had hoped for a longer respite from childbearing, Mette,' she confessed. 'But it seems we are a fruitful couple, Owen and I.'

I felt a little anxious about her diffidence. 'Are you feeling unwell, Mademoiselle? Is there sickness?'

She sighed. 'No, not unwell, just a little jaded. I must not grumble. There are so many who pray for children and do not get them.' Another, longer sigh escaped her lips and she laid her hands on her belly. 'When the warmer weather comes perhaps I shall be more positive about it, especially if Owen has returned. I have let my husband become intrinsic to my happiness and that is wrong because I should put God in that position, but it is hard to worry about my soul when I am worried about my soul-mate.'

Her frame of mind did not improve even when the wildflowers bloomed in the river meadows and the maypole was raised in the churchyard for the spring dancing. There were no protests from the villagers when we went to watch the girls and boys laughing and shouting as they wove their complicated patterns around the pole, their heads crowned in floral wreaths and their feet stamping out jigs played by a band which consisted of the blacksmith on the pipes, the reeve on the rebec and one of the villeins on the tabor. Alys and I tapped our feet as we watched Cat and Louise swirl among the girls, threading their gaily coloured ribbons around the pole, but Catherine hung back near the churchyard gate and kept her children by her side. She could not forget the frightening incident in the church on the feast of St Edmund.

'The man who spat at us is standing near the band,' she said, shaking her head when I came across and asked whether the boys would like to take a turn, 'We will just watch from here.'

Jasper had not been in the church when the villagers turned on us and he was keen to take a ribbon at the maypole, but seven-year-old Edmund stuck by his mother protectively. 'You cannot leave us, Jasper,' he told his younger brother firmly. 'When our father is away we must take care of our mother.'

His sturdy championship of her earned him a hug and a smile from Catherine. In Owen's absence there was something lost and vulnerable about her which Edmund, now proudly seven years old, seemed to have sensed. William, of course, stayed loyally beside Edmund and so Jasper hung his head sheepishly and stayed with them, but his foot tapped eagerly to the music. Little Margaret was transfixed by the dancing and had crowned her doll with a daisy wreath like the big girls at the maypole but, nevertheless, clung close to the big brothers she worshipped. However she did not mind when I lifted her up so that she could see better. We all stayed where we were, a tight little knot set apart; in the audience but not of them. When the barrel of ale supplied by Catherine for the May celebrations was broached and the men began to caper rowdily with the village girls and women, we collected Cat and Louise and crept quietly back to the hall.

41

S oon after this Catherine received an unexpected visit from the Earl of Mortain who had recently been installed at Windsor as a Knight of the Garter, becoming one of the twenty-four who constituted the membership of England's highest order of chivalry.

Catherine was delighted for him. 'Congratulations, Edmund. It is an honour well-deserved. We must have a banquet to celebrate.' Her sapphire eyes sparkled in a way I had not seen for months and she clapped her hands with excitement.

At the time I know Catherine had regretted not being able to marry Edmund Beaufort, and at such a moment as this I wondered if she regretted it still. Now in his thirty-second year, he was a man of remarkable strength and vigour, with a physique honed by almost constant campaigning. The boots he wore over his fine blue hose may have been dusty from the road, but they encased a pair of long, athletic legs and his crimson broadcloth doublet was tightly buttoned over the sculpted sweep of a well-muscled torso. With his hazel eyes glittering hawk-like from under his blue velvet hat, I could not imagine there were many other Knights of the Garter to compare with him.

On his arrival Catherine had taken him straight to her solar and sent a maid to summon me. In such circumstances she liked to have me with her and in this she was wise, for people gossip and sometimes gossip finds a firm foundation.

The earl smiled and shook his head. 'A banquet in your company is a tempting thought, my lady, but I must leave directly; besides there is really little to celebrate. Have you not heard that Paris opened its gates to your brother? More than two weeks ago. Ever since John of Bedford's death, England's cause in France has been crumbling and I am leading a relief force which sails for Calais in a few days. This is a flying visit to check on your family's safety.'

At the mention of the capitulation of Paris, Catherine's hands flew to her mouth. When she could speak, her voice shook. 'Charles in Paris! No – no, I had not heard. I am dumbfounded. Poor Henry must be distraught.'

This observation provoked an incredulous laugh. 'Ha! That would be an understatement. The whole council is in turmoil – so much so that they are actually agreeing with each other for a change, hence my hasty departure at the head of two thousand men. The Duke of York has been appointed Commander in France and sails for Normandy with an even larger force very soon.'

I heard a distinct note of irritation behind this last piece of information, and quickly discovered why as I served them with wine.

'Gloucester insists that we should respect the late king's intentions and reclaim the territory he won in France and to achieve these aims he managed to persuade the council that it is time your son assumed control of his kingdom and began to issue edicts in his own right. Of course these are not the king's edicts at all, but Gloucester's set under the royal seal. Your son has always admired his Uncle Humphrey, as you know.'

Catherine nodded despondently. 'It is true, sadly. So that is why the Duke of York has been appointed Commander in France and not you, even though he is young and inexperienced and you are quite clearly the man for the job. Gloucester is a fool, serving his own ends, although actually it is his wife I mistrust most.'

'Ah yes, the scheming Eleanor, regrettably my wife's namesake, although there the similarity ends.' Edmund took a good gulp from his cup and made a face which I hoped had nothing to do with the quality of the wine. 'Unlike me and my Eleanor, the Duke and Duchess of Gloucester have at last obtained a royal licence for their marriage. It was one of the first documents Gloucester guided the young king's hand to sign. She is now the foremost lady in the land and she makes sure that all know it!'

Catherine's eyes turned icy. 'Does she indeed? Well she is wrong. I am the first lady in England – until my son marries that is.'

Edmund's eyes started to twinkle, as if he found the prospect of a court cat-fight rather amusing. 'You should also know that on the day I received the Order of the Garter, she was declared a Lady Companion.'

'A Lady of the Garter?' Catherine almost squeaked with indignation. 'An honour I received when I became queen. Gloucester does this to taunt me.'

'Then you had better go to court and show Duchess Eleanor precisely who is the first lady of the land. I am sure a daughter of France can run rings around a jumped-up troop-captain's daughter.'

Catherine gave an audible a sigh of frustration. 'I would make a point of going, if I were not with child again.'

'Ah.' The Earl eyed her figure appraisingly. 'I confess I did wonder. You and Owen are richly blessed with children, as are my wife and I. We have three now, but all girls I regret to say. We shall have to try harder. Where is Owen, by the way? He is not avoiding me, I hope?'

'Far from it; he is one of your greatest admirers. He is away in Wales dealing with some violent sabotage on my manors there. You must be aware of the growing prejudice against foreigners, Edmund. Ever since the failure of the Congress of Arras, the English have let their hatred of the enemy spill out into the streets and the countryside. I expect it will be worse now that Paris has fallen. My Welsh villeins fired barns and mills and refused to pay manor dues to a Frenchwoman, even though she is the mother of their king. And the English hate both the French and the Welsh. I have been subject myself to a horrible demonstration of hatred in, of all places, Hadham church.'

'I am very sorry to hear that. I hope you informed the bishop. There should be reprisals – punishments.'

'No, no. That would only make things worse.' Catherine bit her lip. 'I have been foolish to think I could live here anonymously forever. It is becoming too dangerous. Now that Henry is officially head of state, perhaps I should move back to court. If the king were to invite me, Gloucester could hardly object, however much his wife did.'

Edmund looked uncomfortable, his mouth twisting in doubt. 'If you value your marriage and family, I would think twice about that, Catherine. Owen would face jail and you might quickly lose control of your children. Edmund and Jasper pose a very real threat to Gloucester's position. Do not forget that Humphrey has no children of his own and it may be years before King Henry has an heir. If he knew of their existence, Gloucester would consider the king's half-brothers a dangerous focus for conspiracy. He would do anything to prevent them getting near the seat of power.'

'What do you mean by "anything to prevent them"?' Catherine asked sharply. 'Are you implying that Gloucester might want to get rid of them, Edmund? Even kill them?' Her voice rose to panic pitch.

I had picked up my embroidery in order to look busy, but at this point the needle froze and every hair on my body seemed to bristle in alarm.

'No, not kill them. Heaven forefend; I do not think even Humphrey would do that.' Edmund reinforced this statement with an earnest smile. 'But I strongly believe that secrecy is their salvation, at least in the short term.' He stood up. 'Now, am I to see my godson while I am here, or must I depart without a glimpse?'

His complacency only served to make me more fearful. I recalled my conversation with Margery Jourdemayne and wondered how much of her 'image magic' had accompanied Eleanor Cobham's rise. Just how far had she taken her consort with the devil? And if the duchess were to discover the existence of the Tudor children, what kind of magic might she try against them?

Edmund Beaufort stayed only long enough to watch the boys ride their ponies, give tips on how to steer them while holding their wooden swords and shields and snatch a quick meal. I had argued with Geoffrey about whether William should share Edmund's riding lessons, being unlikely to complete the rigorous training of a knight, but I could see no harm in him becoming as competent a horseman as possible. However, now that he was seven I knew that the time was fast approaching when Geoffrey would want him to start attending one of the schools attached to the Inns of Court in London.

As May progressed into June, there was still no news of Owen and his cousins and the women of the Hadham household became progressively more dejected. Only the children with their bright voices and constant activity prevented a pall of gloom settling over us. I fretted about Catherine's health, which had not improved as it usually did when she moved into the middle months of pregnancy. She was constantly tired and complained that there was a nagging pain in her belly.

'Not a sharp pain,' she explained. 'Like a belt around my stomach that is too tight and cannot be loosened. Did you ever feel like that when you were carrying, Mette?'

It was early morning and her pale face was puffed and blotchy. I suspected that she had been crying in the night.

'No, not that I can remember, but there is always something to worry about when you are with child. What you must do is eat well and get plenty of rest, Mademoiselle. I do not think you are doing either of those things. Did you sleep last night or were you at your prie dieu in the small hours?'

She gave me a guilty look. 'I cannot sleep for worrying about Owen,' she said. 'Prayer is the only thing that comforts me. But God does not tell me where he is or why he has not sent any word. I am truly worried, Mette. Perhaps he has run into danger. Do you think I should send someone to make enquiries?'

'It has only been two months since they left, Mademoiselle. I am sure there will be a message soon or else they will be home. I will make you an infusion of caraway. Perhaps that will relieve the discomfort.'

She drank it daily and I did not hear any more complaints,

but nor did she look any better. In my own prayers I included regular pleas for Owen's return.

At the beginning of July Hywell and John at last rode in. They reported hearing of unrest everywhere, especially in the rural areas of England where men had been recruited for the French wars. 'We Welsh are not exactly welcomed when we pass through towns, but the French are detested,' John revealed as we plied them with ale and cold capon to make up for days of bread and cheese in the saddle. 'Once men flocked to fight behind the hero of Agincourt, but now they want to pull up the drawbridge and keep the French out of England. Everyone fears an invasion.'

They had brought a letter from Owen for Catherine, penned in his own hand in script that was crabbed and smudged from lack of practice. She peered at it for some minutes, brow creased with the effort of deciphering its content.

'He says my manors are restored to working order and he has gone somewhere else, but I cannot make out the name of the place. Where is it, Hywell? What has happened there?'

Hywell had picked up little Gladys and was playing with her on his knee, while Agnes looked on happily. At least two of the Hadham women would be cheerful again, I thought, glancing at Alys who sat quietly next to John, pretending not to cast frequent sideways glances at him to reassure herself of his presence. I only wished Owen had come home to put a smile on Catherine's face.

'It is called Penmyndydd, my lady,' Hywell said. 'Owen's grandfather lives there still and it is where his parents are buried. I believe the old man is in need of some help. Does he not say?'

Catherine flung the letter down, tears of frustration brimming in her eyes. 'Perhaps he does but I cannot read it. He might as well have written the whole letter in Welsh. I have heard him talk of the place you mention, but it does not sound the way it is written. How long will he stay there?'

Hywell shrugged. 'I do not know. I suppose it depends on what he finds when he gets there.'

Catherine rose from her seat at the board, marched to the fire and threw Owen's letter on to the flames. 'He had better start to worry about what he finds when he gets back here!' she stormed, her voice breaking on a sob. Swinging round, she headed for the door to her solar and I hastened after her. It was very unlike Catherine to lose her self control in front of others.

I found her kneeling at her prie dieu, tears coursing down her cheeks as she gazed beseechingly at the image of the Virgin on the centrepiece of her altar triptych. I did not like to offer my own comfort when she was seeking it from a higher source, so I knelt quietly behind her hoping she would at least feel my supporting presence if Our Gracious Lady failed to supply sufficient solace. Within seconds she had turned into my arms, weeping in wretched, heaving sobs.

When she could speak it was in sharp jerks, punctuated with juddering gasps for breath. 'Everything is going wrong, Mette. I cannot bear it. We were so happy – and now I feel abandoned. I have lost him. I am sure of it. I do not know what to do.'

I was shocked. How long had this feeling been eating into her? Was it that and not the physical prostration of pregnancy that was making her ill? So much of her personal wellbeing was invested in her relationship with Owen, that if she felt it slipping away it would be devastating for her.

With both my hands I gently lifted her head from my breast where the linen of my bodice had done little to muffle her heartbreak. I looked into the red-rimmed, blurred blue of her eyes and tried to pierce the despair I saw in them. 'You are wrong, Mademoiselle. I am certain you have not lost Owen. He is yours for life. He told you so and swore it at your wedding. He is not a changeable man. He loves you.'

'He loved me,' she said, stressing the past tense. 'But that was before I started to bear this child. I am ugly now and ill and he would rather be in Wales than here with a sickly, unsightly, misshapen wife. He has probably found a beautiful young girl to play his harp to and speak his barbarous native language with.'

'You are not ugly or misshapen, Mademoiselle, you are beautiful. Nor are you ill, but pregnant and finding it tiring and dispiriting. Perhaps you should be glad that Owen is not here to see you in this state. If he says he is going to this place you cannot pronounce to visit his grandparents, then I am sure he is and I am sure they need his help.'

I smiled at her sad little face and wished I could magic all her cares away and that made me think of Margery Jourdemayne again. Could she make one of her image magic dolls that would ease suffering as much as cause it? Should I pay another visit to the wise woman and, this time, make my own purchase? Was there such a thing as white sorcery or did all charms and spells and magic arts deal to a greater or lesser extent with the devil's black demons?

42

From His Grace King Henry VI of England and II of France to Her Grace the Dowager Queen Catherine.

Greetings to our honoured and beloved Mother,

At last we are able to write with some good news. In a few days we shall travel to Dover to bid Godspeed to our uncle of Gloucester who sails to Calais to confront a threatening advance from Flanders by the perfidious Duke of Burgundy. Our cousin Richard, Duke of York, has been appointed Commander in France and has sailed already for Normandy with fresh troops to defend our territories there. Calais itself is valiantly defended by our cousin Edmund, Earl of Mortain. We are confident that these actions will reverse the misfortunes which have beset our cause in France.

As we write of these events we are aware that many loyal members of our court and family are away fighting for our cause in France. The importance of the love and loyalty of family at such times is obvious, for these are the people upon whom we can most confidently rely. You will be relieved to know that until they all return victorious, we will be lovingly tended by our aunt of

Gloucester, who has generously agreed to be our host at Greenwich.

Unfortunately we cannot visit you, my lady mother, as you may have expected. These are perilous days. However, we hope that you will find it pleasurable to come to court when the campaign has ended, to celebrate its success and to thank the staunch band of stalwarts who have defended our kingdoms from French aggression.

Until then we remain your ever loving and respectful son, Henricus Rex

Written at Westminster this Monday the thirtieth of July, 1436.

—ξξ—

This letter arrived for Catherine soon after I returned from staying with Geoffrey in London, having paid a fraught but informative visit to Margery Jourdemayne on the way back. This time I had called at her house, a neat and well-maintained half-timbered cruck-cottage on the outskirts of Eye and close to the woods where I had met her previously. She had not appeared pleased to see me and pulled me swiftly inside, insisting that Walter, who had accompanied me, should take the horses into the woods and remain out of sight. When I told her the reason for my visit, she looked seriously concerned and told me that since our last meeting she had made several visits to Greenwich Palace taking various herbal ingredients and at least one more wax doll to Eleanor of Gloucester. At first I did not make any connection with Catherine's pregnancy woes, but misgivings surfaced alarmingly when Margery went into more detail.

'The duchess wanted a female image,' she revealed, 'and she wanted it to be big-bellied with child but she did not tell me who it was supposed to represent, nor did I ask. I assumed it had something to do with her efforts to conceive.'

That was when I asked her if she thought there was any chance that the new doll was meant to represent Catherine, but she just shook her head and said she did not know.

'There are often other people there, usually two men in robes like priests. They look at me funnily, as if they're trying to read my mind. They give me the shivers and I always try to get away from that place as quickly as possible.' Then she gave me a potion which she said was a mixture of mint balm and powdered blood.

'It will stimulate the female parts and give her strength for the birth,' she said, grabbing my silver florin and trying to push me out of the door.

'What sort of blood?' I asked, clinging to the door-jamb. 'My mistress will want to know.'

'My husband is a cattle merchant,' she said. 'It is bullock's blood. Now go, before anyone sees you!'

On the ride back to Hadham, I could not get the idea out of my head that Eleanor's new wax image was intended to be of Catherine and that some form of sorcery was being practised against her, so I resolved not to give her the potion. Then, when she showed me the letter from King Henry, my thoughts took an even more sinister turn. I sat her down in her private solar, told her about my visit to Margery Jourdemayne and quietly voiced my innermost fears.

'You know that I would not wish to worry you needlessly, Mademoiselle, especially in your condition when you are already fearful about the absence of Owen, but I feel I must tell you what troubles me about this letter. It is not that the king will no longer be coming to visit you, although I know that will be a great disappointment, what troubles me is that he will be staying at Greenwich with the Duchess of Gloucester instead of remaining at Westminster with his household of loyal and trusted retainers.'

Catherine turned her washed-out face to me, frowning. 'Why, Mette, is there any danger in that? I admit that I do not like Eleanor Cobham, but I do not believe there is any real harm in her, barring her vaunting ambition.'

'Well, I cannot be certain, Mademoiselle, but yes, I believe there is great danger in that very ambition. Remember that the Duke of Gloucester is now the heir to the throne. To put it bluntly, if your son were no longer alive, Humphrey would be king.'

Catherine stared at me, a look of bewilderment clouding her expression. 'You surely cannot think that Gloucester means any harm to Henry? He hero-worshipped Henry's father and what-ever bad feeling there may be between me and Gloucester, I believe he is a God-fearing man who would not condemn his immortal soul by committing the ultimate sin. No, Mette. There is no question of that.'

She rose in agitation, but I put my hand on her arm. 'You mistake me, Mademoiselle; it is not the duke I fear in this respect but his duchess.'

That flung her back into her chair as if her legs had lost all power. 'The duchess? You think little Eleanor Cobham means harm to my son? No, Mette! I do not like her, but I cannot believe that.'

I dropped to my knees before her, taking her hands in mine to stop them shaking. 'When she came to Hertford you saw that she is no longer "little Eleanor Cobham", Mademoiselle, she is the Duchess of Gloucester and if your beloved son were not alive she would be Queen of England, a title I fear she may already have bartered her soul to possess. You say that the duke treasures his immortal soul, but he will be away in Flanders and I have good reason to believe that his duchess is a sorceress who is only too willing to pledge her soul, to the devil in return for earthly glory. Only listen and I will tell you why I believe this.'

Catherine did listen as I related the whole story of my encounters with Margery Jourdemayne and her involvement with the ambitious Eleanor. The only element of the tale I omitted was the king's birth 'behind the veil' and the powers believed to adhere to the caul, which meant I could not tell her of Eleanor's acquisition of it and the possibility of using it in magic against the king. I thought it dangerous to burden Catherine with such fears when she was so close to giving birth again.

As my tale unfolded, she appeared to shrink further and further back into her chair as if she wished it might swallow her up. At the end she sat in stunned silence. When she found her voice, however, she was suddenly filled with such energy that, had I not known better, I might have suspected her of having consumed the whole bottle of Margery's blood and balm tonic in one gulp.

'We must go to Henry,' she said, leaping to her feet. 'Pack the saddle bags, Mette, and find whichever men you can to accompany us Thomas and Walter would be good because they know the places where we can seek shelter between here and Westminster. We must go as far as we can today in order to catch Henry before he leaves for Dover.'

I was taken completely by surprise. I had expected her urgently to seek pen and paper, but not to feel impelled to rush to Henry's aid in person.

'But, Mademoiselle, you cannot ride! Not when you are so near your time. Send Thomas or Walter with a letter, or I will go with them and see the king, but not you – it is too dangerous for the babe.'

'Nonsense, babies come when they will and go when they will and not because you ride a horse or fall down a stair. I have lost them for no reason and kept them against all odds. The king is what matters now. He will not listen to you. Only I can persuade him of the danger he is in if he goes to Greenwich. This baby must take its chance. Be sure to pack my most splendid and voluminous mantle to disguise my belly when I get to court. Please, Mette, do as I say. We are losing daylight.'

There was no dissuading her. Within an hour we were in the saddle, Catherine and I riding side by side with Thomas leading and Walter at the rear. I calculated that we had about six hours of daylight and could make it to Enfield before dark if Catherine was able to ride for that length of time. Whenever I glanced across at her she smiled back, a small, determined twitch of the lips which told me nothing other than that she had noticed my glance. She was pale and tense and sat her horse stubbornly astride, despite my suggestion that she ride sideways, as I did. Her swollen belly looked incongruous and uncomfortable, tucked behind the pommel of a saddle which was made to fit a lady of normal girth, not one less than a month from giving birth. Fortunately the weather was fine, if anything rather too hot for comfort and the horses sweated at first until we stopped at Ware to water them in the River Lea. Thomas had been setting the pace at a fast walk in deference to Catherine's condition, but at this point she suggested we pick up the speed to a trot, at least intermittently.

'We must get to Enfield tonight, otherwise we will not get to the king in time,' she fretted. 'I am worried that he might leave for Dover early tomorrow.'

'Perhaps you should ride at the front with me then, Madame, and you can set the pace,' Thomas suggested. 'Then we can slow up whenever you start to feel uncomfortable.'

However, we were reckoning without Catherine's fierce determination and in the end it was not she who initiated a slower pace but me. Neither I nor Genevieve were in the flush of youth and after another two hours I feared my old mare might crumple under the strain of the punishing pace Catherine set. Because she was riding ahead of me, I could not see how she was faring but I began to ease my palfrey up and gradually dropped back into a walk, alarmed at Genevieve's heaving flanks. I could not believe that the heavily pregnant lady, who that morning had been almost prostrate with despair at my conviction of Eleanor Cobham's devilish activities, was now apparently able to drive her horse and herself to the point of exhaustion.

When she finally noticed that Walter and I were no longer trotting at her horse's heels, Catherine drew rein and waited for us to catch up. By now we were on the Great North Highway where there was plenty of traffic on foot, cart and horseback and little danger of attack from footpads. The tower of Waltham Abbey loomed on the horizon to the east and it wanted only three more miles to Enfield. The sun was a huge ball of red in the western sky, marbled with wisps of grey cloud. As Genevieve ambled wearily up to the other horses I noticed that although Catherine tried to remain ramrod straight in the saddle, her aching muscles hunched her forward over the pommel. Her face under her straw sunhat was a white blur against the glaring sunset.

'Do you not want to lodge at the Waltham Abbey guesthouse, Mademoiselle?' I asked. 'The abbot keeps a very good table and the rooms will be cool with their thick stone walls.' I was offering her a reason to halt before she tumbled headlong from the saddle, which I was convinced she must do before long.

But she was adamant for continuing. 'No, Mette. I do not want to risk being recognised by the abbot. Let us continue when the horses have drawn breath. Thomas says the Ermine Inn at Enfield has superior beds. It is not twelve miles to Westminster from there. We can be with the king before Tierce.'

When she finally slid from the saddle in the yard of the inn, it was all Thomas could do to hold her up. Feeling distinctly wobbly myself, I handed Genevieve's reins to a hostler and told him to wash her legs down with cold water before giving her a hot bran meal. There were only two rooms available and since Catherine was travelling incognito, there was no question of pulling rank, so for the first time she and I were to share a bed. Once I might have pulled some cushions onto the floor and left the comfort of the mattress to her but on this occasion we both ate the bread and pottage supplied by the innkeeper, helped each other out of our outer clothes and, clad only in our chemises, collapsed into the cool embrace of the sheets. I assumed that the fierce pains in my limbs and back could have been no worse than Catherine's, but she made no complaint and I heard the words of her night-time prayer mumble into silence as the blessed healing power of sleep claimed her only minutes before me.

Catherine woke me to help her dress before the dawn light pierced the cracks in the shutters and then sent me to knock on the door of the men's bedroom. While we waited for the sleepy grooms to tack up our mounts, we broke our fast on bread and ale in the sweaty reek of the tap room, where the floor was sticky with spilled wine and meat juices. Catherine ate little, but I cajoled her into forcing down a few mouthfuls before we hobbled out to face the seemingly insurmountable task of climbing back into the saddle. Saints be praised there was a mounting block against the yard wall and after a time the agony of being joggled by Genevieve's uneven stride dulled into mere pain. As the first milepost slid by, I sneaked a peek at Catherine's face and her jaw looked just as set as mine was. We did not speak for we had nothing of comfort to say to each other. I prayed silently to St Margaret to help the baby hang on tight.

We all cheered when the spires and towers of Westminster came into view and the king's standard was clearly visible flying from the palace keep. Sure now that Henry had not left for Dover, Catherine fell to thinking out loud about how she should gain admission to the king. She did not wish to declare herself to the guards because of her obvious condition and, anyway, she wanted to change into clothes more fitting for a court attendance. It was Thomas who suggested that we seek accommodation at the abbey guesthouse, where pilgrims from every corner of the land stayed before worshipping at the shrine of St Edward the Confessor.

'The horses can be stabled there as well,' he added. 'They have performed well and deserve a good rest.'

'I will need my mare to take me to the palace,' Catherine reminded him. 'I know it is only a short walk, but I do not think I will be able to manage it. And, Walter, I will give you my signet for the gatehouse guards to recognise. Do not leave my letter with them, you must take it all the way to the king's apartments.'

The monks showed us to a small guest cell where Catherine gratefully lay down on the cot bed while I prepared the robe and mantle I had packed in my saddlebags for her crucial meeting. She had lost so much weight during this pregnancy that the gowns she had worn as Queen of England still fitted, even over her eight-month belly. I hoped that the full-skirted blue silk one I had chosen would almost completely hide all evidence of it, especially when she also enveloped herself in a flowing gem-sprinkled mantle of deep crimson lined with scarlet. At least in that attire there would be no question of the guards mistaking her pedigree when she rode into the palace.

Walter returned after an hour to announce that the king had been shown the letter on the way to Mass and that a squire would come to escort his mother to the royal presence chamber immediately afterwards. I hurriedly completed arranging Catherine's hair into jewelled nets and a gossamer veil and the squire arrived as I inserted the final pin. Unable to disguise my own saddle-sore waddling gait, I followed with profound admiration as Catherine managed to glide gracefully over the uneven stone flags of the guesthouse yard, clutching her mantle around her in such a way as to completely camouflage her protruding belly. Apart from her intense pallor there was no sign of her pregnancy or her hectic ride from Hadham.

43

Although we rode the short distance to Westminster Palace, it was still a considerable walk from the central courtyard, where we left Thomas and Walter with the horses, to the royal apartments overlooking the Thames. Catherine and I more or less held each other up as we negotiated the maze of passages and staircases. We had no energy left for conversation and anyway the silent aloofness of the escorting squire and the curious surveillance of passing courtiers deterred even the most innocuous of remarks. I let Catherine handle the interrogation of the guards at the impressive panelled oak doors of the inner sanctum and kept my gaze firmly fixed on the floor, like a good attendant.

When the king's presence chamber finally opened up before us I heaved a sigh of relief and looked up to see King Henry standing at the far side of the room, deep in conversation with a young priest. Otherwise the room was empty. On a dais set against one wall stood the large and ornately gilded throne under an impressive crimson canopy, at the foot of which a younger King Henry and I had sat together during my encounter with him after his coronation. Apart from that the room held little other furnishing except some richly coloured tapestry hangings showing scenes of famous historical events and, under a diamond-paned oriel window overlooking the river, a polished buffet on which stood an array of refreshments. This chamber was intended for formal court business, during which only the king would sit, while his courtiers stood or knelt. Catherine was swaying with exhaustion, but her incredible fortitude allowed her to sink into a full court curtsy at which the young king barely glanced. She was not able to rise, however, without relying heavily on my hastily proffered arm.

'You, grace, it is so kind of you to see me at this busy time. I trust I find you well.'

Her softly uttered words penetrated the king's conversation and he glanced up frowning at the interruption, whereupon his face registered astonished surprise and he rushed forward to take her other arm. 'Your grace, my lady mother, Madame, you are here already. You look so weary, please let me help you to a seat.'

Since the only seat in the room was the throne, Catherine was solicitously conducted to it, where I hastily arranged her gown and mantle to preserve their disguising folds. Meanwhile, with a muttered word or two, King Henry dismissed the hovering priest, who cast a more than curious look at Catherine as he left the room.

I made full appraisal of the king as he returned to his mother's side. I had already noticed that his voice had dropped and, with approaching manhood, his shoulders had broadened and his chest had filled out. His face was thin, but his cheeks were still boyishly rounded and there was down on his chin. I had previously thought him very like his father with his hazel Lancastrian eyes and above-average height but, noticing how prominently his long nose marched down to his soft rosebud mouth, I realised for the first time that he also resembled his Valois mother.

Catherine looked so pale now that I feared she might not

have the strength to complete her mission but her voice, when she spoke again, was surprisingly strong.

'Was that Master Aiscough?' she asked as the door closed behind the priest. 'I have seen him in the company of Cardinal Beaufort.'

'Yes. I recently appointed him as my confessor and find him a good companion and a wise adviser,' King Henry replied. A wooden board creaked as he sat himself at his mother's feet on the steps of the velvet-covered dais. 'He is younger and more forward-thinking than some of the venerable clerics who have been foisted on me up to now.'

There was satisfaction in Henry's voice when he said this and amusement in Catherine's response. 'So you are beginning to make your own choices, my lord king? I am glad to hear it.'

'Perhaps I take after my lady mother in that,' he replied. 'This is an unexpected and unheralded visit, Madame, and made at a time when I think you should not be travelling.'

'Ah, you noticed,' said Catherine wryly. 'I hoped to disguise my condition from the casual glance, but my reason for coming is more important than my own safety or that of my babe. It is a deadly serious matter I must discuss with you my son.'

King Henry laughed nervously. 'I do not like the sound of that. What can be so serious that you would risk the life of your unborn child?'

'To put it bluntly, the safety of my first-born child – the King of England. You, Henry.'

'Are you saying that my life is in jeopardy?' Henry's voice, still adolescently unreliable, squeaked treacherously on this question.

'Yes and I beg you to do me the honour of hearing me out.

511

For what I have to tell you may not seem immediately believable, yet I assure you it is true.'

In the tense pause that followed, I watched him staring up at her anxious face as if assessing her state of mind. But I knew she was very much in her right mind and eventually King Henry must have come to the same conclusion.

'Well, since you are my mother I will hear your submission,' he said at length.

'Blessed Jesu, you make it seem like a court of law!' The sudden high pitch of Catherine's tone revealed the level of her stress. 'But in a way I suppose it is just that. I have set myself up as judge and jury over someone and I must convince you that my judgement is sound.' She drew a deep breath. 'You are very friendly with your aunt and uncle of Gloucester, are you not?'

'Yes, that is true. I know you and he have sometimes been at loggerheads, but my uncle has always worked hard in my Council of Regency and privately he has been like a father to me. I hold him in high regard.' There was a hint of pique in the king's inflection.

'Which is not surprising,' said Catherine hastily, 'for he is a literate and intelligent man and intensely loyal to the throne, although as you say, sadly no friend to me. However it is not the Duke of Gloucester that I come to warn you against; it is the duchess, the lady Eleanor.'

'But she is also kind and gracious! She has invited me to Greenwich while her lord is absent so that I may use his library. He owns many rare and wonderful books.'

'Yes, Henry, you told me in your letter. That is why I have ridden at speed from Hadham – to tell you that you must not go to Greenwich.'

'Not go! Why not?' His demand was indignant, angry. 'It is a pleasant journey down the river and there are manuscripts there I would dearly love to study.'

'Perhaps so, but it is a journey from which I fear you may never return. Please – just listen to me, your grace – my son! You gave me leave to speak.'

There was a challenging exchange of glances and an awkward silence before Catherine launched into her explanation.

'When your father and I were married, I gave him a wedding gift. It was a thorn from the crown of Christ's Passion. The thorn was in a reliquary which he swore always to wear around his neck to keep him safe from injury, disease and sorcery, but at the siege of Meaux it fell into the mud and was lost. Soon after that he became ill from a flux such as many men suffered and from which most recovered. Your royal father did not, even though he was the strongest of men. He was a conqueror whom his enemies hated and I have come to believe that their sorcery caused his death because he did not have the protection of Christ's blood on the thorn. Witchcraft is rife in England too, Henry, and I believe the Duchess of Gloucester is using it against you.'

'No!' King Henry's denial was loud and emphatic. 'You are wrong, mother – misguided. Lady Eleanor is a kind and beautiful woman and a good Christian. Abbot Wheathampstead has received her into the fraternity of St Albans Abbey. She cannot be a witch.'

'That is only the beginning of my story, Henry. I have evidence.'

My heart was suddenly in my mouth. I thought Catherine was going to call me forward to relate the content of my conversations with Margery Jourdemayne and I began to rack my brains in order to find a way of conveying the information without identifying its source but, to my great relief, she did not.

'I cannot tell you how I know what I am going to reveal, but I assure you that there is reason to doubt the duchess. Have you ever wondered why your uncle married her? Being a prince himself, did you not think it strange that he should chose a girl who was merely one of his captain's daughters? As a mistress perhaps – you are old enough now to understand these things – but not as a wife. The other council members unanimously disapproved of the match, yet you gave it royal approval.'

I saw Henry shift a little on his dais step. 'I thought it odd, but when I met her I realised that it was a love match, like yours with Owen.'

Touché, I thought, wondering how Catherine would react to that. She made a dismissive sound.

'Tcha! Ours is a true love match. Theirs is a marriage contrived by witchcraft. Eleanor obtained love potions from a known sorceress and practises charms and spells to keep Humphrey enthralled. Outwardly she appears to you beautiful and kind but, in truth, she consorts with the devil to achieve her ultimate ambition – the consort's crown. The marriage and your royal approval of it brought her to within one single step of her target. Henry, my sweet son, my lord and king, since the death of your uncle of Bedford only your precious life now stands between her and the fulfilment of that ambition. Humphrey of Gloucester is now your heir and I fear that Eleanor would do anything to put her husband on the throne and make herself Queen of England. While he is here, the very presence of Gloucester keeps her in check but your visit to Greenwich while he is away will be, for her, a devil-sent opportunity.'

I noticed that she had not included any fears for her own

514

health or that of her unborn child or mentioned the sinister existence of the wax dolls and the threat of image magic. As any mother would, she was protecting Henry's youthful sensitivity and only wanted to tell him enough to make him mistrust the duchess and to keep his distance.

'Why do you not discuss witchcraft with Master Aiscough?' she suggested. 'He will tell you that sorcerers conspire together in evil. I do not believe their evil spells can harm you because you are devout and pure and the saints watch over you, but they cannot protect you against poison and if you go to Greenwich you expose yourself to Eleanor's hospitality and to her food and drink. I beg you, as you love me, Henry, do not go there.'

Catherine's earnest entreaties had drained her energy and her face was now as white as her veil. The king took her hand. 'You look faint, my lady mother. Please, do not overexcite yourself.' He beckoned to me anxiously. 'Come, Mette! Help the queen mother.'

I scurried to the buffet table where a flagon and cups were set out. After she had sipped at the rich red wine, a little colour returned to her cheeks. Meanwhile King Henry had taken time to consider her appeal, pacing slowly around the room, fingers pensively stroking the fur trimming of his gown. He returned to Catherine's side, gazing at her anxiously, as if fearful that she might already be in the throes of labour.

'How do you fare, my lady? I hope the wine has restored you.' At her silent nod he bowed his head. 'Very well, I will talk to Master Aiscough, but I do not believe Lady Eleanor is a witch. Witchcraft is a serious charge. It would have to be tested by the Church and I do not think you would wish to bear witness in a consistorial court. But since you are so against it I will not go to Greenwich and I will take care not to eat anything not tasted previously by another. Will that content you?'

Catherine heaved herself to her feet and took his hand to steady her descent from the throne. 'God be thanked,' she breathed, forcing a smile. 'May the Blessed Virgin and all the saints keep you safe, Henry. It is not important that you implicitly believe me, only that you remain safe and well. And now I must leave before word spreads that I am here, for I suspect news of that might bring the Lady Eleanor running.'

'But you will not leave at this hour surely!' The king was aghast. 'It will soon be dark. You cannot travel until tomorrow. I will have rooms prepared for you.'

'No,' said Catherine firmly. 'We lodge tonight at the Abbey Hospice. They do not recognise me there and I do not want my presence here becoming common knowledge. You must prise an assurance from Master Aiscough that he will not speak about my visit. The monks at the abbey are kind and we must start for Hadham first thing tomorrow, else this babe will be born by the wayside.' She gave a brittle laugh. 'It would not do for the king's brother or sister to be whelped in a field like a mongrel pup, would it?'

She still held her son's hand in a tight grip, as if reluctant to let him go. 'But I must ask one more boon of you, Henry. If I die before Humphrey of Gloucester do not, I beg you, tell him of my Tudor family. He is loyal to you as his brother's son, but he hates me and would be furious to learn that I have defied him all these years. He and Eleanor might try to prevent my younger sons' advancement. You know my plans for them and the Earls of Somerset and Suffolk will ensure that my wishes are fulfilled. Will you continue to keep my secret, Henry?'

Catherine looked so frail and vulnerable at that moment that

I wanted to put my arms around her but instead, restricted by the circumstances, I willed her son to give her that comfort.

To my surprise he did lean forward and gently kiss her cheek, then drew back in alarm as tears began to spill down her cheeks, prompting words of reassurance to tumble from his lips. 'You already have my promise to keep your family secret but I will reinforce it if that will make you happy. And I pray that God will preserve you for many years to come so that you live to see them grow to adulthood. But now you must rest. You are right, they will take good care of you at the abbey. God go with you, my sweet mother, and may He grant you a safe delivery.'

He looked at me expectantly and I took Catherine's arm and led her from the room, almost blinded by weeping and weariness. Slowly we retraced our steps, following the same supercilious squire back to the palace gate. Black clouds had gathered in the meantime and drizzle had slicked the cobbles of the main court-yard. Walter and Thomas were waiting with the horses under the gatehouse arch and we pulled up the hoods of our cloaks to walk to meet them. Halfway across, Catherine lost her footing and although I held her arm I was not strong enough to prevent her falling to the ground with a sickening thud and a cry of pain.

I dropped to my knees beside her. 'Mademoiselle, forgive me, I could not hold you!'

There was a strange, sour smell that stirred my memory and a fine mist began to rise around her tumbled skirts. She turned anguished eyes to mine. 'Oh, Mette, you must help me now. My waters have broken.'

44

In the early hours the abbey bell tolled, muffled but relentless and between its clangs came the sound of shuffling feet as sandalled monks made their way from the dorter to the church for Matins. As they passed down the cloister in the fog of sleep they must have wondered about the muted moans they could hear coming from the hospice. In deference to her condition, rather than expecting Catherine to lie among the pilgrim travellers in the long public dormitory, the hospitaller had given us one of the small cells reserved for visiting clerics and, conscious that giving birth within the walls of a monastery was somehow inappropriate, Catherine was desperately trying to stifle her cries of pain. Even so, only the deaf or unconscious would have been oblivious to the plight of the distressed lady in their midst.

After her fall in the palace courtyard, Walter and Thomas had somehow settled Catherine in the side saddle on my Genevieve but she had swayed alarmingly, even with two of us alongside to support her. When we reached the hospice and the men had carried her in and laid her on the narrow bed, I suggested to Walter that he go to Tun Lane and tell his father where we were and the circumstances in which we found ourselves, while brave Thomas undertook to make a night ride to Hadham in the hope that Owen had at last returned from Wales.

'I am worried about this birth,' I confided to him out of Catherine's hearing. 'The queen is exhausted and weak. I fear she may not survive the ordeal ahead. If Owen were here, her spirits might be boosted. Pray God he is at Hadham. And may the Almighty protect you, too, Thomas. Do not take any risks.'

I did not tell them, as I had not told Catherine, what I had seen as we rode away from the palace. Glancing down an alley which led to the river, through the mist of rain I had spied a scarlet-painted galley pulling into the palace dock, torches glimmering at stern and bow, lighting up the royal standard of quartered lions and fleurs-de-lys, its silver border designating Gloucester. Standing at the gunwale, ready to disembark, was the unmistakably glamorous figure of Eleanor, Gloucester's duchess. There must have been an incoming tide to bring her so swiftly upriver from Greenwich when she should have been making preparations for entertaining the king at her gloriously refurbished palace. Had there been time since Catherine was first sighted at Westminster for a fast horse to convey a court spy down to Greenwich and for Eleanor to have been rowed back? I was not familiar enough with the flow of the river to be sure, but with a dread feeling in the pit of my stomach I realised that Catherine had failed to extract a promise from King Henry not to reveal where she was lodging that night. In any case, if he told the duchess that he no longer intended to visit Greenwich it would surely not take her long to put two and two together. It felt dangerously as if we might be riding into a trap.

When Matins was ended, we received an august visitor, drawn by the sound of Catherine's stifled cries, and at the sight that met his eyes the Abbot of Westminster quickly became a troubled man. Abbot Haweden was the very same abbey superior who had officiated at Catherine's coronation. Then he had guided her through the solemn ritual and accepted, as a gift to mark a great occasion, the elaborately embroidered silk stole she had worn during her anointing. Now he gazed down upon her, lying great-bellied on the meagre hospice cot, and was bewildered by her desperate plight.

He turned to me, incredulous. 'God alone knows how the queen mother has come to this sorry pass, Mistress, but she cannot give birth here. It is not a suitable place.'

'We cannot move elsewhere now, my lord,' I protested. 'Her grace's time is near.'

'Yes, I realise that. What I meant was that we must find somewhere more fitting for her to give birth – more . . . discreet. There is a chapel off the infirmary and the walls are thick so that her cries will not be heard.' The abbot thrust his hands into his sleeves, preparing to leave. 'I will send bearers when preparations have been made.'

Before long four strapping young novice monks arrived, lifted the narrow cot with its swollen burden and carried it across the moonlit monastery court, past the looming bulk of the great abbey church and into the infirmary cloister. The chapel was a small lime-washed chamber reached through a separate entrance off this passage and proved to be a candlelit haven of peace and fragrance. An altar bearing a crucifix stood against one wall and a bed had been placed beneath a niche containing a statue of the chapel's patron saint, appropriately St Catherine, holding a book and supporting a wheel, her beatific face frozen in a smile. On the bed a mattress was made up with clean sheets and a woollen coverlet and beside it wafts of steam rose from a tub of hot water, draped in white linen and accompanied by a pile of towels and napkins.

'Father Abbot says to ask for anything else you need,' said one of the young monks, staring in wonder at Catherine's prone and gravid figure. 'We have never had a birth in the abbey before.'

'Please ask the brothers to pray for the mother,' I whispered. 'She is in a poor way. God knows if she will survive her trial.'

Gently I lifted her from the cot to the bed, horrified by her scant weight. Apart from her pronounced belly there seemed to be little of her. Outside in the night sky the clouds must have cleared, for bright moonlight suddenly illuminated a small stained-glass window above the altar, casting pools of coloured light across the white wall beside us.

'Are those angels?' cried Catherine. 'Where are we, Mette?' Her voice was alarmingly hoarse and weak.

'In a chapel, Mademoiselle. It is quiet and private here and look – it is dedicated to St Catherine, surely a good omen.'

She made no comment as her body arched under another violent spasm and she bit down on the leather belt I had given her to stifle her cries. The four monks crossed themselves and made a hasty exit and I dipped one of the napkins in the water-tub and squeezed it out to wipe away the beads of sweat that had broken out on Catherine's brow. When the pain eased, she reached for my hand and I noticed tears sliding slowly down her cheeks, glinting in the 'angel' light.

'Do not leave me, Mette,' she croaked. 'I am so frightened.'

'Shh.' I stroked her head and gently took the belt from her. 'I am here. There is nothing to fear. And you can make all the noise you like now, Mademoiselle. No one will hear. I have sent Thomas to Hadham to see if Owen is back. He may come by morning.'

To my surprise her tears redoubled and my knuckles cracked

under the pressure of her fingers. 'I hope he does not come. I do not want him to see me like this.'

She might have said more but another pain gripped her and she had no breath left to speak. All she could do was moan and, eventually, scream out like an animal caught in a trap. Her bony limbs made sharp angles of the bedclothes around the mountain of her belly. On the statue's plinth I found a jug of wine placed on a tray with cups and poured her a drink, whispering my thanks to St Catherine for being a thoughtful patron. Inwardly I also begged Her to work a miracle, for I felt certain one would be needed before this fearful night was over.

Although a virgin herself, St Catherine proved that she had powers to aid childbirth, for despite the mother's lack of strength the babe did not linger long between womb and world. When he came, however, the infant boy was tiny, apparently perfect in every way but worryingly small, as if he were one of a pair of twins. But there was no second foetus and I had no time to tend the child apart from tying the cord and wrapping him in a blanket because Catherine had given one last, enormous push to expel the babe and then fallen into a faint. Putting my head round the door of the chapel, I called for help at the top of my voice and returned to my charges. Catherine's hands were icy cold and I chafed at them with both of mine, hoping to rub life back into the pale and senseless body. I had pulled the cover off, the more easily to deliver the baby, but now I flung it back on again, even though I knew that I must watch for the after-birth. Although I had attended at least eight births, I had never before been solely responsible for the delivery of a baby and the recovery of the mother as I was now.

When help came it was in the form of the novice monk who

had offered it before. 'Is it born?' he asked entering with caution, like Daniel into the lion's den. 'Is it all right?'

'I need a knife,' I told him. 'A sharp one – to cut the cord.'

'Oh – yes, of course.' He turned away and extracted something from the purse he wore on the belt of his habit. It was his own knife – the one he presumably used to cut his food and trim his quills for writing. 'Will this serve?'

'Yes, thank you.' I took the knife and turned back to the bed. Testing the blade, I found it sharp enough for the purpose and was relieved that I would not have to resort to using my teeth, a macabre practice once gleefully described to me by a midwife, which had surfaced among my random memories of previous births.

I completed my task and adjusted the bundle, immediately handing it to the young monk and suppressing a wry chuckle at his evident alarm. 'It is a boy and he lives, but not for long unless someone finds a wet nurse. And he should be baptised immediately. Tell the abbot his mother said to name him Owen.'

He held the child at arms' length, as if it were an animal that might scratch or bite. 'All the monks are in the church for Lauds,' he revealed. 'I alone was told to wait for your call.'

Tutting my disapproval, I arranged the baby more comfortably, bending the young monk's arms so that the bundle nestled against his chest. 'Hug him close to your body and keep him warm until the Office is over,' I instructed. 'We must hope the Almighty will not take the life of a babe whilst the monks are singing His praises.' He appeared so shocked by my lack of reverence that I was forced to give him a little push towards the door. 'I have to tend the mother. Go!'

In truth I did not hold out much hope for the infant. The circumstances were far from ideal and Catherine's determination to warn the king of the threat to his life had probably robbed the newborn babe of several weeks in the womb. What concerned me more was her condition. I could not tell whether her collapse was sleep due to utter exhaustion, or something more sinister and since I was unable to rouse her I was forced to conclude the latter. However, St Catherine was watching over her her body seemed to function automatically and I was able to deliver the afterbirth without incident.

Having gone without sleep myself for a day and a night, I felt confused and stupefied. I knew that if she was to make a recovery, Catherine would need a long rest and a nourishing diet, neither of which she was likely to receive among the monks of Westminster. I hoped that Geoffrey would come and help me to decide what should be done, for I was at a loss to know. Lacking any other advice for the time being, I knelt down before the crucifix on the chapel altar and offered my confusion up to God.

When the abbot arrived, he must have been gratified to find me thus employed for he seemed a good deal friendlier than he had before, his expression genial under his clerical tonsure. I envied him the few hours' sleep I assumed he had enjoyed between Matins and Lauds. 'I am delighted to hear of her grace's safe delivery,' he said. 'Our hospitaller knew of a nurse who lives nearby and the child has been taken to her. I myself baptised him with the name of Owen, as her grace instructed. I take it that is the name of the father?'

'Yes,' I replied, not wishing to reveal anything more as I scrambled up from my knees. 'Is she trustworthy this nurse? Her grace will need her name and exact location.'

'Of course, of course – all in good time.' The abbot gazed down on Catherine who was still lying, deathly pale and unmoving, beneath the statue of her patron saint. 'How does she fare?'

'She is exhausted.' I crossed my fingers in the folds of my skirt, hoping this was true. 'She needs rest and complete peace to recover.'

'I anticipated such a situation and I have arranged somewhere for her to go that will provide for her every need.'

'Her grace cannot travel far,' I protested. 'Her body is weary beyond bearing.'

'Bermondsey Abbey is only a short way down the river. A boat will be here at the turn of the tide to carry her there. The monks of Bermondsey are a caring community, used to noble residents, both lords and ladies. I have sent them a message that the queen mother will be brought there later this morning, urgently in need of care.'

'Have you informed the king of this, my lord?' My heart was beginning to thump alarmingly in my chest. Things were moving too fast for me. No word had come from Geoffrey last night and at this rate I feared that before he appeared, Catherine and I might be gone. I could not let her go to Bermondsey alone, but nor could I be sure that there was nothing sinister in her swift dispatch from Westminster. I could not help recalling the Duchess of Gloucester's arrival at the palace the previous afternoon.

'Yes, Mistress, have no fear. His grace is fully informed. You look exhausted yourself. I will have refreshment sent to you immediately. Be ready to depart soon after Prime.'

Not for the first time in my life I had a sense of being swept up in events over which I had no control. There was only an hour between Lauds and Prime and by the time I had washed and dressed Catherine as best I could, swallowed a few mouthfuls of the bread and pottage the abbot sent and used the horn spoon to dribble some water down my poor, insensible patient's throat, the four novice monks had returned with a litter to carry her to the abbey dock. In recognition of the rank of his departing guest, the abbot himself came to see her off and, thinking that he could hardly refuse to keep Catherine in touch with her treasurer, I begged him to speak to Geoffrey when he came and inform him of our destination.

I was assailed by doubts as to whether I was doing the right thing by allowing Catherine to be carried onto a barge which bore no mark or flag of identification and whose crew wore no livery badges, but short of flinging myself across her prone body I could not think of a way to prevent it. Even if I tried, there were plenty of brawny monks around to pull me off and lock me up somewhere, which would hardly be to the advantage of either of us.

They laid her litter under a tented shelter rigged over the rear thwarts of the craft. The pink light of dawn did nothing to improve the sight of her expressionless face with its sunken eye-sockets and prominent cheekbones. Despite the jolting of the litter she remained completely unaware of her circumstances and as the six rowers bent to their oars and the barge swung out into the tidal current, I was swamped by an overwhelming desolation, unable to rid myself of the dreadful feeling that I was travelling on some sort of floating catafalque. My brave and cherished Catherine lay in limbo with only me to pray for her.

45

Although I had married a Londoner and stayed in the city on and off for the past seven years, I had never taken any kind of journey on the river or visited the south bank of the Thames, with the result that I did not really understand how much difference there was between the river traffic above and below London Bridge. Downstream from the bridge London was a busy port, with all manner of fishing boats trading their catches at Billingsgate market, seagoing ships by the hundred docked at the wharves around the Tower or waiting midstream in the Thames roads to do so, or else loading and unloading their cargoes to and from barges. Above the bridge the busiest flow of traffic was from boats plying across the river; small cargo wherries and passenger ferries carrying goods and people between the City and the Southwark bank. On these reaches a procession of barges carried cargoes to and from towns upriver, but relatively few craft actually navigated under the bridge and if they did it had to be at the turn of the tide because when it was at full flow, the rush of water was dangerously fast through the nineteen tunnel-like arches of the span.

When Catherine had lodged at the Tower as queen, I had noticed Bermondsey Abbey directly across the river, but from further upstream, in the City itself, it was obscured by the tall houses built across the span of London Bridge. Now, sitting on the barge beside Catherine's litter, I realised that the abbey was on the other side of the bridge. The tide was already ebbing and, seeing the rush of water pouring through, I made the sign of the cross and changed my prayers from pleas to St Catherine for the life of my mistress to appeals to St Christopher for our safe delivery through those turbulent rapids. I did not witness the skill with which the helmsman steered us towards one of the arches because I kept my eyes tight shut, but I heard the swish and swirl of the water and felt the barge lift and surge as it was carried like a toy through the tunnel. There was a frightening thud as we were swept out the other side and the rear of the barge clipped the end of the long pier that supported the foot of the arch.

My eyes flew open in alarm and the first thing I saw was a long line of three-masted cogs waiting in mid-river for their turn to unload, then we swung to the right and the men heaved hard on the oars to take us across the flow of the tide and into the backwater that connected the Bermondsey Abbey demesne to the river. It was at this point that I saw a sight to make my stomach churn anew. Already moored against the abbey wharf was the galley I had seen the previous evening arriving at the Westminster palace dock, scarlet-painted and flying the royal banner of Gloucester. There was no sign of the duchess, but the intuitive lurching of my stomach told me it would not be long before I encountered her.

Like any great river, the Thames was prone to flooding and only poorer houses and workshops were built close to the southern bank. The Benedictines had wisely built their abbey on higher ground and the rowers shipped their oars and carried Catherine's litter for a hundred yards up a sloping cinder path, past a herd of milk cows grazing on the lush grass of the flood-meadow, to a high wall where a river-gate stood open to receive us. I followed behind, dragging my feet, partly out of profound weariness and partly out of a reluctance to confront the situation that awaited me. Within the gate the bearers paused to catch their breath and when I caught them up, passing under an arch built through the thick wall, I was assailed by a sudden chill sense of leaving freedom for confinement.

Built of severe grey stone, the abbey precinct was a busy place and yet uncannily hushed; quiet enough for the summer chirrup of sparrows nesting in the eaves to be the dominant sound. Numerous tonsured monks in dark habits went about their tasks in silence, only the faint slap of their sandals on the flag-stones marking their progress as they moved from place to place. A large church dominated one side of a rectangular enclosure, surrounded on the other three sides by a series of domestic buildings fronted and connected by a surrounding cloister. A formal garden filled the quadrangle, laid out with severely trimmed hedges, paved walkways and a carved stone fountain at its centre; and there, against the muted gurgle of its over-flowing basins, we were met by the abbot and another monk who turned out to be the hospitaller and beside them, conspic-uous against the monochrome surroundings in her brightly coloured robes and scintillating jewellery stood Eleanor, Duchess of Gloucester.

There followed a weirdly formal ceremony of welcome in which both the abbot and the duchess addressed themselves exclusively to a prone Catherine, who remained unconscious and motionless on her litter, scarcely appearing to breathe. I noticed that the hospitaller regarded her closely and with some alarm, but obviously did not feel he could interrupt the ceremonial, even though I frowned, wrung my hands and rolled my eyes at him. Rather than unctuous words of welcome, Catherine needed urgent nourishment and care and I was becoming desperate on her behalf. So much so that when the abbot implied that she should be carried into the church for an altar blessing and prayers to its patron, Our Lord Saviour, I plucked up courage to intervene.

'Forgive me, my lord abbot, what the queen mother most urgently needs is nursing and sustenance. I am certain she will wish to receive a church blessing later, at a time when she is conscious of God's Holy Beneficence.'

Inevitably the duchess felt bound to challenge my temerity, not that she favoured me with any sign of acknowledgement, neither of my presence nor my suggestion. 'My men will carry her grace to the church at once, according to your wishes, my lord abbot,' she said, beckoning to the men who had brought the litter from the barge and were standing at a deferential distance.

I seethed inwardly, partly at her disdain but mostly because her words confirmed my suspicion that Catherine had been brought from Westminster to Bermondsey not by order of the king but entirely at the instigation and organisation of the Duchess of Gloucester. It was her barge, her posse of retainers, and her way of preventing the king's mother from exerting any further influence on her son. I wondered how great a benefice had been promised to the abbey in return for what was effectively a conspiracy to abduct and imprison a helpless lady.

Fortunately the hospitaller did not seem to be in on the conspiracy and spoke up for the first time. 'Her grace's companion is right, lord abbot. The dowager queen is in urgent need of medical care. She should be carried to her quarters immediately and attended by our apothecary. We have a duty of care to the bodies of the sick, as much as to their souls.'

I held my breath and watched as the abbot and the duchess exchanged lengthy and meaningful glances, then eventually the abbot gave a curt nod in the direction of the hospitaller. 'Very well, Brother Anselm. You have prepared our best guest chamber – let her grace be carried there now. We will say prayers for her at Tierce, if you would care to join us, your grace?' This last was directed at the duchess in an apologetic tone.

Within the frame of her elegantly wired headdress, Eleanor's beautiful face had flushed with anger but she did not object. Instead she cast a veiled aspersion at Catherine which she knew only I would fully understand. 'Heaven knows there is much in her life that requires our prayers, my lord, but unfortunately I am obliged to forego the privilege. There are matters that require my attention at Greenwich and I must catch the tide.' She watched her men lift Catherine's litter to follow the hospitaller to the guest quarters, her lips tightening as she took a last look at the unconscious figure stretched out upon it. 'I will send a woman of my household to assist in the dowager queen's care and a messenger to keep me informed of her progress. I trust arrangements can be made for their accommodation.'

It was only then that the lady Eleanor deigned to look at me, a brief, appraising glance before she bent to kiss the abbot's ring in farewell. But in that look I found the information I needed, for although it contained pride and contempt, there was not a hint of trepidation. I assumed from this that Margery Jourdemayne had not told her of my visits or my enquiries about the king's caul and the wax images. Had she known of these I believe I might have seen my death sentence in Eleanor's cold, violet eyes.

To my intense relief, Catherine returned to consciousness towards noon and I was able to spoon-feed her some nourishing barley broth sent from the monastery kitchen. Once out of the abbot's hearing, the hospitaller had proved to be a valuable ally and all Catherine's requirements were met, while the apothecary, having been told the extent of her collapse, had prepared a herbal tonic of lemon balm, parsley and purslane, which I took the precaution of testing on myself before giving to her.

However good it was to see her awake, I was far from happy with Catherine's lethargy. It was only twenty-four hours since she had given birth and yet she asked no questions about the baby and nor did she respond to any reference I made to his whereabouts, his condition or even his name. Her main concern was for religious comfort and I was asked to leave the room when the abbot came to bring her this. Mysteriously her breasts showed no sign of producing milk. I told myself it was early days, and now that she was awake what I found more immediately worrying was the lack of communication from outside. Eleanor's two Gloucester retainers turned up before nightfall and duly presented themselves, a florid-faced woman of childbearing age who introduced herself as Hawisa and a spotty young man wearing the Gloucester badge on his tunic called Edwin. Catherine would have nothing to do with either of them, perhaps because she knew as well as I did that they had come to spy on us, rather than be of any assistance. Edwin mostly made himself scarce, but I knew that he met Hawisa at regular intervals, presumably to acquire information to carry to Greenwich. Rather than let her sit around all day doing nothing,

I made use of Hawisa for work that did not involve contact with Catherine, such as collecting and delivering meals and laundry, fetching water, medicines from the apothecary and fuel for the fire. Despite it being high summer, Catherine was constantly cold and wanted her chamber kept at what was, for me, an uncomfortably high temperature.

To the abbey's credit it was a pleasant room, not large but beautifully embellished with carved and polished panelling, a stone fireplace and two arched windows set high in the outside wall. These let in air and light, but gave no view and anyway Catherine wanted the shutters closed so the room remained dark and stuffy, but it was well furnished with a curtained bed and comfortable cushioned chairs at the hearth. It was in one of these that I slept when we first arrived, before I arranged for a truckle bed to be delivered. I had no intention of leaving Catherine alone or of allowing her to eat anything that I had not tasted myself first. Moreover I feared that even the presence of a crucifix, a prie dieu and the sanctity of our surroundings might not be enough to deter the devil's imps, for I believed it was at the instigation of his acolyte that we were imprisoned in the abbey at all and therefore easy prey to Eleanor's spells and conjuring. I could not dismiss the dreadful feeling that Catherine and I had come full circle, vividly recalling her infancy, when her father's madness had seemed to infect the palace with winged demons conjured by some nameless sorcerer.

The constant presence of Eleanor's spies made me desperate for a friendly face, but there was no sign of either Geoffrey or Owen and by the end of the second day I was extremely concerned. Although Thomas could have been delayed or even, heaven forbid, set upon by thieves during his journey to Hadham or else have lingered there in the hope of Owen's arrival, there was no reason I could think of why Walter and Geoffrey should not have managed to make their way to Westminster, discover our whereabouts and present themselves at Bermondsey within two days, unless the Duchess of Gloucester's influence extended to the abbot of Westminster as well. Could both abbeys have been bribed into a vow of silence over the presence of their royal guest?

As the days passed into weeks, I became more and more dejected at being cut off from the outside world, utterly dismayed by the separation from my family and the total lack of information about them. Every day I went to the gate to ask if my husband had made enquiries, but the porter just shook his head and refused even to let me look out of the grille which afforded the only view beyond the walls of the enclosure, of the inns and houses that lined the pilgrim road to Canterbury. I nursed the faint hope that somewhere in one of them Geoffrey or at least one of Catherine's household might be keeping a vigil. It seemed impossible that no one had discovered our whereabouts. Stressed and miserable as I was, I could not believe that two people, one of them a queen, could be made to disappear from the world of their loved ones in such a way.

Strangely, while I fretted and fumed and pined for my husband and children, Catherine seemed to have undergone some kind of spiritual catharsis during her unconscious state, because ever since regaining her senses she had displayed a complete lack of interest in anything other than her own state of grace and even began to talk of her illness and close confinement as justified punishment for her sins.

'It is no more than I deserve, Mette,' she told me on the day when she at last rose from her bed to sit beside the fire, staring into its shifting embers. 'I thought I deserved the happiness of love and a quiet life with my family, but that was sinful self-indulgence. Queens do not make second marriages, even when they are widowed as young as I was. It disturbs the political balance. I should have obeyed the precedents and taken the veil.'

I could not believe my ears. 'You were only a girl, Mademoiselle. Not twenty-one years old when King Henry died. Why should you have wasted your youth wearing out your knees when you had no vocation to the religious life?'

She raised her sunken blue eyes to mine. They were duller than I ever remembered them, like those of a leper cast out from society, whose spirit has been eroded by pain and rejection. 'Because it was my duty and because it would have pleased God,' she said. 'I have tried to live against the order of things and my sin has caused a canker in my belly. I should not have married Owen and I should not have had his children and now I must suffer the consequences. I shall not leave this place alive.'

I am sure it was the illness that made her so depressed and hopeless; God knows, I felt shattered and helpless myself though I was healthy enough, but she was right when she said that something was growing in her belly, a grotesque swelling protruding in her stomach, like a jester's bladder. Most likely the baby had come early because he simply had no more room to develop in a womb that was being invaded by a growth. I wondered daily whether the tiny boy who had been baptised Owen was still alive.

Smothering my own depression, I did my best to persuade her out of her lethargy. 'You speak as if you came here voluntarily, Mademoiselle. You did not. You were brought here by servants of Eleanor Cobham, the girl you rejected twice as your lady-in-waiting. Perhaps you are paying now for those rejections. This is not a beguinage like those we knew in France, where noblewomen retire from the world of their own volition; this is a prison where women are sent by others because they want them out of the way. I have seen them scurrying to the church, draped in black veils, their eyes on the ground. I have spoken to their servants. You are here because someone – Eleanor of Gloucester and probably Humphrey as well – wants you out of the way, just as your mother did all those years ago when she sent you to Poissy Abbey.'

To be locked away behind walls in a place where the only freedom was to offer your life to God was anathema to me, but to her it seemed to be the most natural place in the world if she was to atone for some terrible and, as far as I could see, totally imagined sin. Always Catherine had turned to prayer and the Church for consolation, proving that the nuns had done their job well when they educated her from the age of four.

The weary smile she gave me at the end of my homily was striking evidence of that. 'What you will never understand, Mette, much though you love me, is that I believe in God's holy purposes. I am here at His will, not that of Eleanor of Gloucester. She may think she has got me out of her way, but in fact she has put me in God's way. And for someone who has not long to live and a lifetime of sin for which to atone, I could be in no better place than in His holy house and among His holy brethren.' She sank down wearily against the back of her chair and closed her eyes. 'I wonder if the abbot could find me the habit of a Tertiary. The next time I dress I should like to wear that. Would you ask him for me, Mette?'

I remembered how she had reacted all those years ago to the awful carnage of Agincourt. Even as a girl of fourteen, she had retreated into the teachings of Holy Writ and the revelations of saints and scholars in grief at the thousands of French deaths in that battle. Now, once again, Catherine turned to prayer and the Church as her means of salvation; she was beyond consolation, and had only her staunch faith.

I shook my head hopelessly and turned away, making the sign of the cross, not in acknowledgement of her piety but in pity for her state of mind and body and, being honest, in consolation for my own sense of desperation. It saddened me profoundly that in fear for her eternal soul she appeared to have erased from her memory the happiest part of her life and all the people who had contributed to that happiness. As well as begging God for Catherine's recovery, my own prayers now were for her children and for Owen, who, unbeknown to them and through no fault of their own, seemed to have lost their place in her heart.

I told myself repeatedly it was the canker, while nursing the ghastly fear that it, too, was the work of Eleanor of Gloucester. How many incantations over Catherine's wax image had it taken I wondered to magic the evil growth in her womb and how many spells and potions and pacts with the devil had Eleanor made to try and conjure herself a crown? Catherine might believe in the power of God and his saints to protect against the devil, but my roots were in a place where everyone believed in sorcerers and their ability to conjure evil. The devil's imps had infected my world when I had been nursemaid to her and her brother Charles; that same little brother who had branded her a traitor and cut her completely from his life and the country of her birth. Now, at my lowest ebb, in the loneliness and abandonment of being shut away with the dying spectre of the person to whom I had given so much of my life and love, those imps had returned to infect the shadows that constantly surrounded me in the room where she would not allow the daylight to penetrate.

Then, one day in the middle of October, I heard a timid scratching at the door of my prison. I opened it to find the small, wizened figure of one of the lay brothers from the laundry. A score of these outside workers were employed in various capacities at the abbey and occasionally, when the spy Hawisa was occupied elsewhere, one of them returned the items of clothing and napery I had sent for washing. Usually they thrust them into my hands and left but, on this occasion, the wizened man stayed long enough to speak in a voice that squeaked with anxiety.

'The laundress says one of the napkins got torn, Mistress. It is at the top of the pile. You should check.' With that he scampered away up the cloister before I could respond.

I closed the door and put the pile of laundry down on a table, peering at the top item in the gloom. Then I picked it up and shook it out. There was no sign of a tear, but a sealed letter floated like an autumn leaf down to the floor. My heart began to beat and I pounced, as if it might vanish before I could lay my hands on it and instantly recognised the looped legal writing beside the seal. It was Geoffrey's. The mere sight of it brought tears to my eyes.

With trembling fingers I broke the seal and spread out the single sheet of paper. The writing was close and cramped, even spreading along the margins as if he could not squeeze enough information onto the page. My mind filled with an image of him sitting at the writing desk in the window of his library, bending over his task, quill dipping in and out of the ink pot and I was consumed by a desperate longing to be there with him.

Catherine was sleeping in her chair as she did so much in those days, so I took the letter and crept nearer to the fire, which burned constantly in the hearth and gave me just enough light to read by.

46

My Beloved Mette,

At last, with the help of the Earl of Mortain, I believe I have found a way through the maze of lies and evasions we have encountered ever since discovering the queen's whereabouts. Knowing that where she is you will be too, I hope against hope that this letter reaches you. My poor Mette, your admirable love and loyalty has led you into a desperate situation which you cannot ever have envisaged and which even yet I do not fully understand. Very soon, however, the queen should receive a visit from Lord Edmund, who will be able to tell you in person news of both your families and bring out to us some much-needed news of you.

In the space available I cannot adequately describe how dreadfully I have feared for your safety and how much I miss you because this letter has to be only one page, so I will reluctantly restrict myself to conveying as much information as possible. We know that the queen is ill and that you are caring for her at Bermondsey. We also know that her baby, Owen, is in the care of the Abbot of Westminster and sickly but alive. The king eventually told us this after we had met a wall of silence at Westminster Abbey and had to follow him to Eltham to hear it. It has been the only news we managed to glean until very recently, for the whole world seemed to have shut its ears, mouths and doors to us. It has been a fearful time, although I am certain no worse than the one you are experiencing.

Owen is a desperate man. He has been ill in Wales with the sweating sickness but when he returned to find Catherine gone and met the same terrible wall of silence, we got together and decided on a course of action. We all went to Hadham, being worried that the Duchess of Gloucester might discover the existence of the Tudor family and take action against the queen's household. Owen took his sons to sanctuary at Barking Abbey and they remain safe there and Walter and I brought the others to London. All are well, including little Margaret Tudor and our own sweet William, but this house was too crowded and Mildy has now taken in Anne and Thomas and baby Hester. Hadham has been closed up for the present. All are anxious for news of you and concerned for the health of the queen.

I have only enough space now to convey the shocking news that last week Owen, John Meredith and Maître Boyers were arrested in the street outside Westminster Abbey by Gloucester's men and thrown into Newgate prison. Having returned from Calais, Lord Edmund is trying to get them released but it is proving difficult. Doubtless the queen will be distraught to hear this, but Lord Edmund may have better news by the time he visits, which should be very soon.

The children pray for you and the queen every night and you are seldom out of my thoughts and prayers.

Your loving and longing husband, Geoffrey

—ξξ—

The last words were crammed up the narrow margin that Geoffrey had left on the page and I pressed them to my lips, my heart full but feeling lighter than it had for what seemed like years.

So at last, after weeks of isolation, we received our first visitor from the outside world. Not that calling on the lady whose beauty had enraptured him as a youth brought any joy to Edmund Beaufort, who was appalled by the frail, pale wraith who sat propped in her chair, swamped by the black Benedictine habit the abbot had supplied, her face a skull-like mask loosely framed in a white linen coif. While walking with him from the gatehouse to the guesthouse, I had warned the earl of Catherine's appearance and condition, but my description had not been adequate to soften the impact of his first sight of her. Proud Knight of the Garter though he was, he could not suppress the profound shock that filled his eyes with tears.

Catherine saw his distress at once and her voice was surprisingly strong as she greeted him. 'Edmund, how very good to see you. Pray do not weep for me; I do not deserve your tears.'

Despite her plea, the forbidden tears spilled down Edmund's cheeks as he bent his knee before her. When he kissed her hand it must have felt like pressing his lips to bare bones. For several moments he could not speak and she let him struggle to compose himself before she continued, her voice gradually becoming huskier and weaker.

'This is my penance for flying against the wind, my lord. I snatched at happiness with Owen when I should have been an obedient dowager and lived a life of charitable works and quiet preparation for eternity. I am trying to atone for it now but I get weary and must save myself for prayer. You speak, Edmund.'

Edmund took a deep breath and dashed the tears from his cheeks, then he stood up and took the seat I had placed opposite hers. 'Forgive me, your grace,' he said thickly. 'I am foolish and waste precious time. The first thing I must tell you is that your children are safe. Young Edmund and Jasper are both at Barking Abbey with Abbess de la Pole and Margaret is with Mistress Vintner's husband and daughter at their London house. The baby is in the care of a wet-nurse appointed by the Abbot of Westminster.'

Catherine had read Geoffrey's letter and made an impatient gesture. 'That much we know from Mette's husband, but what of Owen, my lord? Is he still in Newgate?'

'I am afraid so. Owen was desperate to visit you when he found out where you were but the monks would not admit him. They said you had given the order yourself. Can that be right, Catherine?'

A faint flush stained her cheeks. 'It is true. The first time he took my confession I told the abbot that I wished to see no one. I let them admit you, Edmund, but look how greatly you were shocked by my appearance. I cannot bear for Owen to see me in the grip of this fearful malady. I want him to remember me as we were at Hadham, young and beautiful and happy. But tell me, does Henry know Humphrey has had Owen thrown into jail?'

'I think not. Gloucester knows of your marriage now and I have to be careful in order to keep your other secrets from him. After his recent and lucrative chevauchées through Burgundy's Flemish territories, he is much in royal favour at present. It is hard to get past him to the king's private ear.'

'And I do not believe the Duchess of Gloucester will have revealed to the king the gravity of his mother's illness, my lord,' I interjected. I was still reeling from realising that by choosing to shut herself off from all contact with her family, without telling me, Catherine had effectively enclosed me with her, away from mine.

'Then I will tell him if you wish me to,' Edmund offered. 'Sooner or later I expect to get a private word with Henry. I am sure he would wish to visit you.'

'No!' Catherine's voice cracked with alarm. 'I do not wish it.'

'But he should see you – before . . .' the earl's voice trailed away. After a pause he made a gesture of appeal, spreading his hands. 'You cannot deny him the opportunity to say goodbye, Catherine.'

'There will be time for that – later. I beg you, Edmund, just to do your best to help Owen.' Her voice was growing weaker.

He digested her rebuttal in silence, then changed the subject. 'The Abbot of Westminster tells me the baby he baptised Owen is thriving with his foster mother. Abbot Haweden asked me to request permission for him to remain at the abbey. He feels he is a gift to them from God.'

I held my breath; Catherine had barely spoken of the baby since his birth, ignoring me every time I mentioned him. After another long pause all she said was, 'Yes, I give my permission. That is fitting. And now you must leave me, Edmund. I am sorry but I grow weary. Will you come again?'

'Of course I will, I hope with better news of your husband. Meanwhile, may God preserve and bless you, Catherine.' Lord Edmund stood and stooped to kiss her shrivelled cheek, dry like autumn leaves. I saw him out and as soon as he quitted the chamber he slumped down onto the cloister parapet, head in hands. Deep, wracking sobs set his chest heaving. I stood silently beside him, waiting for the storm to subside.

Eventually he knuckled the tears away. His eyes were red-rimmed when he raised them to me. 'Sweet Heaven, Mette, how can you bear it? She was so vibrant, so beautiful!'

'She says it is God's will.' I crossed myself. 'And perhaps it is; either that or witchcraft.'

His brow creased in a frown. 'Witchcraft?' he echoed. 'Do you have any evidence of that?'

I shrugged. 'Is there ever evidence of sorcery? They burned Jeanne d'Arc on very little. It seems the only thing is to avoid it and I fear it is too late for Catherine to do that.'

Lord Edmund stared at me steadily for the length of an Ave, as if assessing my state of mind, then made the sign of the cross himself, his hand moving slowly and deliberately through the motions. He stood up. 'I will do my best for Owen,' he said. 'Perhaps that will only be by providing him with the means of escape. Have you any message for your kin? I will be seeing your husband within the week.'

Glancing round for possible witnesses, I took from my sleeve pocket the letter I had written in anticipation of his visit and pressed it into his hands. 'It is very short but it will reassure Geoffrey and give him something to read to the children. I tried to make Catherine write something for Owen but she refused point blank. She has changed, my lord. Attaining grace is more important to her now than earthly things. Poor Owen has lost her to the Church, I am afraid. One day perhaps I will be able to explain it to him.'

'How long do you think she has to live, Mette?'

I shook my head slowly. 'It is impossible to say. Some nights I do not expect her to wake in the morning.'

He gazed at me sorrowfully. 'It must be hard for you.'

Tears, never far from the surface, welled now in my eyes. I took a long, deep breath, struggling to find my voice. 'Nothing has ever been harder,' I said.

47

On her thirty-fifth birthday in the closing week of October, Catherine had seemed too frail to live into December, and yet she did. She survived to see another celebration of Christ's birth, while her skin grew thinner than paper and her bones constantly broke through, causing terrible sores which I had to bathe with willow water and wrap in fresh bandages every day. Meanwhile the growth in her belly distended her stomach to grotesque proportions. It had got to the stage when she could no longer leave her bed to go to the church, even carried on a litter and instead of praying for a miracle recovery, I began to beg the Almighty for an end to her suffering.

The Earl of Mortain made a second visit in mid-December, before being obliged to leave again for France at the head of another defensive army. He told us that he had managed to get weapons smuggled to Owen in Newgate, enabling him and his companions to take the keys off their gaoler and make their escape, but had no further news of them except to convey a rumour that they had fled to Wales under the continued threat of arrest or assault by Gloucester's henchmen. Lord Edmund had also managed to obtain a private meeting with King Henry, when he had told him of Owen's unauthorised imprisonment and also of his own visit to Catherine, though not of her illness, as she had requested. When he bid her farewell, they both knew that it would be for the last time.

'I think you should let the king know of your grievous malady, Catherine,' he urged. 'You cannot protect him any longer. I truly believe he has a right.'

She did not speak but slowly nodded her agreement.

'Shall I ask the abbot to write to him on your behalf?' Edmund whispered as he kissed her wet cheek. Once again she nodded.

A few days later, the abbot came to say Mass and bring her the Host and he read her a letter he had composed to King Henry. 'At present his grace is at Windsor but they are preparing for him to spend Christmas at Kennington this year, which is only a mile or so from here, and I am sure he will make all speed to Bermondsey. And when you think it is the right time to make your last confession, it will be my honour to come to you, your grace.'

Catherine chose to make her last confession on Christmas Day and I left her with the abbot for nearly an hour. Afterwards she was exhausted and slept. I could not remember a more sombre Christmas. Had the little wizened man not scratched on the door and delivered a letter from Geoffrey, I should have believed the whole world had forgotten me, but his love and the words of encouragement he wrote tipped me back from the brink of despair.

—§§—

My beloved Mette,

It is Christmas and the whole world is celebrating the birth of our Lord, but I cannot imagine there is any joy for you at this time. However, we are all thinking of you and praying for you and I am holding you in my heart until I see you again. There is now word spreading around town

that the queen's life is drawing to a close, so while I earnestly
pray for her to find a peaceful end to her suffering, I also
hope that her release will at last free you to come back to
me and to your children and grandchildren, who all miss
you and ask for you every day. If it is possible, give our love
and loyal greetings to Catherine and remember that we are
all thinking of you both. Be brave, beloved Mette, as I know
you will be, and bring your tears to shed with those who love
you, of whom the most fervent is your
  Geoffrey.

—ξξ—

Towards the end of December, an icy blast hit England and
sent everyone scurrying to their hearths for warmth. To my delight
Hawisa and Edwin, the Gloucester spies, did not return from their
Christmas break, kept away by snow drifts which obliterated the
roads and piled up on the ice which had stopped the Thames
from flowing. Catherine's bed was moved as close to the fire as
we dared, but even so I could not believe that she would survive
the freezing nights that followed. However, her will to live was
astonishing, driven by a new and consuming need.

Daily, almost hourly, she prayed that her son would come to
say goodbye and, in due course, her prayers were answered. On
New Year's Day they managed to clear the road sufficiently to allow
the king to travel the two miles to Bermondsey from Kennington
Palace. He arrived unexpectedly at the hour of Sext, the abbey
enclosure suddenly filling with the noise and colour of his royal
entourage. Hastily summoned from performing the Office, the
abbot accompanied him to the door of Catherine's chamber, but
when I opened it King Henry would not permit him to enter.

'When she needs the last rites, I trust you to administer them, Father Abbot,' he insisted, 'but now I will see my lady mother alone.'

Catherine had heard the commotion of trumpets and horses' hooves and asked me to prop her up on pillows and pin her white veil over the linen coif she wore. 'He is here. At last he is here.' In their sunken sockets her eyes shone with anticipation and her hands clenched and unclenched on the bedcover. 'Stay with me, Mette,' she whispered. 'Do not leave me.'

'I will be here, Mademoiselle,' I assured her. 'I am always here.'

I remained in the room but retreated to the farthest corner of the chamber so as not to intrude on the king's last farewell to his mother. Being in his presence though, I was obliged to kneel, a position which, having passed my half century, I now found hard to maintain for very long.

His mother's eyes were open wide as King Henry bent over the bed. Although it was not a month since he had celebrated his fifteenth birthday and he was visibly shocked at the sight of her, he did not weep but a throaty hoarseness betrayed his emotion. 'My beloved lady mother,' he said. 'God be with you.'

'And also with you, my liege – my dear son.' Her voice was muffled, scarcely audible.

King Henry leaned in to catch her words and spoke softly back, his mouth close to her ear. 'They said you did not want me to know of your illness but when the abbot learned I was at Kennington, he decided he should send word. I wanted to come as soon as I heard, but the snow has prevented travel until today. They said you cannot be moved or I would have you brought to the palace. Have you suffered grievously?'

'It is nearly over, Henry.' She closed her eyes as if those few words had taken all her strength. I saw alarm flare in his eyes and it occurred to me that he feared she was already slipping away.

'She is very weak, your grace,' I said, raising my voice to carry from my corner, half-hidden from him by the bed curtains. 'But she can listen. Have you perhaps some words of comfort to give her?'

The king glanced across, appearing surprised to find me there. 'What words would comfort her, Mette?'

'The truth, my liege. What has happened to Owen Tudor and what are your intentions for their children? She needs reassurance.'

Henry placed his hand cautiously over his mother's where it lay on the quilt, fragile as a robin's claw. The fire was only a few feet away and the room was stifling hot but he frowned at the icy touch of her skin. 'Owen is being sought, my lady. He escaped from Newgate, I suspect with help from outside. I knew nothing of his imprisonment and I can do nothing for him now unless he comes to court.'

Catherine's lips were moving but no sound escaped. King Henry looked at me enquiringly. 'Do you know what she is saying, Mette?'

I made a guess and rose to move a little nearer. 'I think she wants to tell you that Owen will not come voluntarily until you take full command of your kingdom, your grace. There are people who mean him harm.'

He nodded. 'Yes, I know. But I have spoken to the Earl of Suffolk regarding my brothers, Mother. Have no fear for them. Find peace now in almighty God and die in His grace, as you have always lived. Death holds no terrors. You must have faith.'

There was movement in the hand beneath his and he gave it a tiny squeeze. Her lips moved again but no words emerged. 'Do not speak,' he said, removing his hand and feeling in the front of his robe. He drew out a folded letter with a red wax seal. 'This came secretly from Paris, among some other documents.' He held the letter nearer so that she could see. 'You will recognise this seal, I am sure.'

Impressed into the wax were the three fleurs-de-lys of the French royal crest. A tear swelled and glistened on Catherine's eyelashes. King Henry hesitated. 'Do you want me to read it?'

Catherine moved her head slightly and mouthed a word. 'No.'

'Your lady mother is tired, my liege,' I said. 'May I read it to her later?'

At Catherine's slight nod I approached the bed and King Henry handed the letter over to me, I thought a little reluctantly. Perhaps he was eager to know its content. 'Do not forget it was sent in secret,' he warned.

'It is from her brother,' I acknowledged. 'I will keep it hidden.' Tucking it away, I retreated once more.

The king turned back to Catherine. 'The Pretender is in Paris now – where you were both born. There is so much about your past that I do not know.' He grew bold and bent forward to kiss her cheek. A faint smile twitched at Catherine's lips. 'What a power you might have been in the land, my lady, if my father had not died.'

Suddenly Catherine found the remnants of her voice, but the words came agonisingly slowly. 'You will be – a great king, Henry – as your father was.'

He crossed himself. 'If God wills it. We are all in His hands and we both know that this is our last meeting in this world. I will have masses said for you in perpetuity. May the Angels guard your soul, my sweet mother, and carry it safely to Heaven.'

As he left her side, I saw tears finally well in his eyes. 'I did not know until now how cruel a taskmaster death is, Mette.

Please send word at once when . . .' His voice vanished on a gulp.

'I will, your grace. It cannot be long.'

After closing the door behind him, I found a small cloth-of-scarlet draw-stringed pouch lying on the bed near Catherine's hands. It was the first day of January. He had left a final New Year gift for his mother.

During the early hours of the morning, when she next woke, I showed her the pouch. 'Shall I open it, Mademoiselle?' At her nod I loosened the draw-string and from within slid a tablet of gold on which a crucifix was moulded, set about with pearls and sapphires.

I held it up for her to see and she smiled. 'He wants to pave my path to Heaven,' she whispered.

Then I read the letter to her which the king had brought.

—§§—

To Catherine, Dowager Queen of England from Charles VII of France.

Sister,

I feel able to call you that once more, now that I sit on the throne which your treacherous marriage tried to deny me. To achieve this my rightful place, much blood has been shed and many lives lost, including that of your lord and husband, Henry of Lancaster. Now his cause in France is finished and word has reached me that your life may also be nearing its end. The time has come for us to be reconciled.

I have long lived under the shadow of our father's illness, fearing that the madness might strike me also and I imagine that you may have feared a similar fate but they tell me your malady is not of that nature. We seem to have escaped the curse of insanity and I pray God that it will not afflict our children. Our countries need strong and wise rulers.

I will include this letter among others being sent to the English court, in the hope that it will be delivered to you safely. It brings my prayers for your recovery but should God not grant it then may He send you a swift release from your affliction and gather your soul to Heaven.

I am once more your loving brother,
Charles

Written at the Palace of the Louvre on the feast of St Nicholas 1436.

—§§—

I lowered the letter and peered past the candle by which I had read it. I expected Catherine's eyes to be closed, but they were wide open. Reflected in them were the dancing flame and an expression of intense anger.

'Burn it, Mette,' she said and her next words came in short bursts on a series of laboured breaths. 'Charles never did know – when reconciliation was possible – and Henry should not read – about our father's madness. Burn it now.'

I put it on the fire and watched it shrivel into ash. She was right. It was far too late for reconciliation with the brother who had labelled her a traitor. She was no longer a daughter of France; she would die a queen of England.

Then she said her final words. 'I love you, Mette. Call the abbot. It is time.'

After she had received Extreme Unction, three monks remained in the chamber to sing psalms in muted plain-chant, which set a mood of deepest melancholy. I felt numb as I sat on a stool at the bedside and watched Catherine's face, motionless except for a faint movement of the nostrils and the dancing flicker of candlelight across the parched skin of her cheeks. The king's crucifix tablet lay on her breast, rising and falling on breaths which seemed to come at ever greater intervals. After a time the abbey bell sounded for Matins and the psalmists ceased singing and filed quietly past, each murmuring a blessing and making the sign of the cross over her inert body as they left the chamber, bound for the church.

So Catherine and I were alone when her last, long breath crept slowly and inexorably from her lungs like an invisible wraith. I waited for the next inhalation, but it never came.

For some time I did not move. My body seemed to be in suspension as my thoughts wandered over the course of her life and the momentous events that had shaped it. I recalled the first time she had smiled at me by the light of a makeshift fire in our freezing turret room at the Hôtel de St Pol in Paris – the gummy baby smile that had sealed my life to hers. We had shared so much since; agonising partings and joyous reunions, the heart-rending madness of her father, the negligence of her mother, her flowering into a court beauty, the horror of Agincourt, terror at the hands of Burgundy, injustice and abuse, her all-too-short marriage to King Henry, the solemnity of her coronation, her magnificence as Queen Consort, the fear of barrenness and the triumph of an heir, the death of the king and the endless funeral cavalcade, the spite of Gloucester, the idyll of Hadham, our second loves, children and family life, happiness and fulfilment and then the fateful ride to Westminster that had brought us here to Bermondsey. Now I had witnessed her death and must live in a world without her. I would never again prepare her clothes, pin her veil, pluck her brow-line or arrange her hair. She would never again ask my advice, give me loving hugs or chastise me for being flippant and I would no longer have to chastise myself for putting her before my husband and my children. I had always thought to die first but God does not always permit the child to outlive the parent. The child of my breast, my beautiful princess, cherished queen and beloved friend had left me.

Her hands were clasped over the mound of her belly, the ugly outward evidence of the dreadful growth that had stifled the life from her. For the thousandth time I condemned its cruelty and thought how much more likely it was that such an unspeakable thing had been conjured by witchcraft, rather than inflicted as divine punishment for any sin Catherine may have committed. She was not blameless, but nothing she had ever done or said could have deserved this disgusting and pitiful suffering. I wanted to take her hand in a final farewell but, as I gently prised her fingers from the tablet, something fell from between them which I recognised at once. It was the key to the concealed compartment in her travelling altar, the place where she kept all her confidential letters, some she had received and others she had written but been unable to send. On several occasions I had seen her slip folded papers into it, especially at times of crisis in her life. I reached out and felt gently in the neck of her chemise for the chain she always wore. It held the reliquary I had given her on her eighteenth birthday in order to hide the key safely from prying eyes but when I opened it I found it empty. I glanced from the key to the reliquary and then to Catherine's sculpted face, serene and beautiful again now in the peace of death, and drew from them a message as if it had been penned.

I was the only one who knew that the altar held a secret compartment, the only one who knew what she locked away in it and where the key was and it was I who would be bound to tend her first, after she died. Before she lost all strength and sensibility she must have managed to open the reliquary and remove the key, knowing that I would be the one to find it. She meant me to have the key and the contents of the altar because she wanted me to be custodian of the secrets it contained.

Hearing the sound of footsteps outside the chamber door, I swiftly tucked the key into the purse I wore at my belt, then I bent to kiss the brittle skin of Catherine's forehead.

'Heaven take your grace,' I whispered as the tears spilled down my cheeks. 'God rest your soul, my little Mademoiselle.'

48

'Your task is now completed, Madame. The dowager queen no longer requires your services. Her treasurer will see to it that you are paid. You are free to leave.'

I suppose it was inevitable that it should be the Duchess of Gloucester who was the one to bring an end to my time with Catherine. The thirteen-year-old beauty who had carried the queen's train at her coronation and then been sent home was now the appointed official taking control of Catherine's body, responsible for seeing to its embalming and preparation for the funeral and interment that would follow. I found it satisfactorily ironic that she should not be aware that the treasurer to whom she referred was my husband.

'May I ask where she is to be buried, your grace?' I did not expect to be invited to the funeral, but I believed I was entitled to know where I might be able to pray later at her graveside.

Eleanor folded her hands and shook her head impatiently. 'That is not yet decided. Her executors are in discussion about the funeral arrangements.'

Although there was no possibility of it, I thought it would be fascinating to attend that meeting. The 'discussion' she mentioned was more likely to be a ferocious argument because, in a wayward moment when dictating her last will and testament to a monkish scribe, Catherine had decided to name as her executors the two great enemies on the council, the Duke of Gloucester and Cardinal Beaufort. Perhaps she had hoped in death to become an influence for peace between them, but I rather doubted it. I considered it more likely that it was her de Valois pride at work contriving posthumous payback to both of them for the game they had played with her life.

Eleanor went on. 'Ensure that you take nothing from this room that is not yours, Madame. My woman Hawisa has my full permission to search you on leaving. Any bequests the queen dowager may have made to you will be specified in her will and forwarded in due course.'

I could not believe my ears. I had been Catherine's trusted companion and servant nearly all my life and never so much as pilfered a hair-pin and I took it as an insult to be even suspected of such a thing. Then I remembered the key and sent up a silent prayer to thank whichever saint had caused Eleanor to warn me of the search. Perhaps it had been Catherine herself. I made a mental note to pay a visit to the latrine before leaving and conceal it very privately about my person; somewhere stolid Hawisa would never look.

The duchess turned away and stood for some time gazing intently down at Catherine's body stretched out on the bed. After the abbot and the apothecary had certified her death, I had taken it upon myself to arrange her as regally as possible; dressing her reverently in the blue brocade robe and scarlet, gem-studded mantle she had worn when she made her fateful visit to the king to warn him against the very woman who now loomed over her. Although her sickness had robbed her of her famous beauty, at least the fine clothes made her look suitably regal and the jewelled headdress concealed the terrible sparseness of her once thick and lustrous hair. If they made an effigy of her, like that which had lain on the coffin of the late King Henry, it would probably bear no resemblance to the vibrant beauty the people had called 'the fair Kate'.

'The apothecary says it was a canker that brought about her death,' Eleanor remarked matter-of-factly.

And who conjured the canker? I thought, angry to detect no hint of compassion in her too-perfect face.

Eleanor went on, 'And the Abbot of Westminster tells me that the baseborn son that caused it thrives and may live to become a monk in their community. Her other two bastard sons are in the care of Suffolk's sister at Barking Abbey.'

She does not know about Margaret, I realised joyfully, but her next words further stirred my ire, especially as they came from one who, before she married the duke, I knew for a fact had used sorcery to try and conceive his bastard.

'Three baseborn boys! She has left a shameful legacy.'

I bit back the indignant protest which sprang to my lips and instead asked, 'Have you seen them, your grace? I would be grateful for news of them.'

She turned back to face me then and her violet eyes narrowed. 'No I have not. Abbess de la Pole allows no one but their official guardians to visit her wards in care. It seems we must apply to the Duke of Suffolk for permission. I advise you to stay away from them, Madame Lanière. As I said, there is nothing more you can do for the dowager queen, or her regrettable family. The household no longer exists.'

Within the hour I found myself standing alone outside the gate of Bermondsey Abbey and, despite my enduring sadness at Catherine's passing, I felt a huge surge of relief, an intense feeling of deliverance as if from purgatory. During those five months of our shared incarceration she had deteriorated towards death, inch by inch, and I felt no further sense of duty towards the emaciated corpse I had so carefully laid out on the bed. The real Catherine, the true spirit of the child and woman I had loved and served, had withered along with her flesh until it vanished completely on that last long, final breath which I alone had witnessed.

Together with the deep-seated thrill of liberation, came a sense of satisfaction that not only had I escaped Eleanor of Gloucester's clutches, I had succeeded in smuggling out Catherine's legacy, the key to her altar, safely in my possession. As the abbey gate thudded shut behind me, I gazed into the grey sky over Southwark and took several grateful gulps of secular air before registering, in every part of me at once, that not only was I free, I was freezing. The road was empty and it was deep in snow and I wore only the summer kirtle and light woollen cloak in which I had ridden to London back in balmy July. It occurred to me that Eleanor may have been motivated to release me quickly from the abbey because she expected me to die of cold within a few minutes of leaving. However, when Hawisa searched me it had been a half-hearted effort because during the months of our enforced acquaintance we had come to an unspoken understanding. There was no friendship between us, but no deep enmity had been established either. We served very different mistresses, but we recognised each other's servitude and lack of choice in our circumstances. There had never been any question of her finding the precious altar key but, whether by mistake or intent, she had also overlooked my letters from Geoffrey, which she could not read anyway and the few silver coins I had sewn into the hem of my chemise; more than enough to buy a place by the fire at the nearest inn, hot food and warm outer clothing.

Still thanking God for my freedom, I moved as swiftly as I was able through the new blanket of snow and was rewarded by the appearance of an inn. While I bolstered myself against the cold with a welcome bowl of his pottage, for the rest of my silver the innkeeper sold me a pair of old boots and a moth-eaten fur-lined mantle and told me that I did not have to use the congested London bridge in order to cross the Thames but could make use of a more direct path across the thick ice from Southwark to the Dowgate Steps.

'The ice has borne the weight of ox-carts for more than a week now,' he assured me and added, rather offensively, 'so it should bear you all right, Mistress!'

I learned the next day that by taking this route I may have avoided death or injury, because that very afternoon the build-up of ice above London Bridge caused one of its supporting piers to collapse, throwing several buildings and a number of people violently down onto the frozen river below, a horrific event that was to delay the arrangements for Catherine's funeral well into February.

However, I was unaware of this tragedy as I turned wearily into Tun Lane, where snow had been shovelled in shoulder-high heaps leaving only a narrow path along the thoroughfare and up to the door of each house. The innkeeper's old boots and shabby mantle had prevented me freezing to death, but I was shivering uncontrollably. The House of the Vines, closed and shuttered though it was against the bitter cold, was a truly welcome sight in the smoky dusk.

When old Jem answered my loud knocking, he was so over-come with delight that he forgot all deference and threw his arms around me in a great hug. Never had I been more pleased to be gathered into such an impulsively loving embrace. There were tears in his eyes as he said with fervour, 'Welcome home, Mistress, oh welcome home! The master has been pining away for you. Now all will be well again.'

The sound of his loud and enthusiastic greeting reached the ears of the household who immediately began to tumble down the stairs to the street entrance, practically falling over each other to reach me. There was a confusion of jubilant voices and such a jumble of eager arms reaching out to me that it was some moments before I caught sight of Geoffrey standing at the foot of the stairs, a wide smile on his face and a look in his eyes that, even in the dim light of dusk, told me all I needed to know about where I truly belonged.

Gently but firmly he pulled the children and the young people away from me and put his strong arm around my shoulders. 'Here you are at last, Mette,' he said gruffly, squeezing me tightly to his side as he guided me through the door. 'Here you are at last.'

My head dropped gratefully onto his shoulder as we climbed the stairs and from behind us I heard the piping voice of little Margaret Tudor asking Alys, 'If Mette is here, is my lady mother coming too?' and Alys's quiet reply, 'We do not know, sweetheart. You can ask Mette when she is warm and made comfortable.'

Later, when I was seated nearest the hearth, the fire had been stoked to a blaze and I had stopped shivering enough to respond to their eager enquiries, of all the questions there were to be answered, of course, that was the most important. I lifted the little girl onto my knee and told her, as gently as I could, that her beautiful lady mother had died. I saw the unmistakable reflection of Catherine in Margaret's bright sapphire eyes as they grew round and tearful and I hugged her as my heart ached, for I did not know how best to comfort her, but my love for her recalled me to my love for her mother.

Other than the sad news of Catherine's death and a few details of our life up to that, there was really very little else for me to tell them, and besides, matters had moved on apace in the world I had left behind. Since they so hurriedly left Hadham at the end of the summer, all the family was gathered here at Tun Lane or nearby in Mildy's dockside house. Geoffrey had vacated his ground-floor office in Tun Lane, in favour of rented chambers at the Middle Temple, so that Alys, Cat and Louise could move in there, leaving the upper rooms to Geoffrey, Walter, William and Margaret and, for a time, Agnes, Hywell and Gwyneth.

'But after Owen and John escaped from Newgate and fled London, Hywell and Agnes decided they should also return to Wales and they left before the winter closed in,' Geoffrey revealed. 'Agnes will be heart-sore when she learns of Catherine's fate, there is no doubt.'

'Indeed she will,' I acknowledged, 'but at least she has her own family around her now.'

Once the initial excitement at my reappearance had died down, Geoffrey and I were able to shut ourselves away alone together in his library where another fire had been lit.

'Tell me though, how did Alys take John's departure?' I asked. She was pining for him for weeks after he first went to Wales.'

Geoffrey shrugged. 'She has said nothing about John. Even before he left I had the distinct impression that feelings were growing between her and Walter.'

'Alys and Walter!' There was no disguising the surprise in my voice at this development. I had gleaned no inkling of a relationship between them. 'Is that where Walter went this evening – downstairs to be with Alys?'

Geoffrey nodded and I saw a familiar twinkle ignite in his eyes. 'Yes, as far as I know. Why, do you have some objection?'

'No, not me, none at all but I think the Church might. After all they are brother and sister, even though there is no blood relationship.'

Geoffrey steepled his fingers and assumed his lawyer's face. 'Yes, there is that. But marriage has not been mentioned. It may be that they would need a papal dispensation, which could always be arranged. I have given them my blessing. I hope you feel the same.'

I smiled. 'I do, without question. I cannot think why this has not happened before.'

'I gather that Walter would have liked it to, but John came between them. We shall have to await developments.'

49

Christmas 1441

When the thaw finally came in the middle of February, Catherine's coffin was brought to lie in state, first in the church of St Catherine by the Tower and then in St Paul's, to allow as many people as possible to pay their respects to their sovereign's mother. I went myself, of course, and took the children; William and little Margaret who was understandably confused, particularly when I picked her up so that she could see the effigy on top of the coffin which, as I had predicted, resembled Catherine barely at all.

'Is that my lady mother, Mette?' she asked, puzzled.

'No, Margaret,' I whispered back, glancing furtively about, hoping no one else had heard. 'Your mother is in heaven.'

Her bewildered expression reminded me vividly of Catherine at the same age, when we were forced to say farewell to each other as she was taken off to the convent for her education. Margaret's hair was not as fair and her nose not as long and straight, but those large blue eyes with their thick fringe of dark lashes showed the same sweet, unblinking earnestness as Catherine's had on that day. It seemed to me that this little girl would face the world in the same way her mother had done, with curiosity and candour and a strong streak of stubbornness. I loved her for it and placed a kiss on her peachy cheek.

She wriggled out of my arms then and slid to the floor where I heard her whisper loudly to William, 'Is she the Queen of Heaven now, then?' and his solemn reply, 'Well, yes, Margaret, I expect she is.'

They buried Queen Catherine under the Lady Chapel in Westminster Abbey church, only a few feet away from her first husband King Henry the Fifth. A memorial is being erected, as I write, but I do not anticipate any mention on it of her second marriage and family.

Owen Tudor was never actually accused of any crime but, despite the king's written promise of free conduct to London, when he came he was re-arrested and held in various locations for more than two years, although fortunately never again in Newgate. He faced several council tribunals before he was finally released, after sureties were given for his good behaviour. How they thought he might misbehave was never made clear, but he was at last able to visit his sons at Barking Abbey, where he found them, aged ten and nine, well-fed, well-clothed and happy among their school companions. They did remember him, but three years absence is a long time in a child's life. He also visited his little namesake at Westminster Abbey, a fair curly-haired infant, beloved of all the monks and already able to recite the Ave Maria. During these visits Owen stayed with us at Tun Lane and, much to my relief decided to leave all his children where they were, including Margaret who by now was a much-loved and integral part of our lives. For the time being, he returned to Wales.

The young king was officially declared of age to rule after his sixteenth birthday in December 1437, but over the next few years it became obvious that Henry was out of his depth among the warring factions of his council. The Duke of Gloucester campaigned fiercely to continue the war in France, while Cardinal Beaufort and the Earl of Suffolk constantly opposed his stance and argued for a peace treaty. At the same time, the French towns and cities that King Henry the Fifth had so painstakingly taken by siege were retaken, one by one, by the forces of Catherine's brother, now recognised by most of Europe as King Charles the Seventh of France. England's conquered territory across the Sleeve shrank by the month, so while Gloucester continued to lobby parliament to raise more fighting funds through taxation, his popularity among the people began to wane.

Then his influence suffered a hammer blow from a direction that surprised everyone, except me. In July of this year three men were arrested and held in the Tower accused of using sorcery against the king; the Duchess of Gloucester's confessor was one of them. Within days Eleanor herself was also arrested and then Margery Jourdemayne was taken to join them, so it was not difficult to guess who had incriminated her. Eventually the confessor was released, but the other four were sent for trial and all of England was agog at the sensational evidence. Eleanor admitted to consulting Margery for potions to secure her marriage and conceive a child, but denied casting spells or practising sorcery against the king. For her part, Margery admitted selling the duchess cures and telling her fortune, but claimed any astrology and image magic was done without her knowledge. All four denied the treasonable offence of conspiring to predict the king's death, but the trial judges found them guilty on all counts. Eleanor's desperate desire to become queen had finally caught up with her.

Just as he had done with Jacqueline of Hainault at her time of trial, Humphrey of Gloucester deserted his wife, declaring total ignorance of her nefarious activities. Eleanor was sentenced to perform a public penance through the streets of London and afterwards to life imprisonment. Her marriage to the duke was annulled on the grounds that she had obtained it by sorcery. She was dishonoured, disgraced and deserted, but at least she was still alive.

The other conspirators fared less well. One of the astrologers died in prison before being sentenced, but the other was dragged on a hurdle to Tyburn and hung, drawn and quartered. Poor Margery was also found guilty of treason and, as a convicted witch, was sentenced to be burned at the stake. Her terrible punishment took place last month at Smithfield. We did not watch as many hundreds did, but we could see the smoke rising over the rooftops. Geoffrey said she would have been strangled before the fire was lit and I fervently hoped he was right.

I often think of Margery, irretrievably fettered to Eleanor and ultimately betrayed by her. She did not deserve her fate. Eleanor lives yet, imprisoned in some castle somewhere and no longer Duchess of Gloucester, yet granted twelve servants and an income to support them. I would not have had her condemned to burn, but there is no justice in that.

The Duke of Gloucester may have managed to remain clear of suspicion, but some of the mud has stuck and he no longer has the confidence of the king. He has retired to Greenwich to lick his wounds and the cardinal and the Earl of Suffolk now rule the roost at court. It seems inevitable that there will be peace across the Sleeve before too long, but King Henry still styles himself King of France as well as England.

Meanwhile Geoffrey and I live a sedate life, as befits our age – he is sixty, I am now fifty-five. He has reduced his legal workload, but three years ago he used money and influence to obtain a dispensation from Rome to allow Walter and Alys to marry. Walter has obtained a position as Clerk of Works at the London Guildhall and they have set up house in Cheapside. Their baby boy has been named Geoffrey after his grandfather. Louise is still with them but Cat has recently married into a draper's family.

Our William is now twelve and studies at the Middle Temple School, but he comes home at nights and his favourite companion is eight-year-old Margaret Tudor, growing prettier by the year and reminding me constantly of her mother. No one has come looking for her and we tell everyone that she is an orphaned cousin whom we have fostered. Quite unexpectedly last week we had a visit from Edmund Beaufort, Earl of Mortain. He was back in England fresh from his triumph in recapturing Harfleur, the port in Normandy which had been the foundation of Henry the Fifth's conquest of northern France.

'This is the second time I have had to regain our stronghold on the Seine,' he complained. 'We cannot supply our troops and estates in Normandy without holding its main port, but now that the Duke of York is Lieutenant-General I am afraid I do not have much hope for our hold on France.'

I had heard that there was bad blood between Lord Edmund and the Duke of York, but while I was interested in the situation across the Sleeve I had a more pressing concern. 'Have you been able to visit the Tudor boys at Barking, my lord?' I asked. 'We have heard nothing of them since Owen left for Wales.'

Edmund Beaufort shook his head. 'I have not seen them but

I have spoken with the Earl of Suffolk. They are no longer at Barking but living on Suffolk's estate at Wingfield where there is a well-endowed college. It was decided that Edmund and Jasper Tudor had outgrown the teaching available at the convent and at Wingfield they can pursue their knightly training and receive the education necessary to prepare them for whatever their brother the king intends for their future.'

I pressed him further on that. 'Do you have any idea of what that might be?'

'If I have anything to do with it – and, God willing, I shall – then I will hold the king to the promise he made to Catherine, that he will knight his brothers when they come of age and bring them to his court. It is my intention that her children and the name Tudor shall take their proper place in England's hierarchy.'

'Amen to that,' said Geoffrey.

I said nothing, thinking of little Margaret. Sometimes I look at her and William with their heads together over some book or board-game and I wonder whether Catherine meant them for each other. I have good reason to think that because of what was contained in her altar's secret compartment – her final legacy to me. To explain, I must hark back to the night of my return to my family and my fireside conversation with Geoffrey in his library.

I related how I had found the key to Catherine's travelling altar pressed between her fingers after she had died. 'So I knew she intended it for me. However, I fear that I may never be able to claim it because the Duchess of Gloucester said the household no longer existed and more or less threatened me with immediate arrest if I took so much as a napkin belonging to Catherine when I left Bermondsey. She even had me searched, but I had hidden the key in such a place that no search, however intimate, would ever find it.'

Geoffrey raised his eyebrows. 'Indeed? I think I will avoid probing any further into that matter.'

'Better not,' I said with a wry smile.

Then he went on. 'The duchess was a little behind the times in announcing the closure of the queen's household. We packed up everything at Hadham when everyone came here to Tun Lane and Owen took Edmund and Jasper to Barking Abbey. I took the queen's jewels and coin to the Hertford strong room for safe-keeping and it was just as well I did because a posse of Gloucester thugs raided Hadham soon after the duke discovered that was where Catherine and Owen had set up house. They molested Father Godric and tore the marriage entry from the church records and then, I can only think out of spite, they set fire to the grain stores.'

I was upset to hear all this, but not surprised. 'So there is no record now of their marriage,' I observed despondently. 'The poor children will be branded bastards.'

Geoffrey tried to reassure me. 'Not if the king has anything to do with it – and I am sure he will once he comes of age. Meanwhile I took one precaution, of which I believe you will approve.'

He stood up and went over to the wall-cupboard where he kept his important documents locked away. Taking a key from his purse he opened the door and lifted a large object out. It was Catherine's travelling altar, which I had not dared to hope would have been brought from Hadham. Smiling at my elated expression he put it down on his writing table.

'It was so much a part of Catherine's life that I did not want it to fall into the wrong hands, so I put it in my pack-horse pannier. Why do you not use that key you took such trouble to smuggle out of Bermondsey?'

The finely carved wooden box with its hinged triptych and ivory crucifix sat innocently enough on the table, but my hands shook as I tipped up the cross and inserted the key in the lock hidden under its base. The side panel of the box clicked open. In other travelling altars I had seen this secret compartment used as a container for religious relics, but I knew that Catherine had used hers as a hiding place for her written thoughts, penned at times of crisis in her life. Several piles of folded pages were revealed, carefully tied into bundles. On each one was a label bearing a year date and on the top of these were some loose sheets and a single, sealed packet addressed to me.

Trembling, I drew it out and broke the seal. Inside, pinned to a letter, was the red jasper ring which had helped to bring both my granddaughter Catrine and Jasper Tudor successfully into the world. I had seen Catherine's handwriting many times but the sight of it then and the faint but achingly familiar aroma of attar of roses coming off the paper caused a sudden rush of emotion as I began to read . . .

—§§—

Written at Hadham this 20th day of July, 1436, the Feast day of St Margaret.

To my beloved Mette,
This ring is rightly yours because it was you who told me of the power of jasper. No one will hunt you for it because before he left I asked Owen to remove it from the inventory of my jewels, listing it as sold. I hope you will wear it to

remember me and pass it on to my goddaughter so that she may do the same.

If you are reading this it means that you have stayed with me until the very end as I knew you would and you have the key to open the altar cache as I intend you to. It is my legacy to you, my beloved Mette, for you alone know of this secret compartment and are party to all the events documented in the letters it contains.

I realised some weeks ago that I am dying and I only hope God allows me to live long enough to bring this babe safely into the world. Lately I have fretted much about Owen's safety but now John has returned from Wales and reassured me, I know I can rely on Owen to arrange our children's care as we planned. The king knows all the hopes that are in my heart for Edmund and Jasper and I am confident he will ensure their future once he has taken charge of his kingdom. Meanwhile we must trust the Earl of Suffolk and his sister the Abbess of Barking.

There remains the matter of our little Margaret, who is four today and whose future is less obvious. I would dearly love it if she could lead the kind of life I have lived with Owen, rather than suffer the powerless and circumscribed life of the court or the cloister. If you were to rear her with your little William, Mette, I am sure she would have a happier and more fulfilled life than if she were to be fostered by a noble family, particularly one like the house of Gloucester, may God forbid. Her birth is not recorded anywhere and few people other than those loyal to me are even aware of her short life so far. Is it possible that you might be able to give her all the love and security you gave me and if God should take you, Mette, perhaps Alys? We cannot ever know what life has in store but at least you know my dearest wish on Margaret's behalf.

Oh, Mette, you have been my rock and strength and I know without doubt that you will be until the end. I have come to believe that I am being punished in this world for the sin of seeking earthly happiness and that only through the atonement of suffering shall I be permitted to reach the bliss of a heavenly afterlife with all those I have loved. This has and will be the substance of all my prayers from now until I am gathered into eternity. God's will be done.

Pray for my soul's rest, Mette, for you and Owen have been the source of all my happiest moments. Remember those and not the trials we have also shared and do not weep for me.

I am your daughter of the breast and loving friend into eternity,

Catherine

—§§—

Say what she might about not weeping for her, this was the moment I shed my first real tears for Catherine, breaking down into sudden shuddering sobs as I stood with the ring in one hand and the letter shaking violently in the other.

Instantly Geoffrey was on his feet, his arm around me, kerchief at the ready. 'Let the tears flow, dearest Mette,' he said. 'No one has more right to weep for Catherine. You are crying for your child.'

575

AUTHOR'S NOTE:
FACT AND FICTION

History does not relate exactly what happened to Margaret Tudor. Some records say she died at birth, others that she became a nun. I have made her Catherine's living legacy to Mette. It is an enticing historical fiction.

The memorial which Henry VI erected over his mother's tomb made no mention of the Tudors and so did not serve the purposes of future English monarchs. It was demolished in the 16th century to make way for a new tomb-chapel for Henry VII and during this process Catherine's coffin was disinterred, opened and not reburied. It is a sad footnote of history that through subsequent centuries her remains became a macabre attraction for visitors to Westminster Abbey, including the famous diarist Samuel Pepys who noted after a visit there that he had been permitted a very close encounter: 'This is my birthday and I did kiss a Queen!' he crowed. It was not until Victorian times that the coffin was at last given honourable reburial beside Henry V's tomb and a memorial stone was erected which can be seen today. Unfortunately even that does not give Catherine the respect she deserves since it records the year of her death wrongly as 1438, when it was 1437. The death-mask used on her funeral effigy can also be seen in the abbey museum, in my opinion not a pretty sight or one that anyone would want to be their epitaph.

Nor was Owen's ending a dignified one. He disappears from the record for some years before eventually being given a minor post in Wales by the king and, at over sixty years of age, being drawn into the Wars of the Roses in support of his son Jasper Tudor at the battle of Mortimer's Cross on the Welsh border. On this occasion the Lancastrians were routed and while Jasper managed to escape both death and capture, Owen was taken by vengeful Yorkists and beheaded without trial in the marketplace at Hereford, where a memorial plaque can be seen today.

In order to simplify the narrative of *The Agincourt Bride* and *The Tudor Bride*, I have combined two brothers together into one character – that of Edmund Beaufort. He was the youngest of four brothers and it was his nearest brother, Thomas, who was imprisoned in France and ransomed, but he was made Count of Perche in Henry V's Normandy land-grab and died in 1432. I have used Thomas Beaufort's early life and combined it with that of his younger brother Edmund, who became the Earl of Mortain and sought Catherine's hand in marriage, later becoming the powerful Duke of Somerset, as his three brothers died without male heirs. It was Edmund's feud with the Duke of York which led to the first major bloodletting of the Wars of the Roses – the battle of St Albans in 1455, in which he was killed.

Some historians have suggested that Catherine and Edmund Beaufort were lovers and that Catherine married Owen Tudor after parliament had passed the Marriage Act in order to legitimise the child she had conceived as a result, calling him Edmund after his true father. But there is no historical evidence for this, just as there is no documentary evidence for her marriage to Owen. It has just been accepted that it took place and that the Tudor boys were legitimate.

The coincidence of the names led me rather to pursue the idea that Edmund Beaufort became Edmund Tudor's godfather and a further coincidence is too great to ignore – that in 1453 Edmund Beaufort was riding high in Henry VI's favour as Duke of Somerset, when the king ennobled his Tudor half-brothers, making them Earl of Richmond and Earl of Pembroke respectively. At the same time Edmund Beaufort's niece, the Somerset heiress Margaret Beaufort was betrothed to Edmund Tudor. Their marriage took place in 1455 and she subsequently gave birth to a boy who was baptised Henry to continue the Lancastrian name.

Before he was born, however, Edmund Tudor died of plague, contracted while he was imprisoned by Yorkists after a skirmish in Wales. The baby Henry and his mother were sheltered by Jasper Tudor in Pembroke Castle and it was this boy, reared chiefly by Jasper, who was to defeat Richard III at the battle of Bosworth in 1485 and take the crown as Henry VII, the first Tudor monarch of England. He joined the warring blood lines descended from Edward III by marrying Elizabeth of York and, in Henry VIII, uniting them under the Tudor rose.

I will be following the York journey to the Tudor dynasty through the dramatic and adventurous life story of the Duchess of York, Cicely Neville, in my next historical novel.

Joanna Hickson

ACKNOWLEDGEMENTS

The fifteenth century in France and England was a time when family members fought each other bitterly, both politically and on the battlefield. I find this a distressing aspect of what is otherwise an enticing period of history but I'm happy to say that in my own twenty-first century family life I have experienced the opposite. My husband and all four daughters have been united in their support and encouragement of my writing for which I am extremely grateful. The youngest even delivered her first baby at exactly the time I was writing about Queen Catherine giving birth to Henry the Sixth - a wonderful source of inspiration - and hers was also a 'perfect prince', so huge thank you hugs to Katie and Hugo.

Of course I made research trips to the all the castles in The Tudor Bride – Senlis, Vincennes, Windsor, Kenilworth, Eltham, Hertford - some retaining more of their original medieval character than others. But the most extraordinary experience was a visit I made to the Bishop's Palace at Hadham (now on the map as Much Hadham), where Edmund Tudor was born. There is still a lovely house there, part of which is old enough to have sheltered Catherine and her household but today it is divided into several private residences, whose owners understandably do not seek publicity. So I cannot thank them by name but I am very grateful to the kind lady who let me inside her home to show me the very room in which Edmund Tudor is believed to have been born. For an author seeking atmosphere it was an invaluable kindness.

Similar kindness and of course professional help has been forthcoming once again from the team at Harper Fiction. Many thanks to publisher Kimberley Young, my ever-friendly and forthright editor Kate Bradley, careful and capable copy-editor Joy Chamberlain, well-connected publicist Jaime Frost and to all the designers, distributors, printers, digitisers and marketers who have employed so much skill and effort in sending my sweat-stained words out to the big wide world, polished, buffed and salon-smooth. A hug and a kiss to my ever-diligent agent Jenny Brown, who never misses an opportunity to further the cause of her writers and, most important of all, heartfelt thanks go to you, the discerning reader, who continues to amaze and thrill me by choosing (and I hope enjoying) the fascinating life-story of Queen Catherine and her faithful friend Mette.

Joanna